Praise for

The Low Road

"In his debut novel, Kirk delivers a complicated magical tale . . . Without sacrificing plot for message, [he] offers a subtle critique of the ways humanity mistreats the planet." —*Publishers Weekly*

"In *Elf Realm*, [Kirk] makes a very successful jump to chapter books for young adults . . . [with] an environmental tone . . . and black-and-white illustrations that have a Gothic feel."
—*The Sacramento Book Review*

Named a fall 2008 IndieBound Kids' Indie Next List selection (Inspired Recommendations for Kids from Indie Booksellers)

ALSO AVAILABLE BY DANIEL KIRK

NOVELS

THE *ELF REALM* TRILOGY

The Low Road

The High Road

PICTURE BOOKS

Library Mouse

Library Mouse: A Friend's Tale

THE LOW ROAD

DANIEL KIRK

AMULET BOOKS

NEW YORK

The Library of Congress has cataloged the hardcover edition of this book as follows:
Library of Congress Cataloging-in-Publication Data

Kirk, Daniel.
Elf realm : book one, the low road / by Daniel Kirk.
p. cm.
Summary: When Matt and his family move to a new development, they stumble into the middle of massive upheaval in the Fairy world, and as the elves' territory disintegrates and dark factions try to seize control, an apprentice mage sees in Matt the key to saving the realms from destruction.
[1. Elves—Fiction. 2. Fairies—Fiction. 3. Magic—Fiction.]
I. Title.

PZ7.K6339Elf 2008
[Fic]—dc22
2007039751

Paperback ISBN 978-0-8109-4084-0

Originally published in hardcover by Amulet Books in 2008

Book design by Chad W. Beckerman

Published in 2009 by Amulet Books, an imprint of ABRAMS.

Printed and bound in U.S.A.
10 9 8 7 6 5 4 3 2 1

ABRAMS
THE ART OF BOOKS SINCE 1949
115 West 18th Street
New York, NY 10011
www.abramsbooks.com

FOR RUSSELL
—D.K.

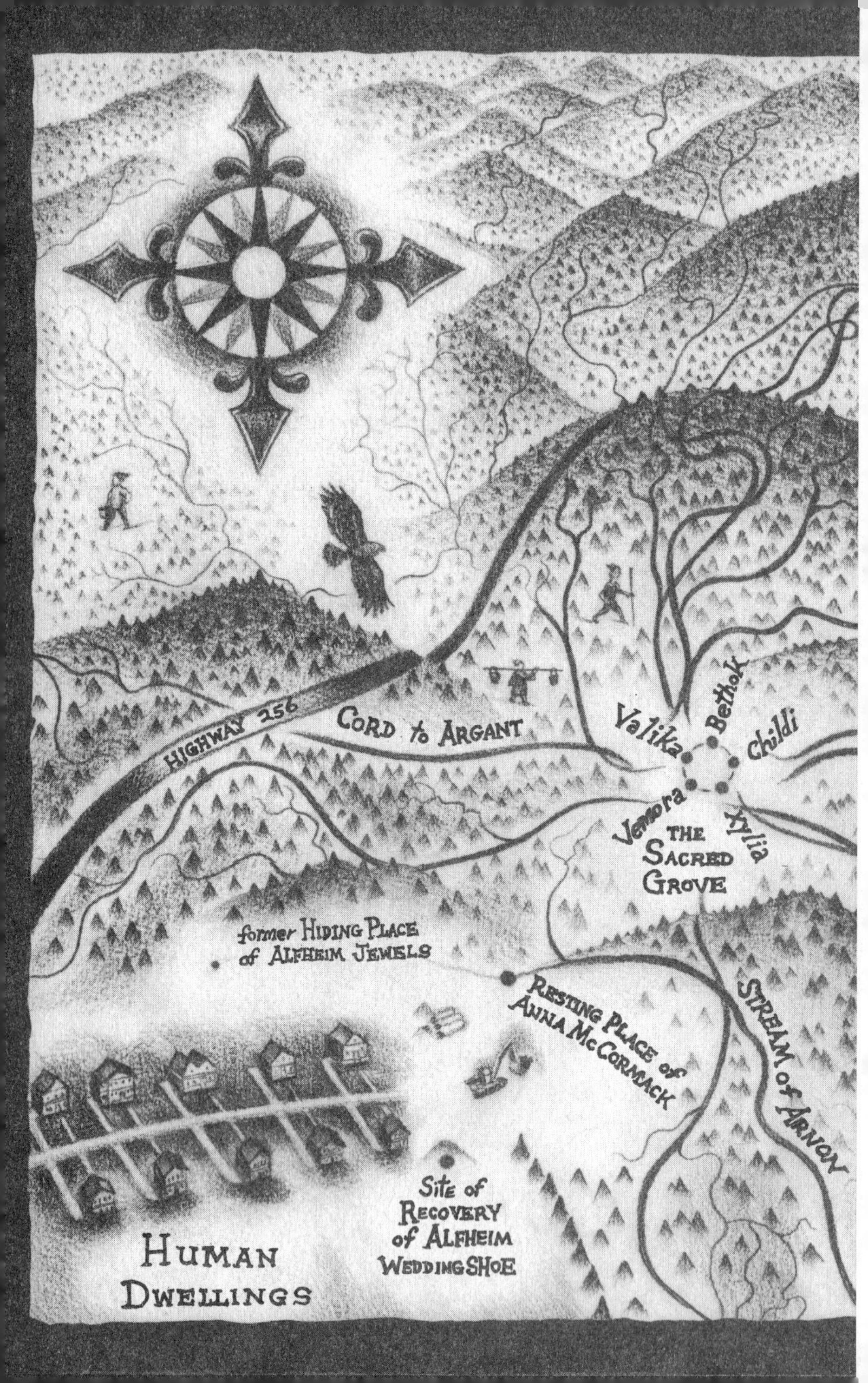
HIGHWAY 256
CORD to ARGANT
Valika
Bethok
Childi
Vemora
Xylia
THE SACRED GROVE
former HIDING PLACE of ALFHEIM JEWELS
RESTING PLACE of ANNA McCORMACK
STREAM of ARNON
Site of RECOVERY of ALFHEIM WEDDING SHOE
HUMAN DWELLINGS

CORD to HELFRATHEIM

home of
Agar the Troll

WILDLIFE SANCTUARY

CORD to LJOSALFAR

ALFHEIM
and ENVIRONS

PROLOGUE

HIGHWAY 256 WAS A COLD, gray line that stretched through the night, splitting the blackness of the woods in two. An hour before dawn the hungry world was waking. A swarm of insects hummed along the paved shoulder. A pheasant, ruffled from sleep, turned a beady eye across the highway and toward the sound. The bird started across the blacktop. *Whaaaap!*

In a spray of blood and feathers the pheasant was hurled to the side of the road. The man behind the wheel of the passing truck glanced in his rearview mirror. Next to him sat his daughter, hunched down in her seat. She yawned and rubbed her eyes. "What was that, Daddy?"

"Dumb bird," he sighed. "Pheasant, I guess. Never knew what hit it."

Jim McCormack was tired. His son, Charlie, was sick and

had spent most of the night throwing up in the bathroom. So Jim had endured the long hours stretched out on the living room couch with a blanket, while his wife tended to the boy. In the dim light Jim had watched the time on the wall clock crawl by, and at 5 AM he sat up, stalked to his daughter's bed, and gave her a shake. "Get up, Anna," he said, "you and me are going hunting."

Anna was not a hunter. She didn't even have a license, and her experience with a shotgun was limited to one botched session at the skeet-shooting range. The gun's recoil had slammed the stock into her chin and sent her crying into her mother's arms. But Jim wanted to go hunting, and he hated to hunt alone. So Anna would have to do.

"Daddy, why are we stopping here?" murmured Anna, when five minutes later her father pulled the pickup onto a dirt road next to a POSTED: NO HUNTING OR TRESPASSING sign.

"Hunting?" her father answered. "We're going hunting."

"But, Daddy, it's posted. *No hunting.* We can't—"

"We can do whatever we want here," Jim explained. "This is our land. I *bought* this property yesterday at auction. Twelve hundred acres. Your mother's mad at me. She thinks we can't afford it. But now it's McCormack land, free and clear. Twelve hundred acres of woods, hills, streams, and all the critters that live there. This is the one place on earth we can do whatever we want. So don't mind the sign. From now on, that's for everybody else but us!"

Jim cut the motor, turned off the headlights, and lifted two shotguns from behind the seat. "Zip up your jacket," he said, stepping out of the truck. He pulled some shells from his pocket and slipped them into the trigger mounts of each Remington. Then he handed his daughter a shotgun, and led the way into the woods. "This is your brother's gun," he said. "Treat it like it was your own."

The forest was much darker than the highway had been. Entering the dense undergrowth, as vines, low-hanging branches, and cobwebs brushed their cheeks, Anna and her father moved slowly into the woods. They made their way by instinct more than sight, by chance more than vision, the girl staying close to her father's side. Their breath came out in puffs of vapor, instantly swallowed by darkness. "Daddy, it's too dark," the girl whispered. "Where are we going? I can't—"

"The sky's getting brighter," her father interrupted. "Look up past the trees, over the hill, you'll see."

Anna looked, but remained unconvinced. "Oh!" she cried, stumbling on a fallen branch, and grabbing her dad's sleeve.

The pair wandered on for perhaps a quarter of a mile. The sky was brightening, just as Jim said it would, and a fiery splinter of sun edged up over the horizon. They trudged a little farther into the uninviting heart of the forest. But neither Jim nor Anna recognized the moment when they stepped across the boundary of their own world, and entered another. It was a place where few human feet had ever trod. Even in daylight the rupture looked like little more than a blur at the edge of sight. But now it was growing, shape-shifting, a gaping hole in the rugged density of the forest. It was a gash in the face of time, and space, and everything that was real. The trees on the other side of the opening might have appeared somehow taller, the air might have had a sweeter smell, but it was, at first, too subtle a difference to tell. Anna and her father would never realize that, as they stepped across the void, they had left the world they knew completely behind.

Anna heard the sound first. It was like singing. The voice was thin and high, but it was a real voice. Not a bird, not the whisper of the wind. "And through sweet seasons spreads our joy, o'er meadow, copse, and hedge, for thee, and this, our Woodland Home, undying love I pledge."

"Daddy, did you hear that?" Anna murmured.

"Ssssh," hissed her father. "I think I see something up ahead."

There was a dim flickering of light. It was like the glow of distant candles, or fireflies, untold scores of them. "Hold up," Jim whispered, and reached an arm out to stop his daughter.

Suddenly the deer were visible. At first they were no more than ghosts, dreamy mounds of vapor, and a heartbeat later they were solid and real. There was an entire herd of them, albinos, with gleaming white coats, facing away into a clearing. Beyond them was a tower, nearly twenty feet high. Tiny creatures of flame danced on the spreading tips of antlers, which stretched out from the skeleton of the structure. The tower was wreathed in flowers. Little figures stood at the tower's apex and descended stairs along its side, joining a vast crowd. Not one of the beings would have reached higher than a human knee.

Jim McCormack held his breath and stared; yet all he saw were the deer, who were there to witness the Faerie wedding of Alfheim. Blind to the alien world and the ceremony taking place, he nudged his daughter's elbow. *"I'm going to get the big one,"* he hissed.

Jim slid the barrel forward, closing the action, and squeezed the trigger. With a loud bang and a burst of sulfur the twelve-gauge shotgun loosed its fury. Anna, startled, dropped her own gun and pressed her hands to her ears.

The mighty Deer King turned his head as death sped through an open space between his antlers. At the top of the wedding tower the Elfin groom stepped forward to sweep his beloved out of harm's way, and the slug tore him in half. His emerald-colored Blood gushed out, and his body toppled from the back of the tower. Pandemonium erupted as the Faerie Folk snatched up their young and ran from the scene of horror. The deer leapt and scattered in every direction. The hunter raced forward. He pumped the shotgun, ejecting the shell, and dropped another into the slot. "Get your gun, Anna, come on!" Jim shouted. "Let's bring home a trophy! Nobody's going to believe what we saw today!"

When Jim reached the center of the clearing he bumped into

something and fell. As he got to his feet he caught a brief glimpse of a toppled tower. Fire Sprites were leaping from the carved ramparts and disappearing in the air. Jim shook the vision from his head and charged after the buck. "Daddy!" Anna called with tears in her eyes, stumbling after him. "Wait!"

Suddenly something small, swift, and silvery made its way around Anna's legs. The creature was muttering words in a language Anna had never heard before. With her next breath her eyes rolled up in her head and she slipped to the ground. Though still conscious, the girl lay paralyzed, unable to move.

Anna's father was in hot pursuit of the deer. He was completely unaware of the Faerie Folk scurrying toward a slight bulge in a ravine just ahead. Down a short flight of moss-covered steps, the skin of a translucent tube, five or six feet in diameter, lay exposed. It resembled a root, or the ribbed back of a gigantic white earthworm. The Faerie Folk called it *the Cord.* Invisible to Human eyes, the Cord was part of a network that spread along the surface of the earth. It wove in and out of the soil, binding their world together like arteries that pulse blood through a living body. The Faerie Folk knew how to enter the Cords where they rose out of the ground and travel on the winds that blew inside them. Now the Cord was their means of escape. As the first Elves, Trolls, Pixies, Gnomes, and Brownies appeared, they used their fingernails to slice through the Cord's thin, rubbery surface. Widening the slit, they bent into the opening to see if the path was clear, and slipped inside. Their bodies hurtled like storm-tossed leaves through the tunnel. The Cord would give them passage to a safer place, somewhere, anywhere, far away.

Ladies-in-waiting guided the Elfin Princess Asra down the green carpet. With her gown torn, and a shoe missing from her bruised foot, Asra knelt at the entrance, where guards held the slit open for the royal family to enter. Her parents hovered at her side, ready for the journey to the kingdom of Ljosalfar. This was the homeland of the dead Prince, and where the Elves of Alfheim would stay until it was safe to return. "Where's your other shoe?" the Queen cried.

"I—I don't know!" answered Asra.

The Queen moaned. "Alfheim brides have worn the diamond shoes for centuries. Without them a curse will fall upon our house. We can't leave here without the pair!"

"N-n-nonsense," stammered King Thorgier, Asra's father. "We'll send scouts to find the shoe and b-b-bring it home."

A distant cousin of the groom, Prince Macta, scurried from behind. "Wait!" he cried, clutching at the broken feathers of Asra's bridal train. "Princess, you needn't be afraid. I'm here to protect you!"

The silver-cloaked Mage, the spiritual leader of the Elves of Alfheim, appeared at the Princess's side. "Asra's not your responsibility. In Ljosalfar she'll be well cared for. 'Tis best you wait at the appropriate Cord for the rest of your Clan to gather, then travel north to Helfratheim."

"This way, Macta," said the monk Jardaine.

Anger spread across the Elf's face. "As you say," he muttered, stepping back.

While most Faerie Folk rode the winds inside the Cord like birds that sail on a breeze, royal families traveled in elaborately carved gondolas. A fleet was tethered inside the Cord, waiting for the departure of Princess Asra and her entourage. Macta watched from a distance. The Princess, whose love he desired with all of his twisted heart, slipped inside. Then the ropes that held the gondolas were released, and they sped away.

Faerie Folk always exercised caution when traveling the Cord. They waited for the precise moment it was safe to enter, for collision meant certain death. Jim McCormack knew nothing as he charged ahead. He tripped and fell against the exposed Cord, the end of his rifle coming down hard and tearing a hole in the membrane. The man's legs were quickly sucked inside. Screaming and kicking, he struggled against the current of wind, but it was too late. He never saw the shape speeding toward him from the milky distance. Black, with red eyes that grew wide in surprise, the Gremlin was moving too fast to change course. In a bone-crunching crash the creature collided with the hunter. The ground was showered with Blood and chunks of flesh, and the rest was swept away in the Cord. "Stay back, my children, stay away from the *Blood*!" the Mage cried out.

Macta lingered nearby, even as the crowd dispersed. When he was certain no one was looking he knelt and dipped his finger in a puddle on the ground. Then he moved the finger to his lips.

He had never tasted blood before. Such an act was expressly forbidden; the Elves harbored an ancient fear of spilled blood and the power of contagion. *And yet,* Macta thought, *just because something is forbidden, that does not mean it is impossible.* Macta had spent his entire life doing things that were forbidden, and he believed that nothing was impossible, if one wanted it badly enough. The Mage raised her hands and cried out in a trembling voice. "Listen to me, children of Alfheim. Today we have borne witness to a tragedy. One of the Humans that entered our realm is dead, and I have cast a spell over the other so that she will do us no harm. Princess Asra and her family are safely on their way to Ljosalfar. Prince Udos, however, has gone to join his ancestors in the Spirit World."

Jardaine and the other monks made an effort to contain the crowd, and to direct their attention to the Mage. It was important that the Elves understand what was expected of them. "Though we are out of immediate danger, the ordeal ahead of us is only just beginning," said the Mage. "We must pack our belongings to leave. Alfheim is unclean; our land is contaminated, fouled with Human and Faerie Blood. Tradition says that three hundred and sixty moons must pass before the Earth has been cleansed and it is safe for us to return."

"NO!" the Elves sobbed, falling to the ground. The mighty oaks of Alfheim represented their Motherland, the only home most of them had ever known. *"Where will we go?"*

"Don't despair," soothed the Mage. "The Elves of Ljosalfar

will take us in. After our time in exile has passed, we shall return. Time heals all wounds, it cleans even the foulest corruption." The Mage gestured toward the clearing where the unconscious girl lay. "But before we go, this Human must be removed from our Sacred Land. All must help. Take leaves from the branches of the oak to keep your fingers from touching her flesh or clothing. The leaves will protect you from contamination while we move her body."

"Is she dead?" someone cried from the crowd.

"Not dead," answered the Mage, "but entranced. Justice must be served. We will put her to rest at the bottom of the stream beyond the grove, and there she'll lie as long as water flows over her open eyes. With my enchantment she'll watch the clouds go by, and see the long years pass. She won't die, but neither will she truly live. She'll have an eternity to consider the damage her kind has done to us."

So the girl was lifted from the forest floor, delivered to the bank of the stream, then rolled into the icy water. The Mage went to the side of a young Troll who towered over the waiting crowd. Tomtar, as the Troll was known, bent over as the Mage whispered in his pointed ear. Tomtar nodded. It was an honor to do the Mage's bidding, and he agreed to stay close by the stream and keep watch over the girl.

Next the dead Prince's corpse was wrapped in cloth salvaged from the celebration tables. The monks pieced together a bier from the wreckage of the tower. Then the Fire Sprites assembled along the platform for the cremation, burning with fierce rage, and sadness, and love, until all that was left of Prince Udos was ash. Silently the Elves went to gather their things. They filed through the woods, and disappeared into the Cord. One day they would return, when time had cleansed Alfheim of the stain of Blood, and the shock from the disaster had settled into numb acceptance. But for now, and for many years to come, the forest was left to the birds, the squirrels, the deer, and the lonely whistle of the wind through the trees.

The Low Road

1

THE MUD-SPATTERED BULLDOZER rested on its crawler tracks, a sleeping giant on a rumpled blanket of dirt. Less than a quarter of a mile away stood the five mighty oaks of Alfheim. Fourteen-year-old Matt McCormack dashed across the construction site. He bent down to squirm through a length of plastic pipe that lay stretched over the soil. Then he raced toward the excavating machine. Matt's father, Charlie, stood at the edge of the forest with a roll of blueprints under his arm. "Matt!" he shouted. "This isn't an obstacle course. I hope you're not going to do what I think you're going to do!"

Matt ran past the wide-toothed bucket and the jointed arm of the steel behemoth and scaled the bumper. Matt had brown, sparkling eyes, like his mom, a round face like his dad, and a pair

of oversized ears which he hoped he would grow into. Growing was something that Matt had thought a lot about lately, as he was a little shorter than many boys his own age. Windmilling his arms, Matt leapt into the air. He landed on his heels in the dirt. Dirt! Glorious, filthy, incomparable, dirty, dusty dirt. "Sorry, Dad!" he yelled. "What did you say?"

"Nothing. I just want you to set a good example for Becky. Don't give her any ideas."

Becky, the older of Matt's sisters, was nine. She brushed straw-colored hair from her high forehead, and squinted into the sun. Then she frowned, apprehension flickering in her pale eyes. She lingered nervously on the concrete walkway that led to the McCormacks' new house. Up and down the short block were ten new houses, all nearing completion, waiting to be sold. Tiny spears of grass sprouted from the straw that covered the yard. Becky eyed the grass cautiously. It would take a lot more than her brother's *ideas* to get her to play in the dirt. "Dad," Becky called, "Mom says you can come in and make some sandwiches, if you want to eat. We're getting pretty hungry."

"Okay, honey. We'll be right in," he answered.

Matt was arranging a row of traffic cones. "Come on, kiddo," his dad said, "you're going to need to get cleaned up before you set foot in Mom's new kitchen."

"But, Dad," Matt complained, "I'm just gonna get dirty again!"

"I know. But can you wait until we've been in the new house for at least a week until you trash it?"

There had been a lot of changes for Matt's family in the year since his grandmother passed away. After working out the details of Grandma's will, Charlie suddenly found himself the owner of twelve hundred acres of undeveloped woodland in rural Pennsylvania. Only, this part of Pennsylvania wasn't so rural anymore, as suburban sprawl had spread its tentacles into forests and pastures, claiming land for tidy developments with names like Glen Acres and Rocky Springs Estates. Nobody but Grandma had known that she even owned the land, and no one could have ever guessed that she was sitting on a potential gold mine.

Poor old Grandma McCormack. After her husband, Jim, and daughter, Anna, disappeared in the woods back in the 1970s, she left the country house and took her son, Charlie, to live in Pittsburgh. Eventually Charlie grew up, got a job in construction, married a girl named Jill, and started a family of his own. They got an apartment on the second floor of an old brick building on the South Side. Space had been pretty tight back then; Matt and Becky had to share one tiny bedroom. The nearest tree was a scrawny maple, sucking up nutrients from a patch of soil next to the trash can at the end of the block. Money had always been in short supply. So when Grandma died and left Dad the property, it was clear that the time had come for a change.

Soon the McCormacks were living in a brand-new house in

what was going to be a brand-new neighborhood, carved into a piece of the family property. Sylvan Estates was Charlie's project, and he was involved in every aspect of construction, from digging the foundations to installing kitchens and painting walls. Even though he hired crews to do the work, he still enjoyed the labor of seeing a job through from start to finish. Matt and Becky were now suburban kids, with a new sister, Emily, they could be proud of. If somebody could really be proud of a toddler who never seemed to do anything but cry and poop and get into trouble. Their mom was always telling Matt and Becky that their baby sister was an unexpected treasure. But Emily kept Jill so busy and tired that she never had time to do the things the kids thought a mom ought to do—like fix their lunch. "Dad, I'm tired of peanut butter," said Becky, as she slathered a slice of bread at the kitchen table. "Can't we have something different tomorrow?"

A toilet flushed, and Matt clomped into the kitchen from the powder room, wiping his hands on a paper towel. He dropped onto the chair next to his sister and tossed the damp towel onto her lap. "I love it here," he grunted, picking up a sandwich and taking a giant bite.

"Mom!" cried Becky. "Matt threw his dirty towel at me!"

"Hey, Matt," their father intervened, "just because you've discovered you like to play in the dirt doesn't mean you can act like a pig."

Charlie stood by the edge of the counter, chomping on his

sandwich. He downed the last of his coffee from a plastic cup. Then, humming absently to himself, he tossed the cup into the garbage and wiped bread crumbs into the sink. "You take the high road," he started to sing, "and I'll take the low road, and I'll get to Scotland before you, for me and my true love will never meet again, on—"

"Daddy, why do you always have to sing that song?" Becky complained. "It gets into my head, and it won't go away."

"Sorry, Becky. It was a song my father used to sing to me when I was a kid. Sometimes when I'm out in the field, the tune just pops into my mind and stays there all afternoon. I didn't know it was contagious, though!"

Matt furrowed his brow. "I don't even know what it's about. What's a high road?"

"I don't have any idea," Charlie said. "Listen, kids, I'm going to have to go into the city this afternoon. I've got to lease some new equipment to replace the machines that broke down. I need to have a talk with our guy at the bank, and then I've got an appointment with a Realtor. There's still a lot of unpacking to do here at home, and I expect you to help your mom."

"But, Dad," said Matt, "I'm tired of unpacking. I wanted to do some exploring and see what it's like around here. Once school starts, we won't have time to do anything."

"Go play for a while," Jill called from the next room. "Emily's going to have a nap and I don't want you in the house making a racket. But stay out of the construction site. You could cut yourself or step on a rusty nail and get tetanus. Just . . . just stay in the yard, okay?"

"Not the yard," Charlie said. "You'll crush the seedlings and we'll have to start the lawn all over. Ours is the first house we've totally finished, so we want it to look perfect."

"What's tetanus, Dad?" asked Becky.

"I don't know. Some kind of disease. You probably have had a shot for it anyway."

"They used to call it *lockjaw*," Jill whispered, slipping into the kitchen. Emily had fallen asleep in her arms. "It's an infection. In the old days people with tetanus would get so stiff they could barely move, and eventually they wouldn't be able to open their mouths or move their joints. Then they died. It's very serious."

"There are shots for it, now," Charlie said. "Jill, why do you say things like that? You're going to scare the kids to death."

"Charlie, will you be back in time for dinner?"

"I hope so, but just in case," he said, turning toward his son, "you're on macaroni and cheese duty!"

Matt and Becky waved from the porch as their dad backed his truck out of the driveway. "Well," Matt asked, "what do you want to do? I set up an obstacle course in the field. I could ride my dirt bike around the cones, and you could time me and see how fast I am!"

"We're not supposed to go over there," Becky warned, squinting at the line of trees beyond the field. "Besides, the woods give me the creeps. Isn't that where Grandpa Jim and Aunt Anna disappeared?"

"Yeah," Matt answered, "so what? That was a long time ago. Before we were even born. But I'm not even talking about going into the woods. Just that field, right there!"

"But what happened to them? Did they die?"

"I don't know." Matt shrugged. "Nobody knows. All they ever found was the pickup truck. Come on, Becky, please? I don't have anybody else to do anything with!"

"I want to get my dolls unpacked," Becky said. "You could help!"

Matt rolled his eyes. He couldn't wait until the development was finished and some more people moved in. With all the new houses, there would have to be at least one family with a boy more or less his age. "Listen," Matt argued, "you heard what Mom said. She gets mad if Emily doesn't have a nap. Come on, let's just hang outdoors. We could even play hide and seek, if you want. You always liked that back in the old neighborhood!"

Matt scanned the construction site for good hiding places as he loped across the dirt. "Stop!" cried Becky, trailing behind him. "I'm gonna tell Mom!"

"I'll hide first!" shouted Matt. He took his sister by the shoulders and stood her with her back to a muddy boulder. "Okay, count to fifty."

Matt dashed around the claw of the broken-down excavator and clambered up a ladder to the cab. He imagined for a second how much fun it would be to get into the excavator and drive it around. But even if he had the key, and even if he had been old enough to drive the thing, the machine was broken. In fact, none of the construction equipment was working. Charlie had said that he was having a run of bad luck. A few days earlier, when his workers went to uproot a few of the big old trees that formed a line across the field, the machines began breaking down. One by one, something went wrong with a motor, or an axle, or an electrical system. Nobody on the crew could figure out what was going on, so work had to be shut down. Charlie said that when you hit a streak of bad luck, you just had to ride it out. But Matt realized it was hard to *ride out* something that wasn't moving.

Becky finished counting to fifty, then looked to her left and right. "Here I come!" she cried, then took a cautious step forward. She crept around the giant shovel, gingerly stepping over the tread tracks, and turned into the shadow of the bulldozer where Matt was hiding. "Bombs away!" he shouted, and leapt into his sister's path.

Splooosh! Matt's feet came down in a puddle, left over from a recent thundershower. Mud splattered everywhere. Becky burst into tears, and as Matt took a step forward to quiet her, his sneaker came off in the muck. When he lifted his right foot, he lost the other shoe as well, and he stood there in wet, muddy socks. "Serves you right!" cried Becky, wiping away her tears and giggling.

"Okay," Matt grumbled, pulling off his socks and giving them a toss. "You can't fight mud. Come on," he said, looking around for some place drier. "I'll race you to the top of that hill!"

Next to an excavation hole a giant heap of soil rose from the ground, and Matt charged up the side. With each step his feet pressed deep into the dirt. "You'd better come down, Matt," Becky warned, but Matt was unstoppable. That is, until something jabbed into the heel of his left foot, and a stab of pain shot up his leg.

"Owww!" Matt cried, flopping onto his back. "Owww, what the . . ." He peered at his foot, looking for the rusty nail or bit of sharp metal or broken glass that must be lodged there. But what he saw sticking out of his skin was the pointed heel of a small, glittering shoe, nearly two inches long. A drop of blood fell onto the dirt. "What is it?" cried Becky. "What's wrong, Matt?"

"Nothing," Matt answered, as visions of amputations, lockjaw, and death raced through his mind. "I just stepped on a—on something sharp, that's all."

Matt squeezed both sides of the little shoe with his thumb and forefinger and pulled hard. The heel was narrow, and it was lodged deep. Matt thought maybe it went into his bone. He twisted it a few times and the spike came out. "Stupid," he muttered. "Stupid doll thing."

Matt slipped the shoe into his pocket, with the heel facing

out. He struggled to a sitting position. Then he slid down the dirt heap to the ground and, keeping his weight on his good foot, brushed soil from his jeans. "Come on," he said. "I want to go inside."

"But, Matt," Becky whined, "I haven't had a turn to hide yet!"

"Look, I got hurt," Matt snapped. "I cut my foot. Mom will be mad at me if she finds out. Promise not to tell, and I'll . . . I'll help you unpack your dolls, okay?"

"I promise," Becky said, trailing behind as Matt limped up toward the house.

2

THE ELF WAS BREAKING a chunk of fungus from a tree trunk when he heard the Human cry out. Hidden in dappled shadows, Byggvir had come to the edge of the construction site to look for food. Once it would have taken magick to bring an Elf so close to Human civilization. But the borders that separated the worlds were continuing to grow more porous, and in many places there were no longer boundaries at all.

After thirty years the Elves were returning to Alfheim. Many spent their days foraging in the woods, gathering food for the kitchen staff to prepare. Byggvir had no idea that he had left Elfin territory. When he heard the Human speak, he froze in shock and disbelief. He peered into the clearing and saw him on the mound of dirt. Then he saw the sunlight flash on the diamond wedding shoe lodged in the boy's heel. Byggvir turned and ran. As he clambered over heaps of dry leaves and fallen branches, chunks of fungus spilled from his basket. But that didn't matter any more. The only thing that truly mattered was that the wedding shoe had been found.

Matt closed the bathroom door behind him and turned the lock. He hoped his mother didn't question why he was getting into the shower without being nagged. He stood in the tub as the water steamed up around him and watched a thin trail of red spread from the bottom of his foot, then circle down the drain. When he got out of the shower he patted the wound to make sure it was dry. Then he rooted around in a box of stuff that was meant to go in the bathroom cabinet, and found a tube of antibiotic cream. He smeared some on his heel and put an oversized bandage on it. After pulling on a fresh pair of socks, Matt hid the little shoe in the back of his dresser drawer. Then he hobbled down the hall to Becky's room. "Remember what I said about telling Mom?" Matt asked in a hushed voice. "I'll help you with your dolls, but you'd better not say anything about me hurting my foot out there in the field!"

Becky just smiled, and slipped a CD into her little pink boom box. Then the pair of them spent the rest of the afternoon taking dolls out of cardboard boxes, getting them into fresh outfits, and standing them on a shelf that stretched all the way from the closet to the window.

3

AS A YOUNG ELF the Mage of Alfheim was called Kalevala Van Frier. Now, centuries later, she was the spiritual leader of her own Clan, and she had given up her name for the title of *Mage.* High in her home amid the branches of an oak tree called Bethok, she stood before a wall of dusty, bark-paper books. Sunlight streamed in through the curtained doorway. Sticks of incense smoldered in ornate holders, as part of the cleansing ritual that had brought the Mage and her monks back to Alfheim. The Mage sighed and dragged a finger along the edge of the books. Next to her were crumbling baskets of scrolls and a tall stack of leaf-wrapped packages. In the packages were the most valued books and manuscripts, returned from hiding places in vaults beneath the roots of massive trees.

Beside the Mage a pair of crickets crouched in an ornate

wooden cage. Slowly they scraped their back legs together, making music that the Mage found soothing in times of stress. And this was, indeed, such a time. During the exile from Alfheim scouts had been sent on a regular basis to make sure the realm was undisturbed, and to search for the shoe that Princess Asra had lost on the day of the great disaster. Without the shoe, the Princess could not be married. The elders of Ljosalfar and their governing body, the Synod, were eager to have the royal family of Alfheim joined to another realm by marriage, to consolidate resources, to create harmony among the Clans. For this reason the missing shoe was a constant source of anxiety. During the latest expedition the scouts had discovered that the woods bordering Alfheim were endangered. They had sped back to Ljosalfar to tell the Mage that the forest was being ravaged. Precious trees were cut down, and Humans were erecting their houses on Elfin soil. In all likelihood it was only a matter of time until the Sacred Grove itself was destroyed. Just thirty years before, two Humans had stumbled across a gap in the border between the worlds. Now the gap was growing ever wider, and it appeared there was no way to stop it.

This was not the end of the bad news. The Alfheim Clan Jewels, a treasure of unfathomable wealth, were gone. Stored away over untold thousands of years, Clan Jewels were never spent, traded, or exchanged. Now even the trees under which the treasure had been buried had disappeared. When the Elves fled this place, the Mage knew that the best protection for the

Jewels would be to leave them in one of their secret vaults, deep in the earth. With a strong spell of distraction woven around the site the Jewels should have been safe. But when it was needed most, the spell over the Clan Jewels seemed to have afforded no protection at all. The loss of the treasure was terrible; but the Mage knew that the real wealth of the Elf Folk was the forest, and the trees of the Sacred Grove. The loss of these would be a tragedy too great to comprehend. So as the thirty-year exile came to its end, the Mage of Alfheim and her monks traveled the Cord from Ljosalfar back to their ancestral home.

Seven long days of cleansing and purifying rituals prepared the ground of Alfheim. Then a hundred more Elves traveled the Cord to help the monks clean, repair, and refurbish dwellings, to till the fields, sow the seed, and stock the larder. Soon the thousands of Elves who had once made Alfheim their home would return. The Mage had assured the Synod that since she was now fully aware of the danger, she would be prepared to defend her little realm. But the way promised to be hard. The Elves of Alfheim were gentle folk, untrained in the ways of war. Their tools were made of stone and wood, and not suited for combat. The few who owned bows and arrows used them only for games and sport. Most Elves refrained from eating flesh, and were bound by a deep respect for other living creatures. Not all Faerie Folk were pacifists, however. In the northern Kingdom of Helfratheim the Elves relished conflict and warfare, and favored weapons fashioned from iron and steel. They loved the power that metal implements gave them, and their Techmagicians developed potions to fend off the nausea and sickness that metal caused their kind. Now they were bargaining at the Synod of Ljosalfar for the authority to go to Alfheim and kill the Humans who threatened the sacred land. Their own Prince Macta had been present at the ill-fated wedding of Udos and Asra, thirty years before. He and his father made a convincing case for the use of violence. But so far, the Synod was willing to give the Mage a chance to protect her own homeland, using the tools at her disposal.

One of the tools she chose to use was the Elfin capacity for magick. The Mage and her monks used the concentrated power of their minds to affect the world of matter. On a late summer's eve they had marched through the woodlands until they found the place where the earth had been defiled by the digging machines. Disgust and terror filled the hearts of the Mage and her monks at the site of the bare soil, stripped of life. They surrounded the awful machines and set to work. Hours of intense, concentrated chanting finally did their job. Though the Elves were nauseated from their exposure to the steel, their magic finally disabled the machines. Never again would these metal monsters tear up the earth, never again would they cut down another tree. But that did not mean that Alfheim was safe.

Outside the door to the Mage's quarters a clay bell clattered, and the gears and pulleys that operated the lift began to turn. On a wooden axle a circular cage spun, and inside it a trio of silky rats raced around and around.

The pulleys hoisted an elevator cage up the side of the tree. The Elfmaid standing inside yanked a cord, ringing the bell again, the signal for the rats to stop. "Mistress," said Tuava-Li, stepping onto the branch, "here are the last of the packages. Shall I put them with the others?"

Tuava-Li was dressed in a burlap smock, belted with a green dandelion stem. Blue tattoos, depicting the wildflowers and insects of the forest, covered her arms and shoulders. Like all of the Elves, Tuava-Li had large, luminous eyes. Her straight brown hair was pulled back from a face that could not hide its weariness. "'Twill be fine," the Mage answered. She lifted three large kernels of corn, the rats' reward, over her head. Poking their noses down from an opening in the ceiling, the rats snatched the corn and retreated. "Tuava-Li," said the Mage, "I have some sweeping for you to do. Dust and dirt have settled o'er everything in this place."

Tuava-Li sighed, and dropped her bundle on the pile. She was tired of feeding the crickets, bringing corn for the rats, and hauling heavy packages of books up by the elevator to the Mage's study. At the age of seventy-three she was really still an adolescent, and all of this hard work put her in a bad mood. The Mage cast her a glance. "Be gentle with my books, Tuava-Li. An Apprentice shows respect for the collected wisdom of the ages. Actions speak volumes, which is why I'm inclined to think there's something you wish to say."

The Elfmaid's ears quivered in frustration. "Well, aye, perhaps there is, but only because you mentioned it, Mistress. I

can't help but wonder if there isn't a spell that could be used to clean up the dust? There are so many important things I could help you with. Organizing the library books on their shelves, for one. I've been your Apprentice for so long, and yet I've had so little opportunity to study spells! You could give me time to study the magick in the books, and I could help you find ways to stop the Humans. 'Twould be a better job for an Apprentice than just . . . just sweeping."

Tuava-Li bit her lip, knowing she had said too much. The Mage's silence let her know just how much. Finally the old Elf spoke. "Tuava-Li, have you been practicing your Discipline?"

Tuava-Li frowned. She had been too busy with her chores to practice the meditations the Mage had taught her. "The Discipline will bring spirit into your body," the Mage said. "'T will teach you patience, which will help you temper your tongue with wisdom. Now, I could answer you with a lash from my switch, like I sometimes do with the monks, but we both know that would teach you nothing."

Tuava-Li tingled with shame and looked away. "Chop wood, carry water," the Mage said. "'Tis how I learned. Hard work for the body builds strength in the Soul. You'll need to be strong to follow in my footsteps. Not to mention knowing when to speak and when to simply do as you're told! I chose you for my Apprentice because you have natural talent, Tuava-Li. My monks work hard and study long, but not one of them has the spark that lives in you."

Tuava-Li was embarrassed to be singled out for praise and criticism at the same time. She pictured the other monks, and wished that she could dissolve back into the ranks. "Ebba is quite gifted," she murmured, "and Parslaine, too. And Jardaine, she stands head and shoulders over the others!"

"Jardaine is very important to us," the Mage confided, "but even she must look up to you, Tuava-Li. 'Tis you who will be my successor, when the time comes."

"Mistress, I pray that day never comes," Tuava-Li admitted, wishing she had gone ahead and swept the floor without a word of protest.

"'Tis not my intention to make you uncomfortable, Tuava-Li," said the Mage. "Each of us has a role to play. Our Asra, for instance, was born a Princess. One day she'll become a Queen. But leadership here is not Asra's destiny. Your fate, on the other hand, is a different matter. The highest level of responsibility awaits you here in Alfheim. In a spiritual community like ours, the Mage is both the head and heart of her Clan. But here's the truth of it. All leaders start their training by following the orders of their superiors, and not complaining about it."

The Mage took the broom from a cobweb-filled corner and handed it to Tuava-Li. She began to sweep, and soon clouds of dust filled the air. The Mage covered her face with her hands. "'Tis foul to breathe it into the lungs," the Mage coughed. "Perhaps this is a problem that a little magick can solve, after all. Watch, Tuava-Li!"

The Mage pulled a strand of beads and animal bones from

the pocket of her robe and held the amulet high over her head. She closed her eyes and began waving her hands in a circle, rocking her head and chanting words that Tuava-Li struggled to understand. Then suddenly the Mage froze. At the very same moment the dust in the air stopped moving. The clouds had become solid shapes, hanging in the air like gray cotton candy. Carefully the Mage stepped forward, gathered the amorphous forms into a clump, and heaved them out through the open door. "Watch out below!" she cried, as a doe and two young fawns stood nibbling leaves from the bushes at the base of the tree.

Tuava-Li peered over the branch to see the strange shapes breaking into pieces as they struck the ground. "There's more than one kind of magick," the Mage instructed. "There's the kind that comes from soliciting the favors of supernatural beings, invisible forces willing to do your bidding for a price. A good Mage would never practice that kind of magick. But then there's the kind of magick that comes from the strength of will you build inside you through prayer, meditation, and practice. That's the kind of magick I'm here to teach. The words we speak aren't meant to draw the attention of outside powers, they're a way to focus the power we have inside. Now 'tis your turn, Tuava-Li."

She handed her Apprentice the amulet, then took the broom in her own frail hands and began sweeping up a fresh cloud of dust.

"A Vitriol torero, ah . . . Ellyn b-b-beyla," stuttered Tuava-Li, waving her hands like she had seen the Mage do. "I'm sorry. Is that right?"

"Focus your mind," said the Mage, "bring solidity to your thoughts, feel the power grow. Don't forget to turn your head, like this!"

The Mage twisted her head a little too sharply to the side, and then she winced in pain. "You may be replacing me sooner than I thought!" she groaned, holding her neck. "Magick is a little hard on these tired bones!"

The Mage shuffled over to the old hammock in the corner of her chamber. She collapsed into it with a sigh, but the fragile fibers tore loose beneath her, and she tumbled to the floor. "*Oooh!*" she cried, coughing amid a cloud of dust. Tuava-Li hurried to offer the Mage her hand. The aged Sorceress, more embarrassed than hurt, regarded her Apprentice with a stern look. She would not choose to have anyone see her in this position. Still, she readily took Tuava-Li's hand and got to her feet. Tuava-Li stood back, her gaze averted through modesty and respect. She coughed once, then covered her mouth to stifle a giggle.

"I'm glad to know that I can so readily amuse you," the Mage muttered. "Now help me tie the hammock back up where it belongs!"

Just then a cry came from below. With a clatter of the bell, the lift was drawn up into the tree. Tuava-Li put down the broom and brushed the dust from her apron as the Mage turned toward the door. "We're comin' up!" a voice hollered. "'Tis Byggvir, from the kitchens. I have important news for the Mage!"

Byggvir stepped from the elevator cage and scurried along

the branch, doing his best to avoid the view of the ground far below. The Elf was accompanied by his own master, the Chef, and a cluster of cooks and dishwashers from the kitchen. At the sight of their leader Byggvir and his fellows fell to their knees, bowing their heads. "In the name of the Mother, and her Cord," they mumbled together.

The Mage nodded. "In the name of the Mother, and her Cord, you may rise. Now what troubles you, friends? Tell me what news you bring."

Barely able to control themselves, the Elves began talking at once. "Your Mage, the Elf—"

"Mistress, Byggvir was walkin' in the—"

"That was when he saw the—"

A withering look from their Mage silenced them. "Please. Now, who saw what?"

"'Twas Byggvir, my Mage," said the Chef. "He saw it all."

"If Byggvir has something important to share, then let him do so without interruption."

"'Tis *the shoe,* my Mage," the Elf said. "Princess Asra's wedding shoe. The one that went missing after Prince Udos was—well, I saw the shoe in the forest when I was—well, it wasn't in the forest, it was in a clearing, out at the edge of Alfheim, and I saw a Human, well, 'twas a Human boy, and the earth was torn apart, and the boy had an accident, and I saw it. The shoe was jammed in the flesh of his foot. There was Blood, and I ran. But I saw it! I saw the shoe, my Mage!"

"The shoe was lost somewhere near the Sacred Grove," the Mage replied. "You say that you saw the Human on the outskirts of Alfheim?"

"Aye, Mistress, that's where I saw him with the shoe, poking out of the heel of his own foot."

"How do you suppose that the shoe found its way to the edge of Alfheim?"

"I d-don't know, Mistress," the Elf stammered. "All I know is what I saw."

"Did the Human touch you?" asked the Mage.

"Nooo," answered Byggvir. "I don't believe he even saw me."

"Good. Now you say you saw the Human take an object that is precious to the Alfheim Clan. Are you telling us that you did nothing to retrieve the shoe and bring it back?"

Byggvir stared hard at the branch, shuffling his feet. "Nooo, Mistress. I was too frightened to do anything but run back to tell you what I saw."

The Mage nodded her head. "All right, Byggvir. That was the appropriate response. Fear is a wise teacher, you know. A direct confrontation with the Human would have been far too risky, especially since you were alone. 'Tis wise not to chance it, especially without a Mage's protection. Now, this is what we shall do. Tonight we will meet in the Glen, every one of us, and I will lead us across the border into their world. We'll go to the place where the Humans live. We'll chant together, beneath the light of the moon, and I will enter the boy's dreams. I'll wrest control of his will, and command him to bring the shoe to the edge of the woods. 'Twill be the safest way of retrieving it. Then the shoe must be cleansed and purified, to free it from contamination. Once we've performed the rituals, and are certain that the shoe is untainted, I will deliver it to Ljosalfar. Once again it will be possible for Princess Asra to marry. This discovery is a gift from the Gods!"

The Mage's smile was a look of pure happiness, and Tuava-Li knew what a rare expression that was. "Thank you, Byggvir, thank you," said the Mage. "You've done well."

The Elves bowed, and bowed again, then turned and bumbled their way to the elevator cage. Tuava-Li gave one of the cords a sharp yank. When the bell rang, the rats scampered into their wheel. "Tuava-Li," said the Mage, "I want you to go to the chapel and tell Jardaine and the other monks that I wish to see them here. We have much to prepare before tonight!"

4

MATT'S DAD CAME IN just before dinner. During the meal Charlie couldn't stop talking about how the company that owned the construction equipment suspected he'd damaged their vehicles through his own negligence, and they were going to pay him a visit to find out what was going on. In the meantime, he'd found another company to lease him a backhoe. Now he could divert the stream that ran down the hill, and clear the way for more construction. Normally Matt would have joined in the dinner conversation. But tonight the pain in his heel made him quiet, and nobody seemed to notice the difference.

When bedtime came, Matt's foot was bothering him more than ever. With the bedroom door closed behind him he went to the drawer and pulled out the little shoe. Lying in the palm of his hand it looked innocent enough. He touched the heel. *Don't toy companies have rules about safety, and stuff like that?* he thought. *Why would they make something this sharp? Who knows. Maybe the shoe's really old and it's been buried in the dirt back there for a hundred years, before anybody thought about kids getting hurt. But then, a hundred years ago, there was nothing but a big, empty forest back there. In fact, just six months ago there was nothing back there but forest.*

Matt put the shoe back in the drawer, tucked behind a stack of shirts. Maybe if his foot didn't get better he'd need to show the doctor the doll shoe so they could do tests on it and find out what kind of bacteria or viruses it might have had on it. If his foot healed on its own, the shoe would stay hidden. He'd have to volunteer to help his mom put away any clean laundry, to make sure she didn't get into that drawer. Matt hobbled over to his bed beneath the window. He crept under the covers and stared up at the ceiling. The light on the bedside table threw shadows around the room. Most likely his foot would feel better in the morning, and he'd forget all about it. Matt pictured the jewel-encrusted shoe. It crossed his mind for a moment that the little jewels might be real, and that the thing was worth a fortune. *But that's stupid,* he thought. *If only I'd kept my sneakers on . . .*

Matt's foot throbbed. He remembered that back in their old neighborhood there was a guy, an Iraq War vet, who lived down the hill in a first-floor apartment. He didn't have any legs, just pants bunched up around his hips. He used to scoot his wheelchair down the block to the liquor store, and then back to the deli where he bought lottery tickets and cigarettes. Matt wondered what it would feel like to have his injured foot cut off. Could the doctors fit him with some kind of high-tech mechanical foot? Would he have to go to a special school? Or would he have to spend the rest of his life on crutches, or maybe in a wheelchair, with his mom pushing him around?

What if the infection in my foot is really, really bad? Matt wondered. *What if it spreads to my leg, or my brain? What if I go insane, like some dog in a horror movie, foaming at the mouth and attacking other people? Why did Mom have to tell me all the nasty things that could happen?*

Matt found himself drifting off to sleep, and the ache in his foot began to pulse. Voices whispered in his head. Something like wind chimes tinkled in the distance. Part of Matt's brain wondered if he had a fever, if he was hallucinating. The voices grew clearer.

"What excuse, what lie conceals,
What fate befalls the Soul who steals?
Who's proven, by his act, a thief?
And is there hope for some relief?
The culprit walks a slippery slope;
To change course is his only hope.
The shoe was never his to own.
Is not his conscience like a stone?
He cries in shame, alas, alack;
And knows that he must give it back!"

Matt turned in bed, pulled the blanket tighter around his chin, dragged his pillow over his head, but the voices wouldn't stop.

They kept repeating the same strange poem, chanting the refrain, *Give it back, give it back, give it back.*

Matt was certain he was losing his mind. He sat up in bed, and held his breath at the sound of footsteps coming down the hall toward his room. Maybe it was just the pounding of his heart, or the throb of pain in his heel. Maybe it was something else. Matt remembered a story from his childhood, something about a ghost who comes to haunt the person who found a severed toe in the grass outside his cabin. *Bony toe,* the ghost in the story called, *give me back my bony toe!*

Little fingers curled around the edge of the bedroom door. A shadow cast by a light at the end of the hall leapt into Matt's room as the door swung wide. "Matt?" whispered Becky, standing there with her hair tousled, and a blanket and a pillow in her arms. "Matt, I had a bad dream, and when I went into Mommy's room Emily was already in bed with them. Can I sleep here with you tonight?"

Becky wasn't used to having a room of her own. Neither was Matt, for that matter, so he limped to his closet, pulled out his sleeping bag, and spread it out on the floor next to his bed. "This is just for tonight," Matt grumbled. "Don't make a habit of it."

Secretly he was glad for the company. Before he fell asleep again, Matt glanced at the dresser drawer where the little shoe lay, and felt very foolish. He also thought that tomorrow would be a good time to get rid of the thing for good.

The morning sun spilled through the window of Matt's room, waking him before he was ready. He pushed his rumpled bedsheet aside and stepped onto the floor. *"Aaaangh!"* he cried. The pain in his heel rocketed straight to his brain. For a moment he thought he might pass out. Becky's face was buried in her pillow, and she groaned. "Is it daytime already?"

Ten minutes later the pair stumbled down the stairs. Charlie raced around the kitchen searching for his keys, while Matt and Becky slid into their seats at the table. Matt sat with his head in his hands as Jill spooned mashed apricots into Emily's mouth. Becky yawned and reached across the table to rub her sister's hair. "Kids," Jill asked, "can you get your own breakfast?"

"I'm not hungry," Matt mumbled.

"Me neither," said Becky. "I didn't sleep too well."

"You didn't have to get up," Jill said. "Why don't you go back to bed?"

Becky stole a glance at Matt, feeling a little embarrassed about having slept on the floor of his room. "I had some bad dreams. It's time to get up anyway, I want to fix my room today. Matt's going to help."

Charlie turned to his wife. "Jill, I'm supposed to meet the crew up on the ridge at eight, and I can't find my keys."

"They're hanging from the ring on your belt," Jill said, rolling her eyes. "Do you have your cell phone?"

"Nah, I forgot to charge it."

"Again?" Jill sighed.

Matt shifted in his seat. The throbbing in his foot was impossible to ignore, and he had to keep his heel off the floor. His mind wandered back to the weird chanting he heard in his dreams. Something about *give it back, give it back* . . . "See you guys at dinnertime," Charlie said, slipping out through the French doors.

Matt hobbled to the window over the sink and stared out at the woods. *"Give it back, give it back,"* the voices kept repeating, and Matt began to feel like the voices weren't just in his brain. They were coming from outside, maybe from the woods beyond the construction site. It was just too weird. He thought of the doll shoe hidden in the drawer upstairs. His chest felt tight; he tried to push the feeling of panic away. "Are you okay, Matt?" his mother asked.

Matt heard her voice like it was a hundred miles away. Somebody, or something, wanted the stupid doll shoe back. What else could it be? It was dumb, he knew, but he couldn't shake the feeling. *"What excuse, what lie conceals, what fate befalls the Soul who steals?"* the voices cried.

"What?" Matt said. He blinked, and stared into the woods. Were those figures milling behind the trees? Matt felt the hair on the back of his neck prickle. He rubbed his eyes and looked again. Nothing. "I think I'm going to go back to bed," he said.

"I hope you're not getting sick," Jill said. "Are you coming down with something?"

"I'm okay," he lied. "Just tired, that's all."

Matt looked at his baby sister, sitting cheerfully in her high chair. He noticed Becky staring at him, her eyes wide. "You promised you'd play with me," she said.

Matt's foot was throbbing. All he wanted to do was get into bed. "I already helped you get your dolls unpacked, didn't I?" he muttered, casting a quick glance at the window. He was certain that he had seen movement among the trees.

5

IN DANK CHAMBERS of the Helfratheim court, a world away from Sylvan Estates, torches were blazing. At the gaming table Prince Macta's face was a mask of calm. He raised his fist, gave the four knucklebones a shake, and flung them onto the table. The Elves on Macta's side of the room jostled for a better view, as the Dwarves on the other side did the same. Rows of candles sputtered in the air as the knucklebones clattered to a stop.

Small black dots were burned into the six sides of each bone, and everyone in the room knew what the combination of dots meant. Macta leaned back, smiling. All eyes were on the table. The Dwarves who were crowded behind the players saw the outcome of the toss and groaned. "Tough luck, my friend," Macta exclaimed. "Three ones and a two. *The Rat*."

The game had been going nonstop since early the previous evening, but in the subterranean chamber where Macta liked

to play, the light of the sun never shone. Zelimir, the fat, pockmarked Dwarf sitting opposite Macta, tried not to frown. In the underground city where he lived, Zelimir was a respected member of the merchant class. Business often brought him to the palace of the Dockalfars. Elves and Dwarves rarely mingled, but money, as Macta often said, has a way of fording many an abyss. Zelimir's eyes never left Macta as he reached for the knucklebones. His translator whispered in his ear. Zelimir grunted, reached into a satchel hanging from a strap around his neck, and counted out a number of coins. He placed them on the table and sat back.

Macta's face was smooth and, for an Elflad, almost pretty. Around his neck hung a silver pendant shaped like a stag's skull, and jeweled rings decorated many of his nervous fingers. His deep-set eyes were green, with flecks of gold. The eyes of all Elves were huge, and much was revealed in their liquid depths. Yet Macta's eyes were veiled by a lifetime of caution. Smoke hung over the heads of the Faerie Folk that crowded into the room, as they drank, puffed their cigars, and gnawed at greasy joints of meat. Servants snaked through the crowd, sloshing ale into mugs. Shaggy Goblins snatched discarded bones.

Macta's brother-in-law, Baltham, stood in the shadows behind him. His soft hands clutched the edge of Macta's chair, and he giggled nervously as Macta dropped a fistful of coins next to the mound that already lay heavy on his side of the table. Baltham was too timid to risk a penny of his own money, but he thrilled to watch his wife's proud, irresponsible brother in action. For his part, Macta thrived on Baltham's envy.

Across the table Zelimir's gaze was steady. He knew that if he lost the next roll of the knucklebones it would cost him everything. He could stop the game at any time, and go home a free, though poorer, Dwarf. Still . . . he had come so far. And what would his wives say if he returned home empty-handed? Zelimir whispered a prayer, then scooped up the knucklebones and gave them a toss. Two sixes, a four, and a one: *the Dog.* Macta picked up the knucklebones and held them in the palm of his hand. "All or nothing, my friend," he said. His bet was reckless, he knew, but it would be worth it all to see the Dwarf suffer. The translator spoke to Zelimir and turned away, giving Macta an icy stare. The other Dwarves shook their heads. Zelimir was livid with rage, and yet his lust for the mountain of coins filled him with a greed he could hardly contain. Finally he sat back, nodding. Just then there was a knock on the chamber door. "See who dares disturb my game," ordered Macta.

A rumpled-looking Elf, out of breath from his long passage in the Cord, stepped briskly into the room. His name was Nebiros, and his official job was to sharpen obsidian knives in the Alfheim kitchens. His real occupation, however, was to pass messages between Macta and his secret accomplice in Alfheim. He pushed his way through the crowd to whisper in Macta's ear. A moment later, the Prince leaned back and grinned. "An object of infinite worth has just been discovered," he said. "'Tis the key to my future happiness, because it is the wedding shoe that will enable me to marry the Elfmaid I have loved since I was a lad. Compared with such a prize, the coins on the table are worth less than the dirt under my feet. And yet, on the day I propose, these coins will buy me some pretty baubles and a bouquet for my beloved!"

The translator did not bother to tell his Master what Macta said; all that mattered now was the next roll. Macta flashed a confident smile and gave the knucklebones a toss. Silence filled the room. One, one, one, and one. It was the lowest of scores, *the Ant.* Zelimir roared with relief as the Pixies pushed the mountain of coins toward him. Macta leapt up, overturning his chair. Losing was not an acceptable outcome. He crashed into the shoulder of his brother-in-law, still standing close behind. "Get out of my way, you idiot," he hissed, and gave Baltham a swift kick in the shin. "I've got more important things to do than stand here looking at you!"

6

IN THE KINGDOM OF LJOSALFAR a different kind of game was in play. A decorative banner hung from an arch over the entrance to the Labyrinth, where Princess Asra joined her friends for a game. Along the winding footpaths, past sculpted shrubbery, a dozen young Elves forgot their sophisticated manners and raced like children through the maze. Asra turned a corner and dodged around a fountain. Her friend Skara followed close behind, giggling, and the beads that hung from the straps of her embroidered cap jangled as she ran. "Hush, Skara, they'll hear you!" whispered Asra.

"But I want them to hear me!"

Asra and Skara reached an archway in the hedge, and on the other side the Elflads were drawing near. When playing the Labyrinth game, the males always entered from the north side, and the females entered from the south. When an Elflad and an

Elfmaid met at any place where the paths intersected, they were expected to kiss. If the same Elflad and Elfmaid should meet three times within the maze, then they were betrothed, which meant that the couple was fated to one day be married. Of course, it was just a game for young Elves to play. It was an acceptable way to act out the rituals of courtship. But Princess Asra felt strange playing the game. Though three hundred and sixty moons had passed since Udos's death, it was but a brief time for the Elves. Asra was the only one of her group of friends to have ever been engaged, and if the hunter's bullet had not felled Udos, she would be married now. Married Elfmaids did not play games, they did not run and chase and kiss Elflads they barely knew.

Asra saw the shadow first. She grabbed Skara by the shoulders and thrust her into the archway. A pair of Elflads tumbled over each other in the effort to stop in front of Skara, and the taller of the two straightened himself and tried to appear dignified. Nevertheless his cheeks gleamed like apples as he leaned forward and kissed Skara on the mouth. Then the pair turned away from each other, laughing, and everyone raced ahead. "Why did you push me in front of you?" demanded Skara. "Vittror was yours for the taking. You've already kissed him once!"

"I know," said Asra, with a shudder. "That's why I didn't want to risk it again!"

"He's handsome," Skara enthused, "not to mention one of the royals of the Ellyll Clan. He'd be a perfect match for you, Asra!"

"'Tis just a game, Skara. I don't want to even pretend to be engaged to someone now. I'm only here because you didn't want to come alone." Asra stopped to peer around the corner of the hedge. "I don't need a perfect match. I don't need *a match* at all. But if my time should ever come again, my parents want me to marry a Ljosalfar lad, like Udos was. They say 'twould be good for the Clans." Asra looked left and right, and then hurried around the corner. "Besides, I lost my mother's wedding shoe. The shoes have been used for a hundred generations. I'm not getting married without them. In fact, no Alfheim Princess will ever be allowed to marry without the shoes."

"A convenient excuse!" noted Skara, as they came to a courtyard with five identical arches. The friends stopped for a moment to catch their breath. "Asra, were you in love with Udos?"

The Princess brushed a strand of hair from her eyes. "My parents arranged the whole thing! I hardly even knew him."

"Then what about his cousin," Skara persisted, "Prince Macta? He's been in love with you forever!"

"Macta Dockalfar?" Asra grimaced. "You must be joking. He claims he was Udos's cousin, but he's from Helfratheim, and the Northern Elves haven't married into the families of Ljosalfar. Macta just uses that cousin story as an excuse to be familiar with me and my family.

"Still," Skara said, her eyes glazing over, "there's something about him . . . he's strong, and willful. And he's not bad-looking, Asra."

"The Dockalfars are the opposite of everything we stand for," Asra said. "Macta makes my skin crawl! And he's not in love with me, he just wants to possess me. Listen, Skara, I'm perfectly happy being on my own. You're the one who's crazy for the lads. Let's find a mate for you, and spare me the romance!"

The paths of the Labyrinth had been designed to represent the pattern of Cords that circled the earth. Seen from above, the weaving paths crossed, and crossed again, and the young Elfmaids and Elflads charged headlong, flirting with chance and hoping to find their future hidden behind an unexpected kiss. "Look!" exclaimed Skara, recognizing the familiar bushy tail of a topiary squirrel. "I think this is the shortest path to the next archway."

She grinned back at her friend, grabbing hold of her sleeve. "Come on, Asra, hurry, there's not much time!"

7

IT WAS LATE IN THE AFTERNOON. Becky was in her room, taking books from cardboard boxes and stacking them on a bookcase by her bed. She tried arranging the books by height, and then by the color of the spines. She had tried alphabetical order, but gave up on that after just a few minutes. Now she was simply trying to get the books out of the boxes and stack them so they would all fit on the shelves. Becky had finally found a radio station she liked, and the music blared from her boom box. Jill stuck her head around the bedroom door. "Can you turn that down a little, honey?" she asked. "Your brother's still sleeping. He's running a temperature. And keep your distance, okay? If all of you kids get sick, I'm doomed."

Becky turned down the volume as her mother disappeared down the stairs. Then she got up to shut her door. But just across the hall she saw Matt, standing awkwardly in his doorway.

"Psssst," he whispered, gesturing to her. "Come over here for a minute."

Becky looked at her brother and hesitated. "Come on, Becky," he pleaded. "I've got to show you my foot!"

Matt retreated into the safety of his room, hobbled to his bed, and lifted up his foot for Becky to see. "Oh, Matt!" she cried, reeling back. "You've got to tell Mom right now, Matt, you've got to tell her! It's disgusting!"

For the thousandth time that afternoon Matt turned up the heel of his left foot and peered into the puncture wound that darkened his skin, and the ooze that pooled at its edges. "It smells bad, I know. I've been putting antibiotic cream on it, but unless I lie down and hold my leg up in the air, it just keeps throbbing."

"I'm going to tell Mom," Becky warned, turning away.

"No, wait," Matt pleaded, "you've got to promise not to tell. I'll—I'll give you something if you promise."

Becky narrowed her eyes at her brother. "I'll tell her," Matt lied. "I will, tonight. But you've got to keep your mouth shut. I want to find just the right way of saying it so that . . . well, I don't know just what to say, yet. I don't want to get in trouble, and I hate it when Mom treats me like a baby."

Matt got up and limped to his dresser. He opened the drawer and took out the doll shoe. "Here," he said, "I want to give you something. I—found it. It's an antique! It's really old, and look, it's beautiful, isn't it? Look at the way it shines in the light! Come here, I'll show you."

Matt led Becky to the window and let the afternoon light play across the little jewels. He turned the shoe this way and that, so that flashes of white and gold danced on his hand.

"Oooh," said Becky, her eyes wide. "It's beautiful! Where's the other one?"

"I don't know," Matt said. "But if I give this to you, will you promise to keep quiet and let *me* tell Mom about my foot?"

"What am I going to do with one shoe?" asked Becky.

Matt pressed the doll shoe into her hand. "I wouldn't even offer it to you if I didn't think you were responsible enough to take care of it. The heel is really sharp, so be careful. And it'll be our secret."

"Oh!" Becky exclaimed, holding the shoe up for a closer view. She nodded slowly. "But why is it a secret?"

Matt furrowed his brow. "Little kids have little secrets. You're nine. This is a bigger secret, just between you and me."

Becky studied the shoe. Finally, she looked up at her brother with a grin. "It's a deal!" she said, clutching the shoe, and she skipped across the hall to her room.

Matt lay in bed, staring at the ceiling. He was embarrassed that he had stepped on a doll shoe and hurt himself so badly. If he'd stepped on a piece of broken glass, it wouldn't have seemed so stupid. And he knew he'd been warned again and again about walking around a construction site in his bare feet. Mom and Dad would be mad that he ignored them. Now that he had let it go so long, they would be even more upset that he had kept the injury a secret. But it was *his* foot, after all. Wasn't he old enough to take care of a little puncture wound? And there was something else. Something about the shoe that made him feel unsettled, uneasy. Maybe he shouldn't have given the shoe to Becky. After she went to sleep, maybe he would go to her room and get it back. The thing was, he had found it, he had paid for it with his own blood and pain. And maybe it was too much responsibility to share. He didn't want Becky accidentally getting cut on it. S*tupid toy,* he thought.

At suppertime the smell of food wafted up the stairs and Matt got out of bed and crept down to join his family. He wasn't hungry, and he knew that soon he would have to tell the truth about his foot. It wasn't going to get better by itself. So much for his right to privacy. He didn't want to die for a secret. The light on the ceiling was harsh, and the noisy clatter of silverware and Emily's happy shrieks jangled Matt's nerves. "Honey, I thought you were going to stay in bed!" said his mother, looking up from the table. With a little pink spoon she shoveled mashed peas into Emily's mouth.

"Mom," Matt mumbled, "I don't feel so good. I think maybe I should go to the doctor. I—"

Emily screamed and flung her sippy cup in the air. It hit the floor with a sharp crack and milk spread across the tiles. "Oh, Matt," Jill said, leaping up and grabbing a fistful of paper towels. "You know, it sounds like the flu to me. I've got some medicine

I can give you tonight. Let's see how you feel tomorrow. We haven't even got a new doctor out here yet. We'd have to drive all the way into Pittsburgh."

Jill knelt to mop up the spilled milk as Emily, reaching over her high chair, giggled and plucked at her mother's hair. "Stop that," Jill sighed. "It isn't funny."

The rest of the dinner conversation revolved around the delays in Charlie's construction schedule. Matt picked at a plate of noodles and broccoli. Suddenly it didn't seem like a good time to talk about his foot. If he could hold out until the morning, his mom would take him to the doctor in Pittsburgh anyway, so maybe it would be better to wait and see. His foot *could* get better by then. Just maybe. And maybe he did have the flu, after all, with the chills, and headache, and fever. A little hole in his foot wouldn't cause symptoms like that, he thought . . . *would it?*

8

THE MAGE OF ALFHEIM lay quietly in the darkness of her study. She stared up past the knots that tied the ends of her hammock to the ceiling, past the rustling treetops, past the swift-moving clouds, and farther still into a darkness deeper than space. Neither awake nor asleep, the Mage lay still, gazing deeply into the past, back to a time that existed perhaps only in legend. She was passing through the Gates of Vattar, in the dreaming ritual that Elves practiced nightly beneath the light of the moon. In her mind's eye she saw the two most ancient Gods, Alvar and Oni. Alvar's home was the sky, Oni's was the earth. Alvar and Oni were neither male nor female, but *both* male and female in one body. Basking in the golden light of their separate realms, they had little need for contact with one another. But one day a flower grew along the horizon between earth and sky. It was a beautiful flower, the most beautiful thing that Alvar and

Oni had never seen, and they both wanted it for themselves.

Full of desire, Alvar and Oni met at the horizon where the flower grew. They drew their daggers, both ready for a fight to the death. Alvar struck first, slaying the female half of Oni. Oni struck next, killing Alvar's male half. The two wounded Gods stood in an ocean of Blood and stared at each other. Oni was now only male, and Alvar was only female. With the realization of the horrible thing they had done, the Heavenly Warriors threw down their daggers and fell into each other's arms, in sorrow and dismay. Each of them was incomplete, imperfect, and mortal. They saw the possibility of Death. Before, the Gods had been solitary. Now each did not draw a breath without the need for the company of the other. The beautiful flower was theirs to share. From that moment on, the sky and the earth were joined. The Gods came together as male and female, and Alvar gave birth to the first Faeries born of this world.

What does the story mean? the Mage wondered. *What does the legend say about the way we must live in the world, the way we must share the bounties of the earth? Is there something to be learned about the Humans, and the borders that have been breached?*

A worried crowd was gathering on the branch outside the Mage's quarters. The Mage had not left her room all day, and now that darkness had descended, the Elves were anxious and fretful. "Is she all right?" the Elves cried.

"The Mage is tired," whispered Tuava-Li, getting up from her place next to the door. "All of our chanting in the Human realm exhausted her. You should all get back to your work. We must be ready for the Clan to return before the next full moon."

The Elves grumbled, shuffling their feet. "Why should we work our fingers to the bone, when the Humans are ready to destroy us?" one demanded. "Soon Alfheim will be nothing more than a memory. We haven't lived here in three hundred and sixty moons. What does it matter?"

"This business with the wedding shoe is just the first of many battles, mark my word," argued another. "What are we going to do about the Human? Will our chanting wear him down? The little magick we have isn't enough. We have to take more drastic measures, if we want to get the shoe back again."

Another Elf wagged her finger at Tuava-Li. "We have to face the facts—the Mage is old. What if she doesn't have the strength to lead us any more?"

"What would you have us do?" Tuava-Li snapped.

"We could cross the border into their realm," an Elf exclaimed, "sneak into the Human dwelling, and take the shoe by force!"

"Elves can't enter a Human's house without an invitation, you know that," Tuava-Li said. "The Mage says the Humans have forgotten that our kind exists. They tell of us in Faerie Tales, to entertain their children, but they don't believe we're *real.* If the Human who has possession of our shoe saw us, he'd be terrified. He'd think he'd gone mad. He would never invite us into his house and give us the shoe. Alfheim would be endangered all the more. Listen, even if we *did* find a way to enter his house without his invitation, the Mage says Human dwellings are full of metal and contagion. We'd be overcome long before we could find the shoe and bring it home. Don't you understand?"

"But we have to do something," cried the Elves.

"Aye," said Tuava-Li, "and we will. When the Mage is rested, she'll take us into the Human's dreams, and we'll wrest control over his actions. The shoe will be ours again, soon!"

"Well spoken, Tuava-Li," said the Mage, stepping into the moonlight. "Twice now we've called out to the Soul of the Human boy. Once during the night, and again in broad daylight. He's not strong enough to resist us for long."

"What about the machines?" argued another Elf. "We stopped some of them. But there'll be more. Alfheim will be destroyed if we do nothing to stop the Humans. We ought to tell the Synod in Ljosalfar now that we need more help—before it's too late. We can't allow another tree to fall, and the boy, and the shoe. It's all too much. Our troubles have just begun!"

"You're wrong," Tuava-Li insisted. "If our Mage didn't have the support and trust of the Synod, they wouldn't have sent us back here. We stopped the machines, didn't we? We can stop them again. You've got to be patient—and patience will help to temper your tongue with wisdom!"

"My children," soothed the Mage, "later this very night we'll return to the home of the Humans. Princess Asra will soon have her shoe. *Conflict* is our enemy, *disharmony* is what we have to fight. We don't need soldiers and armies to achieve what we desire." The Mage raised her arms as one who grasps at something just out of reach. "After all, are we not Elves?"

ONE, TWO, THREE. It was the third little cup of grape-flavored syrup that made Matt gag. "There," said his mother. She sat on the edge of Matt's bed, and slid the bottle back into its box. "That wasn't so bad, was it? Now we'll see how you're feeling tomorrow, and if I have to, I'll call the doctor and make an appointment."

Jill scooped up the washcloth that was draped over Matt's forehead. "I love you, honey," she whispered, and gave him a peck on the cheek. As soon as she had turned away, Matt wiped his cheek with his sleeve. Then he watched his mom switch off the light on the nightstand and disappear into the hall. Matt stared up at the bedroom ceiling. His eyes burned, his head ached, and his foot throbbed. The bed creaked as he tossed and turned. The rhythm of his own breathing finally lulled him to sleep as the medicine quieted his nerves, soothing and dulling his senses.

Matt's eyes opened. He felt like he'd been having a bad dream. Moonlight streamed in through the window. Becky was in the next room, crying. Why hadn't his parents gone to see what was the matter? Was she having a bad dream, too? Maybe they couldn't hear her. Limping, Matt got out of bed and stepped across the hall. Gently he pushed open the door to his sister's room. Becky was sitting up in bed, trembling, with her blanket pulled around her neck. She was staring at the open window. In the light of the bedside table Matt could see what was making Becky cry.

A big doll with a sparkling blue ponytail and enormous eyes, one of Becky's favorites, was standing on the windowsill. The doll was moving its arms and legs, left, right, left, right, and its plastic head banged against the screen, slowly knocking it loose from the window frame. The jewel-covered shoe that Matt had given his sister earlier in the evening was squeezed onto one of the doll's feet. "Tiffany wants to get out," Becky whispered.

Matt went to the open window, grabbed the doll by the hair, and tore the little shoe from its foot. Immediately the legs and arms stopped their clockwork motions. Matt flung the doll onto the floor. Becky leapt up out of the tangle of blankets and sped across the room to Matt. She wrapped her arms around his waist and held on, sobbing. Matt looked out through the screen to see shadowy figures on the lawn. Suddenly he felt his mind ringing with a chant he had hoped never to hear again. *"Give it back . . . Give it back . . . "*

They were looking up at Matt, with their pale, gaunt faces. They had huge, dark eyes and pointed ears. "Oh, my god," Matt whispered, while his mind told him that what he saw couldn't be real.

From her position in the yard the Mage saw the boy looking down on them, and her heart sank. This wasn't supposed to happen. The Human children weren't supposed to wake up. The Mage had let her awareness drift into the air, into the house, and she had read the girl's thoughts. She knew that the girl had put the shoe on the foot of a doll. She had used her magick to animate the doll, and command it to come to her. If the doll had kept banging against the window screen, it would have tumbled from the window and landed on the grass, where the Elves could retrieve the shoe. Tuava-Li, Jardaine, and the other monks were using their own magick to hold Becky's family in deep slumber. But the boy had become a problem. He and his sister were awake, and the Elves had been seen. From the window Matt glared fiercely into the yard. His desire to protect Becky overpowered his fear. "Who are you?" he demanded, thrusting his face into the darkness. "What do you want?"

The little shoe Matt clutched in his palm felt burning hot. His skin tingled, all the way up to his elbow. He wanted to take the thing and throw it out the window, but something inside made him stop. *"Give it back . . . Give it back . . . ,"* the voices continued.

One figure in a silver cloak and feathered headpiece stepped out of the group, looked up, and met his gaze. Matt turned away, but it was too late. He felt a presence in his mind, searching, commanding, *"Give it back."* It was more than words he was hearing, it was as if an alien presence had entered his skull, its fingers weaving through his brain, prodding, trying to shape his actions. He had to get them to stop. Matt ran down the stairs, flung open the door, and stepped onto the porch.

There must have been a hundred of them standing in the grass. They stood shoulder to shoulder in a wide crescent at the edge of the yard. The image of them shimmered before Matt's eyes. Not one appeared to be more than a couple of feet high. Where were his parents? Couldn't they hear anything? Becky was looking out of the bedroom window, with her doll clutched in her arms and tears streaming down her face. "What are you?" Matt demanded. "What are you doing here? What do you want?"

"You have something that belongs to us," came a high-pitched voice, from the one dressed in silver. "'Tis a shoe. Give it back, and we will leave."

"I haven't got anything that belongs to you. Get off of our property, or I'll wake up my dad. He's got a gun!"

"Your father will not come," said the female in the silver cloak. "Your family is sleeping very soundly tonight. We have made sure of that. Now give us the shoe, and we will go."

"I don't have your stupid shoe!" Matt cried, at the same time realizing they knew that he did. "All right, I *do* have the shoe. I thought it was a doll's shoe. A toy. Listen, I found it. I didn't take it from anybody; I found it in the dirt. It belongs to me now!"

Matt was stalling. Something crazy, something impossible was taking place, and he wanted to know what it all meant. He wondered what these creatures were, where they'd come from, what they were capable of doing. Then a thought flashed into his mind. He remembered looking at picture books about trolls and elves and goblins and other fairy things, when he was just a little boy. *They couldn't be real, could they?* "The shoe must be very important, or you wouldn't want it back so much," he said. "If I give it to you, you'll have to give me something valuable in return. Don't you have a pot of gold, or something? Don't you have to grant me a wish?"

Matt was surprised by his own boldness. He watched the creature in the silver cloak confer with the one standing next to her. "Pots of gold are nothing but the stuff of silly stories," said Tuava-Li, "and wishes are for the weak. This is reality. In exchange for the shoe, we will offer you med'cine."

"Medicine?" Matt said, as the pain in his heel throbbed and ran up his leg like a thousand burning spiders. "Medicine? Why would I want that?"

The older Elf glared at him. "Let us not play games. Without treatment you will die."

"You've been spying on me!" Matt exploded. "I'm going to the doctor. Tomorrow. Why should I trust you? What's to say your medicine won't kill me?"

"'Twould not be to your advantage to wait and see what

happens without it," said the old one. "Human med'cine will not help. All living creatures are subject to illness and disease. And all living creatures develop ways to heal their own afflictions. But sometimes contact with others allows a sickness to infect beings who have no capacity to fight it. So it is right that we fear contagion from one another. Direct contact with Faerie Folk can have perilous consequences for your kind. You stepped on our shoe, and your Blood, it appears, has been poisoned. Over time your leg will stiffen and become numb, like a dead thing. You'll become paralyzed. Then the sickness will eat away at your flesh, your muscles, your—"

"All right, all right," Matt winced. He didn't want to hear any more. "Give me your medicine, and I'll . . . I'll *think* about taking it. Once my foot is better, *if* it gets better, then I'll give you the stupid shoe."

Their silence was tense. "The potion must be specially prepared," the silver-cloaked creature finally spoke. "Give us the shoe, and we'll provide what you need later on this very night. We'll deliver it to the base of the maple tree, over there. In a few days you will be well again, and you'll forget what happened here."

Matt took a step and a hot burst of pain shot up his leg. He collapsed onto the porch, nauseated and sweating. How could he trust them? But maybe he didn't have a choice. "Then go back to wherever you come from, and get the medicine. I'll give you the shoe in exchange. Okay?"

The monk Jardaine whispered in the Mage's ear. "The

Human is about to collapse. His will is weak. We can force him to give us the shoe now. We melted the metal veins in the hearts of the machines. We can stop a Human boy, we can kill him and take what is ours. Now's our chance!"

"Nooo," breathed the Mage, turning to her monks. "We've stuck a bargain with the Human, so 'tis our obligation to fulfill it. Deceit is a sickness that spreads and spreads, and has no end. 'Tis not the way of our Clan. I will go and prepare the med'cine, and bring it back. Tuava-Li, you and the others stay here and watch him. The lad is weak, but we don't dare trust him. And we don't want to risk being seen by any other Humans, so I will be quick."

The Mage stood back from the other Elves and closed her luminous eyes. Her lips began to stiffen and bulge out from her face, hardening into a small yellow beak, as she began the transformation that would change her from an Elf into a horned owl. She leaned forward, flapping newly feathered wings, and lifted into the night air.

Matt blinked at the sight, swallowing hard. "Wh-what are you? Where do you come from? And . . . and how come you speak my language?"

In the Mage's absence, Tuava-Li had the authority to respond to the Human's question. But he wouldn't remember any of this, anyway, if the Mage's magic did its job. So why bother talking to him? Tuava-Li drew her lips back in a thin line and shook her head. But the boy made Jardaine angry, and it was she who took a step forward. "'Tis not *your* language, 'tis *our* language," she growled. "Your kind learned it from us. We were here first. We were here long before your hairy ancestors clomped across the plains. We fled from one continent to another to get away from you. This land is *our land*, not yours! You've crossed the boundaries, and cut our Cord, and killed our trees. And for what?"

"If you were here before people," Matt asked warily, "then . . . why have you been hiding? Where do you live?"

Jardaine was amazed by the Human's ignorance. "We used to *share* the world," she snapped, as years of anger and frustration rose up inside her. "But your kind always took our belongings, our homes, chopped down our forests, defiled our sacred places, tried to steal our magick and our power, and then killed us if you could. When it came to war, the Gods were forced to separate us from you, just so we could *survive! Do you know nothing?"*

"Sssh!" warned Tuava-Li. *"Don't talk to him! He doesn't need to know!"*

But the monk was too angry to listen. "The Gods gave us our own world, superimposed right over your own, and none save the Mages are allowed to cross the borders. Everyone knows that! You don't belong here! This land is ours!"

Matt shook his head. "You say you lost a war with Humans? But you're *magic*! You can bring things to life, get in people's minds, you can—"

"We compensate for our size with our skills," snapped

Jardaine, "and our intelligence . . . but *your* kind always finds a way to destroy what you don't understand."

Matt shrugged, and wiped the sweat from his eyes. The throbbing in his foot was making him feel faint. "I never destroyed anything! So try me. Maybe I'll understand."

"Hah!"

Tuava-Li frowned. Jardaine was making trouble where there did not need to be any, but now that her anger was spent, the monk backed away in silence. Matt blinked again. He was getting very tired. Everyone waited as the minutes ticked by, and before long a dark shape swept across the lawn. The owl-Mage approached her apprentice with a cut-glass bottle clutched in her talons. Tuava-Li took the bottle and held it up in the moonlight for Matt to see. "Is that the medicine?" Matt asked, leaning forward. "Bring it over here." He was afraid that if he went down into the yard the creatures would surround him.

"With your permission," answered Tuava-Li, her jaw set in determination.

"Be careful," hissed Jardaine. *"The Human has contaminated the shoe!"*

"I know," whispered Tuava-Li. She crept across the yard, her eyes fixed on the boy on the porch. Then, holding her breath, she reached out and dropped the bottle into Matt's clammy, upturned palm. She snatched the shoe and backed away. When she was safe among the other Elves she knelt on the grass and wrapped the treasure in a large yellow leaf. The owl hooted softly.

Tuava-Li looked into the bird's enormous eyes and nodded, then rose to address Matt. "Ten drops. Every three of your waking hours, under the tongue. Until the bottle is empty. Start now. When you're finished, bury the bottle at the foot of the red maple tree there. Don't let anyone else see it, and don't tell anyone where you got it!"

The Mage of Alfheim, still in owl form, hopped across the lawn. She no longer had the youthful strength and vigor required to turn herself back to an Elf. After her flight to Alfheim, transforming to her Elfin form, making the medicine for Matt, and shape-shifting to an owl again, all of her strength for magick had been consumed. Now she would simply have to wait for the transformation to wear off, though it might take days. The monks surrounded Tuava-Li and the shoe in a circle of protection. They set off on foot into the woods, and the Mage knew that their return to Alfheim would be safe. She flapped her wings and sailed above the treetops. Traveling by air, she would arrive home sooner than the monks. There was much to plan. It was imperative to get to Ljosalfar as soon as possible so that everyone would know that the wedding shoe of Princess Asra had been found.

Matt watched the creatures move across the field and disappear into the blackness of the forest. He opened the screen door and stepped inside, limping with pain. Then he closed the door and bolted the lock. Was all of this just a dream? He didn't think so. Matt went up the stairs, past Becky's bedroom. She was lying on her bed, fast asleep. The doll stood on a shelf next to all the others. Suddenly they all looked strange, and menacing, with their big, dark eyes, pale skin, their awkward, outstretched arms. *It had to be a dream . . .* Matt thought. All except for the little glass bottle clutched in his fist. He slipped into the bathroom and flicked on the light. The bottle looked old; it was crude and misshapen. From the lip of the bottle a bent, rubbery cork protruded. Matt gave it a tug. His breath caught in his throat; the smell was sickening. Everything that had happened outside felt to him like a dream, but the odor of the black, putrid liquid in the bottle was all too real. A greasy-looking droplet hung from the end of the cork. Matt considered that he might wait until tomorrow, and get some antibiotics from the doctor in Pittsburgh. Maybe he wouldn't even have to take off his shoe and show the doctor his heel, maybe the drugs for his fever would take care of his foot, too! Or not. Maybe this was the only way, after all. Holding his breath, Matt shook the cork over his tongue. He closed his eyes and gripped the edge of the sink, prepared for the worst. But surprisingly, the taste was mild and just a little salty; in fact, it was far more appealing than the grape syrup his mom had given him before bed. With a little practice, Matt figured out how to use the cork to lift the drops out of the bottle. When he had counted out ten, he twisted the cork back inside, and slipped the bottle into his pajama pocket. He crept into his room and climbed in bed. *If the stuff doesn't kill me,* Matt thought, *maybe I'll feel better in the morning*. Then he glanced at the clock. It was almost morning already. What had happened in the yard felt like it was all over in half an hour. Yet somehow an entire night had sped by. Matt fell immediately into a deep and dreamless sleep. His foot wasn't throbbing any more.

Cold moonlight lit the forest from above, silvering the tops of the trees. In the night, in the forest, there was no sense of time. Few signs of Humankind were visible here to mark the landscape and claim it for its own. Yet the eyes of the Mage, owl-like though they were, did not have the keen visual sense that a real owl possesses. Lost in the beauty of the night and her joy at the recovery of the shoe, the Mage sailed through the air slightly north of Alfheim. When the tip of her wing brushed a power line stretched along a darkened highway, she spun out of control. She tumbled forward, crashing into every branch between her and the ground. And as the other Elves marched joyfully through the woods toward home, the body of their Mage lay broken and still at the side of the road.

10

THE HIGHWAY WAS A BLUR as rain came down in jagged sheets. Along the road there was a hiss, a distant rumble, and a pair of headlights rolled into view, growing brighter and brighter. It was a state truck, with WILDLIFE MANAGEMENT printed on the side. Somebody had hit a deer the night before on 256. It happened all the time, and the county usually sent somebody out to clean up the mess. But when sanitation reported seeing an injured bird on the shoulder, it was Wildlife Management to the rescue. Carrie was behind the wheel, and Tim, on the passenger side, scoured the shoulder for any sign of movement. "Slow down," he said, "I think I see it. Looks like an owl."

The truck pulled over. When the bird saw the Humans approaching with a heavy blanket, it let out a screech. "Could have gotten hit by a car," Tim speculated, pulling on his thick welder's gloves. "Owls fly low when it rains."

Carrie glanced up and nodded her head. "Or it could have run into a power line."

"Naah," Tim said, coming in from behind. "If it got a good shock we'd be looking at roasted bird right now."

The owl swiveled its head. Its warning shriek was throaty and full of pain, but strong. Carrie winced. "This one's fierce. Come on, let's make it fast."

The pair flung the blanket over the injured bird and wrapped it into a bundle. The owl thrashed, all tearing beak and raking talons. But Carrie held it close as they hurried to the truck. She placed the bird on a blanket inside a kennel cage. Tim pulled it shut, slammed the door, and slid into the passenger seat. When Carrie climbed behind the wheel, the truck sped away.

Matt rolled over in bed and glanced out the window. Rain. The sky was as dark and heavy as poured concrete. The field that stretched from the house to the forest was slick with mud. The big yellow machines lay like skeletons on the dirt heaps, near flatbeds stacked with cinderblocks, bundles of wire, and sewer pipes. So many days had passed since anything out there had moved, it was starting to look like it had always been that way. There was a Portosan standing in the rain, not far from where the trees began. For a moment Matt imagined someone hiding in there, staring out at him through the mesh screen. Then he remembered the night before, and the little people with the pale skin and the pointed ears. The people who could crawl inside his mind as easily as he crawled under his blankets. He remembered their leader, who could turn herself into an owl and fly away. Matt remembered, but he couldn't quite put it all together. It was like a jigsaw puzzle without a picture on the box to guide him.

With a grunt Matt forced himself out of bed and stalked to the bathroom. He shifted his weight from one foot to the other as he stood in front of the toilet, and it wasn't until he had flushed and turned to the sink that he remembered his foot. Why would there be a reason to remember it? It didn't hurt! Matt sat down on the edge of the tub and lifted his heel. He peeled back the bandage. A thin wisp of purple spread from the wound and disappeared at the side of his foot. Matt gently touched the black spot where the doll heel had gone in, then stood up and rocked his weight back and forth, until he was certain the pain was gone. It felt more numb than normal, but that was okay. *Tap tap tap*. A knock at the door. "What?"

"Matt, it's Becky," the voice came from the other side. "Are you all right?"

Matt stood up and pulled the door open. "Yeah," he said, "I'm fine. I had some awful dreams, though. Kept me up half the night."

Becky looked confused. "Me too," she confessed, clutching her blanket as she tried to make sense of her memories. "How's your foot?" she asked.

"It feels a lot better. You'd better go wake up Mom and Dad, though. They must have slept through their alarm. I think it's pretty late."

"Oh!" she cried, and bounded down the stairs.

Matt reached into his pocket and felt for the glass bottle. Then he turned back to the bathroom, and locked the door.

Breakfast passed in a blur. Everybody was glad to hear that Matt was feeling better. Oddly, though, the entire family complained of feeling tired and sore. And there were lots of bad dreams to report. Had it been a full moon last night? Too cloudy to tell. Emily was not in the best mood, flinging Cheerios from her high chair and pounding a plastic spoon. Becky didn't mention anything about the shoe or the doll. She just sat tracing her finger along the grain on the wooden table.

Matt spent the morning lying in his bed, reading a book he'd been assigned to complete before school began. He kept his eye on the clock on the bedside table. When the smell of lunch wafted up the stairs, he went back into the bathroom and locked the door. He took the strange glass bottle from his pocket, swirled it around, and twisted out the cork. He held the tough, gnarly thing up high so that he could feel the drops hit his tongue. It was easier to count them that way, and he wanted to make sure he got them all. He flushed the toilet for effect, and left the bathroom just as his mother called, "Kids, time to eat!"

"How are you feeling?" Jill asked as Matt plopped into his seat at the kitchen table.

She spooned a big dollop of macaroni and cheese into a bowl

and passed it to him. Becky was already shoveling food into her mouth, and Emily was sliding her sippy cup on the plastic tray of her high chair. Matt glanced through the French doors, then quickly scanned the wooded horizon for any signs of . . . *whatever* they were, spying on him. Nothing. His mind wandered back to last night, and the creatures he had seen in his yard. He thought about how stupid it might have been to put something in his body that had been given to him not only by a stranger, but by some kind of weird alien stranger.

"Better," he said.

After the dishes were cleared, Matt told his mom he needed to spend some time on the computer. He explained that he wanted to do some background research on the book he was reading. But when he sat down at the desk in the little side room where the computer was set up, he wasn't really sure where to begin. He needed to do some research, true, but not what he'd told his mom. He needed to look up . . . what? Fairies? Elves? Dwarves? He clicked on a search engine and typed in *fairy* first. *How stupid is this?* he thought. Even the word *fairy* had different spellings: *fairy* and *faerie.* Matt found lots of sites with illustrations of cute little pixies and sprites in skintight long underwear, embroidered on throw pillows and printed on bar signs. *Fairy* seemed to be a general kind of word that included all of the other make-believe woodland creatures one could think of. He found a lot of stuff about Santa Claus. Funny how nobody ever talked about the fact that Santa is supposed to be an elf!

Matt clicked over to a Web site for people who like to role-play at being elves. The photographs showed grown-ups frolicking in the woods, dressed in tights with pointed rubber ears and flowered headbands. Matt realized that if he ever got depressed and thought *he* was a loser, he would just have to think of this Web site. What was wrong with people, anyway? Matt found sites about elf comic books, Halloween fairy costumes with wings and antennae, Dungeons & Dragons, and of course, a million things about Tolkien. Hobbits? *Hmmm.* The things he had seen didn't have those big feet. Elves? Tolkien's elves were human-sized. But then, all of that was fiction.

Matt found a picture, black and white, just a silhouette. It was of a tunnel running beneath a low hill. Tiny figures raced, almost like they were flying, through the passageway. Other small figures with walking sticks trudged along the ground above, beneath a sunlit sky. It was the words printed below that made goosebumps rise on Matt's arms: *You take the high road, and I'll take the low road, and I'll get to Scotland before you, for me and my true love will never meet again, on the bonnie, bonnie banks of Loch Lomond.* These were the words to that annoying song his dad was always singing around the house!

Matt scrolled down. The text said that the lyrics, hundreds of years old, had to do with soldiers who were fighting in a faraway land. A wounded soldier, dying in his friend's arms, is uttering his final words. He says that when the war is over his friend will return home by marching the high road, the road that the living travel on. But the dead soldier's spirit is going to speed back to the land of his birth through fairy channels that lie below the ground, in hidden passageways that can take a soul anyplace on earth. *The low road.* Matt shook his head in wonder. Were there hidden tunnels running through the woods? Beneath the construction site, under his own house? Is that how the creatures he had met got from place to place?

There was more to learn. Plenty more. Matt found some sites with scholarly articles about the history of fairies and elves in European countries. Not all of the creatures depicted here were nice and friendly. Some of them were fierce and hostile, some of them drank blood and stole human babies just for fun. Interesting, certainly, but it didn't seem like the ragtag group of little people that Matt had seen the night before. What he had seen looked more like a bunch of medieval peasants, if medieval peasants were two feet high and had big pointed ears. And the business about getting a wish, that was there, too. Because he had touched something of theirs, and because he had agreed to give it back, they were supposed to grant his wish. Even if they didn't want to admit to it. He'd accepted their medicine, but that wasn't his idea, it was theirs. So what was—

"Matt," said his mother, appearing in the doorway. "What is this? I found it in the bathroom upstairs."

Matt turned his head and saw the little glass bottle clutched in her hand. His heart raced; the cork had been pulled out, and he could see his mother's hand through the bottle. The dark color was gone. The bottle was empty. He leapt up, banging his shin on a table leg. His mind raced for possibilities to explain the bottle as he backed toward the door. *What a stupid mistake,* he thought. Obviously he'd left it on the edge of the sink, instead of hiding it in his pocket. "I—I found it in the dirt, out in the construction site," he lied. "I was going to show it to Dad, but I forgot. It must be an old liquor bottle, or something, maybe perfume, I don't know. It could have been back there in the dirt since pioneer days, who knows?"

"Well I certainly don't know," Jill said. "That's why I poured it down the drain. I rinsed the bottle out, too. Here, you can take it, if you want. But if you find anything else out there, I expect you to show me right away. It was very irresponsible of you to leave that bottle there on the sink, where one of your sisters could have reached it. Who knows what would have happened if Emily or Becky had found it, and drank some of that foul stuff?"

Matt threw up his hands. "Come on, Mom, Becky would never do anything that stupid, and Emily is too little to reach the top of the sink. That bottle was mine. You had no right to dump it out!"

"I had no right?" she said. "I had every right. This is my house, and I don't want you bringing dirty old junk in here. Emily's a toddler, and she can get into a lot of trouble unless we act responsibly. That means you, Matt. Am I making myself clear?"

Matt wondered what he was going to do now that the medicine was gone. Would his symptoms return? How long would it take before the sore on his foot got worse again? He shoved the empty bottle into his pocket. "Very clear," he mumbled, and stormed up the stairs to his bedroom.

11

THROUGH THE LONG, GRAY afternoon, Charlie McCormack worked the joysticks on the backhoe, and the machine raked its shovel through the mud. The demolition crew had cleared away the trees and shrubs with chain saws so the backhoe could get in, tear up some of the streambed, and build an earthen barricade. While the construction team was doing some plaster work in one of the nearly finished houses, Charlie was carving out a path on the other side of the ridge, digging a trench to receive the flow from the diversion. Soon the water would flow away from the land where the rest of the houses were going to go.

Charlie knew it would have been easier to build the houses around the stream, but that didn't fit his vision of the way the development ought to look. Clean, tidy, and orderly, that was the way he saw Sylvan Estates. Charlie had come up with the name of the development himself. *Sylvan* meant *of the woods*, and

Charlie thought it sounded pretty and sophisticated, too. The kind of name that would attract buyers. The cab of the backhoe shuddered as Charlie worked the pedals and levers. Sweat ran down his face as the blade shrieked, unearthing roots and chunks of rock. The tires rolled back and forth, compressing the dirt, and every little weed and sapling was ground beneath the machine's crushing weight. The afternoon wore on.

Down in the field at the base of the ridge rested the damaged bulldozer and excavator. The mechanics had told Charlie that the motors were shot. Parts with high resistance to heat were fused together; the metal in the plastic-coated wires had melted and left silver puddles to harden on the ground. The mechanics had to scratch their heads. Bad parts, maybe. Lightning? Doubtful. But it was obvious that negligence wasn't the cause. According to the lease the machinery would be replaced. The only problem was that there weren't any replacements available for a couple of weeks, until machines came back from other jobs. In the meanwhile, there was the stream to divert, land to level, stumps to uproot. And only one piece of equipment to do it.

At the end of the day, Charlie shifted the backhoe into park and switched off the engine. He pulled off his helmet, tossed it onto the seat, and headed down the hill toward home. A hawk circled above, nearly out of sight. But there were no other immediate signs of life among the trees that lay ahead. The animals in this part of the forest had fled the moment they heard the backhoe lumbering up the hill. Mice, groundhogs, birds, squirrels, snakes, and a thousand other timid creatures raced for shelter, heading for a place, any place, free of that earsplitting, earth-shattering sound. The sound that heralded destruction. The lower part of the stream now lay cut off from its source. The water trickled away and disappeared along the edges of the cold muck. Since Charlie had diverted the course of the stream, the mud had began to crust along the edges of something buried in the sediment.

Something had been placed at the bottom of this streambed, thirty years before. Something lay there still; something conscious, something that had seen things no human being had any business seeing. Over the years, silt and rotting leaves and pebbles had collected around the wet flannel of Anna McCormack's coat. It filled in the space between her legs and gathered around her boots. The rushing water carried mud, bits of broken twigs, and all the refuse of the forest, and it all piled up alongside Anna's ghost-white cheek. Mud and debris had settled in her hair, and the tendrils no longer swayed in the cold current.

Tomtar, the Troll who lived in a hollow place by a dogwood tree, was still keeping watch over Anna, as the Mage of Alfheim had requested. For thirty years he had sat by the girl's side without complaint and without anybody to listen to his words. He was reed-thin, his shoulders barely wider than his narrow face, and he had a mop of hair like straw that hung down over his eyes. Tomtar survived on tender shoots, ferns, morels, and berries, and by drinking the cold water that burbled over the rocks. He played his wooden flute and dreamed his life away, as

Trolls often do. Otherwise, Tomtar was alone with the butterflies and the crickets, the rush of the wind, and the babble of the stream. If the girl beneath the water had been able to reach out her arm, the Troll was so close that she would have touched him. But the only thing moving in the stream was the constant flowing water. For Tomtar, there were no real dangers, no challenges, no surprises in his life. But change always happens, if one waits long enough. Humans had come to devour the forest, bit by bit. Their machines had severed the stream, and from where Tomtar sat, the watch he had promised to maintain was over. The Mage's spell was meant to last as long as water flowed over Anna's open eyes; no one ever said what was supposed to happen when the water stopped flowing and the stream dried up. Was the girl dead? She appeared to be dead. But then, she had always looked that way. Still. Anna's body did not suffer the ravages of decay, abandoned to decompose in the water. Crayfish did not nibble at the bones of her fingers, worms and centipedes and bacteria did not carry her flesh away. But now the stream was drying up, and the reek of steel and gasoline and the shriek of an engine up over the ridge had let the Troll know that if he did not soon abandon his post, it would be too late to get away. The girl's body was nearly buried in mud. It was scarcely visible anymore, even to Tomtar. But there was no doubt it would be discovered if the tearing, clawing metal monster lumbered down and ripped the life out of the earth where he stood. There was no way around it; trouble might well be on its way, and it could arrive at any time. He had to go and find the Mage.

12

TUAVA-LI WAS PANIC-STRICKEN. The Mage should have arrived home before the others. With each passing hour, Tuava-Li waited, her anxiety growing. Just before daybreak she had awakened Jardaine and the monks. Then she had roused the other sleeping Elves, organized them into search parties, and sent them back into the woods, along the path that led to the home of the boy. Tuava-Li had stood on the branch outside the Mage's quarters, praying for her safe return, feeling her worry turn to despair. This was a complete catastrophe. When the search parties returned wet but empty-handed, Tuava-Li was at a loss for what to do. She met Jardaine at the base of the great old oak, Bethok. "'Tis bad, Tuava-Li," Jardaine muttered. "The Elves are coming to me to say that they want to go back to Ljosalfar. Everyone's frightened. With the Mage dead, they're sure Alfheim is finished."

Tuava-Li stiffened. "We don't know that she's dead. We don't know anything. 'Til we can gather more information, we need to stay calm. We can get through this. I know all the routines, the schedules, the plans. I know how things are organized. The Mage has been telling me for years about how one day I would have to take her place."

Jardaine snorted. "I don't think that matters. Nobody trusts you to lead us, Tuava-Li. You haven't lived with us for all that long. You're not from around here. No one's ever understood why the Mage chose you to be her Apprentice. I'm sorry, I'm not saying I agree with them, but they think you're too young, too inexperienced. They don't feel safe."

Tuava-Li turned away from the monk, her face a mask of doubt and confusion. No matter what the others might say, she was indeed their leader unless, or until, the Mage was found. So they all wanted to leave Alfheim, did they? Tuava-Li would have to convince the Elf Folk that everything would be all right, that even if the Mage didn't return, she was ready to take on the role of their leader. And if they didn't trust her ability to lead, she would go to the Synod in Ljosalfar and ask for help.

In the distance, Tuava-Li could hear the monks wailing. The world was a more stable place, a more predictable place, when the Mage was in command. Even though the trees of the forest were being cut. Even though the Alfheim Jewels were missing. But now that their leader, their teacher, their guide, their Mage was gone, so was the faith of the Elves that everything would work out all right. What might disappear next? The future of Alfheim rested in Tuava-Li's hands, if only until the Mage returned . . . *if only.* Tuava-Li rode the lift to the top of the mighty tree. She stepped past the curtain into the Mage's private study, and wept. It did not feel right to be here without the Mage's invitation. All of these books, the personal belongings, the corner shrine, the hammock suspended between heaven and earth, all of it now passed to Tuava-Li, Mage of Alfheim. How could it be? A shiver ran through her body. *No,* she thought, *'tis not time for me to take her place. Something must have delayed her return, but she'll be back. She will, I know it.*

Tuava-Li pulled on a cloak and climbed higher in the branches of Bethok. The Elfin world, overlapping the world of the Humans, was a more fragile, a more beautiful thing than what the Humans ever saw. And its beauty extended all the way to the center of the Faerie Earth, where the Great Seed lay. This was the true heart of their world. From the Great Seed, the source of life, grew the Cords. From the Cords grew the trees. And high atop this tree, among its dense branches, Tuava-Li stood. Practicing the exercise taught to her by the Mage, she held her arms out straight from the shoulders. The Mage had said that strength, clarity, and spiritual power, the foundation of a Mage's character, would accumulate through the practice. With her attention directed toward the eternal, her eyes fixed in the distance, she thrust out her chest and concentrated on her breath. She cleared her mind and waited for the sensation to begin. It started as a tingling in her fingertips, then spread through her arms, and finally into her jaw. Her lips trembled as she began her song, her prayer. The longer Tuava-Li was able to hold out her arms, the more the tingling became a burning, the more her body cried out to her brain that she should let her arms drop to her sides, that she should stop. The longer she held out her arms, the more a part of her began to draw strength from her persistence, and with each breath she began to accumulate energy. Paradoxically, the more pain she experienced, the less it mattered. Her prayer acquired power; her words flowed freely from the cauldron of her heart. She prayed for understanding, she prayed for strength. Finally, Tuava-Li's self took on a radiance that was larger than her physical body. She was crackling with energy. Gently she lowered her arms to her side. She was trembling and drenched in sweat, yet she felt power flowing from her fingertips and her eyes. Slowly she descended the tree to the Mage's quarters, then slipped into the dark room to lie in the hammock and consider what must be done.

Before long a commotion arose from the ground below. Tuava-Li heard the voices coming closer, and felt their excited, chaotic energy from a hundred feet away. She leapt from the sling and brushed past the curtain to the branch outside. Peering down, she could see that a stranger had come into their midst. He was a Troll, no older than she was, and he wore the rough, plain clothes of a country dweller. A score of Elves stood in a circle around him, interested, yet keeping their distance.

Tuava-Li rode the elevator cage to the ground and the crowd parted for her to pass. "In the name of the Mother and her Cord," Tomtar said, making an awkward bow.

"In the name of the Mother and her Cord, welcome, traveler," Tuava-Li replied. It took an effort of will for her to appear calm and in control. "What brings you to Alfheim?"

"I—I wanted to talk to the Silver-Cloaked Mage," the Troll stammered. "I was headed for Ljosalfar when I saw lights gleamin' through the trees and realized the Elves had returned to Alfheim. I had business to discuss with the Mage, so I came here first, hopin' to find her."

"I'm the acting Mage of Alfheim," Tuava-Li answered. "Please tell me your name, sir."

"I'm called Tomtar, but the others just told me the Mage is gone. Have you taken her place, ma'am?"

Tuava-Li swallowed, trying to keep down the panic. She hadn't anticipated having to answer a question like this, not yet. She tried to conjure up the dignity and reserve that her Master had always exhibited. "The Mage is attending to Clan business. As I said, I'm the acting Mage of Alfheim, during her absence. Long live the Mage."

Long live the Mage. The words were a formality, meant to signify that there would always be a continuity of leadership within the Clan. Yet Tuava-Li shivered as she said the words. There was no doubt that she was next in command. But she was far from convinced that she was prepared to lead her Elves. Where was the Mage? And how could the Elves of Alfheim ever hope to find her?

Tomtar bowed again. "Long live the Mage."

Tuava-Li forced a smile. "I believe I've heard your name before, Tomtar. Would you follow me into the Great Hall, please? We'll speak there."

Tomtar furrowed his brow. "I'd feel more comfortable outside, ma'am. I've been livin' in the open for a long time. Maybe we could take a little walk?"

"Very well." Tuava-Li nodded.

Tomtar was much taller than Tuava-Li. With his long legs he was forced to shuffle along behind, as they made their way through the Sacred Grove. They passed a low ditch and a circle of standing stones that lay beyond the trees. Finally, shielded behind a stone tall enough to hide Tomtar from view, Tuava-Li and the Troll came to a stop. "Ma'am, I'd never break my promise," Tomtar exclaimed. "The spell of the Mage was supposed to hold that Human lass in the stream 'til the water ceased to flow over her eyes. That was what the Mage told everyone, three hundred and sixty moons ago. I was supposed to stay there and see that nothin' disturbed the girl in her punishment. I thought the Mage would send someone to take my place—I waited and waited, but no one came. I didn't know what else to do, so I stayed by the stream. And then, just yesterday, some *Tems* with machines cut through the stream, and the water stopped flowin'. The lass is buried in the mud, you can barely see her anymore. I think she's dead. That's why I'm here, and not beside the stream with the body."

"I understand," Tuava-Li soothed. "And now I remember where I heard your name. I should have recalled it before, but I was a stranger to Alfheim when Prince Udos came to marry Princess Asra. The Mage demanded a harsh punishment for the Human after the disaster that happened here. You went well beyond the call of duty, Tomtar, to stay by the stream for so long. I wonder if the Mage even remembered you were there, after all that's come to pass. Thankfully a Human's life is short. All of the Elves of Alfheim are grateful for what you've done. It seems your promise has been fulfilled."

Tuava-Li paused, and she heard the Tomtar's stomach rumble. She looked into his face and saw that his expression was innocent and trusting beyond measure. "If you like," she said, "you're welcome to stay with us tonight and share our company. Our cook feeds us well, and I certainly think you deserve a good meal."

Tomtar glanced around, unsure how this invitation would help him in his quest, a quest with an unknown goal. He was, after all, on his Wandering, a rite of passage for all young Trolls, and he had been on his quest since before the Mage had asked him to watch over the Human in the stream. One of the rules of the Wandering was that a Troll was obliged to accept any invitation offered to him. An invitation was a sign pointing to the next turn in the path of his journey. And as long as the request did not violate any other rule of Troll behavior, he was required to say yes. "Thank you, ma'am," Tomtar said. "I'll stay. But aren't you worried about the *Tems* and their machines? They've come so close. Are you safe, here?"

"We've been holding the Humans at bay perfectly well," Tuava-Li said, her boldness hiding terrible uncertainty. "If you show us where you saw the machine that cut the stream, we'll destroy it, like we've destroyed the others. Elves were in these woods before the Humans arrived; we'll be here after they're gone. Now come with me. I'll see to it that you have something decent to eat. If you'd like to sleep indoors we'll prepare a bed for you. If not, you're welcome to make yourself at home anywhere in the forest of Alfheim that you please!"

"Out of doors is just fine for me, ma'am," Tomtar smiled.

Tuava-Li led the Troll to the dining hall. When they got to the door, he once again hesitated. "In truth I'm sorry, ma'am," he apologized, "but it makes me feel uncomfortable to have a roof like this over my head. If you have somethin' brought to me here, I'll eat outside."

"As you wish," Tuava-Li smiled. She entered the dining hall and strode across the earthen floor to the kitchen in the back. The Elves of Alfheim were accustomed to seeing Tuava-Li bringing trays of food to her Mage. They certainly knew her, and liked her well enough. But now they avoided her gaze, and as she crossed the room, beneath high ceilings crisscrossed with twisting roots, Tuava-Li felt that the Elves were talking about her behind her back. By the racks in the kitchen she bumped into Nebiros, the assistant to the Chef. Lately Nebiros always seemed to be underfoot. "Good evening, ma'am," he smiled. "Is there something special I can offer you tonight?"

"No thank you," answered Tuava-Li, "I'll help myself."

On each of two plates, she spread a row of dandelion leaves, then piled on a heap of crusty oat cakes. Over these she ladled a creamy chestnut sauce. Walking back through the doorway into the dining hall, Tuava-Li held her head high. She kept her gaze steady on the door, and the gangly Troll who waited, like a lost child, for her to return. The two of them took their trays to sit on the trunk of a fallen sycamore tree. "You never told me your name," mumbled Tomtar, his mouth full of food, "or where you're from."

Tuava-Li raised her eyebrows, a little taken aback. "You want to know who *I* am. And all this time I've been wondering about who you might be!" She chose her words carefully. "Very well. I'm called Tuava-Li. Before I came here I was a traveler, making my way from the West, out to see the world."

She picked up an oat cake and took a bite, chewing it slowly. "'Twas nearly three hundred moons ago that I met the Mage of Alfheim, during her stay in Ljosalfar. I had no intention of becoming a monk, or to undertake a spiritual life. But when a Mage chooses you, it . . . changes things. Now here I am. For a long while I've been her Apprentice, and second-in-command."

"We have somethin' in common, ma'am," Tomtar said. "I was

a traveler, too, on my Wanderin' from the city of Argant. I was makin' my way through the woods when I was set upon by a fox, and the Mage saved my life. She was in her owl form, then." Tomtar paused, and eyed Tuava-Li carefully. "Can you turn into an owl, too?"

"Nooo," Tuava-Li sighed. "Not yet."

The Troll sat, chewing with his mouth open, so Tuava-Li went on.

"'Tis part of the Mage's training, to find the right animal form, and the transformation hasn't happened to me, yet. I could be an owl, or a ferret, or a badger, or a hawk. The power to change will come when the time is right, but not before. Tell me, Tomtar, do you sense something of the owl about me?"

The Troll chuckled, and wiped crumbs from his lips. "I don't know why you'd think I could see such things. All I know is that your Mage had a yellow beak and eyes the size of saucers, and she came flyin' out of the night when she heard my cries. She killed the vermin, and the Elves of Alfheim brought me back across the border of the Human realm into your forest, where it was safe. They nursed my wounds and the Mage used her magick to heal me. That's why I spent this time by the stream. The Mage was kind to me, and I owed her my life."

Tuava-Li nodded, thinking of her Mage's face, and of her generosity, and she blinked back tears. Then she and Tomtar finished their meal in a silence that masked as many regrets as it did hopes.

That night, Tuava-Li tossed restlessly in the hammock in the Mage's study. She debated the merits of having taken a stranger into her confidence. The Troll was used to a life of wandering, both within the Cord and on solid earth. What if he found out that the Mage of Alfheim was truly missing, under mysterious circumstances, and that leadership had fallen into Tuava-Li's inexperienced hands? What was to stop the Troll from telling Elves or Faeries in other realms? What was to stop the Synod from taking over leadership of Alfheim? What was to stop them from listening to the Elves of Helfratheim, and driving them all into war with the Humans? The Mage would not have wanted that to happen. It was critical that Tuava-Li find the Mage, and bring her back home. If she was still alive. If she was dead, then everything would change. But that, so far, was unthinkable.

Beneath a troubled sky, the forest held its breath. At the bottom of a muddy streambed, a pair of eyes opened in the darkness and stared blankly into the treetops. The eyes blinked. Then they blinked again. Mud-caked fingers twitched. Then, without warning, the girl shifted laboriously onto her side, propping herself up with one pale, trembling hand. Anna McCormack got up out of the mud and coughed away the sediment that blocked her throat. She rocked back and forth, like a baby preparing to crawl, and whimpered. Her body was unchanged—still just twelve years old. Yet her mind was fearfully altered from all the seasons of grief, despair, and solitude. She rolled into a sitting position and looked down at her muddy clothes, her hands, and her boots. She shook her head and her filthy hair tangled around her face. Then the tears that had been trapped inside for thirty years began to flow, and they would not stop.

13

WHEN THE SUN WENT DOWN, wind howled through the valley, over the ridge, and across the wooded hills. Along the edge of the construction site leaves fluttered on the trees. Crickets thrummed outside the McCormack house. Matt was sitting on the couch in the living room with his sore foot propped up on the ottoman, and the TV set turned low. "Matt, I could use your help in the kitchen," Jill called.

Matt's book was open on his lap, and when he tossed it onto the sofa and got up, he felt a twinge of pain in his left heel. Not a good sign. The windows in the kitchen looked blank and forbidding once darkness came over the valley, and he found himself wishing his mother had found the time to hang curtains. As Matt laid out the plates for supper, Charlie clomped down the stairs with Emily in his arms.

Soon the family settled down to eat. Becky sunk her fork into the spaghetti, then bent to scrutinize her plate. "Hey, are there mushrooms in this sauce?"

"Yes," said Jill. "Just eat them, for once. They won't hurt you."

Becky looked up pleadingly. "But mushrooms can be poisonous! They have spores!"

Jill sighed. "Then pick them out. Maybe your dad will eat them."

"I sure will," Charlie said, reaching across the table. "Hey, you'll be glad to hear I finally got the stream up on the ridge diverted. Now the crew can start clearing way for the foundations of the next houses."

"I thought you were all done with houses," said Matt. "I kind of like living across from a forest, Dad. Are you going to cut down all of the trees?

"Me? No. But if I find a buyer for the rest of the acreage, that'll be up to them."

"What about the animals?" asked Becky. "They won't have anywhere to live!"

"Yeah," said Matt. "I keep seeing deer out by the construction site, and sometimes near the house, too. Where are they going to go if you cut everything down?"

Charlie smiled and waved his fork. "Don't worry about the trees. We cut 'em down here, and somebody will plant new ones somewhere else. And the animals, they'll find a place to go. They always do. If there are too many deer for the habitat, nature will take care of it. That and the hunters. Survival of the fittest!"

Matt squirmed uncomfortably. He was thinking of his secret: the little people in the woods. "Some things might not survive," he said. "They need homes, just like we do. A lot of . . . animals live in those trees."

"Listen, Matt," his dad replied, "this is Pennsylvania. There are probably a thousand trees here for every person. And if you're worried about the animals, cars are way more dangerous for critters than habitat loss. Just check out the roadkill on the highway some morning!"

"Charlie!" Jill exclaimed.

"Sorry," Charlie frowned. "Anyway, I've been thinking about the deer. Hunting season's coming up before too long, and it would be a shame if we kept all of Grandpa's rifles and shotguns locked away forever. I didn't have that gun case built into the hallway wall just for decoration. Your grandma kept them in storage for nearly thirty years—I'm sure she would have been happy to know we were going to use them."

"Use them?" Matt echoed. "For hunting?"

"It's a great way for a father to spend time with his son," Charlie said. "The times I spent hunting with my dad are pretty much the only memories I have of him."

After dinner everyone retired to the living room. The television droned from the corner, and Emily banged the keys on her little electronic piano. Becky busied herself arranging a row of her favorite dolls in front of the picture window. Suddenly she leapt up. "Mom, where's Amber? She's not here!"

"I don't know, sweetie. Didn't you have the dolls out for a picnic in the yard this afternoon?"

"Yes, but I'm sure I brought them all inside. Hey, wait a minute. Ashley's gone, too!"

Becky spun around, making a silent count. "Where's Erin? *And* Jessica? Mom, *four* of my dolls are gone," she whined. "Help me find them!"

"You've got a hundred dolls," said Matt. "How would you know if a few of them were missing?"

Charlie looked up from his newspaper. "Matt," he said, "why don't you take Becky out back, and see if you can find her dolls?"

The security light above the French doors flooded the yard, illuminating the entire deck, the sandbox, the picnic table, and a few scrawny bushes. Beyond that everything was a sea of darkness. Matt stood at the back door. Becky waited close behind him, afraid to step into the open. "Becky, your dolls aren't out here. I'm sure they're in the house somewhere. Nobody would take your dolls. Emily is too little to steal them, and nobody else cares."

"But they're gone!" Becky cried.

"All right," said Matt, feeling fed up. "Maybe they all went camping in the woods together. Maybe they're playing hide-and-seek under your bed or in the laundry room. But they're not out here, are they? Let's just go back inside. I'm sure Mom will help you look for them tomorrow." Matt stared into the darkness and shivered. "Don't worry, they have to turn up somewhere."

Becky wrapped her arms around her chest. "I guess," she said weakly. "I guess."

14

BENEATH PALE MOONLIGHT the nocturnal world was alive, scrabbling in hidden places, whispering its secrets, spreading its influence. For a few dark hours the rule of the night was complete. Then, leaving no trace behind but a blanket of dew, the darkness retreated. A wash of orange spilled over the horizon.

The Cords along the surface of the Faerie world were pulsing. There were countless whispers of movement from inside, like ghosts passing just out of sight. From the pits in the ground where access to the Cord lay, a faint glow shone. Large Cords gave way to smaller ones, tendrils spreading from its major arteries and snaking away into the distance. Cords stretched, forked, twisted, and touched other Cords, joining the far corners of the Faerie realm. Thousands of years had passed since the war that split the world in two. Yet even at their most separate, the Human domain was never far away from the world of Faerie. Natural intersections of the worlds occurred at certain points, like an underwater mountain range whose peaks break the surface of the water. But now it was as if the water was evaporating, leaving larger parts of the hidden realm exposed. The worlds of Faerie and Human were on their way to becoming one. Just as it had been in ancient times.

Four dark shapes sped through the Cord, spinning from the center toward the outer wall. Druga, first, punched his fist through the membrane. Pressing his body into the opening, he pushed with his arms and legs, until the slit was wide enough for him to tumble through. Once he was outside, Druga glanced to the left and right. All clear. Then he gave the signal to his master, Macta, and he, too, squeezed through the opening, followed by a ferocious-looking Goblin who strained on a leather leash. "Come, Powcca," Macta ordered.

Macta's brother-in-law, Baltham, clung to the inside wall of the Cord until it was his turn. The winds rushed past him, tugging at his clothes and pulling at his hair, but he dug in the tips of his pointed shoes and clutched with his fingertips, and held on. Finally he somersaulted out of the Cord onto the deep moss of the forest floor. "Are we there?" he panted.

"Aye," Macta replied, gazing around. "Welcome to Alfheim."

Baltham got to his feet and scowled. "Why can't we make our journeys in a gondola, like all the royal families do?"

"Because it amuses me to travel this way," Macta sniffed, grabbing his brother-in-law's cheek and giving it a painful twist. "Where's your sense of sport, Baltham?"

The three Elves and the Goblin set out at a brisk pace.

Tuava-Li had called the Elves to the Grove before breakfast and prepared them for another sweep of the forest. With a plan in mind, something to occupy them, perhaps they wouldn't think about their new leader's youth. They wouldn't consider her inexperience, or question her judgment. Instead they would be able to devote all their energies to finding their beloved Mage. Tuava-Li had decided to go out this time with one of the search parties; there was no point in staying in Alfheim and waiting passively for the Mage to come back. There was nothing in these woods that would escape her notice. She was just about to lead the Elves into the forest when someone called, "Ho! Ho, there, Elfmaid!"

Tuava-Li spun around to see Macta and his companions striding into the glen. With their leather breeches and fur tunics, their metal buckles and elaborate jewelry, Tuava-Li knew immediately where they had come from. She was no fool; it was easy to tell by the garb of the strangers and the rapiers strapped to their sides that they were from the Northern land of Helfratheim. Tuava-Li's nostrils twitched at the smell of steel, her stomach churned, and she stood back. The Elf holding a taut leash, with a grunting, spiky-headed Goblin straining at the end, she recognized as Macta Dockalfar, Prince of Helfratheim. "Where is your Mage?" Macta demanded. "We're here to see the Mage of this Clan, and we have no time to wait. Bring her to us with no delay."

Tuava-Li swallowed. Blood pulsed in her temples. Half a score of Elves, her entire search party, stood like frightened rabbits. Their eyes darted from Tuava-Li to the Mage's study in the high tree, to the three intruders, to the slobbering Goblin, to the safety of the forest. They covered their mouths with their hands and backed away. Tuava-Li narrowed her eyes at the intruders, then turned her attention to the search party. "Go on," she said, "I'll catch up with you."

The Elves hesitated. "But, Tuava-Li— "

"Is it the metal that bothers you?" asked Macta. "A little steel isn't going to make you sick, you bumpkins. You should try a little med'cinal magick, like we do, to offset the effects. 'Tis an insult to see how you behave in front of royalty."

Tuava-Li turned to the search party. "Go, I said, now!"

Fearful of appearing weak, Tuava-Li stepped forward, her mouth tight. She would teach these fools from Helfratheim a lesson. "Greetings, in the name of the Mother and her Cord. Now, pray tell me, who are you, and what do you want? Make it quick, or be on your way."

Druga, the largest and most menacing of the Elves, showed a mouthful of sharp teeth. He took Tuava-Li's comment as a challenge. "Why, I'll . . . ," he growled, lurching forward, but he was stopped in his tracks by a gesture from his Master. "Perhaps it would be wise," the Prince said, "to begin this conversation on a more cheerful note. I am Macta Dockalfar, Prince of Helfratheim."

He smiled brightly, reining in his Goblin, and took a bow. "In the name of the Mother and her Cord, my companions and I have come to this place as representatives of the royal court. Please forgive me if I appeared to be rude. 'Tis only because of the urgency of our visit that I may appear to lack . . . patience."

Tuava-Li glared at him suspiciously. "Patience will help bring your tongue wisdom, Macta Dockalfar. What business have you with our Mage?"

"I've attempted to be polite with you," said Macta. "We have reason to seek an audience with your Mage, and 'tis none of *your* business to know *our* business. Now I must command you to bring her to me."

Macta's eyes were full of scorn. Tuava-Li's accent was coarse, she was dressed like the poorest country Elf, and to him, her tattoos were positively barbaric. The highborn Elves valued their pure, unblemished skin. They loved to decorate their bodies with gaudy jewelry and elegant clothes, but it would be inconceivable to a royal Elf to spoil the surface of his flesh with something as vulgar as a tattoo.

"I am Tuava-Li, Apprentice to the Mage of Alfheim," she glared, "and 'tis indeed my right as well as my duty to stand between you and my Mage. I don't care for your attitude, sir, and if you don't tell me what you are here for, I shall ask you to leave Alfheim at once."

Seeing that his threats were getting him nowhere, Macta considered other tactics. Humor? Honesty? Ah, now *that* was a choice he seldom made without it being absolutely necessary. But this was, after all, a game, and Macta would do anything to win.

"I'm brought here on the *heels of good news*," Macta demurred, "if I can make a little joke pertaining to a certain *shoe* that has been discovered!"

Druga and Baltham laughed, as if on cue. *"Heels . . . A shoe!"* Baltham sputtered, nearly doubling over with mirth. Druga, too, chortled with merriment, though he didn't get the feeble joke.

"I was present three hundred and sixty moons ago for the wedding of my cousin Udos to Princess Asra of Alfheim," Macta explained, "right here in this Grove."

Tuava-Li glared at the Prince impatiently.

"My cousin was very dear to me," Macta said. "When he was killed, many fled from the site of the murder, fearing for their lives. In the confusion of the moment, Princess Asra lost one of her wedding shoes. As I'm sure you know, royal custom dictates that without that shoe, Princess Asra would be unable to marry . . . even in the event she were to fall in love with another suitor. Out of respect for Asra, I stayed behind on that awful morning to search for the shoe, not without risk to my own safety! In fact, I may be the only one who has come regularly to these woods to search for the shoe. But now . . ." A smile spread across Macta's face, as he prepared to make the request that had brought him to Alfheim. "I want to make it perfectly clear that all of us at Helfratheim are delighted beyond measure to hear the missing shoe has finally been found! The entire Faerie world is resounding with the joy of the discovery."

Macta paused again, scanning Tuava-Li's face for her reaction. "I believe it would be only right to share in this good news by delivering the shoe to Princess Asra, personally. I've brought my brother-in-law and my own bodyguard to accompany me on this mission. Oh, and of course, my little pet!"

Macta rubbed the spiky head of the Goblin, who had just urinated on the ground and was busily tearing up the turf around the foul spot with his hind claws. "Goodbeast, Powcca. Goodbeast. Now, Tuava-Li—it is Tuava-Li, isn't it? Now that your Clan has been so fortunate in finding the shoe, the responsibility of its return should by all rights pass to the family of the departed groom."

"Udos was a Prince of Ljosalfar, not Helfratheim," said Tuava-Li. "If he was related to you, 'twas a distant relationship at best. Northern and Southern families have had little to do with each other for millennia. And what makes you think that the missing shoe has been found? I've heard nothing of it, nothing at all. This is just a silly rumor. You're wasting your time. We here in Alfheim have many things to concern us, but a missing shoe isn't one of them."

"Ah, but the shoe isn't missing; that's why you're not

concerned," hissed Macta. "Will you let me see your Mage, now, or not?"

"Certainly not," Tuava-Li scowled. "The Mage has no time for such nonsense."

Macta threw up his arms in exasperation. "Don't think that I won't report this to my father, the King. He'll personally speak to your Mage about this uncooperative behavior." Macta made an effort to calm himself. "If there can be no courtesy among the Elfin clans," he breathed, "what hope do we have of facing the challenges we all share?"

Tuava-Li threw back her head and laughed. "You speak the truth! Now go and tell your father, before you forget. It was Tuava-Li, Apprentice to the Mage of Alfheim, who stood in the way of your little scheme to get your hands on something that doesn't belong to you. Now good day to you, Prince!"

Tuava-Li stood with her hands on her hips. She watched the Elves turn and stalk back toward the Cord that led to the North, and Helfratheim. Once they were inside, and she saw their shadows disappear, Tuava-Li stepped into the tree lift and rang the bell. The trained rats worked their wheel, the gears turned, and Tuava-Li rode to her high branch. But once inside the Mage's quarters her spirits plummeted. She sat on a stool by the cricket cage, feeling helpless and forlorn. Tuava-Li did not dare to leave Alfheim now to join in a search party for her Mage. If Macta Dockalfar knew that the shoe had been found, and he wanted it for himself—no matter what the reason—nothing would stop him from having it. Another disturbing thought entered her mind. Since Macta *knew* the shoe had been found, it could only mean he had a spy in Alfheim. Tuava-Li went to the bookshelf on the wall and lifted out a particularly heavy volume of magickal lore. In a crevice in the tree wall behind lay the glittering, diamond-covered shoe, wrapped in a layer of dark leaves. It lay at the center of a circle of amulets, tiny carvings, and herbs, magick meant to cleanse it of Human contagion. Tuava-Li stared at the package. Who could she trust to deliver the shoe to Asra's parents in Ljosalfar? Logically, she should make the delivery herself, yet she was afraid to leave Alfheim for a single moment, just in case there was news about the Mage. Tuava-Li's confidence drained out of her. She collapsed onto a stool, staring into the darkness.

Macta loved the Cord. He clutched at his heels, leaned forward, and spun down the center of the passage. "Hang on, Powcca!" he yelled to his Goblin, which he reeled out and in on its leash like a yo-yo on a string. Druga moved with the currents of air like some wingless, muscle-bound bird. He held his massive hands out in front of him. Druga had been Macta's servant since he was a little boy. It had been ingrained in his mind since he was an infant that the sole purpose of his life was to serve and protect Macta, and so he did. Shifting his weight to keep momentum, he swayed back and forth in the wake of his Master. "Are we going home, sir?" he shouted, as the wind howled around them.

"Helfratheim awaits us!" Macta shouted, stretching himself out, and swerving dangerously to the left and right. "I'm sure my father will be interested in hearing about what's going on in Alfheim, and that wretched toady Tuava-Li!"

Trailing behind Macta and Druga in the Cord was Baltham, clutching his arms across his scrawny chest. His long bangs blew into his eyes, so he kept them closed and tried to relax and yield to the current. Baltham shivered. He felt a wave of nausea coming on. All of his life, in fact, he had felt slightly ill. Born into an undistinguished family in a small village in the West, Baltham had met Macta's older sister, Yenri, at an autumnal ceremony. Baltham soon found himself married. His new, high-ranking family wasted no time preparing a special place for him to occupy. He would be the one to take the blame for Macta's mistakes, the one to smooth over rough spots with Macta's enemies. But this was not the end to Baltham's problems. In the space of several years he became father to three spanking-new royal brats. Yenri expected him to fulfill the same role with their young sons that he played with Macta. This meant that Baltham was always at the bottom of the pecking order, cleaning up other Elves' messes, fixing their mistakes, and keeping his mouth shut. It would be a hard life for any Elf, but especially for one as frail and weak as Baltham.

The three leaned heavily to their left as they hurtled through the Cord, approaching a branch that led to another branch, which fed into the major artery leading to Helfratheim. It was a long journey back home. But the traveling was such a roller coaster ride to the Elflads that Macta had nearly forgotten his anger by the time he climbed out of the Cord near his father's stone fortress. Still, he did his best to gather the old indignant rage and fury in his guts as he approached the drawbridge and moat. "Get out of my way!" he shouted at the guards. Ah, but it felt good to push someone around, and have them obey without question. It felt very good, indeed.

The Elves of Helfratheim were partial to a level of cruelty that the Southern Elves would have found appalling. Baltham gagged at the sight of a public execution as they skirted the crowds massing in the main square. King Valdis was in the habit of testing his latest weaponry on prisoners sentenced to death, and today was no exception. The manacled Faerie, whose cries rang out over the crowd, was slowly being roasted by a strange golden beam, emanating from a black box positioned on a high pedestal. The beam sputtered and fizzled; the weapon was obviously still not fully functional. The victim's screams thrilled the crowd. "What do you think he's done to deserve that?" Baltham choked.

"There are so many ways to break the rules," Macta mused, "and only one way to obey them. 'Tis a wonder there are any peasants left alive in Helfratheim."

Druga and Baltham left Macta at the castle and went to deliver Powcca to the kennel. They were only too happy to abandon the Prince to his family business. "Ah, it's you," said Cytthandra, personal secretary to the King, glancing up

at Macta as he entered the room. She sat behind a desk of knotted pine, filing her long, viridian-colored nails and looking bored. Scented candles burned from bee-shaped sconces along the walls of the chamber, and the muted music of pipes filtered in through barred vents along the floor. For security reasons the King always had his musicians play from locked cells on the lower levels of the fortress.

"I want to see my father," Macta commanded.

Cytthandra shrugged. "I'm afraid the King is quite busy. You'll have to make an appointment."

Even in the dim light it was apparent that Macta's face was darkening. It was not the first time he had had this argument. "Cytthandra, for God's sake, he's my father. Open the door and let me in. Something important has happened that he must know about."

Cytthandra glared at Macta and pursed her lips. She twitched a shoulder and the head of a milk snake appeared from inside her collar. It hissed faintly at him, and made a low mumbling sound. "If you want to leave a message," Cytthandra said, "I'll be sure to pass it along."

"So you've acquired one of those ridiculous snakes," noted the Prince. "The perfect combination of fashion and stupidity, I'd say."

Helfratheim's laboratories had recently made a breakthrough in breeding technology and magick, with a generation of superintelligent snakes that had the capacity to speak.

Now everyone of means in the kingdom was hurrying to acquire a snake, much as one might have once purchased an expensive, jeweled dagger as an article of trendy attire. "Cytthandra," Macta said, "I want my father to know that someone has insulted the Dockalfar family name. Someone is keeping secrets that shouldn't be kept. *That someone must be punished.*"

"Oh," Cytthandra cried in mock sympathy, stroking her milk snake's head, "has someone hurt Macta's feelings? Did some nasty Troll step on Mac-Mac's toes?"

The secretary had a long history with Macta. She knew exactly where his sore points lay, and she knew exactly how hard she could push on them. She regarded it as a kind of sport. And the Prince, though he normally loved games, was beside himself with rage. "You tell my father," he demanded, "that his son is about to be married to the Princess of Alfheim. You tell my father that the Mage of Alfheim and her idiot Apprentice are standing in the path that leads to the only happiness I will ever know. You tell my father—"

Macta had lived under the thumb of Cytthandra for as long as he could remember. He hated her more than he hated his own mother. Or, perhaps it should be said, *mothers,* for Macta's father had been married many times. But Macta was a grown Elf now, discovering his own power. *When the time is right,* he thought, *she'll be punished for this insolence!*

"I will tell him you were here," said Cytthandra, with a

look that meant the conversation was at its end. Furious, frustrated, and indignant, Macta kicked the secretary's desk with his pointed boot. It took what little remained of Macta's resolve not to cry out in pain. Grimacing, he turned and stalked out of the room.

15

CLOUDS DOTTED THE SKIES over Ljosalfar. Kites in the shapes of birds, dragons, insects, and all manner of fanciful, multicolored creatures hung in the air, their tails flicking playfully. The kites were beautiful to see, but they also served the purpose of warding off evil spirits. Working the kite strings were scores of Elves, the Kite Masters. From positions high in the branches of pine trees, the Kite Masters made the kites dance, gently reeling them in or letting them soar over the spires of town.

All of the paths below led to the enormous domed building called Jensine Hall. *Jensine* was an ancient word, meaning *God is generous.* Arches looming over the pathways were topped with silken flags, celebrating the various arts: music, dance, sculpture, painting, poetry, literature, architecture, ceramics, jewelry, and more. Slogans were etched into boulders that lined the walkways.

Passersby stopped to read the wisdom inscribed there: HOPE IS THE MOST PRECIOUS TREASURE. HASTE DOES NOT BRING SUCCESS. NOTHING IN THE WORLD IS ACCOMPLISHED WITHOUT PASSION. Strolling Elves gazed at the flags and banners in contemplation, or smiled as they passed other Faerie Folk meandering on their way.

Asra and Skara wandered through the crowd outside the Great Hall. The Faerie Faire was in town, and booths and displays along the curving steps were squeezed together in tight rows. Elves and Pixies, Trolls and Sprites jostled to see the vendors' wares. "Eeh, look out where you're goin'!" shouted an angry Pixie, when Asra turned and bumped into the tiny creature.

"Oh!" she cried, looking down in surprise. "I'm sorry!"

Asra blushed as Skara glanced at her, grinning. "You never know who you might chance to meet in a mob like this," she said, her eyes sweeping the crowd.

Skara was a native of Ljosalfar. Her parents were well-to-do, though not of royal blood, and she and Asra had met at a painting class at the Academy. "Stop looking for him," Asra said. "I know he promised you he'd meet you here, but he's an Elflad, after all. If he should happen to make an appearance, he'll find you."

"Who?" asked Skara, feigning ignorance.

"You know who," Asra teased. "His name starts with the letter *V* and ends with an *R*. And oh, yes, he bears an uncanny resemblance to the Elflad you dream about every night, the one your heart aches for, the one who—"

"Oooh, look at this!" cried Skara, turning to a display of

gauzy scarves. She didn't enjoy hearing that her affections for Vittror were so obvious. "You'd look lovely in one of these!"

Asra strolled on, examining a display of scented candles, one of finely crafted kaleidoscopes, and another of jewelry in the latest style. "Slow down, Princess," scolded Skara. "There's so much to see! I want to take everything in."

She pointed to a banner stretched across the top of a peaked tent, decorated with pictures of the sun and moon, the stars in the night sky, and swirls of color meant to represent the mysteries of the unknown. THE FUTURE IS YOURS TO SEE, it read. Taking her friend's hand, Skara led Asra behind a curtain and into the gloomy fortune-teller's tent. "Oooh!" Skara jumped back, as a Pixie bolted through the opening. Her wings buzzed in fury and angry tears streamed from her eyes as she darted between the girls and disappeared into the crowd. Skara and Asra exchanged glances, then laughed nervously as they walked into the tent. Inside sat the Saga. Her sharp features were gaudily painted in black and white. The Saga's eyes were closed, her bony hands rested on the tabletop, where a candle sputtered. "Which of you will be first?" The Saga looked up, her eyes gleaming.

Asra felt anxious, and a sudden pressure in her chest made it hard to breathe. "I'm going to wait outside," she said.

"Nooo, stay with me, you coward!" Skara pleaded.

"Sit down, one of you," insisted the fortune-teller.

Skara dropped into the seat on the far side of the table. "What did you say to the Pixie that just fled from here?"

"When you ask a question," the fortune-teller answered, "you've got to be ready to hear the answer . . . no matter what it turns out to be! The Pixie wasn't ready for the truth." She gazed into Skara's eyes and smiled faintly.

Asra shoved aside the drapes and stepped out into the fading daylight. The air was full of the smells of roasted chestnuts, herbal candles, scented oils, and the sharp sweat of the crowd. Everything felt alive and vital. Inside the tent, Skara took a coin and laid it on the tablecloth. The old fortune-teller shuffled a deck of cards that had been concealed in her sleeve. She cut the deck, placed the two piles of cards on the tabletop, stacked them again, and finally turned over the card on the top of the deck. Skara went to pick it up, but the old Elf grabbed her wrist. "Not for you to touch!"

After a few minutes Skara shot out of the tent, grinning from ear to ear. She found Asra standing back from the crowd. "You won't believe it!" exclaimed Skara, bubbling over with excitement. "She knew *everything* about me. 'Twas amazing. She did something with a deck of cards, and drew out one that was especially for me. 'Twas the Six of Cups! Can you believe it, the Six of Cups!"

Asra blinked. "I'm so happy for you. What exactly *is* the Six of Cups? And what became of the first five?"

"'Tis a new beginning, Asra. A radical change for me. That's what the card said!"

"You know, change isn't always a good thing," the Princess said in mock solemnity.

Skara clicked her tongue. "Well, let me tell you. The figure painted on the card got up and stood in front of me, right there on the table. She was carrying a big bouquet. Then the old crone told me to look closely, and when I did, I could see that the figure was *me!* Now it's your turn, Asra. Go on inside and find out what the Saga has to show you!"

Asra smiled and shook her head. "There's no point in hurrying what has yet to be, Skara. But, since you mentioned it, I believe the future's telling us that if we don't get something to eat, we're going to starve to death right here next to this musty old tent!"

Laughing, the pair of Elfmaids blended into the crowd, searching for the source of the lovely smells that wafted through the carnival air. Candied burdock? Deep-fried gingerroot? Honey-glazed lemongrass strips with mint sauce? Curds of mole cheese in amaranth pockets? It was all there, and more. On the steps above the crowd a group of Pixies clad in green and gold twirled satin banners. Down the row a Troll with an enormous nose and a tricornered hat juggled a trio of trained Fire Sprites. Farther down the steps a group of beggars lay, scratching the fleas and lice that infested their tattered clothing. They cried out to the passersby stepping around them. "A few coins, sir," one of them moaned, scratching his armpit with one hand while clutching a half-empty bottle of dandelion wine in the other. "A few coins, please, t' buy a poor Faerie somethin' t' eat!"

Skara started when someone touched her sleeve. A grinning Elfin face peered up from under a black cowl. "Have you heard the good news about Brahja-Chi?" the Elf asked. She was flanked by two others, also attired in the severe robes worn by monks.

"Aye, I have," Skara replied, "and I'm not interested in becoming a monk. I have a life of my own!"

"What about you, miss?" The monk turned to Asra, offering a printed parchment. "Those who follow the Canon are doing the will of the Gods."

"No, thank you," Asra demurred, and she took Skara by the arm and turned away. "Brahja-Chi's monks are everywhere these days," she whispered. "I wish they'd stay in Storehoj, where they belong!"

"Imagine if they knew who you were," Skara laughed. "They'd never leave you alone! If that old Mage Brahja-Chi had a Princess among her recruits, what a coup it would be!"

Asra shrugged. "I'm hungry, Skara. And for *food,* not religion!"

At the end of the day, when the vendors were getting ready to close up their booths, Asra and Skara once again passed the fortune-teller's tent. There was hardly another soul around. Skara gave Asra a poke in the ribs. "Come on, you won't get another chance. 'Twill be my treat." She pressed a coin into her friend's hand. "I'll wait outside, and if Vittror happens to come past, I'll tell him to jump off the edge of a cliff for not coming sooner!"

"All right, all right," Asra sighed, rolling her eyes. "If you insist. I can tell you won't be happy until I throw this coin away!"

Asra went past the curtain into the dark tent. "Hello?" she called. "Hello, is anyone here?"

Skara shivered as a breeze darted between the booths. She watched the lights twinkle on the hillside, then a moment later jumped as a soft hand touched her shoulder. "Asra! Finished so soon? What did she say?"

"I don't want to talk about it," Asra answered, grabbing her friend by the arm and giving her a tug.

"What do you mean?" Skara pleaded. "Did the Saga turn over a card for you? What did it say?"

"'Tis none of your business," snapped Asra. "You know too much about me, anyway. This will be my one little secret."

The Elfmaids hurried back to their families and apartments high in the trees of Ljosalfar. And in a dark and musty tent outside Jensine Hall, an aged fortune-teller slipped a card called the Hanged One back into her deck.

16

THE R. D. SCOTT WILDLIFE and Bird Sanctuary and Rehabilitation Center was tucked into a shallow corner of the woods, sheltered from the highway by towering trees. It was here that the injured horned owl was brought after its visit to the veterinarian. There was an empty place in the row of wire cages on the other side of the driveway—a hawk with an injured wing had recovered sufficiently to be released into the wild. But the new owl might not be so lucky. Carrie took a frozen mouse from a sandwich bag and placed it in the microwave. She set it for defrost and perched on a stool by the counter to wait, watching the owl in its pen outside the window. "You know," she said to Tim, who was flipping through a magazine, "the horns on a horned owl are just feathers sticking up. But this new owl actually has some . . . I don't know, like something's happening under there." She chuckled to herself. "It's almost like it has real horns!"

"Or pointy ears," Tim said, looking up and smiling. "I know, I know. The thing's deformed. Remember that owl we used to have, the one that had been raised by a family back in the woods? They tried to feed it fried chicken and biscuits? When it came to us its bones were so messed up from malnutrition that it couldn't even hold its head upright. Maybe this new bird is like that one. I don't know about the soft beak, though. I'm not convinced it's going to be able to get down that mouse you're nuking. Couldn't you just defrost the thing overnight in the fridge? It's gonna smell awful."

Carrie shrugged. "It's what you said about the beak, Tim. That's why I want to make sure the mouse is nice and soft before I put it in there. The part about the owl that gets me is the feathers. Did you ever hear of a feather bleeding when it was broken?"

Tim looked out the window. "Sometimes the pin feathers," he said. "I don't know."

The owl had not yet discovered the stunted tree growing up from the floor of its pen. It hadn't found the wooded nesting box in the corner or noticed the other birds in the neighboring cages. It still seemed dazed, and out of place. "Yeah, she's a funny one, all right," Tim said. "Something tells me that owl's gonna be spending the rest of her days here with us. Some creatures just aren't meant to live out in the wild!"

17

MATT PULLED UP HIS BLANKETS and rolled away from the light. It streamed in through the window and spilled over his face, so bright he couldn't open his eyes. He ached all over. He felt like someone had thrown him down a flight of stairs. There was really no reason to get up. If only he didn't have to go to the bathroom! With a grunt, Matt tossed back the covers, threw his feet over the edge of the bed, and stood up. *"Owww!"*

Matt's knee buckled, and his heart sank—the pain in his foot was back. It wasn't so bad he couldn't get around, if he was careful, but it was bad enough that something had to be done. Soon. He got out of his pajama bottoms, pulled on the jeans he'd worn the day before, and tugged on an orange sweater over his T-shirt. He put the empty bottle into his pants pocket, then slunk down the hall past Becky's room. From her bed, she gave Matt a hollow stare. He nodded and moved on, knowing that he still hadn't spoken to his sister about what had happened that night. He could tell it was troubling her, but what could he do? On the top shelf of the medicine cabinet in his parents' bathroom downstairs, Matt found a bottle of aspirin. He took two capsules, and headed into the kitchen.

His mom sat at the table with a cup of coffee and the newspaper spread out in front of her. Emily was over by the table in her big, blue plastic playpen, working the mirrors and buttons on a busy box. The toy squeaked annoyingly as she banged on it, and she squealed with delight when her big brother appeared. Matt paused to tickle Emily's belly. Then he fell into the chair across from his mother. She glanced up from the paper and smiled. "You're up late, sleepyhead! Feeling all right?"

Matt plucked a banana from the fruit bowl. "I'm fine," he mumbled. "Why, do I look like something's wrong with me?"

"You just look tired," Jill said. "That's all."

Matt poured himself some orange juice. "Mmm-hmm." He rubbed his eyes and crossed his legs, so the injured heel was off the ground. He glanced out the window over the sink and saw something moving in the distance, out by the trees. It was a deer. A young one. He squinted and saw that there were at least three fawns, moving like they were in slow motion, grazing at the edge of the forest. "Mom," he said, getting up, "I'm gonna go for a walk, check out the woods. I want to see what it's like before Dad has all the trees cut down."

Emily fussed in her playpen, reaching out her arms to be picked up. "You make it sound so dramatic, Matt," said his mother. "They're almost done with the clearing, anyway. If there's any money left when your dad pays off the bank loan, it's going to go into a college fund for you and your sisters. So I hope you're not complaining."

"Me? Complain?"

Matt put on his sneakers and set off across the field. He tried to find level ground to walk on, and he did his best not to limp until he was sure he was out of sight. The deer he had spotted earlier were gone. He saw their funny little hoof tracks in the dirt and mud, and he kept his eyes peeled for other tracks, traces, evidence that might lead him to where the . . . the *whatever* lived. Matt knew they were out there somewhere, maybe not even very far. The concoction in that little glass bottle they had given him had begun healing his foot. But since his mother poured the liquid down the drain, the pain in his heel was back, almost as bad as it ever had been. The medicine, whatever it was, worked. And if he wanted to get better, Matt was going to have to get some more of it.

In the forest there were birds singing from the tops of distant trees. It sounded pretty, and lifted Matt's spirits. Then he remembered hearing somewhere that the reason birds sing is because they're marking their territory with sound, so other birds don't go near it. Territory, marking your territory—that was mostly what life was all about. Slogging through the woods,

Matt realized that the trees and vines and shrubs all had their territories. They all grew up as high as they could to block the sunlight from the other trees and vines and shrubs so that they could flourish and so that everything else around them would be stunted and die. The biggest tree branches were high enough not to get in Matt's way. But that didn't stop the little trees and bushes, the weedy, ropy things that seemed to grow to about head level, from smacking Matt in the face. *Maybe if you're small,* Matt thought, *you have to be tough. Like me.*

The forest floor was strewn with damp, slippery piles of leaves, and littered with half-rotten branches. Matt looked around and spotted a branch that would be about right for a walking stick. He picked it up and brushed away the dirt and leaves. It was a good length, sort of soggy, but sturdy and more or less straight. Hiking wasn't easy when you had to avoid putting your weight on one foot. Matt soon got the hang of swinging the walking stick forward in his left hand, leaning in to help support his weight. Looking up, there were little patches of light that filtered down through the leaves, but the overall impression was one of gloomy twilight, even though it wasn't yet noon. Matt looked back over his shoulder and saw the spot of light where he had entered the woods. He could still see the portable toilet, the bulldozer tilted into the mud, and behind that, his house. It looked so tiny and unimportant. Matt wondered for a moment if it would be possible to get lost in the woods. He guessed there wasn't that much of it left, but he was planning on finding out.

He forged ahead, looking for anything out of the ordinary. Of course, it was foolish. He wasn't a tracker; he didn't really know what he was looking for. He wasn't like the kind of character you might see on some nature show on television, who could find a piece of deer poop and tell how long ago it had been left behind, or could spot a broken twig and know whether a raccoon or a groundhog had stepped on it. No, Matt had been for walks in the woods only a couple of times in his whole life. Then there had been blacktop trails to walk on, colored markings on the trees to indicate which path you were on, and markers to tell you what kinds of trees you were looking at. But it was either take a chance on finding the creatures that had given him the medicine, or go back home and tell his mom the truth. And what was the truth, anyway? What had started with a little nonsense about stepping on something sharp in a pile of dirt had turned into something else entirely.

The woods were quiet. Except for the rasp of Matt's own breath and his tramping, noisy feet, there wasn't a sound anywhere. Where had all the birds gone? Matt realized that any living creature would hear him coming from a mile away. He tried to regulate his breath and step more carefully to avoid crackling leaves and snapping twigs. Matt moved through the forest, scanning left and right for a sign of anything out of the ordinary. He'd read online some of the stories about how Elves lived in big trees. It seemed ridiculous, but what else did he have to go on? And where were the really big trees? The ones he passed were little more than wispy tendrils, while others were wide enough to put your arms around and have your fingers barely touch. But nothing more. Nothing really stood out; it was all just more of the same. Matt's foot was bothering him and he had to shuffle a little to avoid putting pressure on his heel. Even with his walking stick the muscles in his calves ached, and he had to stop periodically and sit down to rest. He pulled a little crumpled package of chocolate-filled cookies from his pants pocket. He was glad he had thought ahead to bring a snack. Matt ate all of the cookies, pushed the plastic wrapper back into his pocket, and got to his feet. A breeze whispered past. It lifted the edge of a carpet of dry leaves and tossed them up like confetti. Glancing ahead, Matt realized that everything had changed.

He looked up, blinked, and shook his head. He couldn't be sure his eyes weren't deceiving him. The forest ceiling seemed suddenly higher; Matt felt as if he could barely see the sky peeking through the dense canopy of leaves. The ground beneath his feet was flat and hard. The air was cool and damp. Matt felt as if he were standing at the bottom of a cave. Everything was cast in a gloomy, purplish-blue light. Ahead of him he thought he saw a grayish, mottled tree trunk nearly as wide as a small car. Could it be two trees, close together? No. It was one massive pale trunk, knotted with big, protuberant lumps, and the branches grew out of it like tentacles, reaching into the darkness. Behind this ugly giant of a tree stood another, and then another. As Matt walked toward the grove he saw five trees clustered before him. Could this be the place he had been looking for?

Suddenly, Matt was thrown off balance and lifted feetfirst into the air, with his head dangling in the dirt. He spat out a mouthful of mildewed leaves and rot, and realized that he'd been caught in some kind of snare. A second later a net made of vines fell from the branches and covered him completely. Voices roared up around him. "We've got him, we've got him!" they cried.

Matt could barely make out a crowd of little figures, dressed in rough, earth-colored clothing, prancing and kicking up the dirt and leaves around his head. Most held maple or oak leaves over their mouths and noses. "We've got him!" they shouted, close to hysteria. "Don't touch him!" one cried, her voice muffled by a leaf. "Don't get too close! There may be poison on his breath!"

Matt coughed and coughed, choking on the dust. In the distance he could see a dozen or so black-robed figures moving closer. The vines that were pulled tight around his ankles drew tighter still, and lifted him completely off the ground. Elves stood in the branches of the trees, working the pulleys and levers to pull up the net that had caught him like an animal in a trap. The blood rushed to his throbbing head. He was completely helpless. "It's me, Matt!" he screamed. "I gave you the shoe you wanted. I want to see your leader; that's why I'm here. I don't want to hurt you!"

A round face wreathed in a black cowl came into view. "If anybody's going to get hurt, 'tis not going to be one of us!"

"Stand back!" another voice shouted. Someone was stomping through the crowd, brushing aside the Elves that blocked her way.

Matt recognized the female who had come across his yard to trade the medicine for the shoe. "So 'tis you, again," she said. "You weren't supposed to remember meeting us, let alone follow us into our world. Thank the Gods for this net!"

Behind the Elf was a larger figure, a funny creature with a long nose and a knit cap. Farther in the distance Matt thought he could make out tiny figures peering down at him from windows and open doorways. The branches of the trees seemed to be covered with little hivelike dwellings. When he turned his head slightly to look at them, they simply disappeared. Then when he looked away, the Elfin city was right there, at the edge of his vision.

"The medicine you gave me," Matt said, trying to swallow down his fear, "there was an accident, and it got . . . spilled. I need to get some more of it, so I came to find you. I knew you had to be somewhere nearby."

Tuava-Li turned to Jardaine and shook her head. "So he didn't take all of the med'cine—that explains why he still has his memory of us."

Jardaine pressed a yellow leaf over her nose and mouth, then stepped forward brandishing a sharp twig. She jabbed Matt in the throat and stood back. "We have no reason to help the Human. We ought to do to him what the Mage did to that girl,

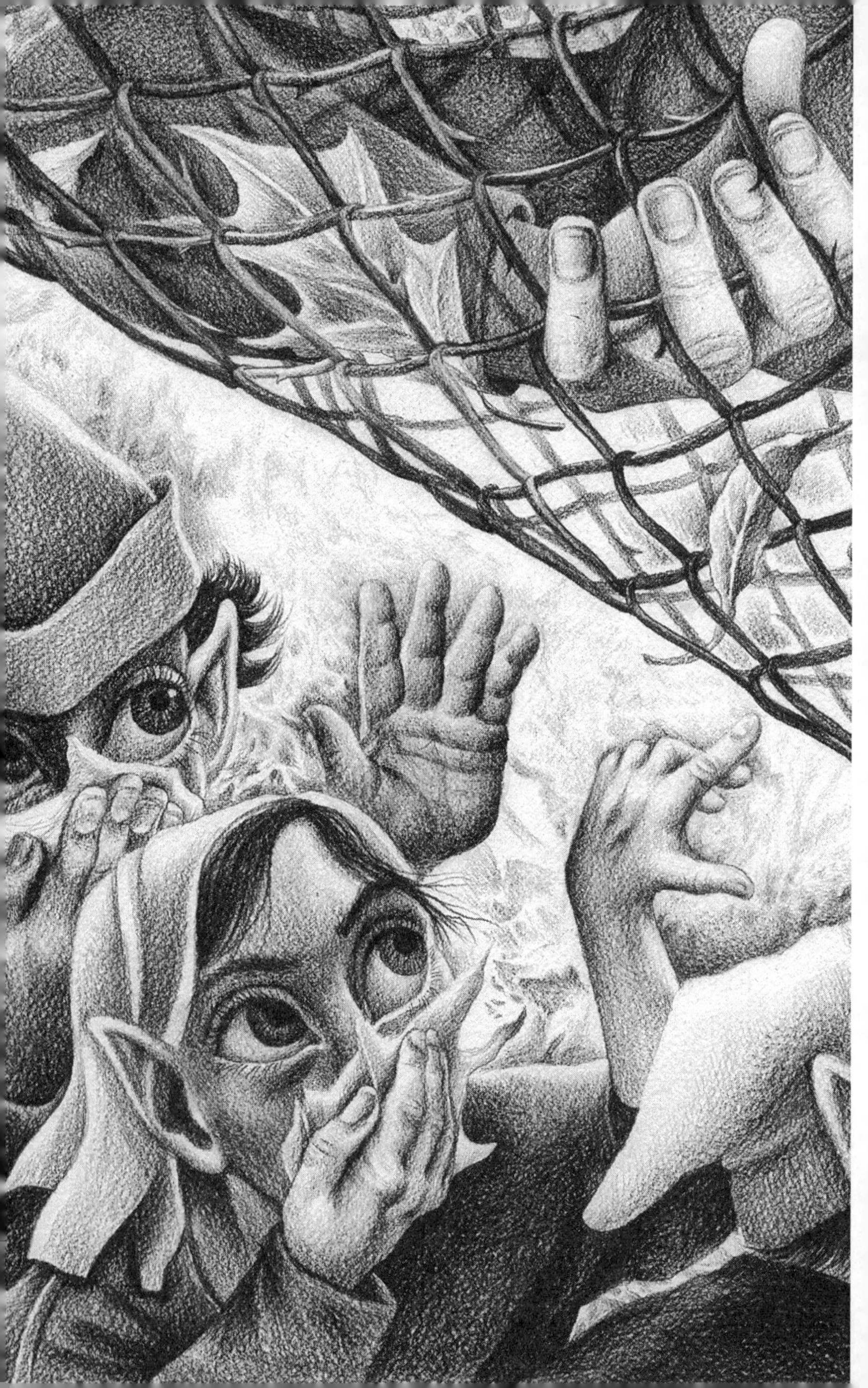

three hundred and sixty moons ago. Now that he's found us, he's threatened us all. We can't let him leave here alive!"

Girl? Matt heard the words, but they made no sense to him. *Three hundred and what? Moons? How many years is that?* But he was too upset to process the information. "My parents know I went for a walk in the woods," he choked. "If I don't come home, they'll tear down every tree and bush and blade of grass out here until they find me. Let me up, right now! So far, nobody but me knows about you. But you've got to give me some more of that medicine, or I'll tell my parents everything!"

The Elves stood around him, their eyes full of suspicion. Tuava-Li and Jardaine stared at each other, wondering what to do. "My head is killing me," Matt cried, twisting and trying to right himself. "You've got to let me out of here, please, now!"

Tuava-Li gestured to the Elves in the trees, who released the pulleys. "I don't really know what I can give you in exchange for the medicine," Matt said, sitting up. "You already have the shoe! I don't know what else I have that you could ever want. All I can really offer you is my silence. I've never said anything to anyone about you, and I won't, I promise. But I need the medicine. I know you can help me."

Matt lifted the edge of the net and hoisted it up over his head. Then he pulled his feet free from the snare and fished around in his pocket until he found the medicine bottle. Tuava-Li, the monks, the Elves, and the Troll all took a step back from the boy, in case he tried anything unexpected. "Stay where you are," ordered Tuava-Li.

The Mage had mixed up the potion for the boy's foot; Tuava-Li had no idea what it contained, if there was some magick, some kind of spell connected with the healing elixir. She wouldn't have a clue how to re-create it. "You will get no more of the med'cine from us, Human," she said. "You should never have come here."

But inside, she was overwhelmed with the fear that unless she came up with a plan to help the Human, the only way the Elves would be rid of the boy was to kill him. Or, perhaps, to put a curse on him, to keep him out of the way forever. Neither prospect was appealing; Tuava-Li had never had to face a choice like this before. Maybe a Mage would choose to commit an act of violence in order to bring peace, but Tuava-Li felt certain that she did not have the wisdom to make such an important decision. Tomtar bent down to whisper something in Tuava-Li's ear. At first she shook her head vigorously, but as he continued to speak she nodded, then sighed, and turned to speak to the boy. "All right. Listen closely. There is a Troll, a hermit who lives in these woods. He has knowledge of cures, and if I explain your situation, perhaps he will help you. We will take you there. But I warn you, if you make one suspicious move, just one, you won't live long enough to regret it."

"Noooo!" cried the monks. "It's a trap, you mustn't go with

the Human! Send him away, you don't know what he plans to do, once he gets you alone!"

Tuava-Li considered what the Elves were saying. She bit her lip and stared at Matt. "The others are right. It is not in our interest to risk further contact with you. I will set you on the right path to the Troll's domain, that is all. You must promise me you will never come to us again for help. Is that clear?"

Matt shook his head doubtfully. "I don't know. Why should this . . . this *troll* want to help me? I'm not a troll, I'm a human, and a stranger. You say he's a hermit. He might have never even *seen* a human before, let alone met one. If you came with me, showed me the way, introduced me, then I'd have a better chance, wouldn't I? I swear, I don't want to hurt you. I just need your help. Please?"

Tuava-Li shook her head. She realized she didn't dare leave Alfheim in order to help the Human; he might present a real danger to her, and besides, it might look like she was too readily assisting the enemy. "Nooo. You will go alone. You have the med'cine bottle; that should suffice to prove to the Troll that it was we who sent you. But . . . ," she hesitated, debating the merits of what she was about to do. "Just in case, I'll give you something else to take."

Tuava-Li knelt close to the ground, and spat on the dirt. Then she dipped a twig into the damp soil and used its muddy point to make a mark on a leaf. It was the mark of the Mage, the letter *M* within a circle. She laid it on the ground for Matt to take, then stood back. "The Troll will understand what this means, and will know that he must do my bidding. Now leave Alfheim, and proceed west. Tomtar, what are the signs?"

"If I recall correctly," Tomtar mused, "he'll pass six hills, a boulder-strewn ridge, then a stream no wider than the shadow of a Pixie at noon. He'll go around the lightning-shot trunk of a giant oak, ummm . . . a ravine full of wild blackberry bushes, and a marsh where frogs sing and dragonflies buzz. He'll pass a ridge, and a burbling brook, then a grove of elms. He'll know where the Troll dwells when he sees a tree 'rounded with nutshells and pinecones."

Tuava-Li wished she knew the sorcery to make the boy forget that he had ever stepped foot in Alfheim. If there was some spell built into the potion the Mage had concocted, there was no guarantee that the Troll's version of the medicine would have the same effect. At Tuava-Li's side, Jardaine silently fumed. She was furious that her superior had allowed the Human to see the inscription of the Mage, furious that he was being allowed to leave alive. Tomtar stood behind the pair and chuckled to himself. The Human was on a journey, just like he was. *We're so different,* he thought, *and yet we're the same!*

Matt got to his feet, picked up the leaf with the marking on it, and backed away. He stared hard at the creatures who stood before him. Because they were small, they looked nearly like humans seen from a distance. Except that they were only a few feet from him—so close that he could smell their musty, earthy odor, and hear their sharp intake of breath as he stood up. Matt turned and walked in the direction the Elves had pointed him, wondering how he would ever find his way.

Tuava-Li glared at her monks. "What were you doing?" she barked. "You were supposed to be weaving a spell of distraction around this place so that no Human could find us. If you'd been paying attention, he would've walked right past Alfheim and never seen a thing!"

"We should've killed him on the spot," hissed Jardaine, "or at least tossed him in the stream with the accursed female. They'd be good company for each other, staring into space for all eternity. How could you allow a Human to wander around the forest of Alfheim like the woods belong to him? Who knows what kind of trouble he'll get into here? Who knows what he'll do to the Troll? The Gods would be happy if we'd killed the Human, and the Mage would have known the spells to do it, Tuava-Li. I'm not sure that you do!"

Tuava-Li stiffened. "For your information, the girl in the stream is dead. And as for magick, I know far more than you, Jardaine. But that's beside the point. Remember your place, and control your anger. The Gods will be happy when they see that we're of one mind. I know what I'm doing." Tuava-Li scanned the row of faces of the monks. What were they thinking? Were they taking sides, and if so, where was their loyalty?

Jardaine, meanwhile, put on her most sincere face. "We've done our job, Tuava-Li, and more. But the veil between our worlds is too thin, and there aren't enough of us to deflect attention any more. 'Twould take a thousand trained monks to draw a curtain between us and the Humans. We've been doing the best we can. We've been praying, fasting, chanting; we've recited the incantations; we've done everything you asked us to do. Now what are *you* going to do about the Human trespassing in our forest?"

Tuava-Li turned to Tomtar, and stared up into his trusting face. "I have another job for you, Tomtar, another favor to ask. 'Tis critical that we know the movements of the boy whilst he's in our territory. No Human has come so close to learning the secrets of Alfheim and lived . . . not in a long time. I'm asking you to trail the boy and see if he goes where we sent him. Just stay out of sight and don't return until he's been to see the Troll, and you've followed him all the way back to his home. In the name of the Mage of Alfheim, will you help us?"

18

HUNTING TIME. From the top of the hollow tree the owl turned her head, taking in every rustle, every sigh, every movement from every tree, every sound from the edge of the stream to the grove of ash along the ridge. She was alive with it all, breathing in the whole, reeling world. Silently she sped toward the mouse that crept from its hole. Claws outstretched, descending through a maze of branches, she glided toward the hapless creature that trembled along the ground.

With one sharp cry the life of the mouse blinked out. The owl fluttered to her perch on the hollow tree, her prize clutched in her talons, ready to dine. Then something began to shift. It was a dream, but it was more than that. It was two dreams, coming together. The table was set. The bowl, the wooden spoon, all was ready. She would dine alone, there in her study, among the books that held the wisdom of her ancestors. It was coming back.

Slowly. It was coming back, and it made no sense. The dream of freedom was over. Only the other dream remained, and perhaps it was not a dream at all.

Why was she trapped here in a cage, boxed in by steel mesh, surrounded by these lonely, lost raptors, flapping against the wire. What was she doing here? The Mage was used to inhabiting the body of the owl; it was second nature for a Mage to hunt. It was second nature to feast upon flesh and then to spread her wings and soar across the sky. The other Elves were not meat eaters; they did not need to be. But eating flesh was the way a Mage grounded herself, centered her power so that she had the strength to lead. The animals of the forest knew, and accepted the reality. Still, there she was, wounded, flightless, sick with disgust from the smell of the metal and the reek of fear and resignation from the birds nearby. It all came back to her, and it made terrible sense. The Human boy, the diamond shoe, the Elves in their fear and their hope and their timid, helpless anger. The magick, the med'cine, the night, the wires, the wet, rain-slick road, the blanket. The awful metal box, the man in the white coat, the poking, prodding, bone-splitting fear.

Before her fingers returned, and her face, and her hair, before any of the Humans saw or even suspected, she must escape from here. And the only one who could help her was her Apprentice, Tuava-Li. The Mage of Alfheim knew how to play at the edges of space. She could close her eyes and move her awareness to the skin enclosing her body. Then she could breathe out and make her awareness move beyond her body, into the air. She had learned to extend her thinking mind far, far beyond the confines of her own brain, and enter the minds of others. Others who would feel the thoughts and emotions of the Mage, no more than delicate shadows, and believe that these thoughts were their own. All that was required was the ability to locate the mind. The Mage closed her great owl eyes and breathed in through her golden beak. She focused her energies and began sensing out into the world. At first, she always saw through the eyes. There were the birds in their cages, of course. The barn owl, the hawk, and the other raptors, all forlorn, hungry, and bored, wronged by fate. The Mage shifted her awareness. She saw through the eyes that peeped out of a nest, high on the branch of an elm, waiting for a mother wren to return. She saw through hungry eyes, low to the ground, darting about in the safety of decayed vegetation. She saw through the eyes of the regal deer as they wandered the forest, nibbling leaves and watching for danger. She saw through insects' gleaming segmented eyes and felt the buzzing of their wings along the branch.

A breeze crept across the boughs of the ancient oak, Bethok. Wooden beads rattled alongside the wicker lift. Tuava-Li sat at the Mage's desk, deep in study. She pored over dusty volumes of Faerie magick, searching restlessly among the musty pages for answers. She needed to know how to protect herself from physical as well as psychic assaults. There must be information amid the endless formulas for healing magick. But how to sort out her enemies? Who were more dangerous—the Humans, or the Elves from Helfratheim, including Macta Dockalfar? Was it possible to fight them both, or to resist them both at once? Were there any other ways to achieve the desired ends—peace and cooperation? And was an uneasy truce an acceptable compromise, should all other efforts fail? The books in the Mage's library offered tantalizing answers to Tuava-Li's questions, but there was so much to know, and so little time to learn. To help create an environment in which making decisions would be easier, she had asked for the help of the monks in concentrating her energies through chanting, prayers, and meditation. But she was obliged to appear strong and decisive to her monks, while deflecting the petty jealousies that arose when she took up the mantle of the Mage. Some of the monks, after all, had been students of the Mage for hundreds of years. Who could blame them for resenting Tuava-Li, and her sudden rise in status? She needed to win their trust, and for that, she needed strength and confidence—hard-won qualities, not the kind of thing found in books. And yet, with the Mage gone, books were all Tuava-Li had.

She opened the old bark binding of a text called *The Three.* The book told of a kind of force that resides in the belly of living beings. The force is awakened when it is recognized by the mind. Then it is strengthened by the imagination and the practice of a certain Discipline. Tuava-Li sighed. More Discipline! Yet all the exercises were meant to open new ways to reach out to the Gods, to develop the capacities that Tuava-Li would need in order to become a Mage. There was a diagram of an Elf on the right-hand side of the page. The Elf was surrounded at the middle by a large, transparent ring, which appeared to be turning. It seemed to be a kind of force field, meant to protect the spirit from harm. Like a spinning belt of power, the ring hovered just below the navel and extended in space nearly a dozen feet. Tuava-Li studied the diagram. Then she closed the book, put it back on the shelf, and walked to the center of the room. She stood with her eyes closed, her body relaxed, and imagined that there was such a ring spinning around her waist. She imagined she could make the ring spin faster and faster, and she could remain balanced at the center. Each exhalation of breath was like a wind that sped the ring around and around. Her nose began to itch. She reached up to scratch it, and the image of the ring disappeared. Then she cleared her mind of distraction and tried again.

The book said that she must maintain the exercise for a quarter of an hour, until she felt a tingling in the center of energy below her belly button. Tuava-Li thought she might be feeling it already. Or was it just another itch that needed to be scratched? Only when she ceased to think about herself at all could she conjure up the powerful gyroscope around her body. *So this is magick,* she realized with a sudden flash of recognition. As much as saying magick words, or directing one's energy outward to change something in the world, magick was about being in control of one's attention, and one's own imagination. Magick was a kind of strength that would come only with practice. All right, then, she would make a better effort to practice. Tuava-Li thought of her own Mage, and how much strength she must have had inside her. Then her spirit sank like a stone. The sense of a spinning ring faded away. How could someone with so much power simply disappear, and leave behind everyone who depended on her?

Suddenly Tuava-Li felt the presence of someone standing close by, so close that she could almost feel breathing on her neck. She spun around. No one was there. Then something flew across the room, something that moved on restless silver wings. And just as quickly as it had arrived, it was gone. Tuava-Li blinked and stared. Her eyes beheld the table, and the book, and the motes of dust in the stream of light from the high window. And at the same time her eyes gazed inward, and there was something else. There was a cage, and a room lit by artificial light, and a bird with a broken wing. There was danger, and time was a race into an abyss. There was a plea. That was all. And yet this fleeting vision meant everything to Tuava-Li . . . *it meant that her Mage was still alive!* It wasn't just imagination, or wishful thinking. The Mage was alive, and trying to communicate with her.

There was no time to rejoice. Within the space of a heartbeat, Tuava-Li heard angry shouting, growling, voices calling out for help. She ran to the branch outside and peered down. Someone was again caught in the trap the Elves had prepared on the outskirts of the Grove. Someone else had gotten past the monks who were using their magick to make Alfheim invisible and direct strangers away. Who could it be?

"Get me out of here! *NOW!*" Macta was livid. His face was flushed, his entire body was quaking with rage by the time Tuava-Li reached the line stretching between two massive trees. Macta, Druga, and Baltham were hung up by their feet. Along with Macta's pet Goblin, Powcca, they thrashed about inside the net. Jardaine and the other monks were already there. "Tuava-Li!" Jardaine exclaimed. "We couldn't stop the intruders until they'd come this far!"

"No matter," answered Tuava-Li, scratching her chin. "Actually, I'm glad to know who's been skulking around Alfheim. Interesting . . . very interesting indeed!"

The green-skinned Goblin in the net howled, struggling, and Druga already had his blade out, sawing through the vines. Baltham was squeezed between his companions, moaning pitifully. A dozen Elves, with looks of horror and helplessness on their faces, stood back. "We've caught the Prince! What should we do?"

Inside the net, Druga dropped his dagger, and it fell onto the dirt below. *"Aaaaargh!"* he bellowed. "Let me out!"

"Will wonders never cease!" Tuava-Li chortled. "Even the quick-witted Prince can fall into a trap! We citizens of Alfheim are gentlefolk, but it seems of late that we must keep our guard up to prevent others from taking advantage of our good nature. What brings you back so soon, my friend? Did you feel the need for some spiritual guidance?"

The Goblin snapped and growled from inside the net, foam dripping from its mouth. Macta's face hardened and he hissed through clenched teeth. "I—said—let—me—out—right now, or I'll—"

"You'll what? Believe me, Macta, you're in no position to threaten anyone," Tuava-Li observed. "But maybe if you tell me the name of the Elf who's been spreading rumors about Princess Asra's wedding shoe, I'll be inclined to take pity on you and your friends and allow you to get out of here."

"Everyone in Helfratheim knows about the missing shoe," Macta replied. "'Tis not a rumor, and you know it. News travels fast when it's as important as this! Now cut me loose. I'm here to give you one last chance to take me to your Mage. My father was very interested to hear that you refused to grant me my wishes. In fact, he was quite offended. You must learn your place, country maid. Cut me loose, and once I'm Lord and Master of this miserable realm, perhaps I'll take pity on you and—"

"You must explain what you mean," Tuava-Li demanded, looking at Macta doubtfully. "I think it's delusional to even entertain the notion that you could be Lord and Master of anything."

Tuava-Li gestured for the Elves to lower the trap line and loosen the cord wrapped around their prisoners' ankles. Macta glared. "That's more like it," he said, getting to his feet and taking Powcca's leash.

Druga leapt up and glanced around, taking mental note of those who had caused him to suffer such embarrassment. Baltham sat on the dirt with his hands clasped over his ankles, looking ill. "The fact is," Macta spat, "the fact is that I'm going to marry your Princess Asra. We are going to be married right here in your very own Sacred Grove, and the assembled multitudes of the Faerie kingdom will be here to celebrate our union. No one will stand in our way, least of all *you*. Take me to your Mage, now. I don't want any excuses. If she gives me the wedding shoe, I'll be happy to leave, and my associates and I will do our best to put this unpleasant incident behind us."

Tuava-Li shook her head. "Amazing. Simply amazing. Twice in a single day I catch bullies in my trap, only to have them telling me what to do, ordering me around, and asking for things I don't have. Why, I—"

"Who else has been here?" demanded Macta.

"I think I know," said Druga, looking at a pattern of large shoe prints in the dirt, trailing up to and away from the Sacred Grove. "I think that maybe these Elves are in league with Humans."

"Druga, I think you're on to something!" said Macta. "First they get the Human who found the shoe to hand it over to them, then, well . . . who knows what they might get the

Humans to do next? I imagine that the Synod in Ljosalfar would be very interested in hearing how the Elves and the Humans are secretly working together."

Tuava-Li looked skyward and slowly sighed through clenched teeth. "All right," she said. "All right. You're right, there was a Human here. The boundaries between our worlds are vanishing, Macta. For one so well-informed, I'm sure you must know all about that. You must also know there's nothing we can do about it. A Human stumbled upon us here, and thanks to the monks of Alfheim, we caught him and sent him back where he came from, before he could do any damage."

Macta exploded. "You *what?* You let him live? And your Mage thought that was an acceptable—"

A sudden realization passed over Macta's face, as if something that had been troubling him became instantly clear. His eyes gleamed with delight. "I think I'm beginning to understand what's going on here. You no longer *have* a Mage, do you? That would account for why you won't let me see her. That would account for the chaos, the bumbling. Of course. That's got to be why you won't bring her to me. She's dead! And who's replaced her as the new Mage? Do you even *have* a new Mage? It's certainly not . . . no, it can't be!"

Baltham got to his feet, and began to laugh. Macta stepped closer to Tuava-Li, aiming his finger at her chest. Tuava-Li breathed in and imagined a ring spinning clockwise around her, a ring of protection that would shield her from Macta's hostility.

Amazingly, the Prince came no farther. "You're wrong," Tuava-Li said, but Macta went on as if he had not heard.

"So *you're* the new Mage of Alfheim. 'Tis true, isn't it? Who would have ever guessed. Well, I'm glad to make your acquaintance, O Holy One! But somehow I don't think your days as Mage will be long. Please accept my apologies for leaving so soon; I've enjoyed our chat. But I think we'll follow these monstrous footprints into the woods, and find out a little more about this Human who's been visiting you here! And whilst I'm gone I trust you'll take that diamond-covered shoe and wrap it up for me. I shall be back shortly to claim it. Druga, Baltham, what do you say we find out where this trail of deceit leads?"

The dark trio, led by their Goblin pet, slipped into the woods and disappeared. Tuava-Li continued to imagine a spinning ring of protection revolving around her body. She realized that she would need a great deal of protection when the news about the recovered shoe and the disappearance of the Mage finally got out. What would the Synod think? What were the chances that Macta was telling the truth about his upcoming marriage? Tuava-Li had no choice but to travel to Ljosalfar and deliver the diamond-covered shoe to the Synod, if only to keep it out of Prince Macta's hands. She would keep the news of the Mage's disappearance to herself, because her vision had convinced her that it was only a matter of time until her Mage was found. The Mage had contacted Tuava-Li once, surely she would do so again. In the meantime Tuava-Li would leave the care of Alfheim in the hands of Jardaine. Jardaine's contempt for the Humans surely meant that she would fight to the death, if need be, for the safety of her homeland. Jardaine was spirited, and quick to anger, and wasn't such passion a kind of strength? Tuava-Li went to meditate and pray for guidance. Until the Mage was home once again, she would need all the help she could get.

19

BREEZES STRAYED AMONG the branches of the forest, lifting leaves, carrying seeds from broken pods, ruffling the feathers of birds and the trembling whiskers of squirrels. The sun crossed the afternoon sky while the clouds cast shadows over everything that lay below. Everything was caught up in a ceaseless flow of time. There was just one place, one place in the forest where time had broken, where it had shattered into pieces. Here the seconds and minutes and hours came undone, scrambling like a million tiny insects racing through the darkness. It was a place where a channel had opened up between the present and the past, where a yawning emptiness formed a passage for fear, and loneliness, and confusion to flood in. It was the broken mind of Anna McCormack.

The girl stumbled through the forest, searching for her father. She clawed through brambles, looking for the way back to the pickup truck. She cried out for her mother, for her brother, for

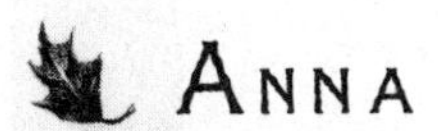

someone to help her find her way home. Anna sniffled, wiping her nose on her sleeve. She wasn't used to breathing air anymore, and the breeze was sharp with the scent of pine. A Christmas tree materialized, floating in a dark corner of her memory. The tree was dripping with lights and ornaments. She fell to her knees.

That's the smell of Christmas, the smell of Christmas, and our tree, just like it ought to be. Just like it always is. There's the angel, the beautiful angel, smiling down from the top of the tree. And the presents, look at the presents under the tree! I'll just reach out, and . . . My hands . . . why can't I see my—my hands?

It's dark, dark in the forest. Briars scratching my cheek, my breath so ragged, my breath, my breath is so loud. Branches, brambles, beetles. A hawk, circling.

And the clouds drifting overhead. Just like when I looked up through the water. There was the funny little troll man, the one who talked to me. There was the snow, falling, falling, the leaves, and the silt, and the silence, the deer, antlers, rifle cartridges, killing, killing, like people do.

So I would learn, so I would see what my kind has done to their kind.

That's what she said. There were the guns, and the fireflies, and the hands lifting me into the air and carrying me through the bushes, when I couldn't walk, or talk, or even move my fingers. There was Daddy, calling for help, and there was nothing,

nothing I could do.

I dropped

the

gun.

Anna was utterly alone. The pieces of the life she had known were blown away in tatters, tethered to a reality that no longer existed. She had become more like a ghost than a girl, more phantom than human, more liquid, in a way, than solid. The water was not just her friend, it was more than that. The water was *her*. She longed for the water more than she longed for the family and home of her broken memories.

Anna found her way to a winding, trickling stream and lay down beside it. She let her fingers dangle in the cold racing water and felt its gentle, comforting power. As long as she was near the water, she could be *real*. She could be alive. Without the water, she would fade away and disappear. As the stream burbled on, Anna closed her eyes and let the darkness carry her away.

20

A WOODPECKER BEAT out a distant rat-a-tat-a-tat on a tree trunk as the wind rustled the leaves overhead. Matt trudged through the woods, his eyes scanning the horizon for a tree whose trunk was heaped in acorns. But there were a million trees, and the forest floor was littered with the detritus of countless seasons. He tried to recall the markers that the Troll had told him he would see, and realized he couldn't tell an oak from an elm, a gully from a ravine, a meadow from a grove. But still he wandered on, trying to keep the weight off his bad foot, and doing his best to see the world the way he imagined the Faerie Folk saw it.

About a hundred yards behind him, Tomtar crept. He moved silently over the fallen branches and decaying leaves, staying out of sight behind tree trunks and foliage, just as Tuava-Li had requested. But the Troll jumped when the boy up ahead let out a cry. *"Whoa!"* Matt stopped, dumbfounded. There it was, just like the Faeries had told him it would be. There was the elm tree, there was the pile of acorns at the base of the trunk. But they hadn't said that the pile would rise up ten feet tall and would be spread around the tree in an impenetrable fan. Neither had they said anything about the discarded deer antler wedged in where the branches met the trunk. No one had mentioned the moldering mismatched gloves and mittens hanging from the antler's points, the old bent forks and spoons, the crushed soda cans, or the bottle caps tied to bits of string and vine hanging from low branches, clattering like wind chimes. Matt nearly tripped over a rusty typewriter as he approached the tree. "Hello!" he called. Then he added, "In the name of the Mother and her Cord," as the Elf had instructed him to do.

Silence. He plodded through the acorns and tried rapping gently on the trunk, like one would knock on a neighbor's door. Nothing. He got down on his hands and knees and dug his fingers into the mound of acorn shells. Maybe there was a hidden doorway or passage somewhere under there big enough for a Troll. However big *that* was. Suddenly a barrage of acorns rained down on Matt's head. He leapt up and stumbled backward, tripping over the typewriter. With a thud he landed on his back and found himself staring up at the tree. Matt saw a squirrel tail, waving frantically from behind a branch. There was an angry chattering sound just like a squirrel would make. But the tail was not attached to a squirrel! At the base of the tail, Matt could see a grubby hand, holding on tight. "Hello there, I know you're there," Matt called. "Would you please come out? The Elves of Alfheim sent me to see you. I don't mean you any harm."

A pinched face peered over a heap of rubble in the crook of the tree. The Troll lowered the severed squirrel tail and stared at Matt skeptically. "Prove it," he demanded.

Matt reached into the pocket of his jeans and pulled out the medicine bottle the Elves had given him, as well as the leaf with the emblem drawn on it. He held the bottle up so the Troll could see. "Look, my name is Matt McCormack. I did the Elves a favor, and in return they gave me some medicine for an infection in my foot. It's some kind of Elf infection. But I need more medicine, sir, and they said you could help me."

The Troll dropped from sight and clattered down a ladder on the side of the tree. He was old and stooped, and the beard on his chin was scraggly and gray. He pulled a dust mask from his pocket and slid the straps over his ears. "I have a fondness for Human stuff," he said, eyeing the boy cautiously, "and I know from experience that it does me no harm. But I've never met a real Human in person before, so I'm not takin' chances. Put the bottle down, and step back," the Troll demanded. "Don't breathe on me. And what's that leaf for?"

Matt placed the bottle and the leaf on the ground and backed up again, this time looking over his shoulder so he wouldn't trip over any of the Troll's junk. "There was an Elf, a girl, I guess, a female Elf, and she looked like she was in charge of things. She said you'd recognize this."

The Troll scuttled over the acorn shells and picked up the leaf. He studied it carefully, nodding. "The mark of the Mage," he said, then reached for the bottle. He held it up in a shaft of light that filtered down through the trees. He turned it over, inspecting the bottom. He yanked out the cork, dipped a finger into the bottle, then popped it into his mouth. "Ah, yes," he mused. "I know this. It *could* be done . . ."

He raised his brow and peered warily at Matt. "And what exactly have you got to trade?"

"Trade?" repeated Matt, like he had never heard the word before.

"Those Elves told you I'd give you somethin' as important as the medicine you need for *nothin'*? No wonder I live all alone. Elves are fools. *All* Faeries are fools. Humans are fools, too. Now what have you got to give me?"

"Look," Matt pleaded, "I don't have—"

"Empty out your pockets!" the Troll demanded. "I'll be the judge of what you have and don't have. Go on, put everything there, on the ground!"

Matt fumbled in his pockets and pulled out a rubber band; a penknife his aunt had given him when he turned twelve; a chunk of crystal he had found in the construction site; four dollar bills; a nickel, two quarters, and a penny; a wadded-up tissue; and a fair amount of pocket lint. The Troll crossed his arms and glared. "What's that on your wrist?"

"Ah," Matt said, removing his watch. He placed it on the pile and stepped back.

"Now give me those strings that tie up your shoes."

"My shoelaces? But . . . oh, all right."

Matt pulled the laces from his shoes, one grommet at a time, and dropped them on the pile. "My name's Matt," he volunteered again. "What's your name?"

The Troll sniffed. He pulled a filthy Human-sized handkerchief from inside his jacket, wrapped up Matt's possessions, then tied the handkerchief up with a shoelace. "You can address me by the name Agar, if you must. Follow me; just keep your distance, and don't touch anything."

"Follow you into what?" Matt asked incredulously.

"In here," said the Troll, kicking at a mound of shells. "I don't trust you outside where I can't keep an eye on you."

The Troll bent low, jammed his arm up to his shoulder in the debris, and rooted around. A look of satisfaction spread across his face as he found the handle he had been searching for. *"Aha!"*

Broken bits of shell clattered into the void when a door suddenly opened. "Come on," he ordered, bringing the bundle of Matt's belongings down into his lair. "Get down! I'm not goin' to wait all day!"

Matt realized the Troll was completely mad. The opening beneath the trapdoor was no more than a foot wide, too narrow for even the smallest human boy to pass. The confusion must have shown on Matt's face, because the Troll took a deep breath, shook his head, and put down his bundle. His lips stretched into what might have passed for a smile. "Get down on your knees, lad, and tuck your head under your arms. That's right, there's a smart lad, now. Close your eyes, and keep 'em that way. Don't move. There . . . there . . ."

The Troll wrapped a scrap of fabric around his fingers, reached up, and yanked a tuft of hair from the top of Matt's head. "Ouch!" Matt cried. "I—"

"Oh, shut up!" yelled the Troll. He laid the hair on a stone, pulled a bent match from a pocket, and lit it with one quick movement. Then he held the flame to the hair and muttered an incantation. He threw a fistful of pungent herbs into the fire and watched the color turn from orange to blue. The stench of the burning hair made Matt feel queasy, but he kept his eyes tightly shut. "Now open your eyes and get up," ordered the Troll, "and don't look behind you, whatever you do."

Matt opened his eyes and got to his feet. Somehow the doorway among the roots of the tree was much, much bigger. Matt would be able to go down the stairs with no problem. The Troll was now bigger, too, bigger than Matt was; and in fact, the acorns strewn all around him were now bigger than tennis balls. Matt looked up at the trees. The massive trunks seemed to be a mile high, like the redwoods in California, only taller. A spider scurrying up the nearest trunk looked as big as a rat.

The scrabbling sound it made was like a claw hammer scraping through a bed of broken glass. Matt froze. Things weren't bigger than they had been before, no—it appeared that he had *shrunk* to a fraction of his normal size. In horror Matt started to turn around when the Troll yelled, "Don't!"

"Why aren't I supposed to look behind me?" Matt asked, cringing. "What *is* behind me?"

"You're behind you, stupid," sighed the Troll. "But if you look back over your shoulder and see yourself, the spell will be broken, and I'll have to start all over again. Now follow me into my humble abode. And remember, don't touch anything."

Behind a fallen tree Tomtar squatted, peering at the strange sight ahead of him. Matt was crouching on the ground with his head buried in his arms. He wasn't moving a muscle. Yet Tomtar heard the old Troll tell the boy to come into his underground hovel, and he heard the creak of the little door as it closed. And still Matt lay there crumpled on the ground. What on earth was going on? It was some kind of magick, he was sure. Tomtar decided to risk moving a little closer to the boy. As he hoisted himself over the dead tree he heard a faint rustling in the leaves. He turned around to see a meaty fist flying at him. "Whaaaa—"

Lights flashed and a burst of pain went through his jaw. Tomtar lost consciousness and fell to the ground. Druga stood over the Troll, massaging his knuckles, and chuckled dryly. "Nothin' harder in all the realms than the head of a Troll!"

Macta got down on his knees and searched Tomtar's pockets for anything of interest. "Bah! He's got a few nuts, some pieces of dried fruit, and not much more. There's a wooden ring on a string 'round his neck. Worthless."

Macta sniffed, then made a face. "And he reeks, too. I wonder why this big-nosed idiot was spying on the Human? Is he working for someone? Tuava-Li, no doubt. Baltham, get over here and make yourself useful. Keep an eye on this Troll while I investigate the junk heap up ahead. Druga, take Powcca's leash. If the Human makes a move, you know what to do."

Macta, Druga, and the hulking Goblin, straining on his leash, moved toward the oddly decorated elm. The Human boy crouched on a blanket of acorn shells did not move; so they ventured closer still. When they had come within spitting distance, Macta lifted his boot and gave Matt a sharp kick.

"Owww!" Matt's Spirit Body, standing inside the Troll's den, jumped and clutched his side. The flesh and blood Matt, however, completely enchanted and still curled up on the ground outside, did not move. "What's going on here?" growled Druga. "Let me have a turn." He gave Matt another kick.

"Don't waste your energy," said Macta. "'Tis some kind of Troll magick. Just a trick. I've seen it before. Come on, we'll go back and make sure that Tuava-Li's spy is still out cold, and once the Human's spirit comes back to his own body, we'll trail him. We'll figure out a way to discover if he's in league with Tuava-Li."

Matt looked around in the dim light of the underground chamber and shook his head in disbelief. "Don't just stand there with your mouth hangin' open, follow me!" demanded the Troll.

Matt stepped carefully down a flight of steps, though there was not much more than a narrow path for his feet. The steps were piled high, along with every other flat surface in the underground dwelling, with mounds of junk. Matt slipped on the stair, causing an avalanche of pebbles, which had been arranged and stacked according to size and color. "Now look at what you've done!" roared the Troll, spinning around. He growled, then disappeared behind a pile of rusting double-A batteries. The place was impossibly cluttered. Heaps of old matchbooks, damp and moldy, sat side by side with plastic bullet casings and stacks of scrap newspaper. Disposable spoons and forks, crushed soda cans, tiny beach shells, and coins were stacked, shoved, and strewn in every corner. A collection of animal skulls filled a shelf alongside one earthen wall, and a pile of squirrel tails, along with some skeletal remains, was heaped on the floor. Bird feathers were bundled everywhere, tied up in colored string, and a complete hawk wing hung from hooks on the ceiling. Odd bits of glass and stone, strange broken metal objects, and familiar hardware items, including bent rusty nails and screws, springs from broken watches, and pieces of crockery, filled up every nook and cranny of the Troll's hideaway. Along the walls were stacked piles of envelopes with their old-fashioned postage

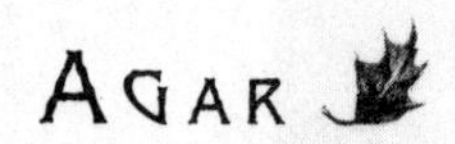

stamps and postcards from faraway places. An assortment of glass Christmas ornaments hung from above.

Matt could hear the Troll murmuring to himself, just around the corner, in one of the tottering corridors of junk. He tiptoed through the mess to find out what the Troll was doing and brushed against an enormous chipped bowl. There was a fine mesh stretched across the top. Matt shuddered when he peered inside. Scuttling around on needle-thin legs, dozens of shiny black earwigs hissed. Matt squeezed past and turned a corner. There stood the Troll, with a book open on the table next to him, busily mixing powders and liquids measured out from an assortment of broken crockery. To take the pressure off his foot, Matt leaned back against a metal box with a handle on the side. Suddenly the lid of the box sprang up and a faded toy clown on a rusty spring popped out. *"Aaaaargh!"* Matt cried, and stumbled over the bowl with the earwigs in it.

The insects pushed against the mesh and scuttled out of their prison. "You idiot!" the Troll screamed at Matt. "Don't let 'em get away. It took me months to catch 'em—there are enough there for a dozen meals!"

"But I—" Matt mumbled, getting to his feet. He hurried down a corridor, past jars of buttons, past a bicycle bell resting on top of a pepper grinder, and a stack of broken colored egg-shells. He wasn't sure what he would do if he cornered one of the gigantic earwigs. Suddenly a large pink figure loomed up before him, and he stopped. "Hey, what's this?"

The Troll was hard on Matt's heels, and now he, too, stopped, his eyes wide. The earwigs disappeared amid the dank clutter. "This is one of Becky's dolls, the missing ones she's been crying about," accused Matt. "I can tell because of the stain on the dress. I got some glue on it accidentally when she left it on the—hey, and look! There's another!" Matt turned on the Troll. "How did you get these dolls? They don't belong to you."

"Finders keepers," said the Troll, looking defensive. "I found 'em outdoors, and I brought 'em here, just like everything else you see . . . all my treasures," he said, thrusting out a nervous hand. "As I said, I don't have any problems with Human things . . . the Elves, you know, they're all afraid. They think they'll get poisoned, or sick. Now a Troll, on the other hand, has natural defenses to— " then he bumped a pile of mismatched buttons, and they tumbled to the ground. Behind the buttons was a stack of baby food jars. Each of the jars was packed full of glittering, colorful stones, along with tiny figurines cast from gold and silver. The Troll jumped in front of the collection, waving his arms and puffing. "This way! This way! I've got to finish the med'cine, now, so you can take it and start gettin' better! Here, come this way! Follow me, and we'll get you right out of here! Come on, I'll show you how 'tis done! Humans aren't ordinarily allowed to see—don't look at that, 'tis just some junk. Hey, Humans aren't allowed to see Trolls practicin' their med'cinal arts, you know, so as a special favor to you, I'll—come on, lad, follow me!"

Matt trailed the mad Troll down the maze of corridors, back to the tabletop where he had his stores of herbs and tinctures. "So nice of you to come by and visit," the Troll muttered, his hand shaking as he added dashes and sprinkles and pinches of powders to the marble bowl. "Eeh, you've certainly made my day a memorable one. I trust you'll be so kind as to forget about what you've seen here! And once your foot has healed, lad, perhaps you'll forget you ever even met me. Ummmm?'"

Matt furrowed his brow. "Look, you really shouldn't take things that don't belong to you. You stole my sister's dolls, and I'm going to take them back with me."

"Ah, yes, the dolls!" the Troll laughed. "Of course, the dolls! I've got so many collections. I found a shoe once, an Elfin shoe, I believe, but I misplaced it, lost it somewhere. So I started collecting the dolls, in case I found the shoe again, and wanted to put it on one of the doll's feet. I might, you know. You never can say when somethin' will prove useful. Lately I've been venturin' to the fields and 'round the buildings of Humans like you, findin' all kinds of interestin' things. My collections just keep growin'; you know, I'm hollowin' out the trees 'round this one, to make room for all my precious things! But I didn't know the dolls belonged to you, honest, I didn't."

"You found a shoe, did you?" Matt asked. "And you lost it? I found a shoe, too. Covered in little diamonds."

"Is that so?" the Troll chuckled nervously. "Well, take the dolls. Maybe the shoe'll fit one of 'em."

"I don't have the shoe any more. The Elves took it back. It belonged to them."

With shaking hands the Troll poured the contents of the bowl into the glass bottle, and twisted in the cork. He spun around and shoved the bottle at Matt. "Well then, here you go! Ten drops, every three of your hours!"

Matt took the bottle and the Troll wiped his hands on his filthy vest. "Now you go back and wait by the door," Agar said, "and I'll drag the dolls out for you."

Within a minute or two, the Troll had moved all four of Becky's missing dolls outside the door of his lair. Then he turned to Matt. "You'll have to back up the stairs, here—I'll hold the door open for you so you can just back on out, that's right, carefully, now. But if you should knock somethin' else over, well, *ha ha,* why would I mind? Now close your eyes, and don't open 'em back up 'til I shut the door! Good-bye, my Human friend, have a nice day and don't forget to take your med'cine. So happy to be of help! Good-bye! Good luck! I trust your sister will enjoy havin' her dolls again!"

Matt backed out the door with his eyes shut. He stood on a plain of acorn shells with the bottle held in his arms. The door at the base of the tree slammed shut. Matt flicked open his eyes. Suddenly he was lying on the ground with his head tucked in, and his knees pulled up under his chin. He stood up. And he was five feet one and a half inches tall once again. The medicine bottle was in the pocket of his jeans, right where it had been before he went into the Troll's lair. He pulled out the bottle and held it up to the light. Full! He pulled out the cork, gave the potion a sniff, and then let ten drops fall on his tongue. Yes! It was definitely the same stuff. Matt gave a sigh of relief. He gathered up the dolls, then turned and tried to figure out which direction might lead him home. "Strange," he mumbled to himself. "Very, very strange. The jewels couldn't have been real," he muttered. *"Or could they?"* He shook his head, searching for a new walking stick. "Probably just plastic. Just more doll stuff. If they had been real, the Troll would have been rich. *Really* rich. He could have lived in some kind of Troll palace, instead of a filthy hovel under the ground. *Aha!"*

Matt picked up a branch, and brushed the loose soil away. It would make a decent walking stick. "Unless," he sighed, "the Troll stole them, like he stole everything else."

Matt clomped down the ridge. The medicine was working; already his aching foot was feeling a little better. He felt hopeful that this was the way back home, and he looked up to see if the trees, the position of the sun, or the direction of the wind might confirm his hunch. *If I ever do this again,* he thought, *I'm going to get myself a compass.*

Macta, Druga, and Baltham crouched behind a boulder and watched Matt walk away. Druga pinched his Master's shoulder. "What are we doing?" he whispered. "I thought we were going to follow him and see where he went? I was going to trip him, dash him over the head, and get him to talk to us. Why are we letting him go?"

Macta frowned. "Don't touch me, fool. There's been a little change of plan. Did you hear the lad mutter something about jewels? I think that's an avenue we might want to explore a little further. Come on."

Macta rapped hard on the trunk of the elm, then the three Elves slipped behind the boulder and waited. In a moment the hidden door rattled open. The Troll stuck his head out. "Back again so soon? Did you forget somethin'? 'Tis ten drops every three hours, just like—hello? Hello?"

Cautiously the Troll climbed up out of his cellar hole. "Hello?" he called again. Behind him the acorn shells rattled, and the Troll spun around. He never saw what hit him. Within five minutes, Macta emerged from the Troll's underground chamber, Druga and Baltham trailing behind, each dragging several large burlap sacks. Druga laughed. "After we found the booty I wanted to trash the place, but 'twas already trashed when we got there!"

Baltham grunted. "Where would a bumpkin like that get a stash of jewels like this? There are more jewels in those jars than in the treasure of an entire Clan! Maybe they *are* the treasure of an entire Clan! Macta, didn't you say that the Alfheim—"

"It doesn't matter *where* the jewels came from," Macta said, sprinting lightly over fallen branches. "The important thing is that they belong to *me* now. I'll have to make another trip back to Alfheim for that wedding shoe. I don't want to risk anyone there seeing our stash. Who knows, that Elfmaid who thinks she's a Mage might even recognize the jewels. Let's take another route home, shall we? I think we might find a tributary of the Cord that goes through Alfheim, running, hmmmm . . . slightly north."

Macta looked skyward, surveying the position of the sun. Then he untied Powcca's leash from a tree. "Lads, today I have become a very wealthy Elf. I'm richer than I could have ever dreamed . . . and I never need depend on my father for anything. In case you wondered, I'm going to be rewarding you both handsomely for your help. I'm *rich*, lads! And no one's going to be the wiser as to how I got that way!"

The three Elves laughed liked children as they moved slowly through the forest. They passed a hillside and a dense patch of brambles, where Macta was reluctantly forced to help Druga and Baltham lift the sacks high in the air. Macta was not an Elf who was accustomed to physical labor, and when the thorns tore his fine leggings, he was furious. But he was about to make another discovery that would change his mood for the better. The sound of running water grew louder as they made their way north. "A stream!" cried Druga, sweating profusely. "I'm dying of thirst. Let's stop for a drink!"

Baltham looked around, flaring his nostrils. "You're going to drink that water? I wouldn't trust it. There's something . . . a . . . a *smell* around here I don't like."

"The only odor around here is coming from you," Druga laughed, kneeling by the stream.

Baltham sniffed the air, and made a face. "There's something, I'm not sure what it is. Something that doesn't belong here. Don't drink the water, Druga; it's contaminated, I'm sure of it. You don't want to get sick!"

Druga threw him a murderous glance. "*I* don't get sick."

"Shut up, shut up!" hissed Macta. Before him, at the edge of the stream, lay a mud-covered form, a filthy, tattered heap with arms, and legs, and tendrils of hair like a mass of eels. The thing's fingers played in the water, and where the mud was washed away, the skin was bone-white. "What have we here?" Macta muttered, moving cautiously to the side to see if he could find the thing's face. There was a whiff of familiarity about the creature, obviously a Human female child. Suddenly he remembered. He tiptoed back to tell his accomplices. "Well, well, well. 'Tis the Human maid, the one whose father killed Udos all those moons ago! The Mage put her at the bottom of the stream near Alfheim. Three hundred and sixty moons now, and she hasn't aged a day. I wonder what she's doing here, out of the water?"

"Obviously," Baltham noted, "the Mage's magick wasn't sufficient."

The girl startled and made a whining sound, but didn't move from beside the stream. "Quiet, lads, quiet!" Macta whispered. "I'll take care of this. But I want you to find some vines. We're going to restrain her before we take her home with us. This whole trip has been an embarrassment of riches!"

Baltham looked stunned. "*What?* Why are we taking this creature with us?"

"A Human," Macta replied, "even one such as this—can be a most valuable tool . . . or a most dangerous weapon!"

Macta crept to the girl's side and whispered in her ear. "Everything's all right," he soothed, "everything is going to be fine now; everything is going to be just the way it used to be. Don't be afraid, my poor girl, we're here now, to take you to your father. Come along and don't be afraid; you'll be safe with us. We only want to help you get back home, back where you belong. Your father has been asking for you! He'll be so happy to see you again! And your dear mother, too. Those bad, bad Elves who put you in the water, they're all gone now. I'm Macta, and I'm here to help you! I'm not one of the bad Elves, I'm good, and nice, and kind. So are my friends! That's it, come on, that's it! Now get up. I'm going to get something pretty for you!"

Baltham returned to his Master's side with a length of vine. "Macta," he gulped, "should you be touching the Human like that?"

"Like what? Why shouldn't I be touching her?"

"Well, she's, she's *unclean!*"

Macta snorted. "She's filthy from being at the bottom of a stream, that's all. Now bring me one of the jewels. Quickly!"

Baltham rummaged through the burlap sack for the biggest, most impressive stone he could find, while Druga held Powcca's leash. Baltham found a ruby the size of a wren's egg and passed it to Macta. "Here," the Prince soothed, "this is for you. Isn't it a pretty bauble? 'Tis a ruby, you know. There will be so many more like it when you get back home. Here. Look at the way the light plays on the stone! That's it, easy steps, now. Let us lead you to the Cord, the Passage, and we'll follow it back home. Soon you'll be home, yes, home, just like I promised."

The world of Anna McCormack had been shattered into so many pieces that only fragments of the Elf's speech reached her. *Father* she heard, and *Mother*, as she crept through broken shards of memory. *There in my hand . . . the stone is so pretty. My great-grandmother's ruby ring, Mother was saving it for me, for sixth grade graduation. She trusts me not to lose it. I'll keep it forever, Mommy, I'll never take it off, or lose it, or*

let it go. The shadows are

growing, pushing in from outside. There's something wrong with me.

When I woke up from my nap, and it was dusk, I thought it was morning, but I was all alone and there was nothing but shadows. I saw the little Elf woman in the long silver robe, and I was like a giant. The tiny, tiny people, running from the giants. And the giants were me and Daddy.

And the water was like a flood, and the sky was pressing me down, like a weight, into the water. The little man is holding my hand. I can't see it, but I can feel it. I've got the ruby in my other hand, and I'll never let it go. Everything is going to be all right. He's going to take me home,

back

home!

When they reached the mound of earth and the crevice, exposing a patch of Cord, Macta smiled up at Anna. "Now, sweet one, we're going to bundle you up so you'll feel safe and comfortable, just like a baby in a blanket. Here, my dear, bend down, and I'll wrap my cape around you so that you can rest. 'Twill be dark and quiet for you. Good, good girl; now I'll tie it in back, not too tightly, just so the light doesn't hurt your eyes."

As Macta tightened the straps of his cape behind the girl's head, Druga and Baltham bound Anna's arms to her sides. She let herself relax, feeling safe and snug. It was a familiar feeling, the way she had felt in the water, held tight in the mud and sediment that piled up around her. Suddenly, freed from the burden of time, she was five years old again. She saw her mother turning off the bedroom light. She saw the little lambs on the revolving night-light go around and around, so she could count the sheep. She felt her father tuck her in, so that the sheet and blanket pressed in around her arms and legs, snug as a bug in a rug, *tuck tuck, pat pat, and good night, don't let the bedbugs bite.* The little man was telling her to kneel down, just like that, then lie on her side. The wind was just a breeze coming through an open window, the sweet, sweet breeze of summer, coming to guide her back home. She was drifting, now, floating, falling, falling . . . falling . . . asleep.

21

WHAT ON EARTH?" Jill exclaimed, hurrying around the side of the house.

Matt was standing by the picnic bench, where he had lined up the dolls he had brought back from the woods. He was spraying them with the garden hose. "Becky lost these," Matt explained, moving the nozzle back and forth. Cold water beaded on their plastic faces, soaked their clothing, and dripped from their little pink hands and feet. The force of the spray made the dolls wiggle on the bench, almost like they were alive.

"Matt, turn that off! If your sister sees what you're doing, she'll—"

"Stop it!" Becky cried. "Stop it!" Matt looked up and saw his sister with her fingers gripping the railing of the deck, and in a matter of seconds she had sped down the steps and across the yard. She grabbed the nozzle of the hose and wrestled Matt for control.

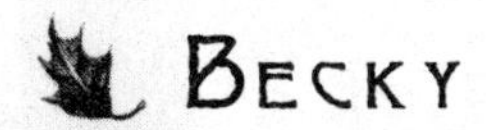

"Matt! Becky!" Jill hollered, then she stalked to the side of the house and turned the water off. "I heard the sound of the hose from inside, and I came to see who'd turned the water on. I can't believe my eyes, Matt! What do you think you're doing?"

"I was just washing them," Matt explained. "I found the dolls over there, in the dirt, and they were all muddy. You know how they disappeared, and Becky was really upset? Well, they were right over there in the field all along, I guess. I didn't want Becky to see them so filthy, so I just thought I'd wash them with the hose, and when they were dry, bring them back in the house. You should be thanking me, both of you!" Matt knew that what was really motivating him was the nagging feeling that the dolls might have been contaminated, somehow, from being in the Troll's lair. The Elves' suspicion that Humans could hurt them with their breath, or their touch, had spread to Matt. He knew what had happened because of the little Elfin shoe, and how stepping on the thing had nearly killed him. So he wanted to wash the dolls, just to be safe. He would have a shower and wash his clothes as soon as he could. But there was no explaining this to his mother, or his sister, and now he was in trouble.

Becky was in tears, lifting each doll one by one, and wiping their faces with the edge of her T-shirt. "I need a towel, Mom," she cried, gathering up the dolls in her arms and heading up the stairs onto the deck.

"Leave them outside and I'll get you a towel," Jill said. She turned and shook her head at Matt. "I don't know what's wrong with you. It's great you found the dolls, but you ought to know better than to line them up and spray them with a hose! Use your head, Matt. You can't wash dolls like you're washing a car. To Becky, they're just like—like little people."

"But they're not," Matt mumbled, thinking of the Elves and Trolls who lived in the forest. "I was just trying to help."

"Then you can help me by getting out of those clothes, young man, and taking them down to the laundry. You're pretty muddy yourself! Have you been back in the woods all this time? I'll never understand how boys get so dirty!"

"Nature's not all clean and tidy, Mom," Matt said, stalking past her. "Don't worry. I'll put my clothes right in the washer."

22

WHEN MACTA WOKE with a vision of Princess Asra floating in his mind, he turned in bed, and smiled. He yawned and sat up, then gazed out his window over the gray spires of Helfratheim. Though his intention had been to return to Alfheim and force Tuava-Li to give him the wedding shoe, the thought of that unpleasantness made him consider a change of plan. It had already been so much work hiding the Human girl and the jewels. A visit to his beloved Princess was in order, and even though he had yet to acquire the wedding shoe, it might be prudent to break the news of its discovery to the royal family. Then, when he arrived later with the shoe in his hands, the shock would have had time to sink in, and plans for the wedding could already be underway.

Skies were clear and blue in Ljosalfar, when many long hours later, the Prince and his gang slipped out of the Cord. They climbed a short flight of steps to a platform hung with banners and decorated in flowering vines. Ljosalfar, a realm always proud of its beauty, had provided an entry point worthy of its artistic reputation. Macta flexed his shoulders. Carefully he brushed his hair behind his ears. He believed that his ears were his most appealing feature. He liked to cock his head to one side or the other, just a little, to display the long, fleshy lobe, the gentle spiral of cartilage, and the graceful curve of the upper ear toward a delicate point. Macta let his hair grow long so that when he pushed it back, his ears seemed to stand out that much farther.

Druga stood at Macta's side, cracking his knuckles. He scanned the boulevard for any hint of trouble. Baltham, still nauseated from the journey, stumbled to the lilac bushes at the edge of the platform. He dropped the bouquet of black roses he was carrying for Macta, and threw up. The Prince rolled his eyes and scowled. He put one boot on Baltham's shoulder and gave him a push. "What did I do to deserve this? How is my true love going to greet me when one of my entourage reeks of vomit? Clean yourself up, Baltham. Give me the flowers, and keep your distance."

When they arrived at the dwelling of the royal family, Macta rapped on the door. A serving maid came to see who was there, and the Prince brushed past her and stepped over the threshold. "Good afternoon," he purred. "Would you be so kind as to tell Princess Asra that Macta Dockalfar, Prince of Helfratheim, has come to pay her a visit?"

Druga and Baltham kept watch outside while Macta slipped into the foyer. With the bouquet held behind his back he stepped from one room to another. "Where is she?" he asked. "She's got to be here!"

The maid stumbled along behind Macta, trying to think of a way to get him out of the house. "She's gone to visit a friend, and she won't be back 'til quite late, so you might as well go away!"

"How disappointing," Macta said, shaking his head. "She must be with her friend Skara. I know where she lives. I'll find her there."

"Oh, no, she's not with Skara; she's gone for her pottery lesson at Jensine Ha—"

"That's enough," interrupted Queen Shorya. She stepped from a doorway flanked by tapestries and stood with her arms folded. "Prince Dockalfar, whatever makes you think that you are welcome in this house?"

"Forgive me, your highness," said Macta, bowing gracefully. "Please forgive my enthusiasm at the prospect of seeing your daughter! I have come to bring news, news of the utmost importance. Good fortune is coming to visit both our houses, madam."

The Queen glared at Macta.

"We all recall," Macta said, "the wedding shoe that was lost in Alfheim on that terrible day. How could one ever forget? I'm sure you'd like to see your daughter happily married, and without the shoe, 'twould be impossible. That is why I'm delighted to tell you *the missing shoe has been found*!" Macta paused. "So many things must be in place for truly eventful things to happen. Like a marriage, for instance—the requirements of tradition, the right families, the right moment. Like the pieces of a puzzle, meant to fit perfectly in only one way. 'Tis a good omen the shoe has been found. Now that all of the proper elements are in place, the time has come. The union of the houses of Alfheim and Helfratheim is at hand. I'm here to tell you how deeply honored I will be, and how pleased my father will be, on the day I take Princess Asra as my bride!"

The Queen clenched her teeth, trying to keep her anger under control. "I speak for the royal family of Alfheim in saying that you shall never, ever be anything more to Princess Asra than a nuisance. That is all, and that is all I have to say to you. Now get out of my house!"

"Madam," Macta said in a wounded voice, "I shall do my best to forgive you for speaking to me in such a manner. But such unkind words are not easily forgotten! Good day, Shorya, until next we meet."

Still carrying the bouquet meant for Princess Asra, Macta stalked past the maid and flung open the front door. "Druga, Baltham," he commanded, "which of you lunkheads knows the way to Jensine Hall?"

Asra sat at the potter's wheel and dug her thumbs into a spinning lump of clay. A burlap smock covered her velvet dress, and her hair was drawn back behind her delicate, pointed ears. "That's it," smiled her instructor, a portly Elf called Varbas. "Deeper, deeper, put your thumbs in there, now squeeze. Just a little, not so hard!"

The pot forming beneath Asra's fingers broke apart, its walls toppling over in a soggy mess. The Princess shook her head and scowled, then wiped her hands on her smock. "I don't know if I'll ever get it right, Varbas. What do I do now?"

"You say hello to your dear friend Macta," came a voice from behind the flap in the tent wall.

The Prince strode deliberately across the floor, glancing at the shelves laden with pottery. Asra sighed. For years he had been coming around, following her like a bad smell, always making his appearance with a bouquet of black roses. Macta wiped one gloved finger across the lip of a bowl, then looked at his finger. "Asra, you never cease to amaze me. Every new challenge you undertake only makes my fascination with you grow, and grow, and grow. Pottery! What a charming hobby."

Druga and Baltham lingered at the entrance to the tent, flicking dirt clods at a groundhog harnessed to a carriage. Asra got to her feet, her eyes darting from one side of the tent to the other, looking for a way out. There was nowhere to turn but to Macta. "Good day," she said, and reluctantly accepted the bouquet.

"It happens that I've just come from a visit with your mother," Macta said, "and she's quite anxious for me to share some good news with you!" Macta glanced at the potter, arching an eyebrow. "In private."

Varbas turned on his heels and left the tent. "That's my teacher you just insulted," Asra said, tossing Macta's bouquet onto a clay-smeared table. "And I'm in the middle of my lesson. What do you want this time?"

Macta smiled at the Princess. "Being of royal blood, we have known each other all our lives, Asra. I remember you in a frilly party frock, and your hair in braids,when we were just children. But the thing I especially remember is how you looked in that wedding gown, and how my heart wished it could have been—well. I always like to think of you in that gown, Asra, so fresh, so expectant, so . . . *perfect.*"

Macta took a step toward the Princess. He smiled, standing so close that she could have counted the hairs on his chin. She tried to back away, and bumped into a shelf stacked high with glazed bowls. "The day I wore that dress is a day I wish I could forget," she said.

"Listen," said Macta, speaking softly. "Come along with me, for a walk to the pavilion. Are you hungry? We could get a bite to eat! 'Tis been forever since we've had the chance to catch up! You'll find that I've grown up quite a bit since the old days. I'm not the rascal I used to be!"

"And those two rascals you left outside?" inquired Asra. "You'll bring them along with us on our little romantic walk?"

Macta glanced over his shoulder. "If you want me to leave

those two buffoons behind, then it shall be so. They only accompany me because I feel sorry for them. Your wish is my command, Asra!"

In a flash the Princess slipped past her awkward suitor, carefully avoiding the hilt of his rapier. Before Macta had time to turn around she was behind him, and free. She shrugged and smiled, gesturing with muddy fingers as she backed away. "Then my command is for you to go, and allow me to complete my lesson. I have things to finish here, Macta. Pots and bowls, pitchers and plates! You already know how important my *hobbies* are to me!"

Macta scowled. "You're making sport of me. My feelings are no secret, Asra; that's the only reason you dare to tease me so. I wanted to be the one to break the news to you, but I can see you're not in the mood to take me seriously. Your mother understands the importance of the message I wished to bring you. Ask *her* about how your future has just taken a turn!"

A picture flashed through Asra's mind. She remembered the banner that read THE FUTURE IS YOURS TO SEE. She remembered the fortune-teller's cards. She remembered the sputtering candle, and the dark, musty tent, and as Macta brushed back the hair from his pale pointed ears and turned to leave, she remembered *the Hanged One*. "Varbas," she called to her teacher, and shivered a little despite the heat of the kiln. "Varbas, are you there? Will you help me get the wheel started?"

23

TUAVA-LI KNELT ON A MAT in the corner of her study, awaiting Jardaine's arrival. With her eyes shut she let her thoughts drift away like an empty boat on a pond. She extended her awareness to the subtle sensations on her skin, feeling a faint breeze, the cool, moist air on her cheeks and arms, the rumble of her belly, and the tightness of her muscles. She relaxed the tension in her jaw, listened to the chirp of a wren in the tree, and let her mind open to even subtler energies. Maybe now the Mage would contact her again. Tuava-Li waited for something to appear in the dark stillness, sensations, images, anything that might give her a clue as to the whereabouts of the Mage. Nothing came. The silence was absolute. *Ring-a-ting-a-ting!* Tuava-Li startled at the sound of the clay bell, then stood up and smoothed the front of her tunic. On her forehead was painted a circle with an arrow at its center, the custom for a monk embarking on a journey. But she was not dressed in the silver-plumed cloak that a Mage wore when journeying throughout the Faerie world. "Come inside, Jardaine," Tuava-Li smiled. "This morning I'll be traveling to Ljosalfar to deliver the wedding shoe to the Synod. In my absence I'm appointing you as the acting Mage of Alfheim."

The monk opened her mouth to speak, but Tuava-Li was not interested in hearing any arguments. "'Twill only be for a few days, Jardaine. I have every confidence in you to take care of things whilst I'm gone."

"But I . . . but you . . . Well, of course, I'll—I don't know what to say!"

Tuava-Li leaned in to whisper in the monk's ear. "We have good reason to be cheerful this morning. Everyone thinks that our Mage is dead. But Jardaine, *I know that she lives!*"

Jardaine held her breath. "She's *alive,*" Tuava-Li said. "I believe that she's caught somewhere, trapped, and she can't get away. But she's alive! I saw it in a vision. Twice now she's made contact with me. She sent pictures, sensations, feelings into the air so that I'd know she was still alive. That's why I want you to stay here, Jardaine, until I return. Spend as much time as you can in the Mage's study, and be open, be vigilant for any signs. Anything that might help us find her."

Tuava-Li turned to the wall and withdrew the wedding shoe from its hidden niche. She laid it on the Mage's desk, then carefully slipped it into her pack. Jardaine looked on, feeling dizzy. The earth seemed to be shifting beneath her feet. "Tuava-Li, I'm stunned. The Mage is alive! 'Tis wonderful news! Wonderful!

And you . . . *your* time will come, Tuava-Li. One day, I know you'll—"

Tuava-Li saw in Jardaine's eyes a subtle gleam she recognized as ambition. With any shift in the chain of command, Jardaine would try to find an opportunity to claim a better position. But this was no time to let rivalry get in the way of what must be done. "What I want for myself doesn't matter, Jardaine. Yes, my time will come, and when it does, it will be an honor and a sacrifice. But all that matters now is that our Mage will soon be back among us, and that I return this wedding shoe to its rightful owner."

Tuava-Li descended the trunk of the great tree Bethok, leaving Jardaine to watch from above. She was certain that the monk could be trusted to keep things in order for a few days. Jardaine would surely relish playing the role of Mage. And once the real Mage was back, all of the problems that had befallen Alfheim would be solved. *All will be well,* Tuava-Li thought, as she strode through the Sacred Grove. *I know it will!*

Tuava-Li sped through the Cord, her eyes shut, arms folded over her chest. The air was hot and humid. Once in a while a Troll, Sprite, or Pixie came within view, but there were few travelers making their way through the Cord. Time had no meaning in this place. There was no day or night, only a faint inner glow to light the long passage. A tingling in her fingertips let Tuava-Li know when she was near her destination. Clenching her shoulders she leaned into the inner wall of the Cord, and slowly came to a stop. A damp wind blew at her hair as she drew a fingernail along the surface, making a fine slit. Then she climbed out of the Cord, stepped onto an elaborately decorated platform, and looked around. No one paid the slightest bit of attention to the serious young Elfmaid as she strode down the crowded boulevard to Synod Hall.

The receptionist looked up from his desk. "In the name of the Mother and her Cord, good day. How may I be of help?"

"My name is Tuava-Li, and I represent the Mage of Alfheim. I would like to see the Secretary, sir. 'Tis a matter of great importance."

"Very well." The receptionist nodded, as he got up and slipped behind a panel at the rear of the chamber.

Tuava-Li gazed around. The room was cool, dry, and silent as a tomb. No pictures hung on the walls. The tabletops were bare. There was a sense that important business went on here. Tuava-Li took a deep breath, and tried to be calm. Since Macta Dockalfar had unraveled her secret, it might be just a matter of time before he spread the news that she had reluctantly assumed the role of Mage. It would be just like him to make life difficult for her. Perhaps the Secretary already knew her secret; if so, the whole story would have to be told. But if the Secretary didn't mention it, Tuava-Li's plan was simply to deliver the shoe, return home as quickly as possible, and wait for the Mage to contact her again.

An aged figure stepped quietly into the room and made a bow. "I am Tacita, Secretary to the Synod of Ljosalfar," she said. "Normally I am visited by your Mage, Kalevala Van Frier. Is she well?"

The Secretary had clear, kind eyes. She was dressed in white linen and the ribbons that hung from the back of her skullcap drifted down to the floor. Tuava-Li smiled and cleared her throat. "She is very well, ma'am. She sends her greetings."

Tuava-Li realized that she was leaving the world of truth behind. Without the safe ground of honesty to stand on, she felt suddenly dizzy. Her hands were trembling as she opened the pouch and withdrew the jeweled shoe. "This is the reason I am here today, mistress, to deliver the wedding shoe of the Alfheim Clan. It was lost for many years, but has only recently been rediscovered. I—we—thought that it would be best for the Synod to deliver the shoe to its rightful owner."

"The wedding shoe," said Tacita, lifting the object in her hands. "Every royal family has its heritage, its customs, to preserve. Now your Princess can feel free to marry again, and carry on the lineage of the Alfheim clan."

She placed the shoe on the table. "Thank you, Tuava-Li. I detect an odor of burdock and blue violet in the air; has the shoe undergone a ritual cleansing?"

"Aye, ma'am."

"Good! You may put the shoe back in its pouch. Was it you who found it?"

"Nooo, it was one of the kitchen Elves," Tuava-Li answered, carefully folding the leaf around the shoe.

Tacita then set the package on a shelf along the wall. "There is a Synod meeting at the next phase of the moon, and I'll share the news at that time. In the meanwhile the King and Queen of Alfheim will be notified, and they can send someone here to retrieve the shoe."

Tuava-Li realized that she was feeling small and insignificant, like a little fish in a very big pond. The wedding shoe of Alfheim had seemed so important. It had occupied so much of her time, so many of her thoughts. Tacita smiled. "Stay for a moment, won't you?"

Tuava-Li's heart pounded. What did the old woman want? Perhaps now the Secretary would tell Tuava-Li that she knew the Mage was missing. Perhaps she would tell Tuava-Li that she was too young and inexperienced to be the leader of her Clan, and that the Synod would be taking over the rule of Alfheim.

"I'm sure you're aware," Tacita said, "that we at the Synod are dealing with some . . . unprecedented matters. The worlds of Faeries and Humans have been separate for millennia. But that may no longer be the case. Now when the Humans level their trees, ours appear to be simultaneously destroyed. When they cut roads across their land, our Cords are severed. We've been encouraging our populations to gather where the borders have become compromised, in hopes the concentration of Faerie energy will hold the changes at bay. This is the path your Mage has taken, in returning Elf Folk to Alfheim. But the time may soon come for more . . . *drastic* measures. Come with me, my dear, I'd like to show you something."

Tacita led Tuava-Li down a corridor and into a darkened room, where an enormous globe hung from the ceiling. On the globe's surface it was easy to make out Faerie villages, cities, and towns, rivers that snaked across the landscape, seemingly endless tracts of virgin forest, all the vast continents, all the oceans—everything was there, even the Sacred Trees at the north and south poles. The major Cords of the Faerie world were shown as white, glowing lines, and they covered the globe like a network of veins. All of the major Faerie realms were represented and color-coded: Elf, Troll, Pixie, Sprite, Dwarf, Gremlin, Brownie, and more. Each clan was also marked to show its corresponding element. Clans of Air, like Alfheim, organized around spiritual principles, were violet. Clans of Earth, celebrating art and beauty, were yellow. Ljosalfar was one of these. Clans of Fire, representing competition, strategy, and the primacy of boundaries, were red. Helfratheim, the home of the Dockalfars, was a Fire Clan. The Drou, the most reclusive of the Faerie world, were allied with water. They lived in underground chambers beneath the seas, and their Clans were marked with dark blue.

"This represents our world," Tacita explained, "in all its complexity and beauty. But if you look carefully, you will see it is damaged. Cracks are beginning to form on its surface."

Tacita moved her finger over the globe. "Look, here are the

places where the borders between our world and the Humans are coming undone. Every day there are more of these tiny cracks. Do you see? Eventually the damage will be too great, and the division between our worlds will collapse. Unless we can discover a way to stop it. Some of the Mages suggest there's a spiritual cause, and suggest a spiritual solution. The Fire Clans would be only too happy to see war break out with the Humans on the other side. Conflict is their answer to everything, and we regard it only as a last resort. At the Synod we try to separate mythology from fact, impulse from wisdom."

"Mistress," said Tuava-Li, "is there a reason why you're showing this to me?"

"Because, my dear, you are our *future.* We're relying on you and others like you throughout the realms—Apprentices, scholars, all those with the passion of youth—to bring new ideas, fresh insights to our problems. Direct confrontation with Humans has never been our strategy. But the Dockalfars of Helfratheim have been very forceful in insisting that warfare is the only solution. Alfheim may be endangered, but other Clans have already been obliterated."

"Are you saying that Alfheim is in that kind of peril?"

"No, I'm not saying that. Not yet. Bring the citizens of Alfheim back to their homeland. Create a thriving, vital Faerie world there, and you may succeed in keeping the Humans at bay. The larger the Faerie presence, the stronger our world will be, and the greater our invisibility to the Humans will be."

The old Elf touched Tuava-Li's forearm. "I'm counting on you to keep me informed," she said.

Tuava-Li stared into the Secretary's liquid eyes. The walls of the room around her seemed to be rising, as she felt something inside herself pulling back, like a mouse retreating into its hole. She had concealed important information about the Mage, because she was certain that she could bring her Master back home without alarming anyone outside Alfheim, or risking a takeover by the Synod. *But would that be so bad, if the Synod stepped in?* Tuava-Li thought. *Perhaps. The Synod might be swayed by the war-makers in Helfratheim to take forceful measures, maybe even to bring war to the borders of Alfheim. The Mage would never approve of war. And isn't the most important thing for me to honor the Mage's wishes, to respect her wisdom?*

"Aye, ma'am," she said, "truly, I understand. I promise that I will keep you informed."

24

MATT SLIPPED UP THE STAIRS to the bathroom. He closed the door behind him, careful not to make a sound, then took the medicine bottle from his pocket. He gave it a shake and pulled out the cork. There was the smell, the dark, pungent, bitter smell. Matt inhaled deeply, drawing in the odor of the strange elixir that had saved his life. His foot was nearly healed; there was just enough of the medicine for another couple of doses, and then he would be done. He counted out the drops as they fell onto his tongue. Then he swallowed, jammed the cork back into the bottle, and dropped it into his pocket. Soon life would be back to normal. School would begin, his dad would cut down more of the trees, build more houses, people would move in. Normal. Matt could put all of the weirdness behind him, and try to get on with his life. He turned the door handle and stepped into the hall, and nearly crashed into Becky. "Whoa!"

"You've got to talk to me," she whispered, blocking her brother's path.

"Go play with your dolls," Matt said defensively. "You're being really annoying."

"I need to talk with you," Becky pleaded, her chin trembling. "That little doll shoe. That's what started it all. Everything was all right before . . . that night."

Matt's breath caught in his throat. "That night?"

Matt looked into Becky's eyes, and she stared back, both of them knowing exactly which night she meant. Matt sighed. There was no use trying to pretend any longer. "Okay. Come into my room," he said.

Becky sat down on the chair next to her brother's desk, waiting expectantly. Matt lowered himself onto the corner of his bed. "You start," he said. "Tell me what you remember."

"I thought it was just . . . just a bad dream," Becky answered hesitantly, "but I can't get it out of my mind. My doll . . . before I went to bed I put that little show on her foot, just to see if it fit. Later I woke up, and it was like she'd come to life, and she was trying to get out the window. You pulled the shoe off and took it, and then she fell on the floor."

"And?"

"I don't know," Becky hesitated.

"Did you see anything else?"

"Maybe I saw . . . people."

"You did," said Matt, "only they weren't really people. It

wasn't a dream, Becky. It really happened. I'm trusting you to keep a secret. A *big* secret." Matt leaned forward on the bed so that his face was just inches from Becky's. "What you saw in the yard were *elves*."

Becky narrowed her eyes and stared, trying to decide if her brother was teasing her. "It's true," Matt continued, realizing how foolish he sounded, how preposterous his story was. "The little people were elves. There's a whole other world out there in the woods, or maybe there's a whole world that you can get to, through the woods; I don't know for sure. But that's where they live—somewhere out there beyond the construction site."

"*Elves?*" Becky whispered, incredulous. "Another world?"

Matt leaned back. "I'm not making this up, Becky. That little shoe belonged to the elves, and they wanted it back. I gave it to them, and they gave me this."

Matt took the bottle from his pocket and placed it on the bedside table, where the light shone down from the window and made the facets gleam. "After I stepped on the shoe I got some kind of . . . some kind of infection. They gave me medicine to help my foot get better. That's what I was doing in the bathroom, taking the medicine. It's in this bottle."

"If what you're saying is true, you've got to tell Mom and Dad!"

"Come on, Becky," Matt said, "you know they'd never believe it. It's hard enough for me to believe, and I saw it with my own eyes. When I went into the woods I saw a whole town, a whole kingdom of elves, maybe a hundred or more, living in the branches of some gnarly old trees. And that's not all. There are trolls out there—all kinds of fairy creatures, I think. It was a troll who had your dolls. I got them back for you. I didn't just find them out in the dirt."

"A *troll* took my dolls?" Becky shook her head. "Matt, if there are elves and trolls and things out there, they might be dangerous. If you saw them in the woods, don't you think Mom and Dad could see them, too?"

"I don't think so," Matt frowned. "You looked out the window that night, and you thought you saw something, but you weren't really sure. Maybe we only see the things that fit into our idea about what's real. I don't know. Maybe I can see them because I stepped on that shoe, and something . . . something changed in me. When I'm done taking this medicine, maybe I won't be able to see them anymore, either. I don't know anything for sure. All I know, Becky, is that this is my business, *our* business, yours and mine, and nobody else's."

"Mine?" Becky swallowed.

"You're involved in this, too," Matt said. "Because of the shoe." Matt put his hand on his sister's shoulder. "You don't have to worry about the elves, Becky. They're harmless, as far as I can see. They don't want to be discovered, or mixed up with people. They're afraid of us. They might not like Dad cutting down their trees, but they can't do anything about it. Before long they'll have to move away, far from here, and everything will be okay. We'll never see them again."

"I want to tell Mom and Dad about this," Becky said, furrowing her brow.

"No," Matt insisted. "You said you were going to tell Mom and Dad that I was up to something, unless I told you what was going on. Well, I told you. Now you have to keep quiet."

Becky bit her lip and stared out the window. The clouds in the sky, the trees in the distance, everything looked still, and peaceful, like a picture in a magazine. She was afraid to imagine what would happen if she turned the page. "Okay," she said hesitantly, "but if anything else happens, you'll tell me, all right? If you see the elves again? Or the trolls?"

"Sure," said Matt, his smile unable to disguise the tension in his face.

25

A CABLE CRACKLED with current, alive with the hum of danger. Trees were stripped of their branches, painted with tar, then lined vertically along the blacktop. They were only telephone and power lines, but the Elves had no words for so many of the Human things they abhorred. Jardaine lay on the woven hammock in the Mage's study. She allowed the images of an owl's nocturnal flight to race through her mind. The Mage was sending her a vision, just like Tuava-Li had said she would. It was nauseating. It was alarming, and very, very strange. It was coming from the Mage—there could be no doubt. From a perch inside a metal mesh box, the Mage showed Jardaine what life looked like through her owl eyes. She saw the trees, just out of reach. She could smell the fear, the disappointment, the longing for the safety and comfort of the forest. The longing for home.

The owl eyes that opened in Jardaine's mind scanned the

miles of green, flowing away into the shimmering distance, and came to rest on the uppermost edge of something man-made. Jardaine did not know that the thing she saw was called a water tower. She recognized the color and the domed shape, and she could even read a few of the letters that were painted on the side of the huge yellow cylinder. The dense foliage, the angle of the lettering, and the blue distance softened the words and made them vague. But it was a sign, at least. A clue. There were the power lines, the road, the water tower. And most important of all, there was the sun, illuminating the tower at this time of day, pinpointing the direction from which the Mage saw these things. Tuava-Li had been right. The Mage was alive, and she was trying to alert the Elf Folk to her whereabouts.

When the images faded, and Jardaine had complete control over her senses once more, she sprang from the hammock and stepped onto the branch outside the doorway to the Mage's quarters. "Did you see any of that, Sarette?" she murmured to the snake, hidden from view inside her dark robes. It was a milk snake, slim and white, with patches of orange and black. It was coiled around Jardaine's shoulder and wrapped once around her waist.

"I didn't misss a thing," answered the snake, "though I tried to block out the *flying* part. A sssnake isn't usssed t' sssuch thingsss. But your mind is my mind, Missstresss. 'Tisss clear what we mussst do now."

It annoyed the monk when the snake talked so much.

Because of Sarette's hissing lisp, snake spittle always dribbled onto Jardaine's bare skin, and it felt cold and clammy. But it was imperative that Sarette remain hidden, so that none of the other monks saw what Jardaine had concealed beneath her robe. She had asked Macta to procure the snake for her when they began their alliance to take over Alfheim. All snakes are known for their cunning and duplicitous ways, and a talking snake was an ideal advisor in matters of deceit and betrayal. As these were Jardaine's chief preoccupations, the snake made a perfect companion.

The monk lifted a tiny whistle to her lips and blew. She blew again. Then she descended to the ground and headed along a path into the forest. When Jardaine reached a grove of white ash, she stopped to watch a figure scuttle silently up the path. "Nebiros!" she called impatiently.

The little Elf was short. He wore a conical hat over a mop of dark curls, and he grinned as he shuffled into Jardaine's view. "I came as quickly as I could, my Devotion."

Jardaine scowled. "Three times, Nebiros. Three times I sent you to Helfratheim to inform Macta that the Mage was dead and Tuava-Li had taken her place. Each time you came back and told me that Macta wasn't there. Each time you said you left the message that he needed to get in touch with me. And yet, Nebiros, I hear nothing from him. Macta's even traveled here to Alfheim to meet with Tuava-Li, and he hasn't given me a single sign that he knows we have urgent business to discuss.

Would it be unreasonable for me to wonder if you're following my orders?"

"My Devotion, I would never fail you," Nebiros said. "But your—how shall I put this—your *associate*, Macta, he's . . . less than reliable. He dreams of conquest, but his focus is scattered. He's too proud to wear one of the advising snakes, as you do. He wants to lead, he wants to be in love, he wants to show his father that he's got the makings of a tyrant. I'm not convinced that he has what it takes."

Jardaine snorted. "Why should I care if you're convinced? I don't pay you to have an opinion. All you need to know is that without me, Macta wouldn't have a chance of building an empire."

"And me, of courssse," hissed Sarette.

Jardaine sighed, knowing that it was she who should be building an empire of her own; she had the talent, the ambition, the vision. But a monk from a small spiritual community had limited opportunities for advancement. She needed Macta, just like he needed her—only Macta didn't understand *how much* he needed her. It made Jardaine seethe with rage. "Nebiros, I want you to go to Helfratheim one last time. I want you to stay there until you have spoken to Macta. Now, this is very important. The message has changed. Tell him that the Mage is *alive,* and that she has been trapped, or kidnapped somewhere outside Alfheim. Tell him that so far, Tuava-Li has no idea where the Mage is, or how to find her.

Tell him I have some important clues. Tell him 'tis critical that we find the Mage before anyone else does. Tell Macta that if he doesn't come to me immediately, our alliance is through. Am I making myself clear?"

The Elf frowned, and sucked in air through his nostrils. "She's alive? Well, my Devotion, I would have bet my left ear that the old bird was dead. Fine, I'll give Macta the news, if I get to see him!"

"You'll get to see him, or I'll be done with you, too, Nebiros. Now get back to Alfheim and make your excuses. Sarette and I have work to do."

Nebiros bowed and scurried down the path. Jardaine threw back the cowl of her robe and shook her hair loose. Birds were singing in the trees, not a cloud hung overhead to mar the perfection of the sky, a flawless, eggshell blue. It was a glorious morning. Jardaine would soon assign Macta the job of finding the Mage of Alfheim and killing her. Tuava-Li would suffer the same fate. Once Jardaine was Mage, and Princess Asra was forced to marry Macta, the first stage of their plan to build a base of power would be complete.

With her advising snake curled contentedly around her shoulder, Jardaine strolled back to Alfheim. She was certain that plans were coming to fruition. As she reached the outskirts of the five oaks, however, she saw a commotion on the ground just below the Mage's quarters. She recognized the Troll, Tomtar, sitting on the dirt with a mass of wet dock leaves pressed against the side of his head. Tomtar's normally vacant face was twisted in pain. Beside him stood another Troll, old, blue-skinned, and wiry, with a large bruise on his pale forehead. He was waving his fists in the air. The little crowd of Elves that surrounded the Trolls stepped aside as Jardaine approached. "What now?" she demanded. "I can't go for my afternoon meditation in the woods without another disaster?"

"Who's in charge here?" the older Troll trilled.

"Who wants to know?" Jardaine demanded.

"My name is Agar. Was it you who sent that Human boy to me? Because if it was, I've got a score to settle with you! And so does this idiot here, who's got an even bigger bump on his noggin than I have on mine."

"Look who's callin' *who* an idiot," Tomtar winced. "You haven't stopped gripin' for a moment since we left that rubbish pile of yours in the woods, and now my head feels like it's ready to explode!"

"That's all the thanks I get, and I'm the one who bandaged up your thick skull? All night long I had to be your nursemaid, listenin' to you moanin' and groanin', 'til you were sure you were well enough to make the journey to Alfheim. Remind me next time to leave your sorry rump lyin' in the dandelions."

"M-m-mistress Jardaine," stammered an Elf, "they came stumblin' up the path crying that they'd been attacked by the Human we found here yesterday. They say he beat 'em both over the head, then stole a fortune from this one, here!"

Jardaine shot a look at Agar. "What kind of fortune could you possibly have?"

Agar made a clucking sound and glanced skyward, as if he were calculating the value of his missing possessions. In fact he was trying to decide how best to hide the fact that the fortune in jewels he kept hidden in the depths of his tree-trunk home was gone. The jewels were his greatest treasure, of course, and he had more than an inkling of their origin. *Finders keepers*, he had thought to himself the day he dug up the jewels from beneath the roots of a tree, which had been felled on the outskirts of Alfheim. As much as he wanted the jewels back, he knew better than to mention them to a servant of the Mage. Agar rubbed his forehead and looked sorrowful. "Can't you see how I'm sufferin'? You think I have a list of what was stolen? I'm not even sure, yet, myself."

The monk scowled at the Troll and folded her arms across her chest. "Make a list, in writing, and bring it to me."

"This is your fault, you know," Agar said, wagging a reproachful finger at Jardaine. "The Human came to me to ask for a favor. Since he said *you* had sent him, I was foolish enough to give him the benefit of the doubt! Just imagine! I was plannin' to help the lad. He said he was in pain. With an innocent, trustin' heart, I went to my alchemick table to mix him a healin' tincture. Then, when I had my back turned, he struck me over the head and ransacked my home! Believe me, 'tis a sad, sad day when we begin lettin' Humans cross over into our forest, and allow 'em to take advantage of our generosity. 'Tis always been like this; you, especially, ought to know."

"It wasn't *I* who sent the Human to you," Jardaine scowled dismissively. "I'm not the Mage."

"No matter," the Troll sneered. "What are you goin' to do about this? I want my possessions returned to me immediately, and I want that Human brought to justice!"

"Yeeaaah!" the crowd erupted. "The Humans must be stopped!"

Alfheim Elves had always been peaceful creatures, yet the stress they felt over the disappearance of their Mage and the proximity of Humans to the Sacred Grove was causing fractures in their calm exterior. "The Human must die!" an Elf cried with unsupressed glee, then covered his mouth, horrified by his own words.

"We'll teach him that you can't steal from the Faerie world without paying the price," another cried.

"Wait!" interrupted Tomtar, wincing. "I know the old Troll got robbed, and I know we both got clobbered all right, but fair is fair, and as far as I can see, we don't really know 'twas that *Tem* who's to blame. We could accuse anybody, but that doesn't make it so. It could have been somebody else."

This was not what Jardaine wanted to hear. The wary and frightened crowd might soon be willing to abandon the old Mage's temperate justice for some real bloodletting. This was exactly the kind of carnage Jardaine had been hoping for. Fear turns quickly to anger, if the flames are carefully fanned. It was no time to allow Tomtar to inject doubt into their minds. But the words had been spoken, and they had to be addressed. "Did you see who knocked you out?"

"Nooo . . . ," Tomtar replied. "The last thing I remember is seein' the *Tem* on the ground, crouchin' in front of Agar's junk-strewn tree."

"Watch your tongue, lad!" Agar bellowed. "That elm of mine is one of the finest trees in the forest!"

Tomtar rolled his eyes. "I saw him on the ground. He was too big to get into the hole under the trunk, anyway. I sympathize, Agar, really I do. We both took quite a beating. But I think we ought to wait for the Mage to return, and then she and Tuava-Li could start some kind of inspection. That'd only be fair, since nobody really saw anything."

The Elves eyed each other in silence. No one dared to say a word. Finally, Jardaine cleared her throat and spoke. "'Tis Elfin business, so no one told you, Troll, but the Mage of Alfheim is dead. She's not coming back, despite what Tuava-Li may have said. Tuava-Li is the new Mage, for better or worse. There'll be a ceremony to initiate her, if any of us lives long enough to see it. But there's no need for any investigation of this latest crime. The Humans have to be stopped. 'Tis the only way. Tuava-Li doesn't understand that Alfheim won't be safe 'til the Humans who've been cutting our forest are dead. For that we would have to call upon the aid of Macta Dockalfar, and the warriors of Helfratheim. That's what a *real* Mage would do."

The crowd went wild. These were the words they had been waiting to hear, strong, resolute, unwavering, decisive. They had feared the worst about the Mage, and now they knew it was true. She was dead, and Tuava-Li was trying to deceive them. Jardaine nodded and waited for the applause to die down. If this is what leadership was all about, then she was certain that she wanted more of it. "Tomtar," she said, "you were told to follow the Human and make sure he left the forest. I understand that you've suffered injury at his hands. But I don't want you to stop now. You must go to the Human's house and watch him, and discover what nefarious scheme he is plotting against us. Find out if it is he who has the Alfheim Jewels. 'Tis the duty of each of us in the Faerie kingdom to hold fast, to be vigilant, to defend our homeland to the very death!" She raised her arms to the cheering throng. And from beneath the monk's robes, Sarette gave Jardaine a congratulatory squeeze.

26

BEHIND THE McCORMACKS' house, the redwood picnic bench was only a foot or two from the wall. From there it was just a short climb up the trellis to Matt's windowsill. Dangling his feet, Tomtar the Troll sat and waited. He would turn around and begin his watch when the boy came into the room, but the windowsill was narrow and uncomfortable. Back in Argant, the Human city where he had grown up, there had been many times when Humans passed Tomtar on the street and never bothered to turn their heads. More recently, in the woods near Alfheim, Tomtar had watched Human hunters approaching the stream. He would crouch on the ground, just out of sight. But it didn't take long to discover that he needn't bother. The Humans walked right by. For this reason he imagined that he could crouch in the window and watch the boy for days, with little risk of being discovered. However, Tomtar was bothered by one small thing.

Or rather, many small, black buzzing things. A papery-thin wasp nest hung in the corner of the window frame, and a swarm of angry insects buzzed around his head whenever he moved to the center of the window. So Tomtar sat precariously on the corner of the sill and waited. There was no point in being stung.

Matt grumbled as he came up from the basement with an armload of laundry. He was obliged to help his mom with chores, and the chores never seemed to end. He clomped up the stairs to his room, flung open the door, and tossed the laundry onto the bed. He let out a sigh. He was just reaching for his CD player when he caught a flicker of movement out of the corner of his eye. His pulse quickened; it was there, just outside the window. Matt spun around and saw something moving with incredible speed. *"AAAAAARGH!"* a voice cried. Then there was a clattering sound, and the creature was gone.

Matt leapt to the window, hoisted up the screen, and looked down. He saw a Troll hanging by his fingertips from the window frame. The creature looked pleadingly into Matt's eyes and cried, "Help!"

Brushing aside a wasp, Matt grabbed the Troll's wrists and heaved him up into his room. He dropped him on the floor, then slammed the window shut. A wasp buzzed angrily along the ceiling. The Troll crouched by the bed, staring wide-eyed at Matt from behind a mop of damp hair. "Are you okay?" Matt asked. "What were you doing outside my window?"

It wasn't the old Troll who had stolen Becky's dolls. He had the same kind of nose, the huge staring eyes, and the same fleshy, pointed ears, but this one looked younger. The Troll crept into the shadows. He pulled the top of his cap down over his face and huddled there, as if he were hoping Matt would forget him and go away. "Look, I'll take you downstairs and let you out the door," Matt said. "You should go back into the forest. You're not supposed to be here. Just being in the same room with you might—might hurt one of us. I saw how the elves got all panicky about breathing the air around me. We could catch something from each other, maybe, like what I got from the shoe."

"You saw me," the Troll whispered.

Matt leaned a little closer. "What?"

The Troll did not reply. "I don't understand," Matt said. "I'm Matt. Do you have a name?"

"I said, *you saw me.* You weren't supposed to see me. And aye, everybody has a name."

"My name is Matt," Matt repeated. "Do you know who I am? I met the elves. They came here, and then I saw where they live in the woods. You're bigger than the elves. You're a troll, aren't you? What were you doing outside my window?"

"I—I was lookin' for food. You know, you don't have to be afraid of gettin' sick from bein' around me," the Troll said. "I've spent most of my life around *Tems,* er, Humans, so I ought to know. Anyway, there isn't much to eat in the woods, so I was lookin' for food, in that, that big bowl thing there."

The Troll climbed up onto Matt's bed and pointed out the

window at the trash can. Matt shook his head. "Bowl? That's garbage. That's a trash can. Anything in there is stuff we threw away. You got something to eat out of there?"

"I was hungry. We're all hungry. We could smell what you put there, all the way into the forest, we could smell it. I thought that maybe, maybe the food was a gift to the Gods, the Forest Gods, and so I came here to eat."

Tomtar was not a good liar, but any story would be better than telling the boy that he had come to spy on him. Tomtar was still surprised to discover that the Human could see him so easily. Humans weren't looking for Faerie Folk; what they didn't look for, they couldn't see. At least that's what he had been told. But he knew that this particular Human was different. Tomtar knew he shouldn't be talking to the boy, but what choice did he have?

"Are you hungry?" Matt asked. "Tell me what you want and I'll get you something."

"I want to eat *food*."

"Eat food," Matt repeated. "Then come with me, down to the front porch. I'll find you something, but then you've really got to go. I don't want to take any chances."

Tomtar smiled, and followed Matt as he stepped into the hall. "Be quiet," the boy whispered. "My mother might see you."

Tomtar shook his head. "Humans can't see Faerie Folk."

"*I* can see you! What does that make me?" Matt replied.

"I'm not sure!" the Troll said, genuinely confused.

Once they slipped out the front door and onto the porch, Matt left the Troll behind a wicker rocking chair. Then he went to the kitchen to get a snack. Tomtar crouched, waiting, contemplating a dash for the woods. But he had promised to stay near the boy, and the one thing he believed in was a promise. And what better way was there to watch him than this? After several minutes Matt appeared with a banana, an orange, a package of cookies, and a can of soda and a straw. "Here," he whispered, "eat fast. You can't stay long."

Matt sat on the rocker and kept his eye on the front door. His mother could appear any minute. Tomtar bit into the peel of the orange, then grimaced and spat. Matt reached down and picked up the soda. He pulled back the tab, popped in the straw, then placed it carefully at the side of the chair. "Try this," he said. "You're not supposed to eat the outside of that orange. Just the inside. Same goes for the yellow thing. It's a banana. And the cookies in the package, too!"

Matt thought about how odd the Human food must seem to a creature who was used to foraging in the woods for nuts and berries and seeds. Then he remembered what he had read about Elves and Faeries on the Internet. "That's metal," Matt observed. "The soda can. Maybe you shouldn't have that. Doesn't metal make you sick? There's metal all around here."

Matt's eyes flashed to the mailbox, the light fixture above the door, the aluminum-frame lounge chair, the iron railings on the stairs. The Troll fiddled with the edge of the cookie package.

Finally he put the foil edge into his mouth and tore it back. "The Elves gave me *trans*," he answered, biting off a piece of cookie. "I'm sorry, I mean *magick*. Transformations. I've got a *Huldu* full of spells. Takes care of the metal. Lots of other stuff, too! The Elves are all afraid they'll catch some sickness from the Humans, but Trolls have been livin' next to *Tems* for thousands of years, so we don't give it a second thought. 'Tisn't *you* we have to fear, at least where sickness is concerned."

"What do you mean by—" Matt heard the sound of footsteps from inside. He jumped to his feet. "We can't stay here. I've got to get you around the side of the house."

Matt leapt down the steps, followed by the Troll carrying the banana and the package of cookies. "I saved your life," Matt said as they rounded the corner. "If I'd let you fall, you'd have broken your neck. You could tell me your name."

"Tomtar, my name's Tomtar. Now 'tis your turn to tell me somethin'," said the Troll, getting straight to the point. "Why are you threatenin' Alfheim?"

Matt was confused. "Threatening? What?"

"Threatenin' Alfheim. Killin' the forest, cuttin' down the trees. Destroyin' what doesn't belong to you."

"I'm not cutting down anything. My dad's cutting down the trees because he owns the land and he's building some houses. But you don't need to worry; he's not going to wipe out the whole forest or anything. What did you call it? Alfheim?"

"It means *Home of the Elves*," said Tomtar. He paused, trying to decide how to phrase the next question. "Now you answer me another. Did you ever take anything that didn't belong to you? Like, for example, some jewels?"

"Jewels? Do you mean that little elf shoe? I didn't steal it, I found it. And I gave it back to them. And I'm going to put that medicine bottle under the tree, just like they asked. Did they send you here to accuse me of stealing?"

"But the jewels, they all think you stole the—oh, I'm not supposed to say anything to you. I'm supposed to—"

"You're supposed to what—spy on me? I thought you said you came here to look for something to eat? Listen, you think I know anything about elves, and faeries, and trolls, and the junk you guys can't keep track of? I never wanted that elf shoe. I never asked to find it."

Matt paused as a thought crossed his mind. "Wait a minute. Now I remember. That other troll, the one in the forest who gave me my medicine, he had a bunch of jewels. At least they looked like jewels, stored away in those baby food jars. I just assumed they were plastic, but maybe they were real. He had my sister's dolls, too, so don't go accusing *me* of stealing. Maybe he's got your jewels. Or do all trolls have jewels stashed away? If you're missing something, why don't you go talk to your troll friend about it?"

"But he's the one who—oh, never mind. I'm sorry. Thank you for what you did for me, truly. And I don't want to accuse you of somethin' you didn't do!"

"Ooookay." Matt scratched his head. "So . . . do you come

from, what did you call it, Alfheim? Do you live with the elves? What are you carrying in that little backpack of yours?"

"Backpack?" the Troll repeated. He still wasn't sure he ought to be having a conversation with a Human. *But why not?* he thought, his trusting nature coming to the fore. *What harm could it do, if he didn't steal the Jewels? After all, the lad saved my life!*

Tomtar reached into the satchel hung over his shoulder and removed a bag filled with bark scraps, no bigger than matchsticks. There were peculiar markings on each of the pieces. "*Tems* aren't supposed to see this," he said conspiratorially.

"What—that bag?"

"Huldu," said the Troll. "But since you asked, I'll show you. Here's a *trans* for metal. I just pop it in my mouth and chew, every time I start to feel queasy."

"Wait a minute," Matt said. "What did you call me? A *Tem?* Does that mean *human?"*

"Here's another *trans,"* Tomtar mumbled, shuffling through his collection of spells. "That means it's for *transformation,* you know? I didn't think you could see me, but if I chew on this, I disappear for sure. No chance you could see me then. Can't have these too often, though, or 'tis permanent. I wouldn't even be able to see myself!"

"The elves gave you these?" Matt said, shaking his head. "With stuff like that, they wouldn't have needed to come to my yard and bargain with me to get that shoe. They could have just waltzed right into my house and taken it."

"Impossible," said Tomtar. "Completely. Couldn't happen. We can't go into your *squat,* not without your invitation. Oh, a *squat* is where you live, 'tis what we used to call the places where we lived in the city where I was born."

"You come from a faerie city?" Matt asked. "A troll city?"

"Argant. A Human city. They built it, but we live there, too. Or at least we did. You call it Pittsburgh."

Matt's eyes lit up. "I was born in Pittsburgh! We come from the same town!" Matt watched the Troll rummaging through the little sticks he called *trans*. "And what's this about me being able to see you, and other people might not?" Matt asked.

Tomtar looked puzzled. "When I lived in Argant we could see the *Tems*, but they didn't see us, almost never. In the city, the borders were always porous, and *Tems* were everywhere. Once in a while we'd be seen. So the monk gave me these, just in case. She wrote the words on the bark, and when I chew on 'em, the *trans* happens. She said that if I chew on one of these, here, 'twill make me look like a Human."

Matt frowned. "What do you mean?"

"It's *magick*. You know how when you see a juicy fungus you want to eat, and it makes your mouth water? Even though you haven't had a bite yet, the smell of the food makes your mouth think the fungus is already there. Well, 'tis the same with the *trans*. I chew on it, and my body puts off an odor. You can hardly smell it, but the magick makes your mind picture what the *trans* wants you to see. When I chew on this, any *Tem* around me will think they're lookin' at a real Human being, instead of a Troll. After a while I go back to lookin' like myself."

"Can you show me?" asked Matt, not quite believing how such a thing was possible. But he'd already had to accept that the world was a far bigger, stranger place than he had ever known. Tomtar placed a piece of bark in his cheek and began to chew. In a matter of minutes Matt's vision began to blur; he felt light-headed as he looked at the Troll and had to blink several times to be sure that his eyes weren't deceiving him. "Awesome," he said, staring at Tomtar. "Completely awesome. And it's all because of a smell?"

Tomtar was no longer waist high to Matt. They were now roughly the same height, and the Troll's exaggerated features seemed to have shrunk to Human proportions. Matt realized he was witnessing an illusion, but it was an incredibly effective one. "How long does the effect last?" Matt asked.

Tomtar shrugged. "As long as I'm chewin'on a fresh *trans*, and as long as you're breathin' the air around me, I suppose! I've never tried it before! I'll tell you what. Invite me into your house."

"What?"

"Just invite me in, that's all!"

"Ooookay," said Matt, "but my mother's in there, and if she sees you she'll—"

Tomtar opened the screen door and stepped inside. "Wait!" Matt warned.

“’Tis all right,” said Tomtar. “You’ll see!”

Jill knelt over the crisper drawer of her new stainless steel refrigerator. Emily was banging on her high chair with a sippy cup when the screen door slammed. “Hey, Mom,” Matt called, trailing Tomtar into the kitchen. His heart was pounding, expecting the worst but knowing it was too late to stop the Troll. “There’s, uh, somebody I want you to meet!”

Jill got up. The boy who stood before her was dressed a little oddly, even for a farm kid. He had a slouchy cap pulled over a tangle of hair, wide eyes, and an even wider nose. “Mom,” Matt said, “this is Tom. He lives across the, um, across the woods, on the other side. I met him the other day when I went for a walk!”

“Pleased to meet you,” said the boy, with a bow.

“Well I’m glad to meet you, too,” Jill said. “That’s an interesting outfit you have on, Tom.”

“Uh, thank you, I, uh, thanks!”

Jill looked down at the boy’s bare feet. “Hmmm. Where are your shoes? You can’t go walking out there without your shoes on. You could step on something and cut your foot.”

Tom smiled. “I know, ma’am. I just left ’em outside so I wouldn’t track mud on your nice new floors.”

“Well, that’s very considerate of you, Tom. Matt, I’m glad to see you made a new friend.”

“Hey!” said Becky, sweeping into the room.

“Becky, this is my friend Tom,” Matt said. “He lives on the other side of the woods.”

"Pleased to meet you!" Becky scrunched up her face at the strange new boy.

Jill made some snacks and put them on a tray on the porch. Becky sipped pink lemonade, while Matt tore open a big bag of cheese curls. He took out a handful and passed the bag to his friend. Tom chewed noisily while Emily toddled along, grabbing the railing of the deck. Jill wouldn't leave the kids alone on the porch for a minute. She kept asking questions, and Matt was feeling nervous. As far as he knew, the spell that made Tomtar appear to be Human could fade away at any moment. Matt hoped the Troll knew what he was doing. Meanwhile, the questions kept on coming. *Do you have any brothers and sisters? What does your father do? Does your mother work? How do you like school? Have you always lived around here?* Matt was so nervous he could barely focus on the Troll's answers; he just hoped that Tomtar wouldn't say anything too outrageous. Finally, when Emily began to rub her eyes and pout, Jill gave up the interview and went indoors to put the toddler down for a nap. Matt wiped his brow with his sleeve. "Well I was getting a little worried, there," he said.

Tomtar grinned and gave Matt a wink. "The *trans* always do the trick!" he whispered. "But I think I should be goin' now. Thank you for the food. 'Twas good fun being a Human bein'!"

Matt smiled. "Don't you mean a *Tem*?"

"No," said the Troll, "*a Tom*!"

"Will I see you again?" Matt called, as the Troll got up and headed across the porch.

"Aye, if you want!" he replied, flinging himself over the railing, and disappearing behind the house.

"What was that about?" asked Becky. "Your new friend's really weird!"

Matt shrugged. "People around here a little different, that's all! You'll get used to it."

"Do you think . . . ," Becky said tentatively, "do you think your friend Tom ever saw the elves in the forest?"

"I don't know," Matt answered. He had told Becky that he wasn't going to keep any secrets from her about the Elves, but he didn't want her getting involved any more than she already was. It would be better for her to move on, and forget about it all. "I don't know. Come on, let's play a game inside. What do you say?"

27

EVERYONE IN THE FAERIE world knew of the House of Dockalfar. Macta and his royal family lived in a fortress built into the side of a windswept mountaintop, surrounded by the factories, refineries, industrial towers, and slums of Helfratheim. As other Elfin realms were built around spiritual ideals, or the pursuit of artistic goals, the House of Dockalfar was founded by a Game Master. Long-lived creatures have much time to spend in leisure and recreation, and the Dockalfars were brilliant at developing amusements based on competition and strategy. In the end, there is a winner, and a loser, and it is not a great conceptual leap from play warfare to real combat. The Dockalfars readily made the jump. As the borders between the Human and Faerie realms weakened, and fear became a motivating factor, the

Dockalfars began to design and sell weapons. It wasn't long before they discovered that weaponry was an infinitely more profitable business than games.

As rain fell from a leaden sky, the Prince, followed by his cronies, climbed from the Cord and stepped out onto the walkway. Macta was in a bad mood; his visit to Ljosalfar had not gone as well as he had hoped. Asra seemed unconvinced that she ought to take his feelings seriously. "There's no place like home," he said sarcastically, gazing about.

The decomposing heads of many Faerie creatures were suspended from poles that flanked the avenue leading to town. They were placed there to warn the citizens of the consequence of misbehavior, of breaking the rules. A bit of gore dripped from one of the heads and landed with a splat on Baltham's shoulder. He brushed at his jacket with a handkerchief, then stopped to retch in the gutter. Macta placed his foot on Baltham's posterior and gave him a push. "When you're finished," Macta muttered, "I suggest you rinse off your shoes in a puddle. I won't have you tracking that into the palace."

Druga held an umbrella high over Macta's feathered cap, shielding his Master from the elements as rivulets ran down his own pockmarked cheeks. As they hurried along the path Macta saw a crew of royal gondola drivers readying the cigar-shaped vehicles for passage in the Cord. He snorted and shook his head; *what a tedious way to travel*, he thought. Only the most important members of the Faerie world rode the Cord in vehicles. The wedge-shaped noses of the gondolas were used to clear other Faeries out of the way, ensuring that none would get too close to a royal personage. Everyone else traveled unadorned, with nothing more than the clothes on their backs, and Macta was happy to join them, for he found the passage thrilling. Even if it meant that he must face the distaste of coming into close contact with the common folk.

"Aye there!" Macta shouted, as he saw the gaggle of Elves making up his father's entourage clustered in the arched doorway of the palace. He knew that at the back of this crowd he would find his own father, King Valdis, undoubtedly preparing to leave home once again on royal business. "Aye there, Father, 'tis I, Macta!" the Prince shouted.

Macta raced ahead, ignoring the rain, and pushed his way through the crowd of accountants, sorcerers, and diplomats who stood in his path, At the back of the hallway Macta caught a glimpse of his father. There he was, staring vacantly as butlers brushed his boots and others adjusted the black-and-yellow carapace he wore over his shoulders. "Father! How fortunate to run into you like this! Did Cytthandra give you my messages?"

The king came to life at the mention of his Secretary, Cytthandra. "What? Oh, Macta. She did say something about you, but I can't recollect just what it was. Lovely lady, Cytthandra. Lovely."

A smile drifted across King Valdis's face. "Well, 'twas nice seeing you again, Macta. I must be off. Important business, you know. We're assembling battalions for a kingdom in the West. Just ironing out the fine points of the contract, but they insist on having me present. I hope you're planning to attend my next birthday celebration. The Experimentalists are working on some killer new games!"

Macta snorted. "Father, it's another eleven moons before your birthday comes again. I need to talk to you about my wedding plans. I—"

"Oh, oh, oh, now I remember!" King Valdis shook his head vigorously. "Listen. You're too young to get married, Macta. And none of your mothers would stand for you marrying that Alfheim maid. Neither would I. We don't need to have Clans joining together, bringing unity to the kingdoms. Since we've reinvented ourselves as arms manufacturers, we've made our reputation sowing discord and hostility around the Faerie world. We make weapons, don't you understand? The Synod in Ljosalfar is hesitant to approve military intervention with the Humans at Alfheim's borders, and the Central Synod just hems and haws when the subject comes up. Why would you want to get tangled up in that? I'm fed up with them all. Listen, Macta, if you're bored and have nothing to do, Cytthandra could find you work at one of our techmagick factories."

The royal advising snake hidden inside the King's costume stuck out its diamond-patterned head and waved its tongue at Macta. "Our gondola isss waiting, ssso good-bye, young Prinsss!"

"Father, wait just a minute," Macta pleaded. "I've got an idea."

As it happened, the idea was not really Macta's, but the monk Jardaine's. And it wasn't really Jardaine's idea, either. The idea originated with the advising snake Sarette. But for the sake of brevity, not to mention pride, Macta claimed the notion as his own. "Just say, Father, for the sake of argument, that I get married to Princess Asra. Everyone would be there; we'd invite Faerie representatives from all over the world. Just picture it. You use my wedding as a pretext for sneaking an army into Alfheim, disguised as guests. Now if some slight altercation should happen to occur betwixt the Humans and the Elves around this time, well, 'twould be a perfect opportunity to rise up and wipe the Humans out—right on the spot. The Synod wouldn't even think to question your motives; clearly you'd be acting in self-defense. You'd come off as brave and righteous. The battle would provoke retaliation on the part of the Humans. *And* the escalating tensions would profit the Dockalfars greatly. The increase in value of your stock and weapon sales would be incalculable!"

King Valdis furrowed his brow. "Hmmmmm . . . ," he mused. "You're more clever than I thought, my son. 'Tis not a bad idea. Not a bad idea at all. Sounds like good sport, and profitable, besides. A perfect combination! You know, we provide munitions for others' warfare, but we so seldom taste the thrill of battle ourselves. How delicious that might be! But the introduction of Humans into the equation adds an unpredictable element that makes me a little wary. What could you possibly do to get them involved?"

"I have it all worked out, Father. There is a family of Humans who live on the outskirts of Alfheim, and at the appropriate time, just before the wedding, they'll be lured into the woods, where they'll make easy targets for your soldiers."

Valdis was skeptical. "Maybe you'd best leave that to me, Macta. I'm sure my strategists could devise a better plan to—"

"No, Father," Macta insisted. "We'll—I mean, *I'll* handle it myself. I'm fully capable of executing that part of the plan. 'Tis time you learned to have a little faith in me!"

Those of Valdis's entourage who had overheard the conversation stroked their chins and nodded in assent. Even Valdis's advising snake hissed approvingly. Macta cleared his throat. "Eh, there's just *one* little problem . . ."

"I should have known. What is it?" queried the King.

"Father, Princess Asra won't be permitted to get married without a special pair of wedding shoes; 'tis some tradition of theirs that's been passed down for centuries."

"Of course," said the King. "Each of your mothers had some antique footwear she was obligated to wear on her wedding day. Why is that a problem?"

"One of the shoes was lost when Princess Asra nearly married cousin Udos. Now it's been found, but there's an Apprentice to the Mage in Alfheim who has the shoe in her possession, and she won't give it to me."

"Well, will she give it to the Princess?"

"She might need some coaxing. I'm sure she wants something in return. And, oh, the Princess's parents aren't really in favor of their daughter marrying me."

"I suppose your reputation precedes you. What about the Princess herself? Is she as keen as you are on this wedding business?"

"Father, I've got Asra wrapped around my little finger," Macta lied. "So a little diplomacy on your part might smooth the way for my plan to go forward. If you went to the Synod and reminded them how important 'twould be to the Faerie world if our kingdoms were joined in marriage . . ."

"Well, Macta," said the King, "under the circumstances, perhaps a visit to Ljosalfar *is* in order. I'll try to fit it into my schedule on the way back from my travels."

"Thank you, Father, thank you!" Macta cried, as a servant opened an enormous black-and-yellow umbrella over the King's head. Macta rubbed his hands together in delight as his father hurried down the path to the gondola.

Finally, progress, he thought. Perhaps it would be a good time to visit the gaming tables in the recesses of the palace and see if lady luck was on his side.

"Uh, Macta?" Druga and Baltham spoke, shivering in the rain.

"You're both still here? What is it?"

"Remember you said that you'd give us our share of the

jewels we stole from that Troll, outside Alfheim?" asked Druga.

"Yes, and you shall get your share. Just be patient."

"I've got a wife and a cartload of children to feed," whined Baltham. "All three brats need ear-braces. Their ears are completely crooked; got that from their mother, I'm sorry to say. and the walls of our dungeon leak like a sieve in this weather. When can we count on our share of the booty?"

Macta sighed. He envied his father in many ways, and one of the things he'd always dreamed of was an entourage, like the one his father had. King Valdis was always surrounded by a group of advisors, bodyguards, and admirers, and whether he was arriving at a boardroom or a costume ball, his sizable entourage was sure to impress. It could help to give a formidable, menacing appearance, when needed, or it could be used to demonstrate that the royal person was a delight to be around. So far, Macta's entourage consisted solely of Baltham and Druga. And typically they were nothing but a nuisance. "We're barely home," Macta explained. "I haven't been here long enough to get the jewels appraised. And did you forget about the Human we brought back from our last trip? I haven't had a moment to look in on her since then. I haven't even had a moment to void my bowels, and already the pair of you are hounding me about your share of the money." Macta waved away his dissatisfied companions and stomped off toward his apartment. "Nothing but thorns in my side," he grumbled.

The fountain in the entryway to Macta's quarters was lit from above by flickering lanterns. Most of the rooms in Macta's private abode were ornamented with fountains of one sort or another; his decorator was fond of oceanic motifs. Burbling sounds rose from the mouth of the statue at the center of the parlor fountain. Mechanical birds perched on high plaster branches chirped. Herma and Holda, Macta's personal serving maids, were polishing their long chartreuse nails when Macta threw open the door and stormed in.

"Well?" he bellowed.

"Long time, sir," said Herma.

"No see, sir," said Holda.

Macta scowled. "What? Where did you learn to talk like that? You sound like idiots."

In the corner of the room there was a small metal box, with a glass screen, emitting flickering blue light and squawking. A tangle of black and red wires connected the box to a larger cable that disappeared into a dark hole in the wall. The sound of laughter spilled from the box, as Macta's housekeepers watched images of a pair of Humans sitting at a table.

"Sit down and watch with us, sir!" said Holda.

"Human stuff," Macta spat. "I should have known. Picking up foreign slang like that will only pollute your minds. I don't know why the Experimentalists keep bringing their versions of this rubbish into Helfratheim—we want to *kill* the Humans, not steal their technology."

"Who sssaysss we can't do both?" hissed the garter snake

that was relaxing in a coil around Herma's waist, obviously enjoying the images moving across the screen.

Macta glared. "Now, where is *my* Human girl? Have you been taking care of her properly?"

Herma smiled. "You mean *Liqua?*"

"Liqua?" Macta repeated.

"We had to give her a name, sir," answered Holda. "So we're calling her Liqua. Because she likes to lie facedown in the arboretum fountain!"

"In the arboretum fountain?" Macta cried. "I asked you to hide her in a cellar, a sub-basement, a dungeon, anyplace she could be kept out of sight. She's my secret weapon. There are so many things I could do with her, but if word gets out that I have a Human hidden away, then I'll completely lose the element of surprise! My father would probably steal her away, and where would that leave me?"

Macta stalked through the hive-like chambers of his apartment, stopping only when he reached the arboretum. A statue of an Elfin nymph spouted water from its puckered mouth. Plants accustomed to the gloom spread their leaves along the edges of the fountain, and slender reeds crept like fingers from the dark pool. The Human lay facedown in the water. "How can she breathe like that?" Macta whispered.

Behind him, on tiptoe, stood Herma and Holda. They peered over their Master's shoulder. "Doesn't seem to need to, sir!" said Herma.

"I hope you didn't pay much for her," said Holda. "We don't

think she's a proper Human, sir. We had her in the root cellar, at first, but she wouldn't stop crying, and before long it turned to round-the-clock screaming."

"Neither of us could get a wink of sleep," said Herma, "so I went down to see what was the matter. That was when we discovered that your Human isn't quite as Human as you thought, sir."

"That's right," said Holda. "She was screaming Bloody murder, enough to shatter your ears, but all the while you could see *right through her!*"

"Transparent, sir!" said Herma, with a smile.

"No," said Holda. "Translucent. But you could still see her shape all right."

"Whatever," said Herma. "Anyway, her screaming got me so vexed that I picked up a bucket of cold water from the next room, sir, and tossed it at her."

"Shut her right up," said Holda, "and soon you couldn't see through her anymore, sir. Solid as rock, she was."

"Not that solid," said Herma. "Just solid like flesh and Blood. But then I got the idea of—"

"*Your* idea, sssay," hissed Herma's slim advising snake, "'twasss *mine!*"

Macta stood with his hands on his hips staring at the Human. She was still dressed in tatters, soaked to the skin. "You say you could *see* through her? I want to witness it for myself. Come on, the pair of you, right over here."

"But, sir, we'll get wet!" cried Herma and Holda.

Macta grinned sourly. "Aye, you'll get wet, and that's exactly why I'm going to be standing over there, out of splashing range, when you lift her from the fountain."

Holda and Herma carefully placed their advising snakes in wicker baskets before stepping into the fountain. Shivering, with the hems of their skirts swaying on the surface of the pool, they reached under the girl's arms. But after a moment of tugging and pulling, it was apparent that they would not be able to lift the girl from the fountain unaided. "Oh, all right," Macta puffed. He hiked up his trousers and waded in beside Anna McCormack's still form. With some struggle, the three Elves got Anna's head out of the water. Herma stood on Anna's back and pulled hard on her hair, while Macta lifted her forehead and Holda pushed up on the girl's nostrils. "She's not breathing," Macta huffed. "She's dead!"

Herma shook her head. "I told you, sir, she's not dead, *but she's not alive, either.*"

"She's a *wraith*, sir," said Holda, "she's not Human! Not any more!"

Suddenly Anna opened her eyes. Macta stood back and grinned fiercely. "'Tis *I*, my dear, your friend Macta. Will you get up, please, and show these two lovely Elfmaids that you're a good girl, a nice girl who needs to get dried off and into her warm bed?"

Anna's thoughts were racing along their tortured path,

bound for oblivion. *Time to get out of the tub! Mommy lifts me out of the tub, she plucks me out, like I'm a flower, a beautiful flower, for her bouquet. Mommy says I'm her little rosebud. Mommy holds my hand. I'm walking away from the tub, and I look down and there are my feet on the ground, walking. And I can see the ground, brown and covered with leaves, and broken branches, and gray smooth rocks, and my feet aren't*

there any more at all. I lift my hand, and my hand is made of smoke.

My fingers are filmy, my fingers are nothing but air, and

I'm disappearing. I'm not here any more, I'm going away. I'm slipping

away, like water down the drain.

Mommy? Mommy? Where are you? Where am I? Mommy? Aaaaaannnngggbhh! Aaaaaaaannnngggbhhbh!

Macta jerked away and pressed his hands against his pointed, oversized ears. In the guest room of his apartment there was a four-poster Emperor bed. Macta had been attempting to lead the girl to the room, hoping that she could stay there, out of sight of the glass arboretum, where others in the palace might happen to glance down from an adjoining tower and see her lying in the fountain. But the housemaids were right; the girl needed water. Once upon a time this child was Human, but now it was impossible to say what she had become. Leaving wet footprints behind her, the part of Anna McCormack that was still visible stumbled back into the fountain. With a splash she did a belly flop into the water. Only a few bubbles rose up from the girl's mouth as her hair floated in straggly brown tendrils.

"All right!" Macta said, sharply. "Holda, Herma, I want the pair of you to move all of the potted plants in the apartment into this area. If the Human—or whatever she is—wants to be in the water so badly, let's make sure it's kept as private as possible. In fact, let's have some trees delivered. We'll make it a veritable forest in here. That's what an arboretum's supposed to be, anyway!"

Macta clapped his hands. "What are you waiting for?" he demanded. "I've got to get my clothes changed; I'm all wet. Find me something to wear, before I catch a chill! And pry that ruby out of the Human's hand, if you can. I'm going to be needing it tonight."

The Prince was slipping into a pair of forest green trousers when a buzzer rang from behind his bed. Only one Elf in all the world besides Macta knew about this buzzer, which had been installed for his use alone. "Nebiros?" Macta frowned.

Outside the gray stone wall that surrounded the compound, the Elf squeezed behind a spreading black rosebush, hidden in the shadows. The rain had slowed to a drizzle. Low on the wall, a chink of mortar had been pried loose, and there was an alarm buzzer buried deep between the stones. Nebiros pushed the button one last time. He swore, and rubbed his neck in irritation. The rose briars had scraped the Elf's sensitive skin, leaving welts on his forehead and up and down his arms. *What a waste of time,*

Nebiros thought, scratching furiously. *I'll have to leave another message, despite what Jardaine said. I'm not going to stand here all night.* Suddenly he saw a patch of turf separate itself from the surrounding earth and slowly descend. Nebiros glanced to his left and right, then disappeared into the hole.

The chamber was a crude affair—dirt walls, oil lamps flickering in the cool dampness, and the apparatus that controlled the secret panel opening on the far side of the wall. "Nebiros," Macta frowned. "What do you want?"

The Elf grimaced. "Never been better, your excellency! Thanks so much for asking!"

"Don't be hostile," Macta said, "it doesn't suit you. Let's make this quick, shall we? I've got things to do."

Macta's hands were jammed deep into the pockets of his trousers. In one pocket he had a pair of knucklebones, and he rattled them nervously.

Nebiros scratched his neck. "What's up, Prince? Do you have some newfound wealth you're anxious to dispose of? Perhaps a fortune in jewels? Yes, I know all about it. Don't squander it at the gaming tables, if that's what you're thinking. Here's an idea: Why not just give the jewels to me for safekeeping! I'm sure I'd hold onto them better than you!"

Macta yanked his hands from his trousers and crossed his arms over his embroidered jacket. "I'm sure I don't know what you're talking about. And anyway, that's none of your business. Now I assume you must have some information from Jardaine to relate, or is this just a social visit?"

"I've got some surprising news about the Mage of Alfheim," Nebiros said.

Macta waved his hand impatiently. "I know all about that. I'm not blind, you know. Kalevala Van Frier is dead, and that little twerp with the burlap jerkin and the tattoos has taken her place. I've had the displeasure of meeting her twice now, and ineptitude is written all over her face. Jardaine must be green with envy. But 'tis only a matter of time. She'll be Mage soon enough."

"Aaah," said Nebiros. "That's good, except for one small detail. The Mage isn't dead, after all. She's trapped somewhere, apparently. Jardaine has information on the Mage's whereabouts, but she's going to be needing your help in getting to the old crone. She wants the Mage out of her way as much as you do; 'twill be easier to install Jardaine as the new Mage if everyone's certain that Kalevala Van Frier is truly dead and we've got her carcass to prove it."

"Indeed. What fun! An adventure. But what do you mean, she's *trapped?* Is someone holding her captive? Humans? Elves?"

Nebiros shrugged. "I don't have all the answers, Macta. Jardaine will tell you more when she sees you."

"Then tell Jardaine that I'll bring my lads to Alfheim. Oh, and I'll bring along my pet, Powcca, as well. He's got a hunter's heart; 'twill be good sport. Once Jardaine's given us the clues as to the Mage's whereabouts, we'll find the old bird and make sure that she doesn't come back alive."

Macta mused, stroking the wispy hairs on his chin. "Whilst I'm in Alfheim, I'll pay a little visit to Tuava-Li. 'Tis high time she gave me Asra's wedding shoe. I want to present it to Asra myself. I'm certain it will convince her, once I place it on her foot, that she's worthy to be my bride."

"Uh . . . Macta, about the shoe," Nebiros said.

"What about the shoe?"

"Tuava-Li already delivered the shoe to Ljosalfar. She's probably on her way back to Alfheim by now. She was going to give it to the head of the Synod, and see what they wanted to do about it."

"What?" Macta said, livid with rage. He rushed at Nebiros with both arms extended, and knocked him off his feet. Then he scrabbled on top of the startled Elf, pinning him to the ground. "If she thinks she can score points with the Synod by giving them that shoe, then . . . then . . ."

"Wha—what are you doing?" Nebiros cried, struggling to get up. "I had nothing to do with the infernal shoe! What's done is done. As long as the shoe is back where it belongs, you're still on track, right? Now let me up!"

There was a fantasy that played out in Macta's mind, a dream that repeated itself over and over. It was a scene that featured Macta on his knees in a fragrant grove, kneeling before his beloved, with one jeweled shoe cupped in his hands. Sitting before him on a carved bench was Princess Asra, already wearing the match to the shoe in Macta's hands. In Macta's fantasy Asra's eyes glistened with love. Her ruby lips formed a perfect smile as she extended her bare foot. Then Macta slipped the shoe onto it. As a look of pure bliss passed between them, Macta reached into his pocket and withdrew a ring, crafted around one of the giant diamonds he had stolen from the Troll's lair. He slipped it onto Asra's finger and then—the fantasy fell apart. Just like that.

Macta stalked to the other side of the underground chamber and leaned hard on the lever operating the lift. "Tell Jardaine I'll be there as soon as I can," he said to Nebiros, as the rectangle of turf shifted into place. The disgruntled Elf got to his feet and brushed dirt from his trousers. Macta grimaced at him, rattling the dice and the jewels in his pockets. "Tonight, I'm in need of a little amusement. Oh, and be sure and tell Jardaine not to worry. The Mage of Alfheim is as good as dead!"

28

TUAVA-LI HURTLED ALONG the milk-white passageway of the Cord. In the Cord Tuava-Li always felt that she was free. In the Cord Tuava-Li could forget the troubles that weighed her down, for here she was weightless. Now, coming home from Ljosalfar, she felt even lighter than before, for Princess Asra's wedding shoe was safe in the hands of the Synod. There would be no more trouble from Macta Dockalfar. Now she could focus on finding the Mage.

Tuava-Li moved to the right as she felt the approach of something with massive bulk. A brown, leathery creature rushed by her, suddenly huge, and hot, throwing its shadow across her for a second, then gone. The low, flat *wooosh* of sound returned. It was nearly useless to try to concentrate, to hold onto a thought when the winds were rushing so fast. Then, with hardly a warning, the air began to pop.

Tuava-Li shook her head. What was happening? Her eardrums fluttered, her head began to throb; she pressed her hands against her ears to try to stop the pain. But the quick, pulsing suck-suck-suck of air continued. Tuava-Li could hear screaming around her, groans and cries of surprise, and these, too, came in bursts of sound. The interior walls of the Cord, normally a soft, shimmering white, suddenly appeared gray and mottled. Shadows filled the air. Tuava-Li realized that she was seeing a blur of foliage and tree trunks; the Cord was nearly transparent where it opened to the daylight. The walls billowed and flapped inward like a canvas tent. Then came the tear. A huge flap of the Cord was pulled back, ripped open to the daylight; the rushing wind, the very breath of the Cord, was escaping like air from a balloon. Creatures smaller than Tuava-Li were being flung outside and to the ground. She managed to jackknife across the width of the Cord and sheer momentum sent her hurtling past the tear. Still, the walls closed in on her and then bulged out, then closed in again. Tuava-Li banged hard against the Cord, ripping it further as she bounced along. The Cord was falling apart, beginning to collapse on itself. Yet Tuava-Li continued to hurtle forward. Soon the walls of the Cord were smoother and more opaque than they had appeared just moments ago. The rippling sensation seemed to pass, and the sucking feeling in her ears faded away. She was safe, and moving as effortlessly as before, but Tuava-Li had seen firsthand that something was terribly wrong. The Cord was damaged. The Cord was ill. Deathly ill.

This was more than damage from Humans unwittingly cutting Cords as they deforested their world. This was something else.

With the tingling sensation that told her she was approaching Alfheim, Tuava-Li curled her body into a ball, then pushed her feet straight out in front of her. She dug her heels into the wall of the Cord, uncertain of what to expect. The familiar rubbery resistance of the membrane made her breathe a sigh of relief. She cut an opening with her fingernail. When she slipped through, landing on solid ground near the grove of the five trees, Tuava-Li watched the opening slowly seal itself. She ran her fingers over the Cord. Did it feel a little too soft? Did it feel a little cold to the touch? Were the capillaries that ran from its main branch as thick as they had been, were they growing as they should as they stretched and rooted themselves in the soil, nourishing and bringing the strength of spirit to the trees? The Cords of the earth had never needed tending; they always provided the sustenance on which everything else relied.

Behind Tuava-Li a group of Elves were on their knees, working along the edge of a worn bed of moss. Their eyes were closed, their hands pushed the air before them in a motion that resembled kneading bread. Their mouths moved silently and Tuava-Li knew at once that they were using magick to make the mossy carpet grow. "What do you think you're doing?" she exclaimed. "Who told you to do this?"

Tradition dictated that magick was meant to be used only in rare circumstances. And even then, such powers were to be used with guidance and supervision. The Mage had taught Tuava-Li that lesson, and the Mage had also been called upon to remind Tuava-Li of it many times.

"'Tis Jardaine's idea," said an Elf, leaping to his feet at the sight of Tuava-Li. He bowed awkwardly, unsure of the proper protocol. "She told us that we weren't working fast enough, that we weren't doing our jobs properly."

"She made the other monks teach us the spells to do our work with magick," another added.

"'Tis the easiest way to get everything done!" said a third.

"Magick isn't the easy way," Tuava-Li frowned. "'Tis the *hard* way, but you never discover that for yourselves until it's too late."

She knelt and ran her fingers along the ground. "When you work with your hands, the time and effort required will show you the real value of your goal. This moss, for example. It requires devotion and care. If you rely on tricks of mind over matter, the moss suffers. It suffers because you didn't give it the attention it needed. You might even say it suffers from lack of love. The Mage taught me that. If you repeat magick words, cast a spell, you force things to change in ways that may benefit you in the short term. But then the beauty of the moss you grow not only comes too easily, it's nothing but an illusion. And illusions don't stand up to the passage of time."

"Mistress," argued one of the Elves, "we've seen *you* use magick. We've seen the Mage use magick, too."

"Aye, because she *is* a Mage. Because the Mage's desires are not just her own. When she performs magick, she does the work of the Gods. *We* can be the hands of the Gods in this world. Learning these things is a process. I'm just learning. It takes a lifetime. I don't know what the Gods want, and neither do you. You just know what Jardaine wants."

Tuava-Li paced up and down. "Listen. Think of what the Humans are doing. They build their machines, and they use them to chop down the trees and flatten the earth. Their machines work like magick, because in an instant they do the job that a thousand hands would otherwise have to do. They use their machines to cut roadways and build cities and shape the world to their own desires. But their desires aren't the desires of the Gods. If the Humans had to use the strength of their own backs and hands to do their work, they might hear the spirits of the trees and the earth speaking to them. They might choose to do their work *with* the world, instead of against it. Do you understand? Alfheim is a community of spirit. Elves come here to learn to listen to the quiet voices of the Gods, and to be their hands in the world. Only those who are trained in the ways of spirit—the Mages, the monks—only they can really begin to understand how and when to use magick."

"Does that mean we have to stop using the growing spells, Mistress?"

"That's exactly what it means," said Tuava-Li, as she stalked off toward the Grove. High in the branches of the oak tree Bethok sat Jardaine. She leaned across the Mage's table with a score of books open before her. Three of the monks stood behind, gazing down upon the bark-paper papyri and volumes of spells. The monks' dark, enormous eyes scanned the inscriptions, the figures drawn in faded inks. The clay bell tinkled in the doorway. The rats in their treetop wheel began to run, eager for the corn they would get when the elevator reached its stop. Jardaine lifted her head. "Tell Orette to come in. Orette, do you have the object?"

"What object?" Tuava-Li demanded, stepping past the curtain. Immediately the monks leapt back, and Jardaine swiveled on her seat. "Tuava-Li!" she smiled innocently. "I wasn't expecting you back so soon. Did you deliver the shoe to the Synod?"

Tuava-Li turned to the monks who stood, heads bowed, on either side of Jardaine. "Would you excuse us, please?"

The beeswax tapers at the sides of the altar were unlit. Tuava-Li took the candle from the desk and went to light the first twelve, which represented the seasons of the moon. The gold leaf on the carvings of the altar shone. There were the Gods, the heroes, the whole, rich tapestry of Elfin life that had unfolded through the millennia, etched into the face of the altar. The wood had been taken from a fallen limb of the first Sacred Tree, so long ago that it was more like stone than wood. "Pray with me, Jardaine," said Tuava-Li, and the pair of them knelt before the altar.

After many minutes of silence, Tuava-Li opened her eyes.

Around the altar wound a ring of vines. Tuava-Li reached for a vessel of sacred oil and poured the precious liquid into a bowl. Jardaine also poured a portion of oil into the bowl, then lit the surface with a candle flame. The fragrant oil swirled in dark curlicues of green. "There is much I need to ask you," Tuava-Li said. "Whilst I was gone, did you have any visions? Did the Mage come to you, as she did to me?"

Jardaine shook her head. "I did as you asked, Tuava-Li. I stayed here in this place and waited. I sat at the desk and studied, I knelt at the altar and prayed, I lay on the hammock during the nights you were gone and let myself pass through the Gates of Vattar, and the only thoughts I heard were my own. The only messages I received were from the Elves, who are overwhelmed with the work you've asked them to do. You imagine that the Mage is alive and trying to contact you, because you want to believe it so badly. But the Mage is dead, Tuava-Li, and you'd best be ready to take her place now, because the Elves need a leader. If you're not prepared to do it, the Synod will appoint someone who is."

Tuava-Li felt her chest tighten as Jardaine got up from the floor. "Since you left me in charge, Tuava-Li, I've taken the liberty of making a few changes. If we intend to bring back the rest of our Clan to this place, we'd best make sure 'tis ready. That's why the monks have been meeting by day with the Elves in the fields and the Elves in the Grove, to teach them the spells that will help them get their work done on schedule. We eliminated the dreaming rituals, and shortened our time at the Gates of Vattar by two hours. Tuava-Li, you wouldn't believe how much we've accomplished. The monks and I have been searching the libraries, and we found a formula for a med'cine that will protect us from Human contagion. If we're going to run the risk of being exposed to the Humans, we need to protect ourselves."

Tuava-Li was stunned. She didn't even know where to begin. The clay bell clattered in the entryway and Jardaine turned. "That ought to be Orette. We've learned to paint a special tincture on wood chips to offset the nausea from exposure to metal and poisonous vapors from the Human world. Orette used it to protect herself on her mission."

"I've seen tinctures prepared," Tuava-Li said.

"But you've never seen these!" Jardaine put on a smug grin. "I'm not afraid to take on my own education. You can't wait for permission to rise to an occasion, Tuava-Li."

Orette arrived in the doorway. In her arms she carried an unwieldy bundle. "Didn't I tell you to leave that outside the glen?" Jardaine demanded. "You can't bring something like that in here! You're putting all of us in danger!"

Orette panicked and dropped the leather gardening glove. It brushed the high branch of the oak and drifted to the ground, far below. "We needed to have a Human thing to start with," Jardaine said. "Something their flesh has touched."

She turned to Orette and barked her orders. "Get down there

and take it to the spot we've prepared. I don't want anyone else coming near it."

Jardaine went to the Mage's desk and began tidying the stacks of books. "We'll boil the glove in mouse milk," she explained. "O'er the course of three nights we'll extract its Human essence. The monks will wave willow wands over the cauldron while reciting the incantations from the papyri. We'll dilute the solution, and every one of us will consume a small portion. That should be sufficient to protect us from Human illness."

Tuava-Li looked doubtful. "How can you be certain the formula's safe, how can you know if it truly works? And why is such a thing even necessary? Who's to say that—"

Jardaine snorted. "We can't escape the Humans any more, Tuava-Li. We're going to have to start preparing for what's to come."

Tuava-Li heard Jardaine's words, she saw the proud, defiant expression on the monk's face, and a wave of despair washed over her. Maybe the Mage was truly gone, Tuava-Li thought, maybe the visions had all been her own imagination at work, trying to cloak her own weakness. Maybe she wasn't smart enough, wise enough, confident enough. Maybe the Mage had been wrong about her. Maybe Jardaine was the one who should be the Mage. And yet, the single thing the Mage had left Tuava-Li was the assurance that it was *she* who should take on the mantle of power, when the time was right.

"I can tell your heart is in the right place," Tuava-Li said, "but Jardaine, I have to question your methods. This is not what our Mage would have done. The dreaming rituals, the hours we spend at the Gates of Vattar, these are our traditions; they're not meant to be tampered with. The magick you gave the Elves isn't meant for them. And the Mage always said that—"

"Sometimes the best ways are the quickest ways," Jardaine interrupted. "Just look around you! How can we tend the gardens, bring in the harvest, prepare for the change in seasons; how can we do that without using magick? We've all been trained in the Mysteries; we've learned spells, incantations, charms to change the flow of little things. If we had the luxury of time, we could do things the way they've always been done. But there isn't any time left." Jardaine pushed past Tuava-Li. "Now, I'm sorry, but I've got work to do. Orette needs help with the preparation of the med'cine."

Tuava-Li reached out her hand. "The med'cine is a good idea, and I appreciate your work on it. But tonight we return to the old rituals. Tomorrow the Elves return to the old methods. I couldn't do this without you, Jardaine, and if you think we're falling behind, I'll request that more help be sent from Ljosalfar. But *I* make the decisions, until the Mage returns. You have to remember that."

Jardaine let out a scornful laugh. "I wonder, Tuava-Li, whilst you were in Ljosalfar delivering Princess Asra's shoe, did you feel compelled to tell the Synod about what's going on here? I'd be surprised! The Mage isn't coming back, Tuava-Li, and I think the

Synod really ought to know Alfheim has a new leader. I wonder if they'll agree with your methods. I wonder if they'll agree with the Mage's choice of a successor. Perhaps you'd like me to tell them?"

"You'll do nothing without my permission. Do you understand?"

Jardaine spun around and marched out of the room. Tuava-Li trembled in the shadows, breathing hard. It was all too much to bear. She had wanted to tell Jardaine about the Cord, the accident on her return from Ljosalfar. She knew it was vital that the Synod know of the damage. But if the Cord was failing, how could she even get back to Ljosalfar? She turned to the altar. The flame of the candles still flickered, and so she knelt with her hands resting on her knees. The rituals, the techniques, were doorways. They were places to begin, not places to end. Tuava-Li was sure of this, at least.

So she began another ritual. In her mind she stood on a cliff top, overlooking a precipice. She imagined, one at a time, all the things she desired for herself; and in her mind she became these things. In her mind she became a body built solely of her desires. Tuava-Li wanted peace. So she became peace. She didn't want to fight with Jardaine. She didn't want to argue with the Elves. But peace was more than the absence of conflict, so she became that as well, saying yes to her life, whatever it brought. She wanted harmony, so that there would be no conflict, within or without. She became harmony. She wanted strength so that she could lead the others, and defeat their enemies. She wanted confidence so that the others would trust her judgment. She wanted to be the Mage. There it was! Sometimes the truth is frightful to behold, but still it must be seen. She became it. Another desire lurked just behind; she *didn't* want to be the Mage. With a passion, she wanted to avoid the responsibility, the hard work, the sacrifice. It made no sense, but it was true. Both desires lived in her, fighting for dominance. Tuava-Li became her desires, all of them, conflicting and pure, dark and light, selfish and giving. She wanted the Humans to go away. She became her desire. She wanted the Humans to be dead. She became that, too. She wanted her Mage to return so that things could go back to being the way they had been. Tuava-Li was so full of desire that she could barely stand it. Tears streamed down her cheeks. In her mind's eye, she hovered at the brink. And then she let herself fall.

Down she tumbled into her imaginary abyss. The wind screamed at her, and her clothing billowed around her body. So full of desire, and her eyes saw the void below, and there was nothing she could do to stop it. Down she fell, and the winds tore at her flesh, stripping her limbs to the bone, and the clothing fell away in tatters. The Blood streamed away, the bones crumbled to dust in a cloud of gray: the eyes that saw, the mouth that cried, everything disappeared, and the desires that filled Tuava-Li and clouded her mind from grasping the truth fell away, too. There was nothing left to fall. There was nothing. Nothing. Tuava-Li opened her eyes. And she saw in that moment, stripped of all desire, with nothing to cloud her vision, what needed to be done.

29

FROM THE OUTSIDE the cage looked empty. When the owl came out at night to inspect the dead mice that the Humans had left on the stump, the other birds thrashed around in their cages and screamed. They knew instinctively that something was wrong. But in the daylight hours, the owl hid in the box, its back turned to the light. Tim opened the cage door and stepped inside. There was a round hole in the wall of the box. Tim could just make out the tail feathers of the owl, so he knew she was still inside. But the bird obviously didn't want to be seen. Tim shook his head and sighed, certain it was only a matter of time until he went to look in the box and found her lifeless body.

It was true; the owl didn't want to be seen. But not for the reasons the Humans believed. At the ends of its feathered wings the owl was growing hands and delicate, Elfin fingers. Its beak was separating into a nose and mouth, and teeth were forming where the beak dissolved into skin. Even the talons were softening and turning into feet and toes. The horned owl was once again becoming the Mage of Alfheim. And it wouldn't be wise to allow the Humans to see that. The Mage concentrated on the Human, and tried to gain control over his mind. All she needed was a few seconds, when the Human left her cage—the moment when the door was pulled shut and the rusty metal lock snapped in place. If she could create a kind of blur, a slip of the mind, just a few seconds of forgetting, the Mage was sure she could get the Human to leave the cage unlocked. And if she could get out of the cage, she had a chance of getting home.

For many days and nights the Mage had cast her awareness through the forest, for miles in every direction, looking for a familiar place. Over and over she had tried to find a Soul she knew, some consciousness that saw something, anything that she knew, too. Finally her prayers had been answered. At first she had seen only a ring of lights. Could it be stars, or the lights of some distant Human home? Then the vision grew clearer, and the Mage had recognized that the lights were flickering candles, surrounding an altar. The picture had become clearer still. It was the altar of her own study, high in the branches of the sacred tree. As joy leapt in her heart, the Mage knew that she had located Tuava-Li. Then she'd projected her own senses, her own memories outward across the miles, giving clues to help her Apprentice find this place, and come to her rescue. But it was exhausting work, casting a psychic net into space. Exertion like this was more than she could endure for long.

The Mage needed rest. When next she found the strength to look for Tuava-Li, she sent images and feelings into the area where she had found her before. If she could have just formulated words, it would have been so much easier. But the following day when she sent her awareness to the space where Tuava-Li had been, she found to her surprise that another mind had taken its place. The Mage could feel darkness lurking there. There was conflict, and rage, and contempt hidden beneath walls of pretense. This was not Tuava-Li. It couldn't be. But if it wasn't Tuava-Li, then who could it be, sitting at the Mage's own desk, reading the books, the papyri scrolls, praying before the altar? One of her monks? There was no time to waste. So when the Human came to leave another mouse in her pen, the Mage closed her mental talons around his will.

The wind ruffled Macta's hair as he stood on the dome of the water tower, gazing into the distance. "It's beautiful!" he cried, cupping his hand to his mouth. "I don't think I've ever been this far from the ground."

The Elves had spent hours making the ascent to the top of the tower, scaling the human-sized ladder with hooks and rope. Special tinctures, as always, protected them from exposure to metal. "'Twas worth the climb to the top, just to see this!"

Macta and his companions stood facing south. They had left Powcca tethered to the foot of the tower below, where his howling was drowned out by the roaring wind. The Elves had traveled the Cord to Alfheim, then continued their journey on foot. If much of the boundary between the Elfin and Human worlds remained here, there was scant evidence of it now. The Elves spotted a highway snaking through the trees. Human civilization was a complete mystery to them. A gas station, a convenience store, a hunting and fishing supply shop, and the endless network of electric and telephone wires that stretched across the landscape caused Druga to scratch his head in wonder. The first time Baltham heard a truck roll by on the highway, he dropped to the ground in fear. The noise of the truck soon passed, but the terror remained. He kept a wary eye open for predators. Foxes, weasels, and raccoons could pose a real threat to Elves. For this reason each of the gang had a rapier secured to his belt, and each took turns shouldering a new weapon called the Dragon Thunderbus. The body of this weapon was a cast-iron rod with an S-shaped lever. It was fashioned to contain a measure of serpentine powder, and when ignited by a Fire Sprite, an enormous fireball would explode from the end of the barrel. Druga, in particular, enjoyed using Macta's weapon to blast birds and squirrels from the trees.

Despite the fact that they were traveling over foreign territory, the Elves had followed the markers provided for them by Jardaine. The tower was a remarkable sight, enormous, smooth, and horribly out of place among the trees. The metallic smell carried on the breeze for miles. From their high vantage point the Elves could survey the landscape below, and pinpoint the direction from which the Mage may have made her psychic distress calls. "There," said Macta, pointing to an area of brown and gray. It appeared to be a cluster of small buildings. A dirt road connected to a wider ribbon of black, which grew thicker as it wound through the woods. "I believe we've found what we're looking for," Macta grinned. "The Mage of Alfheim should be down there, somewhere. We're looking for a horned owl, maybe with a broken wing. Now let's get this over with. I've still got a wedding to plan!"

It worked! The Human had failed to put the lock back through the metal latch, and the door was open. Freedom was just a few feet away. The Mage left the wooden box, hopped onto the perch, then flopped to the ground. Her wing burned like it was on fire. But she leaned against the chicken-wire door, and prayed that she could make it budge. The door squeaked open. And then she heard the distinct barking of a Goblin.

Macta released Powcca from his leash. On short, powerful legs the creature tore into the compound where the animals were caged. The Humans came running when they heard the terrified shrieks from outside. They searched up and down the dirt driveway, around the cages and the edge of the woods. They saw nothing.

"Baltham, go around the front of that structure and make some noise," said Macta, handing him the Dragon Thunderbus.

"I don't believe the Humans can see us, but 'twill make our job easier if they're out of the way."

Baltham crept to the front of the wildlife sanctuary. He took a small iron box from his satchel and opened the lid to reveal a tiny, orange-tipped Fire Sprite. Gently he placed the box on the windowsill. The Sprite darted out, leaving a line of flame to dance along the window's edge, bubbling the paint and charring every inch of wood along its path. Baltham opened a pouch containing three vials of powder, and he mixed the charcoal, sulfur, and potassium nitrate together. Then he stuffed the mixture into the end of the iron rod, and called to the Fire Sprite. With a flash of light and a belch of smoke, the front of the building erupted in flames. The overhanging porch groaned, then collapsed. Tim and Carrie stood frozen in disbelief. "The animals!" Tim finally shouted. "The ones in the infirmary. We've got to get them out of there!"

And as the desperate Humans hauled cages from the back of the burning building, the trio of Elves and their Goblin searched the outdoor pens. From a nearby bush the Mage peered through foliage and tried to estimate her chances at escape. She recognized Macta, and understood that he and his cohorts had not come to rescue her. Fortunately, Powcca was easily distracted. The smells of the other animals, the ceaseless racket of the hawks, falcons, owls, and mammals in their pens all drove the Goblin mad with Bloodlust. But

Macta held a scrap of fabric and feathers in his hand. It had been torn from the silver cloak of the Mage. He held it over the Goblin's slobbering muzzle so that Powcca would know the scent he was there to track. "Now find your prey, my little pet!" Macta crooned.

A quick search convinced Macta and Druga that the owl-Mage was not in any of the outdoor pens. Yet when Druga yanked open the door of one empty cell, the Goblin went wild, thrashing and foaming at the mouth, "She must have been in here," he grunted.

Tim lumbered from the doorway. With his eyes streaming from the smoke, he lowered a tank to the ground. Then he caught a glimpse of something out of the corner of his eye. When he looked up, the Goblin met his gaze. That was all it took. Powcca bounded across the yard and lunged for Tim's throat. Columns of black smoke stretched into the sky. Rangers all across the county would see it; in a few minutes there would be fire trucks, police cars, rescue workers. And they would be too late. "Powcca!" Macta called. "Come!"

The Goblin raced back toward his Master, Blood dripping from his jaws. Carrie stepped out of the smoke. She was choking, her eyes burning with tears. She thought she saw something blue and furry, with legs like a pit bull and ears like horns, moving toward the forest. Then she looked down and saw what remained of her friend.

The Mage was hopping, flapping, crashing across a carpet of needles, plunging behind tree trunks to catch her breath, trying to put some distance between herself and the Goblin. But she knew that at any moment the creature would pick up her scent. The Mage pulled herself onto a low branch, then heard the ragged breath of the monster behind her. "Get her, Powcca, get the owl!" a voice called. With all the strength she had left, the Mage flapped her wings. And she rose into the air. Whether or not she intended it to be so, it was magick. She left worry behind. She left hope behind. These things had weight to them, so she let them go. She flapped her wings, with the tiny fingers sprouting from their tips, and she left the pain of her broken wing behind. She wasn't flying straight, she wasn't flying elegantly, but she was airborne, and she had a chance. The Mage sailed through the low branches of the trees, her wings somehow avoiding them all. Suddenly the trees came to an abrupt end. The Mage soared up over the highway. *Honk! Honk!* The pickup truck swerved as the owl skimmed across the hood and flapped to the far side of the road. The blue thing that leapt out of the woods behind her was not so lucky.

The driver slammed his brakes and skidded to a stop. He flung open the door and climbed out, unsure of what had just happened. Thirty yards behind him, Macta Dockalfar stepped out of the forest and onto the gravel shoulder. He let out a cry of despair. Besides Princess Asra, the pet Goblin was the only other thing Macta had ever loved. Powcca's body was smeared along the blacktop. Macta scurried up and down the edge of the road, searching for the head. "What the—" the driver of the vehicle swore, rubbing his eyes in disbelief. Figures flickered on the road before him. He wasn't sure he was seeing anything at all, and yet when he blinked he thought he could see two tiny men. Then a third figure leapt out from the trees. It heaved something black and shiny to the first of the creatures, who pointed it at him. Thunder split the air. A ball of flame blew past the man's head. His rear windshield exploded in a cascade of broken glass, and the inside of his truck filled with fire. The man ran for his life.

Macta lay sprawled on the blacktop. The recoil of the Dragon Thunderbus had slammed the barrel into his jaw, and knocked out three of his teeth. He spat green Blood onto the pavement and cursed. "He killed Powcca! The Human deserves to die!"

Druga stared at the wall of trees on the other side of the road. "Did you catch a glimpse of the Mage? The owl-thing?"

Baltham shuddered. "'Twas horrible. A nightmare. The creature had hands and feet like claws, and a face somewhere betwixt an Elf and a bird. It makes me sick to think of it. And what was that—that metal thing that crushed Powcca?"

Macta's tongue felt thick. "Just a Human vehicle, nothing more. 'Tis exactly like the gondolas my father rides in the Cord. Except ours move on a current of air, and theirs travel along the ground. We have to be very, very careful here. We—"

A sudden explosion and a gust of scorching wind knocked the three Elves off their feet. The flaming pickup truck, blocking a lane of the roadway ahead, had exploded in a massive ball of fire.

Druga shuddered and moved his bulk to protect his Master. "Macta!" he yelled over the roaring sound. "I saw a Cord back there among the trees. 'Twasn't a very big one, but it might be enough to get us out of here quickly!"

Macta shook his head and peered into the woods. "I don't know. We promised to kill the Mage. But there's no way she'll survive for long in the wild. You all saw how she's injured. Jardaine won't be happy to hear that we failed, but we did what we could. 'Tis obviously too dangerous for us to be here. Let's allow some other predator the pleasure of doing our dirty work. I want to go home."

Macta plucked a leaf from the undergrowth and held it against his swollen jaw. He knew that his missing teeth would grow back, but not before the time of his wedding. With Powcca's head tucked beneath his arm, and Druga carrying the Dragon Thunderbus, they clomped through the woods. A siren screamed from the highway. A burning smell stung Macta's nostrils. *This is no work for a Prince,* he thought, contemplating who he might blame for his failure. Macta was no friend of responsibility. *And every bit of it,* he concluded, *every single bit is Jardaine's fault!*

The depression in the earth where they found the Cord was hidden in leaves and brambles. The Cord itself looked frail, but when Macta punched his boot through the membrane, he felt the warm, rushing winds. It made him smile. This Cord would not take them all the way home, but at least it would get them away from the chaos they had caused here. "One at a time," he said. "I'll go first!"

Later, when the Cord widened, Druga made swimming motions to catch up with his Master. "Poor Powcca!" he shouted. "His head will make a lovely mount on your wall."

Globs of emerald-colored gore still dripped from the Goblin's neck, as Macta cradled the thing in his arms. *Splat!* Baltham winced as a chunk of green flew back and struck his cheek. He was about to complain when he saw that just ahead, the walls of the Cord were ballooning out. Something was wrong. "Watch out!" Macta hollered, dragging his boot to slow the momentum. Roots shot through the tear the boot had made, and Macta cursed as they ripped his leggings. Macta's body wrenched to the side and spun out of control, just as the Cord made an unexpected twist. Druga hit the curve straight on. His body tore through the membrane and flew through the open air. There was a sickening thud as his head struck the trunk of a tree. The air in the Cord escaped with a loud hiss as Macta climbed out still holding Powcca's head. Baltham was caught in the Cord's collapse as the walls folded on top of him, pressing on his chest, squeezing the breath from his lungs. He was suffocating. In a moment Macta was there, yelling, "Get up! Get up!" Grimacing, he yanked away great fistfuls of the Cord. It was coming apart in his hands; it was suffused with rot and decay and flecks of mold. The smell was horrible. Macta tugged his brother-in-law from the mess and got him up on his hands and knees. "Look what you've made me do," Macta snapped. "Just look at this mess! My clothes are ruined!" Then he shoved Baltham back to the ground.

"We've got . . . to get to . . . Druga," Baltham choked.

Macta turned, glancing at the body of his servant. "I think not," he said. Druga lay at the foot of the tree like a broken doll, his neck twisted at an impossible angle. "Death got to him first!"

30

ALL AFTERNOON the scream of chain saws echoed through the forest. Birds took flight, deer scattered, and small mammals burrowed deeper into their holes. The Elves kept watch, peering from behind great trunks of aspen, birch, oak, and pine. With their hands pressed against their ears, and their noses burning from the stench of gasoline, they saw the Humans perform their ghastly work. The mighty trees fell, and the machine lumbered in to scoop up the trunks. The Elves watched the destruction with a mix of horror and awe. Trees died; that was nature's way. In the natural course of things, it was no reason to mourn. Their carcasses littered the forest floor, providing food and shelter for many living creatures. And for each tree that fell from age or disease, there were a thousand seedlings ready to take its place. Some trees, however, were more important than others. The Cord was connected to every one, sometimes with delicate capillaries no bigger than a thread, and some with interwoven veins a hundred heads tall. The Cord was the circulatory system of the world. Its scope was so immense that it could withstand a certain degree of abuse from the unwitting Humans. But the Elves knew that if the five ancient oaks were cut, it would be a disaster for Alfheim. It was unthinkable, and could never be allowed to happen.

Against a wall of green the arm of the machine moved hypnotically. It stood as tall as the largest trees, moving back and forth, snakelike, in the clearing. Some of the Elves stood transfixed. Others ran back to report to their new Mage the horror they had witnessed.

"We could stop the Humans right now," Jardaine pleaded.

The monk sat with Tuava-Li in the Mage's quarters. "I know there are spells that can stop a beating heart, spells that bring sickness and death. Spells that would bring down lightning on the Humans' houses and burn them alive. Why won't you listen to me?"

"I'm listening, Jardaine," Tuava-Li replied. "But I don't like what I'm hearing. You might find spells like that in the library of some other Mage, but not this one. From the way you speak, you'd feel more at home in Helfratheim than you do here. What became of your monk's vows? What happened to your heart of compassion, your mind of wisdom, your spirit of peace, your—"

"Everything is changing, Tuava-Li," interrupted Jardaine.

"And I'm just changing along with it. I'm moving in the flow of life, but you're standing still. 'Tis you who should be reconsidering your vows, not me. The Humans' machines are getting closer to us every minute! What are you going to do to stop them?"

Tuava-Li was tired of hearing about how she had to do something. She was tired and scared, because the fear that the Elves felt was nearly tangible. She could feel their fear in her bones, their panic in her heart, and it made it difficult for her to think. "We know how to disable the Humans' machines with chants and simple incantations. We did it before, we can do it again. We can do it again and again and again, if need be. Humans are short-lived, and easily distracted. Eventually they'll give up, and go away. We'll have peace again. This won't last forever."

Jardaine's eyes burned like pits of fire. "But maybe they'll come with more of their machines and cut down the entire forest! Would you listen to me, then? It's got to stop, Tuava-Li. You're afraid to make a decision; you're scared to be our leader. You're afraid that you'll fail. Maybe 'tis time you—"

"It isn't easy to make decisions when so much rides on the outcome," Tuava-Li said, Blood pumping in her cheeks. "But tonight we'll go to that infernal machine and do just what we did before. All of us."

The night was chill and moonless. The Elves filed into the clearing as the midnight hour began. They joined hands and encircled the backhoe, a towering steel skeleton on a bed of dried mud. Their fingertips tingled as their leader began the invocation. "I, Tuava-Li, Mage of Alfheim, Mistress of the portents of Good, which are as the trunk and branches of my Soul, have turned toward thee. How I have established thee! How my grateful tears have nourished thy roots. How highly I have sung thy praises! In the name of the mulberry, the beech, and the tulip, in the name of the locust, ash, and witch hazel, in the name of the hemlock, larch, and box elder, in the name of the pine, the maple, and the oak, may you heed my cry! In the name of the eyes, the nose, the ears, the heart, the tongue, and body, may you deal graciously with me.

"Great spirits of heaven and earth we beseech thee,
All praises be sung in thy name,
May you stand in our midst with the strength of the sun,
In a glittering halo of flame.
We bow to your wisdom, and pray you may grant
The fulfillment of our sole desire,
And yield command of the transmuting flame,
Your unquenchable cauldron of fire.
May you grant us one orb of devouring heat,
An inferno whose radiance you feed,
And quicken the white-hot combustion inside,
Like the life force that stirs in a seed.
May this spark be exalted in pure incandescence,
May you grant us one power this night,

May you lift up the veil of your luminous world

In one searing pinpoint of light."

The invocation complete, the Elves began their slow, steady chant. *"Bring down, bring down, one coal from your furnace,"* they intoned. *"Bring down, bring down, one coal from your furnace."*

Five minutes passed. Ten minutes. The Elves repeated the chant, over and over, and waited for the white-hot ball of fire to appear, hovering in the air like it had done when last the Elves disabled the Humans' machines. A half hour passed, and doubt was beginning to weaken their resolve. Tuava-Li stood in the circle and felt their failure of nerve. She felt their fear, and the slightest touch of anger spreading through the group, growing larger, denser, looking for a target, and finding it in Tuava-Li herself. Perhaps it would have been better to wait for a clear night, with the moon and the stars shining down on them. Perhaps it would have been better if the group had not taken Jardaine's potions. Perhaps they were weakened, not strengthened, by the thin, bitter liquids meant to protect them from human contagion and exposure to metal. *Perhaps,* Tuava-Li thought, *I said something wrong, perhaps I left something out of the invocation. Perhaps this is another sign that I'm not meant to be the Mage of Alfheim.*

With her eyes closed, Tuava-Li felt the doubt and negativity rushing at her, tearing at her, clinging, pulling her down. She knew she had to be strong, and let the assault of weakness and fear wash past her. She had to find the fire in her own core. And suddenly it was there. The Elves opened their eyes and saw it hovering, a blinding spot of light in the sky, smoking, crackling with energy, rolling slowly in place, waiting. Waiting for the Elves to send it where they willed.

And though Tuava-Li did not know it, this was the moment when the real battle of wills began. *Close this window, quench this fire.* Jardaine and her followers began their own silent, unspoken chant. For days they had planned for this moment, when the humiliation of Tuava-Li would occur, when they would spoil her plans to destroy the Human machine and make her appear foolish and incompetent.

Close this window, quench this fire,
Unyoke its power from desire
To place such might in Elfin hands,
And yield not to their demands.

Jardaine focused all her strength to hold the ball of fire in place. Her followers, too, worked to keep the fiery orb from following the will of Tuava-Li, from moving into the mechanical heart of the machine. The blinding sphere sputtered. Orange sparks fell to the ground. The light contracted, condensed, dimmed. Then it flared up again, brighter than before, smoking, snapping, whirring in place. It moved slowly, deliberately, toward the cab of the backhoe, to the metal hood over the engine. The determination of the Elves held the ball of light and guided its movement. *Close this window, quench this fire . . .*

Jardaine chanted in silent fury. Rivulets of sweat ran

down her forehead and she drew in the forces of her fellow traitors to stop the movement of the orb. It hovered over the cab, flared and flickered once again, and then with a loud popping sound, vanished. Jardaine groaned and fell to the ground in a dead faint. The Elves pulled their hands apart and the circle came undone. Some rushed to Jardaine's side, others fled to the forest and clung, crying, to the trunks of trees. As the crowd dispersed Tuava-Li stood by herself. Grim determination hardened her face. Then she strode to the cab of the backhoe, climbed inside, and began to pull, tug, push, and bang on whatever protruding pieces of metal or plastic looked like they might have some mechanical function. Suddenly the hood on the backhoe popped up. Tuava-Li swung out of the cab, climbed the side of the machine and flung the hood wide. "Don't, Tuava-Li!" someone shouted. "The metal!"

Tuava-Li had refused to take Jardaine's medicine. She was completely unprotected. Holding the hood high with one hand, she reached into the pit of wires, tubes, black cylinders bolted to steel blocks, and all the other organs of mechanical life, and grabbed at anything that would yield. Tuava-Li's fingers blistered as she tugged on a coil of wire. Blind to the pain she pulled and pulled, realizing she would need both hands to make any headway. She let go of the hood and it came down hard on her back, tearing her robe. With a strength Tuava-Li never knew she had, she yanked on the wires until they came undone. Then she fumbled in the darkness. Her hands moved over the surface of the engine, probing, pulling, clutching, digging at everything that would move, while her skin was corroded, scalded, and charred, until her mind was as condensed with pain as the scorching fireball had been with unearthly power. When the Elves finally pulled her from beneath the hood it was as if all there had ever been of Tuava-Li was concentrated in one long, terrible scream.

31

THE FOLLOWING MORNING Charlie McCormack loped across the construction site to the trees at the end of the clearing. With its metal arm gleaming in the sun, the backhoe looked like a steel skeleton. Charlie stared in disbelief. "What the—"

The hood over the engine was ajar. Scratches and streaks of color marred the shiny metal. It had been a crude job, this time, nothing subtle. Frayed and torn wires stuck out everywhere. Hoses had been yanked from their clamps, the rubber and plastic torn apart. Charlie shook his head and swore. *This time it's vandalism,* he thought. *Who would do this to us?*

Humming a little tune, Becky peered into the refrigerator. The new shelves sparkled, but there wasn't much on them that looked appetizing. Eggs. Mustard. Pickles. Some white cheese in a drawer, and apples in the crisper. Cold hot dogs. Mystery meat. An opened jar of cream of carrots. "Mom?" she called. "Mom, there's nothing to eat!"

"Get yourself some cereal," Jill answered from the basement stairs.

"I ate cereal all week. Can't we go to the store?"

Jill came into the kitchen with a laundry basket and plopped it on the floor. She pulled an envelope of coupons from a drawer, then tossed it onto the table. "Here, Becky, you can help. Find the coupons that haven't expired yet, and make a pile."

Just then Matt and Tom came into the kitchen. Tom had been Matt's nearly constant companion over the last few days, showing up every morning, and staying until suppertime. "Hi, Matt," Jill said, looking around. "Oh, hi, Tom! Do you guys want to give me a hand at the grocery store?"

"Can we get pretzels?" Matt asked.

"Can we get slushies?" Becky chimed in.

"Oh, I suppose so," Jill sighed.

"Then let's go!" said Matt, grinning at his friend. "I'm hungry."

At that moment the screen door slammed, and Matt's dad stalked into the house. "Hi, honey," said Jill, but Charlie stormed past her, mumbling to himself, and began rooting through a stack of papers near the telephone. "Charlie," Jill asked, "what's wrong?"

"You don't want to know," he sighed. "Have you seen the contract for the backhoe? I thought I left the file here."

"Oh, Charlie, don't tell me there's something wrong with the new backhoe!"

"Wrong? What else could go wrong?" he said. "Now I have to call them and say that somebody got into the engine last night and tore everything apart. Nobody's going to trust me to rent a tricycle around here."

"But that's crazy, Charlie," Jill said. "Do you really have to call the company? You're always working on your truck. Maybe you could try to fix it yourself this time!"

"I sure don't have time to wait for somebody else to do it," Charlie sighed. "Maybe I'll give it a try. There's an automotive place out by the mall; I could see if they have the parts."

"I don't get it," Jill said, with a frown. "What kind of person would intentionally damage somebody else's things?"

"I don't know, you tell me," Charlie said, turning toward Matt and his friend. "What about you, Tom—are there any troublemakers around here? You have any idea of what kind of idiot would do something like this?"

Tom shrugged. Matt looked at his friend, then at his father. "No idea, Dad!"

The Elves clustered behind a tree trunk, waiting for the Humans to leave. Prince Macta held a deerskin leash, tethered to Anna McCormack's arm. Covering the girl's head was a kind of crystal helmet. Streams of water trickled down her face, then collected in hollow tubes around the neck of the helmet. From there the water was pumped back to the top of her head, to be released again in a perpetual flow. Rivulets trickled from the loose seal around Anna's neck and soaked the collar of her shirt. But the water seemed to calm her, and prevented her from fading away. The pickup truck pulled out of the driveway first, followed by the minivan. "We're in luck," said Nebiros. "I think they're all leaving."

"Of course they're leaving, idiot!" Jardaine snapped. Her forehead was damp with sweat, and she was exhausted from trying to read the minds of the Humans in the house. She was just learning the trick, and the effort took a toll on her temperament. "We'll have the house to ourselves, and not have to bother with any magick to hide our presence. They'll all be gone for hours."

"'Tisss a good omen," hissed Sarette, lifting her head from Jardaine's robe. "The fatesss are on our ssside!"

"We make our own fate," Jardaine said.

Macta frowned as he watched Baltham and Nebiros dragging the burlap sacks toward the house. "I don't know why we needed to sacrifice so many of the jewels," he grumbled. "Surely just a few would have been enough to implicate the Human boy in the theft. Besides, my father's plans for the wedding day make this little scheme of yours irrelevant."

"Those were my plans, too," Jardaine snapped.

"And mine," hissed Sarette.

In irritation, Jardaine rubbed at the spittle on her collar. "Whatever your father does, Macta, whatever part he chooses to play in inciting war between the Humans and the Elves is his business," she said. "What we do here today is about Tuava-Li and me. And since you failed to kill the Mage, you owe me this. When Nebiros told me about the Human girl you found by the stream, I knew we could find a way to put her to use."

Macta scowled. "What? How did Nebiros find out about the Human? I've told no one outside of my own inner circle. Do you have Nebiros spying on me, or is there an informant within my ranks? We're on the same side, Jardaine. I came to Alfheim when you asked, didn't I? And I brought the jewels, just like you said. I've been completely honest with you."

"No one is completely honest," Jardaine snorted derisively. "And you didn't tell me about the Human girl, so don't go bragging about how honest and trustworthy you are. If there are spies in your household, it's no doing of mine. I send Nebiros to give you messages in Helfratheim, and he's an observant fellow. Not much gets past him."

"Well, don't blame me for failing to kill the Mage," Macta replied. "You have no idea how dangerous it is in the Human world. And you didn't see the condition the Mage was in! She's dead by now, I'd lay odds on it."

"You no longer have the resources to back up your wagers, Macta," Jardaine snapped. "This time you'll play by my rules. Once we hide the treasure in their dwelling, I'll go back home and rant and rave to Tuava-Li that I'm sure it was the Human who stole the Jewels of Alfheim. She'll reply that there's no way to prove it, since Elves can't go into a Human house without being invited. Then you'll show up in the Sacred Grove with Liqua, your new toy. I'll act all indignant, like I've never seen the creature before. I'll be angry, scream about contamination and so on and so on. You'll say that she's not dangerous anymore, after all those years in the stream, and we've got nothing to fear. Then, in a flash of inspiration, I'll come up with the brilliant idea to use Liqua to help us get into the Humans' house, and search for our stolen treasure. Tuava-Li will come along, reluctantly, no doubt. But when she sees the jewels for herself, she'll understand that the boy is to blame. You and I will insist that the Humans deserve to die for what they've done. We'll whip the Elves into a frenzy of hatred, but Tuava-Li, good, kind Tuava-Li, won't agree to do what must be done. Then they'll turn against her. And as for the jewels, Macta, once you're married you'll have them all to yourself. I allowed you to keep a few to do with as you please, so don't complain."

Macta sighed. "It's all very complicated. Too much depends on what Tuava-Li will do. Is this your plan, or Sarette's?"

The snake lifted her head from behind Jardaine's collar. "We're not ssso egotissstical as to need to claim ownersssship of a plan," she hissed. "We all benefit from sssuccesss."

"Tuava-Li is wearisome and predictable beyond measure," said Jardaine. "I know exactly what she will do."

Macta tugged the leash attached to Liqua's arm, to get her to follow. The girl was thin and pale, and her muscles were weak from disuse, but at more than four feet tall, she was easily twice the height of the Elfin Prince. Macta led her across the yard and up the steps of the front porch. Then he untied the strap from her wrist. "Liqua," he said, "I've got a little game for us to play. 'Tis called Find the Key."

Behind the crystal surface of Liqua's helmet, which had been fabricated for the occasion in King Valdis's laboratories, the girl's eyes came to life. "Now, there is a pretty, shiny key hidden here," Macta said. "I want you to look for it, and as you search, I'll tell you if you're getting warm or cold!"

Macta knew that the key was hidden under the welcome mat by the front door. Nebiros had seen one of the Humans put it there. "Ah, you're getting cold!" Macta said, as the girl stumbled past, banging her crystal helmet on the wall.

Anna turned. "You're getting warmer!" Macta exclaimed. "Warmer!"

For Anna, the past and the present ran together in a blur of feeling, each new moment a gateway to a memory of something long gone. Her mind conjured up a party, and she was just six years old. *I love games,* Ann thought, smiling as she stood on the porch. Then her expression turned to a frown. *The key, how am I going to find the key when I can't see the ground? The little man is angry with me. The woman with him, she's jealous, because the little man is my friend. But once I have the . . . the key, where is the key? Everyone's waiting for the key. It's hidden somewhere on the porch. The key. I hope, I hope, I hope I find it first. I want to win the prize, I . . .*

"You're getting very, very warm!" Macta said, excitedly. "You're getting hot!"

Why didn't I realize it before? Anna thought, her mind shifting ahead. Now she was twelve, sneaking in to her own house, late at night. *There's only one way in. The windows are all locked, the doors bolted. It's got to be under the mat. Mom and Dad won't ever know I went out after I was supposed to be in bed. They'll never—*

The key was in her hand. Then the key was in the lock, turning, and the door swung inward, and Anna stepped across the threshold. *This isn't my house; I've never seen this place before. Who lives here? What's going on? What's this, this thing on my head? Why is it so hard to see?*

Suddenly her memory delivered her to a swim meet, waiting for her friends. *It's my goggles, my new swim goggles. That must be why*

it's hard to see. I'll get used to it. The goggles will keep the water out of my eyes. I was the first one in. The water's so cold! I hate it, I hate being alone like this. Where are my friends? Why don't they come into the

water? I'm

shivering. It's so cold, so cold in here. And it's dark, too.

It's getting harder to see my hands.

"My dear girl," Macta soothed, "aren't you going to be polite? Aren't you going to ask us in?"

Anna looked at her new friends, down on the lawn. They

seemed so small, so far away. She nodded her head and a faint smile turned up the corners of her lips. It was so nice to have friends. Life without friends would be a terrible, lonely thing. *Yes,* Anna mouthed from inside her crystal helmet, and gestured with a pale hand. Jardaine was the first one up on the porch.

Tomtar had never tasted anything so wonderful in his life. "Giant salted pretzel with cheese," said Matt. "You like?"

The Shopco was too big to fathom. Light fixtures hung from steel ceiling beams, as high as the tallest trees in the forest. A sparrow swooped from rafter to rafter. The place was full of music, the chatter of shoppers, the rattle of hundreds of carts as they moved up and down the aisles. Tomtar could only shake his head. His mouth was full of something that was at once crunchy and soft, creamy, hot, and salty. The flavor was so intense that his vision swam, and goose bumps rose on his arms. "Haven't you ever eaten a cheese pretzel, Tom?" asked Becky.

Tom shook his head, his smile ecstatic. "Here, try my slushie," Matt said. "It's blueberry."

Tom loved blueberries. He took a breath and sucked hard on the straw protruding from the bubble-topped lid. Ice-cold slush coursed through the striped plastic tube.

"Not so fast," Matt warned.

The Troll first felt the sensation in his throat. It was tight, contracted, and he winced at a feeling that was like a thousand icy needles jabbing him in the neck. His head throbbed, exploding with pain. His ears burned all the way up to their pointed tips. In his belly, sharp, stabbing things seemed to be racing back and forth. Then, just as quickly as they'd come, the sensations drifted away. With a horrible grimace he pushed the drink over to Matt. "Brain freeze!" Becky laughed.

Matt tapped his friend on the arm. "Come on, let's catch up with my mom. Maybe we can find some free samples on the way!"

There was more food than Tomtar had ever seen, even at the biggest harvest banquet back home. Something called a salad bar. An entire aisle of baked goods, cakes, muffins, and cookies in every size and shape. Food in packages, frozen solid, hard as rocks. Food in metal tins, stacked up in pyramids nearly to the ceiling, food in plastic bags, food in cardboard boxes. Enough food to last an entire city of Trolls for years. And it was all for the taking!

Tomtar followed Matt and Becky down the aisles. Past the shelves of crackers, chips, soda, bread, and candy, looking for Mrs. McCormack. It seemed like it might take hours to find her. People ambled past, their carts piled high, loaded with impossible riches. At the end of an aisle, a woman stood behind a table with a little metal grill on it. Next to the grill was a tray laden with tiny brown sausages, each finger-sized nugget pierced with a yellow toothpick. She glanced up and smiled. "Free samples, try one!"

Matt sampled a sausage. Becky shook her head and made a face. "No meat for me! And Tom, those are sausages, you don't—"

Tomtar popped a sausage into his mouth and let the hot, spicy juice roll around on his tongue. "Tell your mom they're on sale!" the woman said.

Tomtar plucked another sausage from the tray and stuffed it into his mouth, and then another. He didn't even take time to chew before he gulped the meat down. The woman behind the table furrowed her brow. "One per customer," she warned. "Don't be greedy!"

Tomtar shook his head, happy tears forming in his eyes.

Becky frowned. "Tom, I thought you were a vegetarian!"

"Aye," he replied, still running his tongue over his teeth. "What's that, again?"

"You don't eat meat?"

"Nooo, I don't eat that. Meat's not *food*. These sausages aren't made of meat, are they?"

"'Fraid so, Tom," said Matt, shaking his head. "You're now an official carnivore. Come on, I'll bet there's some more free samples over in the cheese department. You can eat your fill there."

"Wait for me!" cried Becky, dancing down the aisle behind them.

Inside the McCormacks' house, the Elves were chewing the pieces of bark that Jardaine had promised would prevent contamination and sickness from exposure to metal. Nebiros hung back, his eyes wide, as the others followed Liqua from room to room. "I'll help you find a place to hide the presents, my dear," said Macta, eyeing the pouches of jewels in the girl's hands. Jardaine and Baltham peered behind draperies, under couches, inside cupboards, looking for a suitable hiding place. Baltham shook his head in disgust. He chewed the bark chip in his mouth with fury as nausea crept into his stomach. "How can they live like this?" he muttered, brown saliva dribbling down his chin. "Everything is dead. There's no air in here."

"Stop your bickering and look at what I just found!" shouted Macta. He was standing on his tiptoes and peering into a cabinet built into the wall. "Metal," uttered Jardaine, coming around the corner. "Sticks made of metal. Does that hold some special fascination for you, Macta?"

"They're weapons, you empty-headed bumpkin. My father's Experimentalists have developed technology like this, based on something the Human dropped in the woods when Asra was nearly married to Udos. Perhaps one day you'll have the pleasure to experience the Dragon Thunderbus in action. What do you think, Baltham, can we break into this cabinet and liberate one more of these weapons without destroying the glass? I wouldn't want to leave a telltale mess behind us."

"Look here, you overprivileged excuse for a Prince," Jardaine snapped. "Don't you think the Humans would know if you stole one of their weapons? We've come here to plant evidence of the Humans' thieving ways, not to steal anything ourselves."

Sarette peered from the corner of the monk's cowl. "When

the battle'sss begun, you can come back here and sssteal to your heart's content. 'Til then, let's ssstick to the plan."

Liqua turned a corner. Scraping her shoulder on the door frame, she staggered to the side. Water gushed from the bottom of the helmet. The pouches of jewels slipped from her twiglike fingers, and hit the floor. "Careful!" shrieked Macta. He tugged on the burlap sacks that lay at Liqua's feet, but had to struggle to lift them.

Nebiros giggled from the other side of the room. Macta shot him a murderous glance, then turned to smile at the ghostly, ragged girl. "Here, my sweet one," he said, "pick up the presents, won't you? We still have to find a place to hide them. 'Twill be so much fun to come back later and watch our friends search for them!"

The door, she thought, *behind the door.* First the kitchen, then the basement. The stairs were very steep, and she negotiated her descent with care. Water trickled down her arms and dripped from her wrists.

I need a place to hide. A place to get away. Hide.

Past the furnace, past the workbench, where Daddy fills the shells he uses for his guns. Past the fireplace, and the shelf where Momma keeps her preserves. Past the old couch. There, the trunk is down there, the trunk

with the dolls in it, the ones I don't play with anymore. I'm saving them for my girls, when I grow up. I'll hide the little bags in the trunk.

Even though the house she was imagining had been abandoned for years, and her mother and father were both dead, the trunk in her memory was, in reality, just a few feet away. Liqua reached the bottom of the stairs. Macta, Jardaine, and Nebiros followed, backing down the steps one at a time. Baltham clung to the leg of the kitchen table. When he realized what he was touching, he opened his eyes wide in horror. "Metal!" he spat, and examined the palm of his hand. Was that red mark a burn? The chunk of bark in his mouth had been reduced to a rubbery pulp. He slumped to the floor as his stomach churned, burped, and a rank bubble burst on his lips. "Jardaine," he cried, "the metal is making me sick; I need some more of the bark!"

But Jardaine was already in the basement, watching Liqua as she moved toward a black trunk. "Yes!" Macta said, with a gleam in his eye. "Yes, my dear, I believe you've found the *perfect* hiding place!"

Anna lifted the lid of the trunk, the same one she had had as a girl. The dolls she had loved were moldering inside, untouched for more than thirty years. Matt's mom had discovered the trunk among her mother-in-law's things when the old woman went into a nursing home. Though her daughter had disappeared so long ago, the poor old woman never had the heart to get rid of her child's playthings. Jill brought the trunk back to her own house, thinking that Becky might enjoy looking at the dolls when she was a little older and could appreciate the painted heads and hands, the old-fashioned clothing.

My dolls, Anna thought, *here they are. Momma saved them for me.* She dropped the bags of jewels at the bottom of the trunk. Then, with incredible tenderness, she took an apple-cheeked doll in a satin dress and cradled it in her arms. *My doll,* she thought. She held it against her breast, just beneath the tubes that wrapped around the base of her water-filled helmet. Her tears merged with the recycled liquid that trickled in her eyes, flowed into her ears, and bubbled at the corners of her mouth.

"I don't feel good," moaned Baltham, upstairs. "I've got to get outside, I—"

And then he threw up. "We don't have time to clean that mess," Jardaine groaned, when they led Liqua back up the stairs into the kitchen.

"But the Humans will be suspicious if they see that on their floor," Macta said. "Baltham, I'm getting sick of your getting sick everywhere we go. Take off your jacket and wipe up that disgusting puddle."

"But—" Baltham started to complain, then saw the look on Macta's face and thought better of it. Anna wandered into the hallway, then the living room. It felt so strange, being inside a house after all this time. She drifted past the fireplace. She stepped closer to the mantel, peering at the framed family photographs arranged there. *The beach,* she thought, as something familiar caught her eye.

We were at the beach. Daddy and Mommy and Charlie and me, a fisherman took the picture for us, on the dock, with Daddy's new camera. The wind blew my hair into my face, I was squinting into the sun. Daddy had his arm over my shoulder, and my sunburn hurt.

Daddy.

She picked up the photograph and tucked it under her arm, next to the doll.

There was another family photo. Unlike the other picture, this one was just a few years old. And though the girl thought it was a picture of her daddy, it was really her brother, Charlie, all grown up, and with a family of his own. Matt and Becky were just little. Emily hadn't even been born yet.

Daddy.

After thirty years, Charlie looked an awful lot like his father. The eyes, the nose, the hair, the crooked smile, the similarities would have been hard to miss, even through the crystal helmet and the water running over her sorrowful eyes.

Daddy, she thought.

She picked up this photograph, too. And when the little band of Elves slipped out the front door, and Macta attached the deerskin strap to her wrist, the girl stumbled into the woods with the doll under her arm and the pictures pressed tightly, desperately, against her breast.

"I was beginning to wonder where you were," said Jill.

She had one of the shopping carts with the red plastic car attached to the front so that Emily could sit in the seat and play with the steering wheel. The cart was brimming over with boxes, jars, cans, and plastic bags full of food. "I got most of the shopping done while you were in the snack bar," Jill frowned, looking over her list. "But I forgot the sandwich bags. Would you go and get them? I think they're a couple of aisles over, that way."

"I'm tired, Mommy," Becky whined. "Can I stay with you?"

"Fine," Jill said. "Matt, you and Tom can get them. Oh, we could use another loaf of bread. Big slices, for sandwiches. You remember what the package looks like?"

"I know what bread looks like," said Matt, rolling his eyes.

"Then you can catch up with us at the checkout line."

As the boys rounded the corner, Matt's heart leapt into his throat. The illusion that made Tom look like a human being was quickly fading away. The upper half of his body was translucent. When Matt glanced down, the Troll was plainly visible, pointy ears and all, barreling along next to him. "Tomtar!" he hissed. "That stuff, that stuff you've been chewing; it's wearing off. Look at yourself, you're little again! You've got to take some more!"

Tomtar reached around for the pocket of his jacket, where he kept a handful of the pieces of bark he needed. But the jacket was gone. He stood in his shirtsleeves and shrugged, staring wide-eyed at Matt. "'Tis *gone*! I think I took it off in the snack bar, when we were eatin'."

"Well, you'd better hope it's still there," Matt said. The aisle was clear; no one was approaching from the other end. "Come on, this way!"

At the corner of the next aisle, Matt and Tomtar passed an unattended cart. There was food in it, but the owner had gone around to the next aisle for something, and left her cart behind. Matt looked both ways. Then he grabbed Tomtar by the shoulders and hoisted his friend into the cart. "I'm going to hide you in here," he whispered, and Tomtar slid beneath a sack of dog food.

Matt clutched the handle of the cart and skidded around the corner, heading for the snack bar. "Hey, stop!" he heard a voice cry out. "That's my cart! Stop!"

From a distance Matt thought he could see Tomtar's jacket still hanging on the back of the chair where he had left it. "Hold on," he said to Tomtar, "we've got to make this fast!"

Tomtar giggled and grabbed the bars of the cart. The illusion spell was completely gone, the nausea spell was nearly gone, too. The metal felt hot to touch, but not yet capable of doing damage to his hands. He grinned, then bit into the sack of dog food that lay on top of him. Moist kibbles spilled across his face. The aroma was intoxicating. Tomtar couldn't remember the last time he'd had so much fun.

32

THE OWL COULD BARELY lift her head to look up. A hawk circled somewhere above; she could hear its cries. As far as she could tell she was no longer being hunted by Macta Dockalfar and his gang of thugs. She hopped along the forest floor, looking for a safe place to hide. Part of her mind was given to the problem of how the Prince had found her, and why he wanted her killed. She was certain she had heard someone speak Jardaine's name in the midst of the melee. An alliance between Macta and Jardaine? For what purpose? Greed? Power? Revenge? Such sad motives, such shallow, foolish desires.

The Mage blamed herself for Jardaine's betrayal. She should have known when she brought Tuava-Li into the community and made her Apprentice that something like this might happen. How could she have understood so little of Elfin nature? How could she have thought that all the baser instincts could be erased, just by choosing a life dedicated to spirit? It had been naïve of her to think that all of this could have unfolded any other way. She had failed to pay attention. She had failed Alfheim. It was a costly error, and she only hoped that the mistake wouldn't have to be paid for in Blood.

The Mage held her injured wing close to her body. She was hopping along the forest floor, keeping a wary eye open for predators, when she saw the Cord. It was partly hidden by decaying leaves, but by the gnarled roots of an ash tree, the Cord was completely exposed. Even a slight breeze made the surface of the milky-white tube flutter. The Mage's heart went out to the fragile, sickly thing. The sight of it made her long for her home. As she got closer to the Cord, she could see that there was a place where the surface was shredded and torn, and gusts of warm air blew from the opening. She reached out to touch it.

The Mage gasped as she was propelled into a vision, and the universe opened before her. She suddenly knew that everything in her long life had been leading to this moment. The Cord was gone; the sun-dappled woodland was gone; the Mage herself was gone. Now she was nothing but pure awareness, with no eyes to see, no fingers to touch, and yet she was aware of it all, from the farthest reaches of the galaxy down to the smallest atom. The universe was enfolded in absolute silence, and yet the heavens rang with a billion voices singing together in celestial harmony. Time was compressed, speeding up, birth and death followed by birth and death, and there was the Cord, holding the world

in its interwoven fingers, spreading across the surface of the planet, an impossibly thin membrane of life stretched over a ball of rock. There were the trees, the holy Adri, reaching out from the north and south magnetic poles. Impossibly tall, their branches stretched into the void of space, their trunks like ramrods piercing the globe with pure white energy, and meeting at the center. There the Seed, the heart of all living things, radiated its power. And the energy of the Seed, the Mage could see, was nearly spent. The Adri were saving their energy now, conserving, redirecting what remained toward one single hope. One single fruit growing on one slim branch revealed that a new Seed was beginning to form. As the veins and arteries of the Cord were cut, neglected, abused, and their strength waned, and the Seed at the center of the earth cooled and drew inward like a dying star, the promise of a new Seed was the only chance for survival.

The vision ended. The Mage's awareness, strung like bright lights along endless filaments of spirit, returned to her body. She regained the use of her eyes, now more Elfin than owl, and she felt her Elfin fingertips on the sticky white surface of the failing Cord. It was collapsing in soft folds, its fibrous body coming apart like a dandelion blown in the wind. But before her vision of the Holy Adri and the Seed shrank into memory, the Mage focused her energy and broadcast what she had seen to the mind of Tuava-Li.

On a downy bed she lay. The monks had woven a protective spell around her. White and egglike, it hovered around Tuava-Li, glistening, translucent, holding within its seamless shell the tender heart of healing. The monks had found the spell on a parchment in the Mage's study. Spells and incantations were special tools reserved for special occasions, and the monks who performed their miracle on Tuava-Li's behalf had concluded that this was one such occasion. Now Tuava-Li would stay within the magical egg until she was healed. Her body was wrapped in milk-white leaves, their liquid essence beaded up like tears along the length of her. She slept under the watchful eye of Parslaine. The monk spread ointment on Tuava-Li's damaged skin and changed the leaf dressing at regular intervals. Elves from the community took turns praying through the long hours of the moon and sun, kneeling at the foot of the great oak tree.

Suddenly, Tuava-Li cried out, her body convulsing like a bolt of lightning had struck her. Her chin flew back. Her hands contracted into fists so tight that the salve squeezed out from her bandages. "Get Jardaine, quickly!" Parslaine shouted to the Elf keeping watch at the rectory door.

The vision the Mage had witnessed now flooded Tuava-Li's own consciousness. Its power, though, overshadowed its source; Tuava-Li did not sense the presence of her mentor. The pictures in her mind seemed instead to be a direct revelation from the Gods, blinding in their intensity. She felt the emergency in the vision; she saw the Cord, she saw the world and the Adri trees and the tiny, fragile fruit, and she, too, understood what was happening. She felt it in her bones. She saw that it was within the power of the Elves to save their world and rebuild the wall that had fallen between them and the Humans. Tuava-Li lifted one eyelid. The light was painful. She opened her mouth to speak, but her tongue felt heavy and dry as ashes. She rose up on one elbow, but collapsed back onto her bed. It was all still too much, too soon. The burns on her hands, arms, legs, and face were such that even with the use of magick, her recovery would be slow.

But Tuava-Li had seen the look on the faces of the Elves of Alfheim. There in the field with the Human's infernal machine, when she was so badly burned, she saw the look in their eyes as they carried her back to Alfheim. They knew what Tuava-Li had sacrificed on their behalf, and she knew they loved her for it. She knew that whatever else might happen, she now had their trust, their devotion, and their loyalty. And these things were what would give her the strength to be their Mage.

Tuava-Li blinked. Smiling faces swam around the edges of her sight. There was a warmth inside her, a comfort that came with a new feeling—confidence. Tuava-Li knew that she would be a good Mage. Perhaps Jardaine had been right all along; perhaps Kalevala Van Frier was gone forever. Perhaps it was time to accept the truth of it. The vision that had just burned through her Soul was unlike the glimpses she had seen of the Mage in her owl form. Tuava-Li had been so certain that the Mage was alive and trying to communicate with her from afar.

Perhaps that was all just wishful thinking, daydreams, illusions born of her own insecurity. *When I'm better,* she thought, drifting away, *I'll step up to my responsibility. If this is my fate, I'll tell the Synod, I'll tell Macta Dockalfar, I'll tell the world that I am the Mage of Alfheim. I'll show the Elves that I'm ready to lead them and that their faith in me will be rewarded. The vision I just saw was an omen. A good omen. The Gods must surely be looking upon me with favor.*

Tuava-Li was overcome with fatigue. She let go of the tension in her body and surrendered to the cloud-soft bedding, where sleep was waiting to embrace her once again.

Nebiros raced after Jardaine as she hurried toward the rectory tree. "Maybe she's died," he puffed.

Jardaine snorted. "'Twould be too much to hope for."

"We stopped the orb of fire, maybe we could . . . maybe we could *help things along.* Her burns must be quite painful. You could say we'd only be putting her out of her misery."

"Nay, better to keep her alive and humiliate her," Jardaine reasoned.

"Yesss," hissed Sarette, from inside the comfort of Jardaine's warm and cozy robe. "Better to ruin her rosy reputation, find waysss to make them all hate her. Better a live failure than a dead hero, yessss?"

Nebiros sighed. "I suppose you're right. Somehow, Sarette, you always manage to take the pleasure out of everything."

33

A GAUNT SLIVER OF MOON hung in the sky as gatekeepers welcomed the Synod members to the meeting hall of Ljosalfar. By gondola they came, from many far points of the Faerie realm, for their monthly gathering. Elves, Pixies, Brownies, Gremlins, and Dwarves arrived, dressed in their finest attire. Slajjar the Laureate led the invocation in the Great Hall. He cleared his throat, then recited the poem he had written in honor of the moon.

"Beneath a dome of night we lie
And wonder at the moonlit sky,
Pierced through and through that we might see
The light of Heaven shining.
Through you, O lunar aperture,
Serenely gleaming, bright and pure,
The Gods look down and smile upon

The lands of their designing.

Your nightly progress we behold,

And watch your cycle there unfold,

With your celestial spinning wheel

Our dreams you gently weave.

And here until the end of days

We lift up our voices in praise,

While humbly, basking in your light,

Your blessings we receive."

When the Laureate returned to his seat and the applause died down, the Synod members opened the folios containing the evening agenda. No one, however, needed to read what was written there; they all knew they had come to discuss the Cord. Several members had been late to the meeting due to Cord damage, and several others had not arrived at all. The meeting began. First there were suggestions for Cord repair and maintenance, including building reinforcements, the application of magickal spells, organized prayer to the Gods, and various herbal treatments to the surface of the Cord itself. Then resolutions for funding were proposed to continue the study of the health and well-being of the Cord. Other speakers addressed the border problems that more and more communities had been experiencing. Nearly everywhere Humans and predatory animals were freely wandering into formerly secure Faerie territory. The tension in the room rose as the Synod members argued. The only thing everyone could agree on was that there were many difficult problems that ought to be addressed and everyone should work together to overcome them as soon as possible.

Several Mages were present at the meeting to discuss the spiritual ramifications of the damage to the Cord, and the ways in which fear and uncertainty were affecting the realms. It was suggested that the rise of a Mage called Brahja-Chi, leader of the Storehoj Clan, was directly tied to the increase of anxiety felt by Faerie Folk. This Brahja-Chi was gaining converts from spiritual communities everywhere, and her peculiar brand of rigid, authoritarian leadership, as well as her allegience to a mysterious text known as the Canon, was frightening to some. One speaker suggested that the Synod attempt to limit the number of disciples of Brahja-Chi, but none could agree on a method to accomplish this goal. As the evening proceeded, the frustration of the Synod members grew palpable. Faerie Folk squirmed and fidgeted in their seats, and when members spoke, the tension in their voices served only to raise the level of discomfort.

The final issue on the evening's agenda was introduced by Valdis, King of Helfratheim. In his black-and-yellow armor, Valdis looked formidable as he strode to the platform. Most Synod members were afraid of him and the power he commanded. "Gentle Faeries," he began, "I come before you tonight to propose a solution to one of the dilemmas that has long plagued us. My travels as chief executive officer of Helfratheim Security Operations have shown me the importance of well-equipped armies to the safety of our homeland. Our security can only be assured if we're armed with weapons of peace. As you know, the House of Dockalfar specializes in such weapons. For years we've offered our traditional line of competitive battle games, swords, knives and daggers, cudgels, longbows, axes, maces, and so much more. But never let it be said that we ride on the success of our past glories. Just this year we were pleased to introduce an exciting new innovation we call the Dragon Thunderbus. Our advising snakes and other morphologically adapted animals have proven to be quite popular! We work around the clock to manufacture the best articles of protection and peace of mind. Our next innovations will take the Faerie world by storm! At this very moment my Experimentalists are putting the finishing touches on our new, sorcery-enhanced biological weaponry. As enticing as that sounds, I dare not say more."

King Valdis paused, and looked around the chamber. "My friends, I want to assure you that the chief guarantee of the safety of our homeland is a strong military force, armed with the appropriate weaponry. But this is not the only key to our protection . . . no. The safety of our people depends on all of us working *together.* By this I mean to say that we need to be prepared to put aside many of our traditional values and belief systems that have kept us apart, and think toward the future, building new strength through cooperation."

Tacita, the Secretary of the Synod, rose to her feet. "King Valdis," she said, "the hour is late. If your proposal is to arrange for the sale of your latest weaponry to members of the Synod, perhaps there is a better time for—"

"I have nothing of the kind in mind," the King said, interrupting. "What I wish to talk about is marriage. Not for myself, mind you; I've already had a number of wives, and my marrying days are behind me! I have come here tonight to seek the Synod's blessing for the marriage between my son, Prince Macta, and Princess Asra of Alfheim."

Hushed murmurs spread across the room. The King waited for the announcement to sink in: Members of Northern and Southern clans, embodying the opposite principles of light and dark, had not been joined in marriage in thousands of years. "I don't need to remind you why such a union," Valdis concluded, "would be highly beneficial to us all. There is strength in unity, and the more our Clans are connected by bonds of marriage, the stronger the foundation we have to protect us from our enemies. We will have a deeper sense of purpose, of a common goal, unobstructed by petty squabbles. Our interdependence will give us reserves we do not have on our own."

King Thorgier leapt up, his face burning. But, as usual, he found himself at a loss for words. "I—you—I—w-w-well—"

Queen Shorya stood up next to her husband, clutching his hand. "I am disappointed," she said, "that King Valdis has seen fit to bring this matter before the Synod without first discussing it with us privately. In any event, 'tis all well and good for us to speak of unions and bonds. For countless millennia, Faeries have been bound by our dependence upon the Cord. We're bound by our loyalty to the Gods and to the sanctity of the forest homeland we all share. However, there is one bond I will never allow to be formed. We've known Prince Macta since he was a youth. He is shallow, spoiled, and greedy. He is a bully, like his father. And I suspect he is dangerous, also like his father. Northern and Southern Clans do not mix. We all know that. We must confront our common enemies, while understanding and honoring our differences. Macta will never marry my daughter."

King Valdis nodded. "As I'm sure you know, Shorya, most young men of means would not find your daughter to be a suitable mate. Superstitious though they may be, many would interpret your daughter's bad luck at marriage as a curse. My son happens to be *in love* with Asra, and doesn't believe that marrying her would put him in danger. By all rights you should be overjoyed to accept my offer. I know for a fact that a large contingent of Elves is at this moment preparing Alfheim for your return. Therefore I propose to the Synod that this wedding take place in Alfheim seven nights from today. Let this announcement be our invitation to you all to the wedding of Prince Macta and Princess Asra. As the Alfheim Clan makes its triumphant return home, we'll join forces to ensure that the borders of our world are no longer overrun by the Human scum."

The eyes of the Synod members darted around, seeking reinforcement or denouncement of the King's scheme. A moment later someone stood up and began to applaud. Others joined in, and soon the entire hall was on its feet, applauding and shouting, "Here, here!"

"But this is ludicrous!" cried Queen Shorya, trying to be heard over the ruckus.

"My lady, perhaps you should not be so impulsive in your rejection of Valdis's proposal," King Adon of Ljosalfar suggested. "'Tis unconventional, I'd be the first to admit, but joining the Northern and Southern Elves in marriage would be an act of courage, a leap of faith! Are we not ready to make such a move?"

There was a rumble of assent from the crowd, and even Secretary Tacita gave a nod. "'Tis customary for the Synod to seek balance among the realms, and not to interfere in local disputes, or to force unpopular or unwanted changes. We'll take a vote on the proposal so that the will of all is known; but the final decision is up to you and your husband, Queen Shorya, and perhaps your daughter as well. Consider that if this wedding takes place with your blessing, it may well inspire others to undertake such unions, binding the realms in a web of relationship we've never seen before. Let the Elfin world be as one, and we will be united in strength. Your own courage and cooperation could well be the first step on the road to our salvation."

Tacita turned toward the Synod members. "If I may begin. When your name is called, please let your will be known with an *aye* or a *nay*."

"What?" Princess Asra exploded, when her parents arrived home and shared with her what had transpired at the Synod gathering. "And how did you respond, pray tell, when Valdis insisted that I marry his cretinous son?"

"Well, we d-d-didn't say for sure," answered her father. "But he did make a number of good p-p-points."

Queen Shorya went to take Asra in her arms and comfort her, but the Princess pulled away in disgust. "Well, I can tell you that it isn't going to happen," Asra hissed. "*You're* my parents, you're supposed to look out for me!"

"We *are* looking out for you," said Queen Shorya, trying to be the voice of reason. "Not all marriages begin with love. A Princess must always consider duty before her personal feelings, 'tis a reality that comes with the territory. Believe me, I'm no fan of Macta Dockalfar, and if you decide not to marry him, your father and I will support you completely. On the other hand, should you refuse outright, it will look very bad for us in the Synod."

"Well," Asra fumed, "this *is* the end of it. How could you stand up for that arrogant fool, for his father, for something that you know is wrong? How could you do this to me?"

"But, my sweet, your m-m-mother and I—"

Princess Asra stormed out of the room and disappeared down a long corridor. King Thorgier and Queen Shorya jumped when they heard a distant door slam. "She'll c-c-come 'round," the King said, doubtfully.

"Perhaps," the Queen sighed. "I'm just not sure *I* will."

34

A TINY SPOT OF BRASS appeared in the northern sky, growing larger as it came closer to the town. But this craft, unlike all the others the Kite Masters of Ljosalfar had seen, was not a Human thing that the scholars called an *airplane*. As the borders of the Faerie world dissolved, airplanes were frequently seen passing overhead. But this craft was headed directly for them. Kite Masters, keeping watch over the skies, sent messengers to warn the King's guards. This new vessel had no wings or tail, it made no sound at all as it zigzagged through the air. The strange object did not move of its own volition. Instead, a long brass basket hung from the belly of something that was barely visible, something that moved remarkably like a living being. Directly overhead now, a great, wormlike creature appeared to be coursing through the air. If the view of the kites on the other side of it had not been distorted by the creature's enormous, nearly transparent bulk, it would have been almost impossible to see. The beast moved like a snake, sidewinding across the sky, and it was descending toward an open field. The grass and shrubbery beneath the great cab flattened as the shadow of the thing moved across the park. And emblazoned on the front of the vessel was a large, ornate letter *D*.

When it touched ground, a team of Elves clad in black and yellow emerged from doors along the length of the cab. They fought against the winds made by the translucent creature above them to tether the vessel to the earth with stakes. Only when the vessel was secured did Macta Dockalfar and his companion, Baltham, dare to step onto solid ground.

By this time crowds had gathered around the clearing. Huddling close to each other for safety, the Elves gasped with disbelief at the gaseous, ethereal creature that hovered over the metal cab, impatiently twitching its tail of vapor. Macta walked with a purposeful stride along the avenue. With his head held high and his eyes gazing ahead, a smug smile crept across Macta's face. He could feel the fear of the crowd. It felt good. *It was worth the risk,* he thought, *to sneak the craft out of Helfratheim, just for this! My father would never have approved, but who could resist such an opportunity?*

Messengers had already brought the news to King Thorgier and Queen Shorya by the time the Prince arrived, rapping his knuckles on the door. Baltham stood behind with a huge bouquet of black roses in his arms. Inside the stone building, the Queen hurried past the servant, flung the door open wide, and stared at Macta. "You know why I am here," the Prince said.

"She's gone," answered Shorya. "And you are not welcome here. Good-bye."

Macta took the roses from his brother-in-law and forced himself into the entryway, gazing about. "I'm not in the mood for playing games. I want to see your daughter, or shall I say, my fiancée. Tell her I've come to take her for a little ride."

"Then you're wasting your time, Macta. As I said, she's not here. She's gone away."

"No!" Macta shouted, and flung the roses onto the stone floor. "That's not the answer! That's not what I want to hear! Tell me where she is. I didn't come all this way to be treated in such a manner!"

"Send him in!" shouted the King, from an adjoining room. "I'm not going to w-w-wait forever!"

The Queen bit her lip, Blood pulsing in her temples. "Follow me," she muttered, and held up the palm of her hand to let Baltham know that he was to wait outside. "Pick up those flowers on your way out," she commanded. "I can't stand the smell of black roses."

In his high-backed chair sat Asra's father, dressed in a robe and wooden sandals. "Excuse me for not g-g-getting up," he stammered. "I'm not feeling particularly well today. And I'm sorry to say my w-w-wife is rather overwhelmed at the moment. Our daughter, you see, is less pleased than I am with the prospect of her marriage. I suppose she would have liked to p-p-pick a husband for herself. Now, it seems, Asra has unexpectedly left town. None of us has any idea where she has gone, or when, or even if, she'll r-r-return to us."

"Come on, Thorgier," Macta sneered. "You don't expect me to believe that, do you? You're just trying to get out of this wedding. And after my father made such a convincing case in front of the Synod, the Faerie world won't stand for a betrayal like this. Everyone wants this marriage to take place."

The King struggled to his feet, and his face blanched. "Macta, believe me, I wouldn't tell you this if it weren't t-t-true. We heard that Asra may have been seen entering the C-C-Cord late last night. She didn't take a gondola, and she started off in a westerly direction. That's all we know."

"My God," Macta said, turning pale. "The Cord? It's not safe to travel. Not a week ago I lost my companion Druga in an accident near Alfheim. I've got to go and find Asra. She's making a terrible mistake."

King Thorgier cleared his throat as Macta turned to leave. "We've already sent her friend Skara with some soldiers to f-f-find her. Skara knows Asra better than anyone. They'll surely c-c-catch up with her soon and bring her back. Believe me, she'll be angry that we followed her, and she certainly won't want to s-s-see you right away. Don't worry, Macta, the wedding will p-p-proceed as planned."

Macta sighed. *Perhaps I'm being rash,* he thought. *'Twould be pointless to be at the rear of the trail when others are tracking her down. If I couldn't be the first to find her, it wouldn't be worth the effort.*

"I suspect you're right," the Prince said. "She won't like me following her. But I must be sure that she's safe. I want you to get word to me as soon as you've brought her home. Can I rely upon you for that?"

The King nodded and breathed a sigh of relief, glad that the Prince was asking him, not telling him what to do. "You know, Macta, the whole town's talking about the unusual means of t-t-transportation that brought you to Ljosalfar today. I'm anxious to see it for myself!"

"You mean the *Arvada*," Macta said with a haughty smile. "The word means *eagle*—a predatory bird from the Human world. 'Tis a new advancement in cross-selection. Sprites are elemental, I'm sure you know. They can take on a number of shapes. So the Experimentalists collect Fire Sprites and Air Sprites, and with a bit of conjuring, breed them. They're capable of breathing fire, just like the dragons that once roamed the skies. Yet because they're part Air Sprite as well, they can ride the winds in flight and they're translucent, so you can see right through them. Since the Cords are too dangerous for traveling, we'll be using the Arvada for all of our transportation now. I'll be delighted to escort you and the Queen on the Arvada when you journey back to Alfheim for the wedding." Macta planted a finger in the King's soft belly. "Send word to me as soon as you have Asra back home.

I'd still like the chance to win her heart before she stands by my side at the altar."

Through fair skies the Arvada pilots sailed the vessel home to Helfratheim. From the windows of their cab, Macta and Baltham peered at the forest below. Soon, however, there was nothing to be seen but green and brown rectangles, little white boxes, concrete roadways, and other signs of human dominion over the land. Baltham choked as he clutched a small sassafras leaf bag. He was feeling nauseated again. Macta, his eyes glazed over, pondered his glorious future. Somehow, he never tired of thinking about it. He smiled faintly, and pictured his reluctant bride. Someday she would come to love him, he was sure. When his wealth and power exceeded that of her own father, as it surely would, then she would see that Macta was the one she had always wanted. *Perhaps,* he thought, *I should consider following the path of the Cord in my Arvada, and finding Asra before the others reach her. 'Twould show my forceful side, my passionate side, my gallant side. 'Twould show her how much I really care . . .*

"Driver!" he shouted. "There will be a change in course!" And at that moment the cab lifted into a haze of white. The vaporous creature to which they were bound rose high over the clouds, opened its mouth in an expression of sheer joy, and a jet of flame belched into the air.

35

MAY I POUR YOU ANOTHER CUP?" asked Becky, sitting on one of the pink stools at her bedroom table. The table was set for a tea party. There were tall plastic cups, utensils, and even slices of plastic cake on a lacy doily. Tomtar smiled and held up his cup for a make-believe refill. "Aye," he said.

Tomtar was practically living with the McCormacks. Every waking hour was spent with Matt, and sometimes Becky, either at the edge of the forest, at the picnic table in the yard, or in the house. Matt couldn't help but wonder where Tomtar was spending his nights, when the family was asleep. All he knew for sure was that Tomtar's supply of *trans*, the bits of bark that he chewed for various magical effects, was running low. While he was indoors, Tomtar always chewed the medicinal bark that kept him from getting sick when exposed to metal. Matt was surprised to discover how much metal there was in his house. Tomtar could point it out to him, even when it was hidden behind the walls. Each room was framed from inside with metal. The wiring for electricity was sheathed in metal. The kitchen and bathroom were full of metal, and the metal plumbing bands on the pipes for fresh water and sewage ran like arteries throughout the entire home. Until Tomtar returned to Alfheim to refresh his supplies, he had to ration the bark Jardaine had prepared for him. And so far, he showed no signs of interest in returning to the forest.

Tomtar loved his time with Matt. After all of the years he spent in solitude, it was a welcome change to have someone actually listen when he talked. Every morning he popped a piece or two of bark into his mouth, climbed out of the hollow in the earth where he slept, and trod across the field to Matt's house. Tomtar had learned, through careful practice, to change the way his clothing appeared when his identity was shielded by the effects of the bark. This reduced the chance that Matt's mother would be suspicious if he showed up every day in the same odd, rustic outfit. Now he appeared to dress in clothes identical to Matt's.

Apart from a vague discomfort he experienced at being in enclosed spaces, Tomtar loved everything about Matt's house, his family, and the complex world of Human beings. Tomtar enjoyed watching Matt play his Game Boy, especially the fantasy games that featured alien warriors, battling Faeries, and sword-fighting demons. "Someday I'll teach you the fightin' games I learned when I was a lad," Tomtar would say, as if he intended to be there for a long while.

Tomtar also loved the snacks that Matt's mom gave the kids. If the food came out of a plastic package, he was sure to appreciate it all the more. He took pleasure each time he reached into Emily's playpen and tickled her under the chin. He also truly enjoyed playing with Becky, who was always asking Tom if he wanted to come to her room for a visit. She appreciated his willingness to play with dolls and drink imaginary tea, when he wasn't busy with Matt.

One morning, Matt and Tom were in Matt's room, with the door closed. Tomtar was sitting on the edge of Matt's bed, unshielded by his appearance spell. *Tap, tap, tap.* "It's me," Becky said, hoping to join in. Until school started, and she met some new kids, Becky didn't have any friends to play with.

"Come back later!" Matt called. "We're busy."

Becky pushed the door open and leaned her head into the room. "Matt, I was just—"

Matt leapt up from his chair and gave the door a shove. "Owwww!" Becky cried, grabbing her forehead.

Matt rolled his eyes and cursed. He'd neglected to lock the door. He took his sister by the shoulders and turned her away from his room. "Becky, I didn't mean to hurt you. Come on. Let's go downstairs and get an ice pack from the fridge."

But it was too late. Through her tears Becky had seen a little figure leap from Matt's bed and dash behind the dresser by the window. She pushed her way into Matt's room. "Is everything all right up there?" came Jill's voice from the kitchen.

"Everything's fine!" Becky hollered in a trembling voice. Then she turned to face her big brother, standing, arms folded, in front of his dresser. "I—I *knew* there was something going on. I just knew. You promised you'd tell me, Matt. You promised!"

"I'm sorry," Matt sighed. "Let's all just go outside, okay? I'll explain everything."

Behind the dresser Tomtar grabbed his pouch of *trans,* popped one in his mouth, and chewed it as Matt put on his shoes. Minutes later the three of them were trudging across the construction site, headed for the woods. It was there that Becky heard the whole story, as Matt and Tomtar confessed their secret. "I knew you weren't just a regular boy," Becky said to Tomtar. "You're even stranger than the friends Matt used to have in Pittsburgh."

"That's not fair," said Matt.

"Anyway," Becky mused, "I'd much rather know the truth than have everybody lie to me. Now let me take a look at that, that *Huldu,*" she demanded, and Tomtar handed her the pouch. Becky stuck her nose into the top of the bag and inhaled. "They don't smell so bad. What do you think would happen if I chewed one of these things? How about the one that makes you invisible?" Becky giggled. "Matt, maybe there's something here that would make you taller!"

Matt glowered. "I said I was sorry about hitting your head. You don't have to be mean."

"I wouldn't try it," said Tomtar. "The *trans* aren't meant for the likes of *Tems.*"

Becky dropped the pouch in Tomtar's outstretched palm. It fell straight through the illusion of a human hand, landing on the ground. "My real hand's down here," Tomtar explained. "I just chewed a little tiny piece of bark that time. I guess it's not enough to keep the spell workin'."

Tomtar peered into his *Huldu* and rooted around. "Ah! There are a few left in here after all. I'll save 'em for when I go back to your house."

"What do you mean when you say *trans* aren't for *Tems*?" Becky asked. "I know you said a *Tem* is a human being, but why not say *people*, or something?"

Tomtar looked at the ground. "Faerie Folk live a long time, a very, very long time," he said, "and Humans, well, they just don't. 'Tis the nature of time in the two worlds. So we call Humans *Tems* 'cause they're only temporary, just here for a while."

"What about when you get exposed to metal?" Matt asked. "Could that make you sick enough to die? And what if you spent your whole life on the human side? Didn't you once tell me about an elf who got shot by a hunter and died? Everything has to die sometime."

Tomtar shrugged. "It *can* happen. But it isn't natural."

"What do you mean, *natural*?" asked Becky.

"Natural . . . ," Tomtar repeated. "Ummm, I suppose 'tis like, things happen a certain way, for certain reasons. For instance, there's a reason for me bein' here. When a Troll comes of age, he always goes on a *Wanderin'*. When I was a lad I watched Trolls leave their homes and families when they came of age; male and female, they all just went away for a spell. The time each was gone was different, but every one came back, with their *Gift.* On the first night of their return, everyone would come together to share it."

"We get gifts on our birthdays and Christmas," Becky said. "We don't have to share them with anybody, though."

"The Gift isn't necessarily a *thing,*" Tomtar said. "Or if it *is* a thing, 'tis just somethin' you use to show everybody what you've learned. After you get back from your Wanderin', though, life's a whole other story. No more waitin', or watchin', or dreamin'. Everybody gets assigned a job to do. We used to grow our own food. Mushrooms in the cellar, roots and tubers 'round the foundation, herbs and flowerin' things that needed a lot of sun on the roof. When I was really young I remember standin' on the roof at nighttime, lookin' up at the purple sky, and pretendin' that I lived in the forest."

"I can't believe all this was going on around us in Pittsburgh, and nobody knew anything about it," Matt said.

Becky nodded. "Did you take back a gift when you were done with your wandering?"

"I've not been back yet," Tomtar replied. "I don't know what my Gift is goin' to be, so 'til I get it, I can't go home." Tomtar's eyes glazed over. "There's that, and then there're other reasons for not goin' back. Someday I'll tell you."

The next afternoon, Matt and Becky lay with Tomtar on a hill next to the woods, and watched the billowing clouds pass overhead. During a lull in the conversation, Tomtar took out his wooden flute and began to play. He improvised a melody, fingering the holes along the hollow reed to change the notes. "That's pretty," Becky said. "I wish I could play like that."

"It's nothin'," said Tomtar, blushing. But encouraged by the praise, the Troll launched into some of the tunes he had learned as a child. Matt and Becky tapped their toes and nodded, while staring up at the sky. The music was a little odd, but not unlike folk songs they had heard in music class at school. Then a familiar series of notes made both children sit up and stare wide-eyed. "That's not your song," said Becky. "My daddy sings that song. It's called 'You Take the High Road, or the Low Road,' or something. Where did you learn it?"

"Maybe it's not a human's song, Becky," said Matt. "Maybe it comes from—"

Becky shook her head vehemently. "Then how did our daddy learn a faerie song?"

"'Tis an old melody," said Tomtar. "I don't know who wrote it. We call it 'The Low Road.' I suppose it must come from the old days when *Tems* knew about the Faerie world, and understood what happens to 'em all when they . . ." The Troll paused, confused for the hundredth time about what he should or shouldn't feel free to say to the children.

"I read something about the low road. What is it?" Matt asked.

Tomtar nodded, then rested the flute in his lap. "The High Road is a *Tem* road, see? The Low Road is the Faerie passage, under the ground. 'Tis called *the Cord*. I know I mentioned it to you before. Anyway, 'tisn't like a tunnel dug into the dirt, the Cord is more like, aah, I don't know; in a way it's like a—a kind of tube, or a long, hollow root, like somethin' that . . . well, 'tis hard to explain. It's our way of gettin' from place to place, and they say it's the way spirit moves through the Faerie world. Do you understand? They used to say that when *Tems* died far from home, their spirits would travel back through the Faerie Cord to the place they were from. So the song is about a pair of *Tem* soldiers in a battle, and one of 'em gets wounded, near to death. He whispers to his friend that he's goin' to die, and his Soul will fly through the Cord back home. His spirit'll travel faster than the *Tem* who's still alive, who has to walk all the way back, on his own two feet."

Tomtar felt embarrassed and awkward as he picked up his flute. Then he put it back down. "Well, eeh, maybe that's enough. You've probably had plenty of my music!"

"No, please." Matt said, "I'm sorry we interrupted. Let's hear how the song sounds when you play it!"

Tomtar let his fingers dance on the flute. The tune was strong and rhythmic, but a little forlorn, a little haunting. When he came to the end, Becky let out a sigh. "It's just the way Daddy does it. Now I'm going to have that song going through my head all day."

"Matt! Becky!" their mother called from the house. "It's time to come home!"

"Well, I guess we'll, uh, see you soon," said Matt. He turned away, feeling badly that Tomtar seemed to have no place to go at night. Becky, meanwhile, bent down to give Tomtar a quick hug, then skipped down past the trees that bordered the construction site. Matt lingered for a moment. "You know, Tomtar, we could probably hide you in the house so you'd have somewhere warm to sleep at night."

"Nooo," said the Troll, "but thanks anyhow. I prefer sleepin' 'neath the stars, right here on the ground is as good a place as any for me!"

Matt nodded. He had known what the answer would be, but he felt better for asking. "Okay, then, we'll see you . . . tomorrow?"

Tomtar stood up, and his face crinkled in a broad grin. "If the sun rises in the east and the wind whistles in the trees, you'll find me standin' at your front door!"

Tomtar watched the children hurry to their big, white house. He winced as their feet pounded across the dirt. The sight of so much land stripped of vegetation made the Troll's Soul ache. The bare land was like an open wound, and the sorrow he felt inside kept him from noticing the rustle in the bushes behind him. "Well, if it isn't a spy I'm spying, keeping a close eye on his prey!"

Tomtar whirled around. "Nebiros!" he exclaimed, as the Elf tiptoed through the brambles.

"Jardaine wishes to know what you've learned of the Humans, so as her favorite errand boy, I've come to make the inquiry. But I must say I'm not entirely sure she'll be happy to find out you're on speaking terms with the enemy. You were just supposed to watch the Humans."

Tomtar struggled to find the words he knew Nebiros wanted to hear. "I been watchin' 'em, just like I was told. I pretty much know the lay of their property by now, as they've asked me through the entrance to their house on more than one occasion. The place is full of metal, though, so it's apt to sicken the likes of us."

"But you have potions and charms for that, don't you?"

"Aye, I do," answered Tomtar, his eyes avoiding contact with the dark-haired Elf. "I've learned that the *Tems*, the young ones anyway, they like games, and stories, and music, 'tis a joy to behold, and they're a jolly, trusting lot. They take it for truth, whatever I tell 'em."

"Then did you tell them that you were sent here to spy on them? You can't be friends with Humans, you ignorant Troll. They're our enemies. Perhaps 'twas for the best you took them into your confidence and got them to trust you. 'Twill be to our advantage if they believe we mean them no harm."

"I *don't* mean them any harm," Tomtar insisted. "I'm just here to do a favor for the new Mage, that's all."

"But have you heard anything about the Alfheim Jewels? Have you talked to them about that? About the terrible machines

they use to ravage our homeland? About their plans for the rest of the forest? What have you learned that's useful to us, Tomtar?"

The Troll looked at the ground and shrugged. "They're not *bad,* Nebiros. They're not out to hurt us."

A wave of anger came over the Elf's face, as he shook his stubby finger. "That's not the news we sent you here to find. I'll be back in two days' time, and I expect you to tell me more of what I want to hear. Understood?"

"Aye," Tomtar mumbled, as he watched the Elf vanish back into the forest. "You know where to find me, Nebiros, 'tis plain to see."

When he was sure that the Elf was not lingering in the darkness, spying on him, Tomtar got to his knees and pressed a mound of loose grass and fallen leaves into a shallow pit. He worked slowly and carefully. It was a scooped-out area of dirt, just the right size for a Troll to lie down in. And it was there that Tomtar spent another solitary night, beneath a swirl of stars in a cold, black sky.

36

I WANT YOU TO DELIVER this to Tacita, Secretary of the Synod in Ljosalfar," Tuava-Li said, handing Jardaine a sealed scroll. Through the use of magick and medicine her wounds were healing quickly, but a week after the accident, Tuava-Li was not yet strong enough to undertake a journey. The pair stood outside the Mage's quarters as the morning sun warmed the leaves of Bethok. "The message explains that Kalevala Van Frier has disappeared, and the Elves of Alfheim have repeatedly searched for her, to no avail. It says that as the Mage's successor, I've taken charge as the spiritual head of this Clan, and assumed the role of Mage of Alfheim."

Jardaine could feel Sarette twist uncomfortably around her waist. She nodded and stared at her feet as Tuava-Li continued. "I don't want there to be any secrets between us, Jardaine; that's why I'm sharing this information with you. After all, you're next in line, should anything happen to me. The message explains that we're finally prepared for the return of all the residents of Alfheim, that the land has been completely cleared of spiritual contagion from the Blood that was spilled here. Now I want you to leave for Ljosalfar immediately, and return as soon as you've given Secretary Tacita my message. Is that clear?"

"Perfectly clear, my Mage," replied Jardaine, the Blood pulsing in her temples.

"Very well," said Tuava-Li. "I thought you'd be pleased that I've come to this decision. I also want to warn you about your journey. It may not be swift, or direct. There are tears in the Cord, dangerous places. Rely on your intuition to guide you on an alternative route, if need be. If you sense anything amiss, a weakness, an odor, a change in color, be very, very careful. Much depends on you reaching Ljosalfar safely."

Jardaine hesitated before responding. "And what about my safe return to Alfheim?"

Tuava-Li was taken aback. Jardaine was weighing the importance of the mission against her own safety. "If I am Mage, then you are my Apprentice," Tuava-Li said. "I need you to go to Ljosalfar, and I need you to come back home safely once your mission is through. You should think of it as an honor to do my bidding. Now hurry, Jardaine. For the good of all."

A violet-gray dawn was just creeping through the branches as Jardaine rode down the trunk of the great oak Bethok. Sarette slithered around the monk's shoulder and lifted her scaly head. "You're not going to deliver the message, are you?"

"Of course I am," grumbled Jardaine. "Valdis has sent messengers to all the corners of the realm informing them of Macta's wedding to Asra. Everyone knows about it. If I don't take the news to the Synod, 'twill be clear to everyone when they all arrive for the wedding that I didn't do as I was told. Then where would I be?"

"Well, if all goesss according to plan, Tuava-Li can be dealt with after the wedding, when the battle betwixt the Humansss and the Elvesss beginsss."

"Exactly," Jardaine said. "'Til then, I'll be the dutiful monk, and do just as I am bidden. 'Twon't be long until the tables are turned."

Sarette wrapped herself comfortably around the traitorous monk's shoulder. The others were just crossing the glade on their way to morning meditation when Jardaine slipped into the Cord and disappeared from sight.

Deep in the forest a cry rang out. It was like the bark of a dog, a small, fierce dog, and there was something sharp and wild in the sound that made Kalevala Van Frier tremble. She had spent the night huddled against the trunk of a hickory tree. Her feathers blended in perfectly with the bark of the trunk and the blanket of leaves on the forest floor. Yet despite her camouflage, she knew that her smell would give her away to the family of foxes nearby.

The Elf smell, the bird smell, the smell of Blood, fear, whatever it was, it was only a matter of time until they found her. In fact, they probably already knew where she was. She would do what she could to distract or confuse the beasts, but the danger was coming closer. The sound came first from her left, perhaps a few hundred yards away. Then the bark was answered by another, a little deeper in the woods. Then another. Kalevala looked at the fingers growing out of feathered hands. She looked up at the tree. The nearest branch was a dozen feet above her; with her wings slowly changing back into arms, there was no way she could fly that far.

She turned to face the trunk and dug her fingernails into the bark. Though her hands and feet had returned completely to Elfin form, the nails on her toes were still hard and clawlike. She was just reaching the lowest branch of the hickory when the first of the foxes appeared. Black-eared, beady-eyed, the mother fox thrashed its white-tipped tail as her offspring drew near. Then the foxes circled the trunk of the tree. The Mage looked down on them. In her mind she began to form the image of a black bear. She let her attention form every detail of the bear, its strong, dank odor, its stiff, bristling coat, the gleam in its eyes, and the terrible sharpness of its claws and teeth. *Magick begins in the imagination,* she thought. The Mage took the image of the bear in her mind and began to move it out of her body, projecting it into the mind of the mother fox. It took all of her strength, all of her energy to perform this feat of deception. She nearly lost her footing and fell from the branch, but the claws of her feet held to the rough bark. The mother fox's mind was suddenly filled with the sense that there was a bear close by. She looked around in terror, imagining that at any moment she would see the awful beast crashing through the foliage toward her and her young. She could smell the bear, she could almost hear its fierce roar. In panic the fox turned to run, and her mystified offspring scampered after her.

The owl's strength was spent. As the illusion of the bear fell apart like a trail of vapor, she wavered on the branch. She opened her mouth and let out a cry of despair. It was a terrible wail, part the screech of an owl and part Elf. Her skin tingled with the exhilaration that comes from facing danger and then escaping it. Her body shook with an inner fire; she had come back from the brink, only to find herself still alone and far from home. What was this life of hers all about? Back in Alfheim she was Mage, and that gave her life meaning and purpose. But what purpose was there in her survival here? She dug her claws deeper into the tree and forced herself to climb higher and higher, toward the crown of the tree, the topmost branches, the sky. Her breath came ragged and torn, her nails were bloody and raw. The passion in her heart, like a rope tethered to an anchor of air, was cast overboard, cast out into the breeze, and it sailed far and away, seeking purchase in something familiar, something that would allow her to pull the tired vessel of her body back home.

Tuava-Li sat cross-legged on the platform. Her eyes were closed, her hands still wrapped in bandages, but her posture was strong and erect. Around her, deep in meditation, sat the monks of Alfheim. They breathed in harmony, drawing in each other's energy, pulling it into their hearts, then letting it rise up through the crowns of their heads and disperse into the air. The sun was still coming up when Tuava-Li felt a strange sensation in her chest. She had the sense that someone was staring at her, a pair of eyes, gleaming and powerful, were holding her in their grip, lifting her bodily from the platform where she sat. Her eyes flashed open and she saw that she was still on the platform, the monks were still sitting calmly in their circle.

Tuava-Li blinked and closed her eyes. Immediately she was hovering again, being drawn up by an invisible thread. She realized the body being lifted was not her physical body; it was the Spirit Body inside her. Carefully she opened the eyes of her Spirit Body, and looked into the face of the Mage. Tuava-Li's newfound confidence was like a beacon that had allowed the Mage to find her again. The Mage's eyes were burning into hers, not imploring, or demanding, or insisting that Tuava-Li come to her aid. It was simply an invitation. Their bond was like an umbilical cord, a rope of connection, and Tuava-Li's Spirit Body used it as a guide to take her to the crown of the tree where the Mage was waiting. When they joined, Soul to Soul, a white-hot burst of light exploded in Tuava-Li's skull. She found words rising from some distant, timeless place, searching for form. "The Mage is among us," she gasped.

"Aye, mistress," nodded the monks.

"No, you don't understand," Tuava-Li said, leaping to her feet. Her heart was pounding in her chest. "I'm not talking about myself. I didn't truly understand until just now . . . all my confusion, my uncertainty; I was right in my intuition that it wasn't yet my time to lead. Our Mage is alive, and now I know where to find her. I've got to go and bring her home. Now!"

37

THE NEXT AFTERNOON, Matt and Becky hiked with Tomtar to their favorite spot on the hillside. Warm sunlight burnished the leaves as the trio sat and talked about the differences between the Human and Faerie worlds. Tomtar was explaining the relative sizes of Brownies, Pixies, and Dwarves when Becky leapt up with a cry, brushing frantically at her hair. "Oooh! There's something on me! Is it a bug? Help me get it out!"

"It's just a leaf, Becky; sit down," Matt laughed. "You'd think you never saw a tree before. The leaves aren't going to bite you! Tomtar, you have no idea how much Becky must like you for her to sit out here on the ground and take a chance on getting dirty and having a bug crawl up her leg. She's always hated being outdoors."

"But I'm different, now," Becky argued. "I'm changing, Matt. Just like you."

"What do you mean?"

"You're not the same as you were before," said Becky. "Everything is different, now that Tomtar's here."

"Matt! Becky! I made cookies!" It was their mother, calling them home.

Matt stood up, his knees a little sore from kneeling on the ground, and strode past the trees so that he could just see his mother standing on the deck. "We'll be right there!" he hollered. "Tomtar, do you want to come down for a snack?"

"Eeh, do you have to ask?"

Tomtar followed his friends as they made their way back across the field. "Hello, Tom," said Mrs. McCormack, when she saw the shaggy-headed boy trailing behind her children through the screen door. "I've got chocolate macadamia nut cookies, straight from the oven."

Tomtar had never tasted anything so delicious in all his life. When he finished his cookies he sat at the kitchen table and noisily sucked the smears of melted chocolate from his fingers, then slurped milk from a plastic cup. Emily sat in her high chair and laughed at Tomtar. "Let's play a game, Tom," said Becky. "How about some hide and seek!"

"Whatever you say," the Troll grinned, wiping a milk mustache from his face. "Just as soon as I've finished my snack."

Becky scrunched up her face. "Tom, you close your eyes and count to twenty. I'll go hide, and you try to find me!"

"I think I'm going to sit this one out," said Matt. "Tom, when you're tired of chasing Becky around the house, I'll be up in my room." He padded up the stairs and his sister rushed past him like a gust of wind. Tomtar stood in the hallway and closed his eyes, as Becky had instructed. He still couldn't quite believe his good luck at making friends like Matt and Becky. He wished that he could stay forever, but he knew that soon it would be time to return to Alfheim. His *Huldu* was nearly empty. In another day, Nebiros would be back to ply him for more information. Maybe that would be a good time to leave. Tomtar only wanted to assure Nebiros and Jardaine that the Elves had nothing to fear from the Humans, even though he knew they weren't interested in the truth. And he didn't want to say anything that might bring harm to his new friends. Tomtar took a deep breath. It was time to look for Becky. It would be easy to find her. Tomtar could detect the telltale odor of Humans from anywhere in the house. Still, he made the pretense of looking in the upstairs bathroom, glancing into Becky's closet, and traipsing down the stairs calling in a loud voice, "I wonder where Becky could be, eeh? Maybe she's in . . . *the kitchen*?"

Tomtar glanced out through the window. Mrs. McCormack was weeding her flower beds, while Emily fussed nearby in her playpen. On the kitchen table lay the plate where the chocolate cookies had been. Tomtar took a leathery piece of bark from his mouth and held it in his hand while he lifted the plate to his lips and licked away the crumbs. Life was very good. He put the bark back into his cheek and opened the pantry door. "Is she in here?" he called.

Hmmm. There were so many cans in here, so many packages, noodles, grains, it could feed an army of Trolls. Tomtar opened another door. Steps led down into darkness, and a funny smell, a little damp and moldy . . . "She's not in here!" he shouted, and closed the door.

Tomtar walked to the living room and sniffed the air. "Let's see . . . is she . . . back here?"

He pulled aside the edge of a chair by the window and peered around it. Becky was crouched behind the sofa, her body tight as a coiled spring, her hand over her mouth to stifle her giggles. When Tomtar finally strolled over to her hiding place, Becky leapt up with a shriek. Tomtar actually jumped back in surprise, and for a second the illusion spell broke. Becky looked down and saw the Troll staring at her wide-eyed. "You scared me," he said.

It only took a moment for the spell to flicker back into place, and Becky was once again looking at a boy just about her brother's height. "Now it's your turn to hide," she said.

Becky buried her face in her hands and began to count. Tomtar glanced around. He didn't have much time to hide! Then he remembered the door in the kitchen, and he raced out of the room and down the basement stairs. The basement was musty, even though the house was new. It had an odor of fresh concrete and decaying paper, for so many of the boxes that had been moved from storage and Matt's grandmother's place were stacked here. Tomtar ran his hand alongside a shelf and felt the entire stack of cardboard boxes wobble a little. He pressed himself against the wall, hidden in shadows. No. There was another spot, even better, even darker, on the other side of the room. "Ready or not, here I come!" Becky shouted from upstairs.

Tomtar saw a plastic sword sticking out of the top of a box. He took the sword in his hand and tested its weight. Then he peered over the top of the box to see what else was there. Little plastic figures, heavily muscled, dressed in odd, painted outfits. There must have been a hundred of them! Next to the box was a trunk. Old and battered, the trunk had faded stickers glued to its sides. Tomtar shook the lid. It was loose. *I wonder if there's enough room in here for me to hide?* he thought. He lifted the lid, and his skin began to tingle. There was something from the Faerie world in the trunk, he could sense it. Tomtar climbed in and put his hand in among the worn and dusty dolls. It took him only a second to find the jewels. There was no doubt about where they had come from. So Jardaine was right—Humans could not be trusted! All the things Tomtar had told the boy, and his sister, all the secrets he had revealed, how stupid he had been! How blind! Why hadn't he been able to see through the deceit? The boy had stolen the jewels and hidden them there, it was plain. The Clan Jewels of Alfheim. Maybe the boy's parents were involved.

SCOTLAND
WALES

None of them was innocent. Not even the baby. All of them were Human. All of them were the enemy. Tomtar heard the thudding footsteps of the girl upstairs; his heart was in his stomach. It would be a while before she thought to look in the basement. He had believed there was no reason to blame the boy for the cutting of the forest. Just because his father was doing something stupid didn't mean that the boy was guilty, too. Or so he had thought. And he had been wrong. Here was the proof of the Humans' intentions. Cut down the homeland of the Faerie Folk, steal their treasures, then . . . then there was the incident with the gun, and the murdered Prince, and the girl in the stream. Three hundred and sixty moons he had wasted, sitting by the side of the Human. Suddenly it all made terrible, perfect sense. Tomtar gritted his teeth. There was no making peace with them after all. He slung one of the sacks of Jewels over his back. He had to be quick; someone would have to come back for the rest. Then he fumbled around in his *Huldu* pouch until he found the piece of bark with the sign for invisibility on it. He popped it between his lips and began to chew, and there was only the taste of bitterness in his mouth. He was up the stairs, out the back door with the sack of Jewels, and well across the field before Becky discovered the open basement door and hollered, "Look out, here I come!"

38

THE ELFMAID'S HAIR trailed out behind her as her skirt flapped in the harsh wind of the Cord. Asra had not taken a royal gondola. It was important to make this journey without being recognized or followed. With anxious eyes she scanned the length of the passageway unfolding before her for signs of injury or weakness. Several times already she had found tears, fluttering gashes, paper-thin walls bulging out nearly to the breaking point. Already she had been to Skrydstrup, to Huldremose and Egtved, hoping to find the traveling carnival that had passed through Ljosalfar. She needed to talk to the fortune-teller and demand to know what the Hanged One meant for her future. Storehoj was her next stop, and as a tingling sensation raced up her arms, she was certain that her destination was near.

Moving closer to the side wall, Asra thrust an arm against

the membrane to slow her movement. But her fingers slashed through, and she hurtled forward with her arm jutting out, tearing an opening nearly thirty feet long. Finally she tumbled out into the dirt. The wounded Cord fluttered, wind billowing out of the hole, and Asra waited in vain for the membrane to seal itself. She smoothed the surface with her hands, trying to move the skin back into place. *There's no turning back now,* she thought, as Elves raced from every direction to see what had happened to the Cord. In the raucous confusion that followed, Asra slipped away from the scene, not wanting to draw attention to herself. There was nothing she could do to help, anyway.

Asra strode toward the busy treetop village. The foliage above was so dense that the Elves who scurried across the high, rope-strung pathways carried torches to light their way through the gloom. The pathways were a chaos of activity. Asra glanced up toward the ceiling of branches and saw the bridges swaying, torch-lit, level after level, until the flames flickered like distant stars. Asra had just slipped into the crowd along the forest floor when a pair of young monks approached her. "Greetings, traveler, have you heard the good news of the Canon?" one asked. "Would you like to hear about the teachings of Brahja-Chi?" the other inquired.

"No, ah, I've heard mention of the name," said Asra, a little taken aback. "She's the Mage of this place, isn't she?"

"Aye, she is our beloved Mage, and we seek recruits for her cause."

Asra snorted, attempting to bypass the monks. "Where I come from, Faerie Folk are afraid of her."

"Nooo, they're not!" declared the older of the monks, blocking Asra's path. "That can't be. Here in Storehoj we follow the teachings of the sacred parchment known as the Canon. 'Tis written in a language so ancient that only the Mage and her monks can understand it. The book contains all the laws and teachings of the Gods, all for the good of those who follow her!"

"I'm sorry, I'm not interested," Asra waved her hand, taking a step forward.

"Take this, please," the younger monk said, slipping a tiny piece of parchment into Asra's hand. "It'll tell you all about Brahja-Chi, and the favors bestowed upon those who join her."

"Indeed," Asra replied, "and I hear your Mage also metes out strict punishment for those who disobey her rules."

"We believe that the Gods speak through the Canon, and Brahja-Chi interprets it for the faithful," insisted the older monk. "Elfmaids come from all over the realm to study here, to sit at Brahja-Chi's feet and learn about the Law."

"All right, I promise I'll read it," Asra lied, slipping the crumpled parchment into a pocket.

"You won't be sorry!" the monks said in unison.

Asra found the carnival set up along a broad avenue in Storehoj, much the same way it had been arranged in Ljosalfar. High torches flickered, lighting the revelers who crowded the great broad way. Elf children strained at the hands of their elders, and adolescent Faeries raced from one amusement to another. The banner with THE FUTURE IS YOURS TO SEE printed on it was hung over the top of the Saga's little tent. The cries of the barkers and the raucous laughter of Faerie Folk sounded almost hysterical as Princess Asra slipped inside. The Saga sat by herself in the guttering candlelight. The cards were spread out before her, face up, and the card characters danced together on the tabletop. A tiny string quartet played a waltz as the High Priestess danced with the Magician, who held hands with the Fool, Temperance, Death, and the Devil. The Hanged One swung upside down from the tree outside the Tower, and the Hermit crouched by the Wheel at the edge of the table. The Saga lifted her head, then in one swift move swept the cards up in her withered hands. "I wish t—" Asra ventured, but the old woman stopped her with a glance.

"I know what you wish. Come, Elfmaid, come closer," the fortune-teller said.

Asra peered at the Saga's face. Her eyes were red-rimmed behind the black-and-white makeup, and her lips were crusted and dry. The tooth that hung over her lower lip wiggled slightly, as if it were nearly ready to fall from her mouth. "You spend your time pursuing me instead of pursuing your fate," said the crone, "or letting your fate take you. Sit at the table, and I'll show you again."

Asra slipped into the chair, glancing at the table as her eyes adjusted to the dark. "The card I drew last time was—"

"Nooo," interrupted the old woman. "Perhaps this time 'twill not be the same. Dip into the waters of fate, and each time you'll find yourself standing in a different place."

Once again the Saga went through the ritual of shuffling and cutting the cards, and once again when Asra's card was drawn from the top of the deck, the Hanged One swung upside down from a rope, head down, hair dangling. The tree and the tiny figure popped up from the card, a convincing illusion of a macabre scene. The Hanged One's eyes shone, then winked at Asra. The Princess gasped and leapt up from her seat, toppling the chair. "Don't be afraid of what you don't know," the Saga said. "If you hadn't fled before I had time to explain, I would've gladly done so the last time. Now be calm, Elfmaid, the Hanged One is not a death sentence. Look closely at the figure. 'Tis hanging by the feet, not the neck. That's it, come up as close as you dare."

Asra took a deep breath and leaned in toward the table. The figure hanging from the tree seemed to be female, with long amber hair flowing from the head in a halo of light. Since the figure was upside down, it was hard to make out the expression, so Asra cocked her own head to the side, the better to see the tiny face.

"Oh!" she cried. "The Hanged One is—is *me!*"

"'Tis a symbol, that's all," soothed the fortune-teller. "It reveals your inability to find your way to action. Whether 'tis because you're too young, or because those you respect don't take you seriously, you search in vain for freedom. You must put self-interest aside and think of the higher good. You must surrender to what life has to offer you, and be patient."

Asra stared at the old crone. "I don't think I understand," she said, finally. Inside her, however, there was a nagging voice, perfectly clear, that shouted an answer the Princess did not want to hear. She pushed it back down and stared in incomprehension at the Saga.

"You'll only get what you truly want by surrendering, not by the effort of will."

"But it *is* an effort of will to surrender," said Asra. "Who am I surrendering to?"

"That's for you to decide," said the Saga. "And the time has come to make your decision."

The frantic pounding of feet on the midway outside and the harsh cries of Elves and a dozen other forms of Faerie Folk brought Asra to sudden attention. "What's going on?" she asked.

"The time has come," answered the Saga.

Asra felt dizzy as she got up and stumbled from the tent. She grabbed a Pixie by the sleeve. "What's happening?" she demanded.

"There's been an accident in the Cord, a bad one!" the Pixie cried, her eyes full of fear. "I heard that a party from Ljosalfar traveling in a royal gondola tore through the Cord. There are bodies and Blood everywhere! We've got to get away!"

Asra moved against the tide of Faeries who were fleeing the

site of the carnage. At the place where the Princess had exited the Cord the gondola lay in ruins, bashed to pieces against the trunk of an enormous tree. Hundreds of torches lit the air, illuminating the scene. Plumes of smoke drifted into the treetops. Brahja-Chi, the Mage of Storehoj, stood with her monks amid the wreckage of the gondola, working their magic. As the bodies from the accident were lifted from the surrounding foliage, each was gathered up in an orb of blue light, and suspended in midair. It was an attempt to keep Elfin Blood from contaminating the soil of Storehoj. "The Blood!" cried an onlooker, peering from behind a boulder. "'Tis unclean! We'll have to leave our homes!"

"Nooo!" shouted another. "Brahja-Chi says the magick in the Canon will protect us!"

The air was thick with the smell of fear, and cries of despair and sorrow rang out. Asra hurried past the broken prow of the gondola as another body was lifted from the forest floor. "This one's still alive!" shouted one of the monks, and Asra's heart sank as she recognized her own best friend. "Skara!" she moaned. "Oh, nooo, Skara!"

Asra hurried to her friend's side. She wiped away the Blood from Skara's cheek, overcoming her instinctive fear, then kissed her friend's face. "'Twas the Six of Cups," Skara whispered hoarsely. "The old Saga told me to expect a radical . . . a radical change. I never expected it to be like this!"

"Never mind," soothed Asra. "Never mind all of that. I'll take you back home, Skara. Everything will be all right!"

"We—we came to find you," Skara croaked, managing a faint smile. "Your mother sent me to f-find you and bring you . . . home. Why didn't you . . . tell me you were leaving? I—I would have come with you."

"I'll take you home," Asra cried, pressing her tearstained face against the bosom of her friend. "I'll take you back home, and I'll stay by your side, and care for you, in the name of the Gods, this is all my fault! Stay with me, please, Skara, don't . . ."

The light in Skara's eyes faded like the moon behind a cloud. The monk who stood behind the Elfmaids gestured, and a blue orb took shape around Skara. Asra shook with sobs as her friend's body was lifted into the air. She felt hands clutching at her shoulders, and she stepped back as a group of monks got down on their knees to search the soil for any trace of Blood.

Suddenly a hot wind blasted down upon the scene. All eyes peered into the treetops, as Brahja-Chi's monks abandoned their work and scurried for shelter. All around them torches were snuffed out from the sudden rush of wind. Then a blinding burst of flame shot from the heavens, withering trees and setting a rope bridge ablaze. A brass gondola emblazoned with the letter *D* drifted through the smoke. Flames licked from the Sprite's gash of a mouth as the gondola settled to the ground. Black-and-yellow garbed Elves emerged to tether the vessel, and Asra was shocked to see Macta Dockalfar step down into the clearing. Baltham peered out from behind a window, afraid to leave the vehicle and come near the site of the disaster.

Brahja-Chi and her monks hurried to surround the Prince. "The trees!" cried the Mage. "The trees! Everyone knows not to destroy trees. If we were not here to keep this blaze under control, the entire forest would go up in flames!"

"But it didn't," Macta replied. "The flames were necessary to illuminate the path for our vessel. It is very dark here, and our pilots are new at maneuvering the Arvada. That means *eagle*, you know. We were following the others from Ljosalfar, but I see tragedy arrived before we did. 'Tis a good thing I directed my pilots to follow their path here, in order to rescue our Princess Asra and bring her home."

Asra charged into the clearing, pushing her way past the monks, who stood awestruck before Macta's Arvada. "You could have offered to take them in your—your *flying thing*, Macta," she spat, "you could have done that much. You knew that the Cord isn't safe for travel, you could have stopped them and come here together, if you truly had to find me!"

Asra was close enough to strike Macta. Her fists were clenched, and her eyes glowed with rage. The Prince was just about to protest when the Mage of Storehoj spoke in a withering voice. "The Canon is quite clear about the penalty for destroying trees. You will come with me, both of you." The Mage shouted to her monks. "Take the others who are hiding in that abomination into custody. They must all be delivered to the catacombs, at once!"

"You must be joking," Macta said, staring incredulously at

Brahja-Chi. "Who do you think you are? You have no right to arrest me or my servants. Call off your minions or you'll be sorry you ever decided to undertake this course of action."

A pair of monks slipped up behind Macta and Asra and grabbed them by the arms. "The penalty is death," Brahja-Chi rasped. "The Gods demand that your lives be sacrificed as punishment for what you have done here. Now will you come quietly, or will you force us to take your lives here and now?"

Asra cried out in surprise, but Macta slipped from the monk's grasp and withdrew his dagger from its scabbard. He leapt forward and grabbed the Mage by the throat, pressing the blade against her wrinkled neck. He grinned menacingly. "We will leave here with your blessing, hag, or we will leave without it. But we will leave here alive, nonetheless." The Prince shouted at the monks who held Asra in their grip. "Stand down, or your Mage dies!"

"Do you not think I could stop your heart with a simple spell?" Brahja-Chi hissed, staring coldly into Macta's face.

"Do you not know who my father is?" Macta replied.

Brahja-Chi sneered, her face a mask of disgust and calculation. Then she ordered, "Let the Elfmaid go," and she slumped out of Macta's grip.

The monks backed away from Asra and the Arvada. "Come," Macta snorted, grabbing Asra by the shoulder. "Let us not stay where we're not wanted!"

"But we must bring our dead back home!" Asra cried, looking

over her shoulder at the dozen glowing orbs that hovered near the wreckage of the royal gondola. "I can't leave Skara here!"

Macta shuddered. "I'm afraid we must, Asra. Your parents need you at home. Come inside the Arvada. The accommodations are quite comfortable, I assure you!"

Moments later the vaporous tail of the Sprite began to swing back and forth. "There will be retribution!" Brahja-Chi shouted, and her monks wailed and swayed as a cloud of dust enveloped them.

The monstrous creature gulped air, gulped again, shuddered, and lifted into the air. Soon Asra would be able to look down upon the forest, and the frail white arteries of Cord lacing through the darkness. She would be able to see where the rescue party and her best friend had met their fate. But for the moment she contemplated her own fate, and turned to gaze upon the smiling face of her future husband, Macta Dockalfar. "I saved your life!" he exclaimed, inflated with his own sense of bravery and self-importance.

"Only after you put it in jeopardy," Asra replied.

39

WHEN DAWN ROSE in the forest, Jardaine was already awake. Her eyes gleamed in steely resolve as she gripped one of the Mage's crickets in her hands. She looked at it with interest; it would take at least several bites to consume the thing. The insect's antennae waved as Jardaine contemplated the task before her. *Soon Tuava-Li will be out of the way,* she thought. *Finally, I'll be the Mage of Alfheim. Soon I'll acquire the Mage's ability to transform into an animal, and I must be ready to hunt. Insects, first, and then mice, and lizards, voles and moles, and rats.*

This was part of the Mage's way to learn to draw powerful energy from living flesh. She had delayed the inevitable long enough. In one swift move, Jardaine bit the cricket's head off and gulped it down. The taste was bitter, the texture a revolting mixture of hard shell and slippery innards. *But not bad,* she thought. She shivered and stood up. Grabbing a water-filled gourd, she took a long draught.

It was time for Jardaine to meet the other monks for their morning rituals of meditation and prayer. But that could surely wait a little longer. Jardaine's eyes were drawn once more to the pages of a book that lay on the Mage's desk. For many hours she had pored over the pictures of predatory creatures, hoping that one animal in particular would elicit some emotion, some feeling of kinship, some sense of identity. These were the animals that the Mages of the Elfin world had as their familiars, their totem animals. Not all of them were fierce predators; there were raccoons, opossums, badgers, ferrets, bears, bobcats, red foxes, and weasels. Any of them *could* be dangerous. But Jardaine thought it would be far preferable to change into an animal that possessed some dignity, and not one of the clumsy, lumbering little scavengers that scurried along the forest floor. Jardaine knew her inner nature only too well. When one day she was ready for her transformation, it would undoubtedly be a fearsome creature, an animal worthy of respect and fear. Nothing less was even conceivable. The birds in the illustrations included hawks, such as the falcons and the kestrel, as well as the many varieties of the owl, and the vultures. It was quite a range. Then there were the snakes. *How awful,* she thought with a shiver, *for one Mage to be transformed into something that slithered along the ground when another might soar through the heavens.*

"What'ssss wrong?" hissed Sarette, from inside the Monk's garment.

"Not a thing," Jardaine replied, eyeing the reptile critically. "Sarette, how do you like being a snake?"

"There'sss nothing wrong with being a sssnake," Sarette answered.

Jardaine shrugged. "I didn't say there was."

The bell clattered on the limb outside the Mage's quarters and Jardaine jumped. Who would be calling on her at this hour? She hurried to peer down the trunk of Bethok. With a sigh of relief she stepped back and folded her arms. It wasn't long before Nebiros stepped from the door of the cage onto the massive gnarled limb. "You wear that red hat, and anyone will see you coming," Jardaine said. "Maybe you ought to try blending in a little more. There's something to be said for the art of subtlety."

Nebiros scowled. "Greetings to you, too, Jardaine. Don't forget, there's something to be said for the art of courtesy. It would show you appreciate the work I do for you!"

"I'll show some appreciation when you tell me what news there is of Macta and the Dockalfars."

"Everything is going according to plan," the Elf said.

"Of coursssе it isss," uttered Sarette, her forked tongue darting next to Jardaine's pointed ear. "'Tisss *my* plan, after all."

"'Tis not just *your* plan," hissed Jardaine, "We're a team, don't forget. We're all working together for the same goal. We all share the work, and we'll all reap the rewards."

"Don't forget what you promisssed me," Sarette breathed.

Nebiros rolled his eyes and snorted. "A snake, with legs. 'Tis preposterous!"

In a blur of motion, Sarette lunged at the Elf, twisting around his throat as he toppled to the floor. "When Jardaine isss Mage," the snake whispered, "and her magick has given me legsss to shadow your every ssstep, we will sssee who is prepossterousss."

Disentangling himself, Nebiros leapt back, wiping spittle from his cheek. "Honestly, Jardaine, I can't believe you promise that reptile—"

"It *can* be done, and it *will* be done," Jardaine reprimanded, her eyes wide. "Sarette knows 'tis possible for a Mage to use her power to create a set of legs for a snake. The only question," she smiled, stroking the snake's scaly head, "is how many legs does she want?"

Sarette's eyes glazed over dreamily, as she contemplated her appearance with four legs, six, eight, even a hundred.

"Now, what news do you bring?" Jardaine demanded. "You nearly scared me to death when you rang the bell. For a second I thought it might be Tuava-Li, back from her latest hunting expedition for the Mage. But then I saw your ridiculous red hat and realized 'twas only you."

"Tuava-Li's still looking for the Mage?"

"Listen to this," Jardaine enthused. "I went to Ljosalfar to deliver Tuava-Li's message that she was taking the old hag's place as Mage. But by the time I got back to Alfheim, I found Parslaine and Ebba in charge, and Tuava-Li off on another of her wild goose chases."

Nebiros scowled. "What chance do you think she has of coming back with the Mage?"

"None whatsoever," Jardaine chuckled. "Macta told me the Mage was near death when he lost her in the woods before. I was furious that he didn't finish her off, but after giving it some thought, I concluded he was right. A creature like that couldn't survive for long. Tuava-Li won't find her precious Mage, and I'd be surprised if she comes back herself, this time. She'll be too ashamed to return empty-handed once again. 'Tis completely exhausting keeping up with Tuava-Li—*the Mage is alive, the Mage is dead. The Mage is alive, the Mage is dead.* After the wedding, and I'm sworn in as Mage of Alfheim, there won't be any more of that nonsense. Now tell me about your latest meeting with Macta, and make it quick. The monks are waiting for me."

"Macta tells me that his father has been putting the finishing touches on some new secret weapons," Nebiros began, "and assures us we won't be disappointed! Princess Asra's safely back in Ljosalfar, getting used to the feel of her wedding shoes, and Macta is training his Human pet, that ghost girl he found in the stream, to—"

The bell startled them both. Someone was pulling on the cable to the wicker lift, and the rats in their treetop cage scurried into the wheel. "Oh nooo," muttered Jardaine, as she leaned over the limb and peered into the foliage. "'Tis that Troll, the one I sent you to spy on. What does he want?"

"I'm stayin' out here," Tomtar told Jardaine, when he arrrived on the high branch outside the Mage's quarters. "I don't need to come any closer. I was pacing back and forth through the woods all night long, tryin' to decide what to do. I don't understand anything any more. All I know is, this property is yours, not mine. Just take it, and I'll go."

Jardaine and Nebiros exchanged glances as the Troll emptied the contents of a burlap sack. Great chunks of ruby, peridot, sapphire, and tourmaline spilled out, and Jardaine bent down to examine the stones. From the glittering heap she plucked a small Elfin figure cut from a piece of chrysolite, and turned it slowly in her hand. "The Jewels of Alfheim. I can't believe my eyes."

The monks of Alfheim were gathering at the base of the mighty oak. Concerned that Jardaine had not yet arrived for morning prayers, they had come to find her. It wasn't long before many other Elves joined them there. "Where did you get these Jewels?" Jardaine demanded, loudly enough for all below to hear.

Tomtar pointed into the woods. "I trailed the Human, like you asked me to. But there was an accident, and the boy saw me, and we began to talk. I know I wasn't supposed to, but I got to know him—at least it seemed that way. I thought you were wrong about the Humans. I thought they were my friends. But Matt, and the other *Tems*, they fooled me. They stole the Jewels. You were right all along. The Humans are our enemies—Matt, and his whole family. Now you know what I know. Good-bye."

"Wait," ordered Jardaine.

"I'm sorry," Tomtar said, turning away. "I don't want to stay here anymore."

"You're not going anywhere yet," Jardaine snapped.

Nebiros whispered in Jardaine's ear. *"This is better than we could have expected! Who'd have thought the Troll would find the Jewels we planted in the Humans' house? Now we don't need to make a show of searching—"*

"Ssssssh!" spat Sarette, lifting her head inside Jardaine's tunic.

Jardaine held up the chrysolite figure and stalked to the edge of the branch so that those on the ground could look up and observe how she was handling this unexpected situation. "What you've brought us is only a small portion of the Jewels of Alfheim, just a fragment of our Clan treasure. How many more Jewels were there in the Human house?"

"I don't know," Tomtar replied. "I just wanted to get out of there. You can go get 'em yourselves. Now will you let me leave? I've got a long way to travel before I get back home."

"Home?" Jardaine echoed. "You're on your Wandering. Are you saying your journey's finished? And you're going home empty-handed? No gift for your Clan?"

Tomtar's eyes were moist and red-rimmed. He shook his

head. "Just me and the story I'll tell, 'bout how my trust was betrayed by . . . by the Humans."

"No, Tomtar," Jardaine said. "You can't go home with nothing but a story. I'd like to reward you for your loyalty and good work. Please, choose among the stones. Go ahead, take whatever one you like. 'Twill be our way of saying thank you, of affirming the bond between you and our Clan."

"Nooo, not that, that'sss againssst Clan tradition," hissed Sarette. "You know you can't go againssst tradition! The othersss will not approve!"

"I can do whatever I like," Jardaine mumbled. "Tuava-Li isn't in charge here any more, I am. 'Tis my opinion that we make some new traditions around here."

Tomtar stared at the gleaming Jewels, and struggled to find his way through a maze of confusing thoughts. He was obliged to return to the Argant Clan with a special gift, when his Wandering was done. Was his gift meant to be one of the Jewels of Alfheim? It was possible. Bringing a Jewel home would certainly make for a good story, one that the Trolls would remember for generations to come. But there was a more obvious reason for not taking one of the Jewels from Jardaine. There were so many sad memories, hurt feelings, so much of a sense of betrayal connected to the precious stones. Tomtar never knew his heart could hurt so badly. He had allowed himself to feel like a part of Matt's family, and they had deceived him. The Jewels would never mean anything but sadness to him now. "I won't take one of your stones," he said. "You don't need to reward me."

"Then so be it," answered Jardaine. "But I insist that you stay with us a while longer. 'Tis important that the Synod hear your story. There are many questions that still need to be answered."

The monk directed her attention to the crowd gathered below. "Children of Alfheim!" she shouted. "This only proves what vile, thieving vermin the Humans are, and what a danger they pose to us. At this moment they're butchering our forest, and claiming the land of our ancestors as their own. Is it any wonder that they stole from us not only Princess Asra's wedding shoe, but the precious Jewels of Alfheim? We won back the wedding shoe, but we jeopardized the safety of our Clan in bargaining with the Human. I give you my promise, we'll not rest 'til all of the Alfheim Jewels are back where they belong, and the Humans are driven out of our homeland, once and for all. No matter what it takes!"

Shouts of "In Truth! In Truth!" rose from the crowd gathering on the forest floor.

"We must stop them from digging in our Sacred Earth. We will use whatever means we have to make sure they don't continue to threaten our survival. As soon as we are able we'll take back the rest of our fortune, and burn the Human houses to the ground!"

Tomtar watched Nebiros shovel the gems back into the sack

as Jardaine, grinning from ear to ear, turned away from the edge of the branch. *"That wasssn't very sssmart,"* hissed Sarette. *"The plan was t' sssave the aggression for when the Humansss show up unannounced at Macta's wedding. Now everyone knowsss your real intentionsss."*

Jardaine wiped snake spittle from her neck. *"Shut up,"* she whispered. *"The more we fan the flames of hate, the easier 'twill be for the fires to spread. Don't you think I know what I'm doing?"*

40

TUAVA-LI COULD FEEL it before it happened. She was passing westward in a narrow Cord, drawn to the Mage by a force greater than fear, or love, or her own willpower. The Cords, once bustling with Faerie life, were now nearly deserted; only an unsuspecting few still made their passage along the Low Road. A family of Pixies rocketed past Tuava-Li. The little father nodded, and his children giggled as they went by. Suddenly Tuava-Li heard a pulsing, sucking sound ahead. She felt the pressure change in her ears. "Stop!" she cried out, alarm turning her voice into a command. "You've got to slow yourselves, there's danger—"

The little cluster of Pixies, startled by Tuava-Li's voice, did as they were told. Following her example, they clutched at the walls of the Cord. Farther along, Tuava-Li saw shadows.

There was a flapping sound coming from where the tattered Cord had opened up. *Better to leave now than chance the force of the wind ahead,* she thought, forcing her fingers through the wall and prying an opening above her. *"Aaaaaahhh!"* came a cry from behind. One of the children had lost her grip, and was instantly yanked away in the torrent of air. Tuava-Li shot out her free hand and grabbed the little Pixie as she hurtled past. Then she flung the child out through the hole above, and held back the edge while the other Pixies climbed to safety. Just ahead, the Cord bulged into the open air, its torn walls flopping. Tuava-Li climbed out to join the others on the ground. "If you come close to one of those flaps, 'twill hit you like a hammer. This Cord's not safe. You'll have to find another way to get where you're going."

"We can't thank you enough!" cried the mother Pixie as she gathered up her children, her enormous eyes blinking in the sunlight. Then she turned to scowl at her mate. "I told you we shouldn't travel in the Cord!"

The father fluttered around Tuava-Li's head, with his youngest daughter in his arms. She reached down to touch the Elfmaid's hair. "What happened to our Cord?" she asked.

The father shook his head. "Hush, child, nobody knows the answer to that."

"Actually, I *do* know," Tuava-Li said, still out of breath. "The Cord is old. It's dying. For the Cord to be reborn, a new Seed must be planted."

The Pixies stared blankly at the Elfmaid, which only made her want to explain all that she had learned in her vision. "A new Seed must be planted at the center of the earth, as it was in ancient times. That's the only thing that'll save it . . . that's the only thing that'll save *us*."

The father snorted. "A Seed? I can see by the way you're dressed that you're a monk, and I don't want to show you any disrespect, especially after what you did to help us. But if anything is to blame for the state of the Cord, 'tis the Humans, cutting our forests, hacking away at our Cord everywhere in the world, that weakens it like this. But planting a Seed? That's just an old story!"

"It doesn't help us to blame the Humans," Tuava-Li said. "They don't even know we exist. To make this forest *our* world again, the legend must be lived anew. Don't you remember the story of Fada?"

"Well, I—"

"In mythic days," Tuava-Li explained, "the Faerie Prince Fada and two companions journeyed to pluck the fruit from one of the Holy Trees, and to take the Seed that grew inside. They traveled to the Underworld to plant the Seed in the earth where the old one was dying. When the sacrifice of Blood had been made to awaken the Seed's power, the Faerie world was restored. It must all happen again, for us to survive."

"We owe you our thanks for helping us in the Cord, but now we've got to find our way home," the Pixie father said, frowning.

"Follow me," he said to his family, and they opened their wings and fluttered into the forest.

"Stay close to the trees," Tuava-Li called. "The forest is a dangerous place, too."

"Aren't we going to visit Grandmama?" cried one of the children.

"Not today," the mother said.

Tuava-Li brushed at a gnat on her cheek. Like the Pixie family, the insect flew off into the warm afternoon air. Tuava-Li kicked the ground in frustration. *If only . . .* she thought. *If only I could fly.*

But no. Wishes were for the weak; the strong acted to make their desires into realities. So what if she couldn't fly? She would stay close to the earth, and still she would find her Mage at the end of this journey. No one could take her confidence away. So what if it would be easier to sail above the trees, so what if it would be faster? No one would take away her resolve. Tuava-Li gazed into the cloudy sky and saw a hawk drifting on a breeze. Once more the longing swept into her heart. If she were a bird, she would fly with purpose. She would use her wings to reach her destination. She would soar high into the sky, and then—and then—Tuava-Li blinked.

The hawk was plunging straight for the fluttering Pixie family. Tuava-Li opened her mouth to warn them. But her cry was strangled, her tongue felt thick in her mouth. And before she knew what was happening she was rocketing through the air toward the hawk, a fierce *Craaaaaawwrrr!* forming in her throat. Tuava-Li glanced down and saw the ground falling away beneath her. A blur of rust-hued feathers swept a path where her arms should have been. Pink fingers jutted from the tips of fully formed wings. Her speckled breast swelled in downy white feathers. As her clothing dropped from her body, her new wings pumped up and down. She glanced at the trees below, and her kestrel body was flooded with panic. She clutched at her stomach, and felt her fingers forming once again. Then, in terror, she realized that she was changing back into an Elf; the fear was taking over and reversing her transformation.

Whooomp! She lay on the ground for a moment, trying to catch her breath, her heart pounding wildly in her chest. "Owww!" she cried, turning on her back and reaching for her injured shoulder. Nothing was broken, but the pain and the shock were overwhelming. Was this the transformation she had been longing for? She climbed to her feet, naked, dirty, and sore, and glanced at her scraped and bloodied hands. Then she heard a cry, looked up, and saw the hawk sweeping below the treetops. *The change happened because I imagined it to be so,* Tuava-Li thought. She tried to rein in the chaotic energy pulsing through her body, making an effort to direct the power toward her fingertips. Immediately she discovered that it was not willpower that directed the change. It was more like bringing her attention to a place in the mind where the material world was ready to transmute. Right before her eyes, Tuava-Li's

fingers softened and blended into a smudge of brown feathers. It wasn't exactly painful, but it bore no relationship to any pleasure Tuava-Li had ever felt before. *Not an owl,* she thought, *not like the Mage, but still a bird. Still I can fly!*

The Pixie children shrank in terror as the hawk snatched their mother in its claws. The father flapped alongside the fearsome bird, pounding on its flank with his fists. "Let go!" he bellowed. "Let go!"

Then, as if from nowhere, the kestrel appeared. With a wallop she plunged headfirst into the hawk's belly. The hawk reflexively opened its claws and dropped the Pixie. Straight toward the ground the tiny creature plummeted. At the last possible moment, her husband fluttered into range and swept her up in his arms. The hawk, meanwhile, soared away; it didn't like having to work so hard for a meal.

Tuava-Li came to an awkward landing in a patch of pine needles. She flexed her wings and squawked. The Pixies trembled, and watched in awe as the body of the kestrel seemed to turn in on itself and become the Elfmaid who had rescued them in the Cord. "'Tis twice in one day I've had to save your lives," Tuava-Li said breathlessly, gathering up her clothing. "Now, will you promise me you'll be more careful? I don't have time to be your guardian angel."

With that, she closed her eyes, drew in her energy, and became a kestrel once more. As the Pixies watched, Tuava-Li clutched her garments in her claws and flapped to the low branch of a tree. She hopped to a higher branch, and then a higher one still. Then she lifted her wings and sailed fearlessly into the air. As the wind rushed over her feathers, Tuava-Li allowed the joy inside to flow like a torrent through her new body. It lifted her, soaring, to heights she had never even guessed were possible.

41

"I NEVER THOUGHT we'd find this place," Jardaine muttered, staring at the pile of acorns piled up around the trunk of the elm tree. Nebiros grunted, wiping the sweat from his brow. They scanned the forlorn place, with the tangles of briars, the deer antler, and the human gloves hanging from the branches.

"My feet hurt," said Jardaine. She winced and sat on the edge of a boulder to take off her slippers and massage her blistered heels. "If you'd been able to locate Macta, we never would have needed to come all this way. His father's Experimentalists could have given us what we want."

Nebiros batted at one of the moldy gloves and watched it swing back and forth. "I suppose the Prince is preoccupied with his infernal wedding."

"'Tis what' comes after the wedding that ought to concern him more," said Jardaine. "There's a war about to begin. And the blisters on my feet are killing me!"

Sarette darted her scaly head from Jardaine's collar. "The one blesssed with feet complainsss of blissstersss, while ignoring the missery of the one who hasss no feet at all."

Suddenly a squirrel tail appeared in the crook of two large branches, waving frantically. A rain of acorns came down on the Elves' heads. In one swift motion, Jardaine drew a piece of sharpened flint from her robe and flung it at the squirrel tail. With a quiver the weapon lodged in the branch. A little Troll dressed in a grubby vest leapt out from behind, waggling the squirrel tail in front of him. "I know magick," he cried, "so you'd best back off, if you know what's good for you!"

"Simmer down, Agar," Jardaine demanded. "Don't you remember us? When you showed up in Alfheim to complain about the *robbery* that you said took place here? 'Tis me, Jardaine, the next Mage of Alfheim, and my servant Nebiros. Now come over here this instant."

"You, you," the Troll huffed, "you tried to kill me! Now get out of here, before you make me do somethin' I'll—"

"Relax, Agar," Nebiros advised. "Nobody wants to do you any harm."

"I wouldn't have thrown the flint if you weren't such a hostile old coot, putting on that display with the acorns and the squirrel tail," Jardaine said. "We're not frightened of squirrels, you know.

Anyway, if I'd wanted to hurt you, you'd already be lying on the ground in a pool of your own Blood. We need your help, Agar. Let's go somewhere a little more private and discuss it, shall we?"

The Troll scratched the bald spot beneath his cap and gazed about, his suspicious eyes searching the woods. "Well, then, follow me," Agar huffed. "You can come inside. I've been doin' some house cleanin', so you'll have to mind your step."

The Elves followed the Troll down the cluttered stairs. Gingerly they worked their way around piles of rubble, stones, shells, bundles of dried leaves, and colorful plastic toys. Jardaine whistled and shook her head at the mess. "Human things. Only a fool would risk contagion like this. Nebiros, make sure you don't touch anything. Now, Agar, why don't you show us where you kept the Jewels?"

The Troll turned in alarm. "Wha—?"

"Aye, we know all about it," Jardaine continued. "Don't worry, we'll keep your secret. Nobody has to know that you stole the Jewels of Alfheim. And don't feel too badly about losing them; the Jewels are back in our possession once again . . . at least some of them. Your friend Tomtar found them hidden in the Humans' house. He didn't bring them all back to us, but at least we know where they are. And that brings me to the reason we're here, Agar. You see, we want to kill the Humans. Not all of them, just yet, only a few. The problem is, we can't figure out a good way to do it. The monks of Alfheim are trained in the mystical arts, you know, for the purposes of healing, of bringing unity and peace, and that sort of rubbish."

"Why did you ever become a monk, if that's how you feel?" asked Agar.

"Not that it's any of your business," answered Jardaine. "But in this life, there are few paths to power. I took the steps that were available to me. Now—we've searched the Mage's library for spells, incantations, poisons that would help us eliminate the Humans, but we've found nothing. We know that contamination from Elfin things can harm Humans if it enters their Bloodstream, but it takes too long for the effects to do their damage."

Jardaine walked a slow circle around the Troll. "You're known to have a special talent in the realm of med'cinal arts, Agar. If you provide us with what we're looking for, we'll make sure that business with the Alfheim Jewels is kept just between us."

Agar stared up at the tangle of tree roots on the ceiling. He stroked his grizzled beard. "Hmmmmm . . . I happen to have read a book or two on the very subject. Somethin' that'll work quickly, you say? Do you want somethin' fancy? Somethin' that'll result in great Blood loss? Pain? Somethin' that'll cause bodily tissues to dissolve, somethin' that'll burn, or rot? Something that'll keep the mind alive whilst the body falls apart? A fast-acting poison that could be injected into the Bloodstream through the use of darts, perhaps?"

Jardaine turned to Nebiros and grinned. "I think we've come to the right place," she said.

The bulldozer rattled over the rough terrain, lifting tree trunks that had been cut into sections for easier hauling. Some of the pieces weighed hundreds of pounds, yet the bulldozer lifted them as if they were toys and hoisted them into the clearing. Charlie McCormack sat behind the controls. He blinked away the sweat that rolled down from beneath his hard hat. It had been a stroke of good luck to find a leasing company with a bulldozer ready for delivery, when he hadn't yet managed to get the backhoe repaired. If he got these trees out of the way by noon, when the rest of his crew arrived, they'd be ready to start cutting back the edge of the forest once again. Enough land for a few more houses, enough work for another six months or so.

Five feet into the trees, the gloom of the forest was oppressive. In the shadows lurked Tomtar, accompanied by three Alfheim Elves. All of them had their fingers stuffed into their ears. Tomtar grimaced at the roar of the motor, but peered through the foliage to keep his eye on the machine and its Human driver. Then he noticed one of the Elves creeping into an open space between two trees. "Get back," he ordered, grabbing him by his collar. "Stay out of sight!"

"The Human can't see me, can he?" warbled the Elf, scurrying back into the shadows. "I'm supposed to be invisible!"

"You weren't listenin' to what I told you while we were hiking here," scolded Tomtar. "I think the young *Tems* can see us, and maybe some of the big ones, too, some of the time, and maybe all of the time. Everything is changin'; nothing's like it used to be. You can't rely on anything you've ever heard about what *Tems* can or can't see and do. Just stay back and keep covered by the trees. Be on the lookout for more *Tems* comin' across the field. Sometimes there are lots of 'em here, and then they do a lot more damage, in a lot less time."

The Elves hopped up and down in frustration, covering their ears with trembling hands. "We can't hear you! The machine is too loud! What do we have to stay here for? We know that *thing* will be hauling off dead trees all morning. 'Tis too late to save 'em. There's nothing we can do here! Can't we go home, where it's quiet, and come back later when the Humans are gone?"

"Listen," Tomtar said. "Jardaine ordered us to watch the Humans and their machines, and that's what we're goin' to do."

The Elves turned to each other. "Eeh? What did the Troll say?"

"I don't know," answered another. "I can't hear anything but that horrible racket. I'm going deaf from all the noise!"

The smallest of the Elves trembled. *Why did they choose me to come here?* he thought. The Elf's brow was dripping with sweat and his eyes squinted into the sunlight beyond the line of trees. Every minute here in proximity to the metal monster was agony. Now it was coming closer, so close he could feel the earth shake beneath his feet. He had to get away. Now!

When the bulldozer scraped against a boulder, causing an unexpected scream of metal on stone, the small Elf let out a shriek of terror and bolted. Tomtar shot after him. "Stop! You're goin' the wrong way!"

Sunlight glared on the bulldozer's windshield. Charlie McCormack blinked when he saw a flash of movement out of the corner of his eye. *What was that? An animal? A kid?* He jerked his head toward the place where he thought he saw—and there it was again! No, it was something different this time. There was more than one of them. Two, three, no, four children, running along the edge of the woods. Who could they be, out here in the forest? A tiny face turned toward Charlie, and for an instant their eyes met. Charlie shook his head and reached for the hand brake. But by accident he lurched forward, the great wheels of the bulldozer plowing over a fallen log, over a small embankment, toward the trees and the children. He grappled for control as he saw them scatter before him. One of them screamed and leapt past the bucket. Another was heaved onto the front of the cab, his hands smoking as he knuckled across the metal. These were no children! Flustered, astonished, Charlie was overwhelmed by the roar of the motor and the frantic shrieks of the little creatures. He jerked the steering wheel to avoid plowing into the trees; and then he lost control. The bulldozer toppled to the right. With its tires spinning in the air, the vehicle ground to a stop. Charlie tumbled sideways out of his seat. With a loud crack his helmet struck a boulder, and his world faded to black.

Tomtar scurried over a log to see what had happened. The motor of the machine was squealing, an awful, high-pitched sound of metal grinding against metal. The Elves clutched at the Troll's legs, trying to hide behind his scrawny body. Tomtar instantly recognized Matt's father. His stomach convulsed in a knot of confusion. It was more than the mere nausea that he got from being so close to metal. "Let's get out of here!" he shouted to the Elves. "We'll head back to Alfheim, fast. This is big, big. Jardaine'll want to know what happened here."

Tomtar glanced across the field to Matt's house, and his heart ached. He thought about the cookies he had eaten in their kitchen, the pretend tea he had shared with Becky. Where were Matt and Becky, and their mom? Prying the Elves from the legs of his trousers, Tomtar strode back to the toppled bulldozer. He pulled the sleeve of his jacket down over his hand, then pressed hard on the steering wheel horn. The Elves leapt back in surprise. "It's a warning," said Tomtar. "I saw the *Tems* do this when I was . . . spying on them."

Tomtar leaned on the horn three times. Then he pressed three more. "Is he dead?" asked the Elves, peering through their fingers. "Is the Human dead?"

Tomtar glanced down at the man sprawled on the ground next to the vehicle. "Come on!" he yelled to the Elves. "There's nothin' more we can do. Let's go."

42

INSIDE THE BASKET THE SHOES gleamed and sparkled. Queen Shorya knelt at Asra's feet with the basket in her hands, smiling up at her daughter. The Princess sat in a high-backed chair and glowered. Then she lifted both bare feet and sighed in resignation. "They're only shoes," she said. "'Tis only a wedding," she added. "'Tis only my life."

"I don't know how many Elfmaids in our lineage have worn these," Shorya said, gently slipping the shoes onto Asra's feet. "Perhaps a hundred or more. I pray there'll be a hundred more after you!"

Asra bristled. "And what is that supposed to mean? Do you say that because of what happened to Skara? Or because I'm to marry Macta? Is there something I don't know?"

"Parents always worry for their children, that's all," the Queen said. "The future's unknown. And the unknown always inspires fear. I've lived long enough to see many happy things turn out . . . unexpectedly. But listen, dear, we got the shoe back, didn't we? 'Tis a good omen." Shorya leaned back to admire the shoes. "Well, they're beautiful; you can't deny it. Listen, Asra, we all grow up. You had your years to play. Now it's time to put childish things aside. Before you know it, you'll be a mother, too, chasing around babies of your own."

A gentle knock sounded at the chamber door. Asra looked up sadly. "When I think of Skara, it makes me—"

"Hush, child, 'tis morbid to wallow in sorrow the way you do," said the Queen, turning her head to the arched doorway. "Come in!"

A host of Elfmaids slipped into the room. Each carried an article of adornment from the Princess's wedding trousseau, including the mandrake-leaf wig, the spider-silk gown with the feathered train, the ribbons and bows. The seamstress in charge of the wardrobe gathered the Elfmaids in a row. "Time for another fitting," she exclaimed.

"For heaven's sake, n-n-not yet!" cried a voice from the doorway. King Thorgier padded across the floor. "Shorya, Asra, there's something I'd like to sh-sh-show you."

Behind the King, a pair of engineers trailed. With thick spectacles perched on their noses and hands clutched behind long, black coats, they eyed Princess Asra and glanced away.

"Take a l-l-look at this," stammered the King, as the engineers knelt at the foot of Asra's chair to spread out a roll of parchment. It was decorated with images of the Cord, propped up at strategic locations with an elaborate framework of supports. "None of us wants to ride in those infernal eagle-contraptions that the Dockalfars t-t-travel around in," said the King. "So I've asked the engineers to devise a grand p-p-plan."

"Allow me to explain," said one of the engineers. "As you know, the primary artery of the Cord between Ljosalfar and Alfheim has become weakened in several locations, making conventional travel problematic. We've designed a series of reinforcements that can be installed quickly at the weak points, buttressing the walls of the Cord. This will allow you to travel safely to Alfheim in your royal gondolas, just like you've always done."

Queen Shorya nodded. "If this is possible, why didn't the Synod vote to use this technology to shore up the Cord in all of its major branches?"

"Your highness," said the other engineer, "in places where the Cord lies deeply buried, the earth holds it in place like a corset. But in places where it runs closer to the surface, 'tis possible for the walls of the Cord to rupture nearly anywhere. The means we've devised to bolster the Cord for your travel is intended just for the day of the Princess's wedding, just for the weak spots and lacerations that currently exist. We've already experimented with supports for the Cord in several places. But with the winds, and the weakness of the Cord itself, the effects are temporary at best. We can't make any guarantees for the future, when more fissures are certain to occur."

The engineers peered over their spectacles at Asra, who gave them a frown. "What will you need to build these supports?" asked the Queen. "Timber, I assume. Is there any magick involved?"

"Aye, there is."

"What about the wood? How much?"

"Quite a bit, I'm afraid."

"Do we have enough fallen timber to build these supports?" asked the Queen.

King Thorgier and the engineers exchanged nervous glances. "My dear, I'm afraid it requires the s-s-sacrifice of a large number of our living trees. That's why I've come to d-d-discuss it with you."

"So it's come to this," mused the Queen. "Then have the botanists and caretakers of the forest select weak or sickly trees for sacrifice. 'Tis *survival of the fittest* now, may the Gods forgive us."

43

MACTA KICKED OPEN THE DOOR leading from the underground gaming chambers and stepped into daylight. Candles along the corridor were snuffed out as wind rushed into the passageway. The Prince stalked into the cobbled street, his fist clenched. Baltham followed, letting the door close quietly behind him. He shivered and tugged at the collar of his jacket. At close range, anything or anyone could become Macta's target, so he kept a safe distance from his master. *Bam!* The doors were flung open once more as Zelimir the Dwarf and his two cronies stumbled into the gray afternoon air. Macta spun around and glared at the Dwarves. Zelimir chortled, pointed, and nudged his translator in the ribs. The third Dwarf, the one who carried the sack of money, laughed out loud. "Why, if it isn't *the Ant,"* mocked the translator, referring to the toss of the dice that had lost Macta the money he had made from selling off his stash of the stolen Jewels of Alfheim. "*The Ant,* and his little cockroach!"

The three burst into gales of raucous laughter as Macta stood staring at them with contempt. "Hello, again, Mr. Ant," said Zelimir, stepping forward. "Fancy finding ye're still here, after the tragedy what happen'd inside!"

Macta was incredulous. "Zelimir, you—you speak our language? Then why do you have a translator? Why did you pretend—why, you scoundrel, you cheat, *you!*"

"Just part o' game," the Dwarf snickered. "Say, young Prince, perhaps ye'd be intereste'd in making little wager? What are the chances thah sweet-faced Princess from Alfheim will show up at wedding o' ye'rs t'morrow? What are odds . . . two t' one? Five t' one? Zelimir's willing t' bet she is a no-show. But, oh dear, I forgot, Macta, you have nothing left t' gamble! Sorry!"

Exercising uncharacteristic restraint, Macta turned his back to the Dwarves. The rage screaming in his ears drowned out the sound of their horrible laughter. *Control,* he said to himself, teeth clenched, *control.* Meanwhile his life was spinning out of control. The tidy sum he had extracted from the gem merchant? Gone. He never should have risked it, but Macta was so swept up in his emotions that he had believed he couldn't possibly lose. Everything of value that Macta owned was squandered, thrown away at the gaming tables. *No matter,* he thought. *This will soon be forgotten, once I'm married, and the war with the Humans has begun. Then the real money will begin rolling in.*

"Forgive me," mumbled Baltham, hanging back a few paces, "but Macta, if you have no further use for me this afternoon, I have some obligations at home. Yenri is expecting me to take the children to their fencing lesson."

"Then go," spat Macta. "Abandon me in my darkest hour. What do I care."

Baltham scurried to Macta's side. "No, if you need me, Macta, I'll stay. I will! Yenri can send the children with the servants. You know how she is, she expects me to do everything, even when she knows how important my job is assisting you!"

"Your problem, Baltham, is that you've got to decide who your Master is. You can't serve two, you know."

Baltham swallowed. Being married to Macta's sister presented him with a vexing dilemma; he *did* have two Masters. But he had learned that the Master to whom he should bow was whichever Master stood before him. Baltham bent low and clicked his heels. "My Prince," he squeaked, "I am at your command."

"Then I command you to go home and tend to your family. I have no need of your company today. I was just testing you, Baltham. I made a little wager in my mind that you would yield to me, and I won. I won! If only there had been some money riding on the bet. Now go, before I change my mind."

As Baltham scurried out of harm's way, Macta pictured Princess Asra's face. It floated before him, indistinct and fuzzy. It hovered for a moment before crumbling away, revealing behind it the green, slobbering visage of his pet, Powcca. Macta forced back a sob.

My confirmation dress, it's so pretty, the satin, the bow for my hair, Mommy is putting in the hem. Like a princess, Daddy said, I look like a princess standing on the chair, while Mommy pins the hem. Daddy says he'll be so proud, and I'll be proud, too . . . when I look down, my new patent leather shoes are so shiny, so bright!

But I'm in the water, always,

the water.

It's too late, now, too late for me, too late for Mommy and Daddy, too late. I want to lie down in the water, I have to lie down, for it's just about

over.

"What in the name of—" shouted Macta. There in his apartment, by the lava statue in the parlor fountain, were his housekeepers, Herma and Holda. Between them stood the Human girl he had taken from the stream near Alfheim, the one they called Liqua. She hovered, staring into space, with the doll and the photographs in her arms, with that same stricken look her face always wore. Herma and Holda had draped the girl in wide swaths of cream-colored fabric and were pinning the seams of the fabric together for stitching. "Long time," said Herma.

"No see," said Holda.

Mechanical birds cheeped from the plaster branches above, as Macta stalked into the chamber, flailing his arms. "What are you doing? This creature is my weapon, my tool, and you're playing dress-up with her? Look, I can see right through her arms. Her hands, my God, they're almost invisible. She's fading away. You're killing her, keeping her out of the water. Stop this nonsense and get her back in the arboretum pool!"

"We're dressing her for the wedding, sir!" Herma mumbled through the pins clutched in her teeth.

"For the wedding," said Holda. "You said she was coming, and we wanted to make sure that she looked presentable! Isn't it going to be lovely?"

"Pretty asss a picture!" hissed Herma's snake, slithering around from behind her collar.

"This isn't *your* idea, is it?" Macta fumed. "You're just as stupid as . . . as a snake. You know nothing, none of you! She's not part of the wedding, she's not a guest. Everyone would be terrified if they saw her at the ceremony. And that's exactly the point—she's my trump card, the ace up my sleeve; she's the key to the house none can enter. She's an implement, a living machine, part of our strategy. But she's not coming to the wedding; she'll be out in the woods near the Humans' house. She doesn't need a pretty party dress. The rags she was wearing when I found her were perfect camouflage. Get her back in those clothes. And for God's sake, get her back in the water so that she doesn't evaporate right before my eyes!"

Macta could hardly see Anna now, except for the head and a hint of her shoulders, and the cloth hung there like a sheet on a ghost. The doll and the McCormack family pictures looked like they were floating in space. Macta reached out and waved his hand where Anna's arm should have been. She was like a vapor, a fume. But she felt the Elf Prince's touch and recoiled.

It's nearly over. The coming and going, the waking and the dreaming, all done. There he is, the dark one, coming for me. It's in his touch,

the shadow . . . like

water, in my nose, and eyes, in my throat and my lungs. The water is everywhere, black, and cold, and the water

will take me away. No more of the past, no more

memories, no more hopes. Gone, gone, gone. I want to

go home. I want to to go to

sleep.

Herma and Holda were ushering Anna down the corridor to the arboretum when they heard a knock at the door. "What now?" Macta muttered, stalking past the rainbow-colored lanterns. He stood on tiptoes and peered through the peephole in the door. Through the fish-eye lens he could make out his father's personal tailor standing impatiently with a team of seamstresses. Macta flung open the door. "What do you want?"

The tailor breezed into the room. "We're here for your fitting, sir, time's running out."

"I'm well aware of that," Macta replied, eyeing the mounds of yellow-and-black fabric carried by the seamstresses. His heart sank as the realization hit him. "Wait—what is this? Yellow and black? I'm not wearing the Helfratheim Security colors. I won't be a walking advertisement for my father. I've been planning this day for years; I know exactly what I want to wear—a suit made of the finest moss, with an embroidered deer antler across the breast, a high collar and—"

"Your father, the King, has spoken," interrupted the tailor, "and his word is my command."

Macta stiffened. "Then I'll just have to have a little talk with my father, won't I?"

"I don't believe I see your name on today's calendar," said Cytthandra, the King's personal assistant.

"Then you'll just have to write my name down, won't you?" Macta hissed, storming past her desk.

He raised both fists and smashed them against the doors to his father's quarters. When the doors sprung open, Macta stalked inside, only to discover that no one was there. He swung around to see Cytthandra leaning against the door frame. The advising snake around her neck eyed him warily.

"Why didn't you tell me he wasn't here?" Macta inquired, his face burning with rage.

"You didn't ask."

"Then I'm asking," Macta fumed, so close to the Secretary that she could feel the heat of his breath. He grabbed Cytthandra by the collar, then whipped out his dagger. He pressed the point of the knife to her throat. "Where is my father?" he growled.

For the first time in her long relationship with Macta,

Cytthandra experienced a taste of fear. "In the Experimentalists' chambers," she croaked.

Macta stormed across the palace grounds, pushed his way past a cart of executed criminals, and snarled at anyone unlucky enough to get in his way. He found the King standing with his entourage outside the bunker known as the War Room. "Macta!" Valdis said, a smile pasted on his face. "What a surprise!"

"Father?" Macta narrowed his eyes. "I'm confused. Why are you standing out here?"

"Waiting for you, my lad. Cytthandra sent word that you wished to see me."

"But, how—I came right here from your quarters. How did she—"

"A little bird told me," said Valdis, as he glanced at a crow nodding on the gutter overhead. "I also heard that you behaved very badly toward Cytthandra. Very badly, indeed. So I am standing here in the cold and the damp in order to ascertain if you and I are still on the same side. I look upon life as a game, Macta, but one can't begin play until the sides have been drawn."

"I—I'm your son," Macta stammered, tugging at his collar, "but I don't believe we can win this game without each other's trust."

"Indeed!" The King spread his hands. "Then I trust that you will make an effort to rein in your anger, my son. Now, what have we got to talk about?"

"I'm here to discuss my wardrobe for tomorrow," Macta

said. "'Tis important that I look my best, Father. So despite your insistence, I wanted you to know I have no intention whatsoever of wearing yellow and black to my own wedding."

The King's face darkened as his advisors clicked their tongues in disapproval. "'Tis perfectly appropriate for the son of a King to honor his father and the family corporation by dressing in a manner that pays proper respect to the company. Everyone knows what the yellow and black represent—they are the colors of a bee, and they stand for the twin virtues of industry and aggression. You will play the game, son," the King exclaimed, "and your reward will be my blessing for your future happiness. Now come inside, and let's find out what the prognosticators have to say about your wedding day!"

In the chambers of the Experimentalists, the sound of moaning came from behind a pair of ironclad doors. As the pair entered the chamber, the King swept an arm around a room abuzz with activity. "The Diviners!" he said. "You can't plan a wedding or a war without them!"

A circle of black-clad Elves, their eyes squeezed shut, were rattling bundles of reeds. These bent and huddled figures were the source of the miserable groaning. "Father, what makes them—"

"Ssssssh!" ordered Valdis. "You'll destroy their concentration!"

In a low, carpeted area another group danced in circles, spinning furiously until Macta was certain they would tumble into a heap of broken arms and legs. At the center of the room stood a stone slab where an animal had been strapped, belly-up. Above the slab a Fire Sprite hovered, illuminating the squirming rodent with a fierce intensity. "We've been waiting for you, your Highness!" grinned an Elf, standing by a smoldering brazier. He was the leader of an assembly of hooded monks, who looked up anxiously when they saw their King approaching.

"Well, there's no need to wait," Valdis smiled. "Let's find out what the entrails have to say about our success in battle tomorrow! How glorious will our victory over the Humans be?"

With one deft slice from an iron blade, the Elf opened up the rodent's belly. The monks hovered over the carcass and examined the color of the liver, the shape of the heart, the arrangement of glistening organs spread out before them. Then the Elf wielding the knife stood up. He gulped, the color draining from his face.

"Well?" Valdis inquired.

"There—there's something, your Highness, something that doesn't bode well. There's something amiss, though I'm not yet certain what it is . . ."

"Let me look!" Valdis bellowed, pushing his way past the monks who surrounded the slab of stone.

"There," said the Elf, his finger trembling, "do you see the discoloration, toward the top? And do you discern the odor?"

The King sniffed, then grimaced. "So . . . it's something to do with our air offensive?"

The monks grumbled, shaking their heads. "Nooo, your

Highness, 'tis not an airship that's the problem. Leastwise not *all* of it. We're in agreement about that. It has something to do with—with *you*, sire. You see, it's—"

"I come to you for the answers I want to hear," the King bellowed, "not for some vague mumbo jumbo that can't possibly be verified. What do the divining sticks say? What about them, over there?"

King Valdis stalked across the room to a low pit. There a half dozen Elfmaids, all deep in trance, lay in a circle. At the center sat a grizzled old Elf with a film over one eye and drooping, pendulous ears. The Elfmaids' lips moved silently, their eyes stared blankly toward the ceiling. "Well," said the King, "what do *they* have to say?"

From his chair the interpreter cocked an ear, squeezing his eyes shut. He nodded, his lips forming a pained smile, then nodded again. "Their message is unclear, my King. We must try again, later."

"There won't *be* any later, if I wait around for you to tell me what's going on," the King fumed. "I suppose no news is good news, at least compared to that nonsense about the arrangement of the rat's innards. Take courage, Macta. Let's go have a talk with the generals. That should cheer us up. Confidence is the best weapon, in business and in warfare!"

"And marriage," said Macta.

"Confidence or foolhardiness," his father corrected. "Sometimes 'tis hard to tell the difference!"

44

MATT WAS THE FIRST ONE into the hospital room. In the bed next to the window he saw his dad sitting up, eating breakfast from a tray. There was a bandage on his forehead, but when he looked up and smiled, Matt felt a wave of relief. "Hey," Matt said, leaning over the bed railing to give his dad a hug. He felt the bristles on his father's cheek and realized that he was smiling so hard that it hurt. In a flash, Becky was there at his side, too, and his mom with Emily just behind. *"Waaaaa!"* the toddler cried out, reaching for her father.

"Good morning," Charlie smiled, pushing the breakfast tray out of the way. Then he took Emily in his arms. "Funny meeting you in a place like this!"

"Are you okay, Daddy?" Becky asked.

"Good as new," Charlie said. "Or at least I will be, when I get out of here!"

"How's your head feel, Dad?" Matt asked.

"Like gremlins were banging on it with a two-by-four. You know, it isn't easy sleeping in a hospital. They wake you up every hour taking your temperature, or checking your blood pressure. I could use a good night's sleep about now. Too bad I have to get back to work."

"You are not going straight back to work," Matt's mom declared.

"Don't you remember what happened yesterday?" asked Matt.

His father shook his head and shrugged. "I don't know. My memory's a little fuzzy. I figure I must have dropped into that ravine at the edge of the woods. I've driven equipment by there a hundred times before, so I don't know why I went over this time. I guess I must have passed out after I honked the horn. Good thing your mom heard it, or I could have been out there all day. The only thing I'm worried about now is the bulldozer."

"The only thing I'm worried about is you," she said. "When we get you home, I want you to stay in bed and rest."

Charlie took a bite of toast and chewed. "I can't afford to fall behind, Jill. I talked to my foreman this morning and told him to keep the guys on-site, and I'd be back this afternoon. They're counting on me to show up."

Jill bit her lip. "I think you're afraid that if you're not around, the other guys will find out that they can do the job just fine without you. They're going to be all right on their own for a couple of days, Charlie. You'll see!"

Agar moved crablike at the edge of the trees. "I've been savin' this stuff for ages," he muttered, unwinding a coil of rusty razor wire. "If you wait long enough, you'll find a use for everything."

"What's a little metal wire to a Human, anyway?" Jardaine complained. "That won't hurt them."

The Troll grumbled and withdrew a vial from one of his many overstuffed pockets. "The secret of *part one,*" he said. "We hang the wire just off the ground, all across the path. Then we paint the sharp edges with this liquid. When the Humans come to work, we draw their attention with these." He gestured at a bundle of feather-tipped darts that were tucked into another pocket. "We use blowguns to shoot 'em. Then—"

"If we can kill them with darts," Nebiros interrupted, "why do we need to waste our time with the rest of this nonsense?"

The Troll glared. "As I was sayin', we get the Humans' attention. The tips of the darts have already been soaked in a liquid that enters the Bloodstream, but only does its damage when *part two* of the poison comes into play. Now, when the Humans see us, we run down the path, and they're sure to follow. We jump to safety, but they tumble over the razor wire and cut their ankles. The poison on the wire blends in their Blood with the poison on the darts, and starts to eat away at their flesh from the inside. They follow us 'til they're deep in the woods and completely out of sight. Then they drop dead, lyin' in a pool of their own Blood. In an hour or so there'll be nothin' left of 'em but the clothes on their backs, and a nasty odor. No bodies to dispose of!"

Jardaine chuckled, and Nebiros rolled up his sleeves. "Give me the end of that wire," he demanded. "The Humans could arrive at any moment. We've got work to do!"

Tuava-Li sailed over the forest on kestrel wings. Flight was bliss, sheer joy. She looked down at her world and was overwhelmed by the beauty of it all. She saw a mouse darting through a pile of leaves, a hare's quivering nose protruding from a hole, a school of fish gently swaying at the bottom of a pond. Though the journey had been long, she knew where the Mage would be found; she could see it, she could feel it like she could feel the wind rushing over her feathered wings. *I'm coming,* the words formed in her mind, and the purity of her intention radiated from her heart. *I'm coming!*

The tree where the owl was perched was lightning-struck and hollow. Her eyes took in the panorama of the forest, the falling leaves, the light streaming through the mighty trunks and the brambles and the slender shoots growing low to the ground. Her inner eyes, though, saw a dark place, where light was swallowed up, extinguished in depths too deep to fathom. *I am coming,* a voice had said, echoing in the depths of her solitude. *This is the end,* the Mage thought. *My Death Angel is coming to take me away.*

She wanted to see everything when the end came, so she hopped from branch to branch, moving higher in the tree. And she thought she saw it coming now, at first just a pinpoint in the distance. But as she watched, the pinpoint grew and grew until it was clear that what she saw approaching her was a bird. It was a predator, a kestrel, surely capable of taking the Mage's life. But this was not death arriving to claim her. *I'm coming,* the voice said again, and then Kalevala Van Frier knew. As Tuava-Li swooped toward the branch, the Mage saw her in a blazing halo of gold, a savior come to bring life, not death. And when the kestrel's claws touched the branch, her transformation into an Elfmaid was nearly instantaneous. Tuava-Li's inner powers had grown slowly, invisibly, until she found her ability to take on animal form. Now she was capable of tapping a level of spirit that gave her immense energy. She radiated such power that it filled the Mage, and made her strong, too. The Mage's Elfin ears appeared, as did her lips, her chin, and her hair as the feathers faded away and her arms were once again free to take Tuava-Li in their embrace.

"I always knew I'd find you," Tuava-Li whispered, her voice choked with emotion.

"I tried to let you know I was alive," whispered the Mage. "I thought I was too weak, my powers too dimmed. But you came. Your strength saved me. And now you've learned the transformation! A kestrel, no less. You'll make a good Mage, Tuava-Li!"

"If I'm strong, 'tis only to serve you," Tuava-Li said. "We must hurry. Alfheim is in danger, and all of us need you."

"But who watches over Alfheim now? You can't have left our homeland unattended."

"Jardaine, of course!"

Darkness came over the Mage's eyes. "Macta Dockalfar and his henchmen tried to kill me, Tuava-Li. And 'twas Jardaine who ordered it. Together they plan to eliminate you, too, and take control of Alfheim."

Tuava-Li shook her head. "It makes no sense. Macta Dockalfar is preparing to marry Princess Asra, in our own Sacred Grove."

"How can that be?" cried the Mage, her mind reeling.

"The Synod has practically forced this upon us! There was nothing that I could do; it's all been decided in Ljosalfar. Asra is only going along with it because they say the union of our Clans will give us solidarity."

"Baaahh," spat the Mage. "We've been betrayed. The marriage will be a sham, just a path to some new deceit. And nothing will protect our borders anymore. The Cord is dying; the division of the worlds is coming undone. Do you remember the legend of Fada? The Seed that was planted at the center of the earth?"

Tuava-Li's eyes grew wide. "I had a vision. 'Twas about the trees, the Adri, and the Seed. I saw it all. Did you—"

"We're part of something much larger than ourselves. Something drew you to me when we first met in Ljosalfar. Something drew you to find me here. The vision came for a reason; we've been chosen to safeguard this world, Tuava-Li. But the first thing we must do is put a stop to Macta and Jardaine's schemes. This bone was broken," she said, holding up her arm, "when the wedding shoe was recovered, when I first disappeared. I doubt that I could fly now, even if I managed the transformation to an owl again. Can a kestrel carry a Mage in her talons?"

Tuava-Li looked skyward. The sun was going down. Once it was dark her vision would surely be limited, and the thermal winds that held her aloft during the day would be gone. She would have to flap her wings to stay airborne for the long journey home, and she was not yet sure of her strength as a kestrel. She also had no idea of how long the trip would take without access to a safe Cord. But there was no other choice. She took her Master's hands and stared into her eyes. A current of living energy rode on her words: "Let me try something. I will use my strength to help you change."

"Nooo," insisted the Mage. "You will need your strength. It doesn't matter if I—"

But the change had already begun. *Magick begins in the imagination,* Tuava-Li thought, bringing attention to her arms. She pictured the feathers growing there, the bones lengthening and becoming hollow, and what she imagined became real. As Tuava-Li's pale flesh disappeared beneath a layer of feathers and her mouth and nose hardened into a beak, her kestrel eyes saw her Mage's eyes grow into huge, yellow orbs. The Mage's hands and arms changed into owl wings, healed and whole, and ready for flight. When the transformation was complete, the kestrel and the owl took to the air.

45

IN A CLEARING CARPETED with emerald moss, the wedding was about to begin. Soon the destinies of two Elfin Clans would be joined, their union sealed by marriage. At the top of the wedding tower hung a canopy of leaves, lit from inside by scores of tiny Fire Sprites. Jardaine stood in the glow with the silver Mage's cloak around her shoulders. "Stop that blubbering!" she cried in exasperation.

Some of the monks clustered around Jardaine were rocking back and forth and chanting in a strange tongue. Parslaine, expert at the healing arts, was the latest convert to the brand of worship practiced by Brahja-Chi, Mage of Storehoj. Though the monks' ability to travel in the Cord had been impaired, Brahja-Chi's teachings were spreading like wildfire among the Clans. "We're doing what the Canon insists we do in preparation for a wedding," Parslaine murmured. "'Tis the Law, the way it must be done."

Jardaine was indignant. "*I'm* the Mage of Alfheim, and you must do as I say, not what you learned from Brahja-Chi. The answers to life's questions aren't in some musty old parchment. The traditions of this Clan aren't those practiced by the fools who chase Brahja-Chi. You can't even read that infernal Canon for yourself; you're just repeating what Brahja-Chi says. If you love that witch so much, then go and join her in Storehoj. I won't allow any of that chanting here. And why are you wearing those heavy cloaks? 'Tis not cold this morning."

Three of the monks, Parslaine, Ebba, and Crotalus, were dressed in the thick robes normally worn during the coldest part of winter. "'Tis written in the Canon," Crotalus said, "that—"

"We were . . . chilly, Jardaine," interrupted Ebba.

"And the insects were biting us," said Parslaine. "We know 'tis not tradition to wear these robes at a wedding, Jardaine, but at the top of the tower, no one will see us anyway."

Jardaine shook her head in disgust. "From now on I expect you to refer to me as your *Mage*, not my given name. I demand your respect. Now, you may wear the robes, if you insist, but I will not allow that ridiculous chanting. You're monks of Alfheim, and I expect you to behave accordingly. You know what kind of chanting is acceptable here. Worry yourselves with what I desire, and nothing else. Now, there are other matters to which I must attend. I'll be back before sunrise to lead Macta and Asra in the wedding vows."

Jardaine turned her back on the monks and proceeded down the steps. "You should watch out for thossse onesss," hissed Sarette.

When the sound of the new Mage's footsteps died away, the three monks in their thick black robes began their chant anew. "You should stop that now," said the monk Gyttha. "Jardaine—I mean, the Mage—would be very angry to know that you disobeyed her."

"Just wait," said Parslaine. "By the time the wedding is through, Jardaine will have nothing to worry about from the three of us again."

"What is that supposed to mean?" asked Gyttha. But the monks ignored her, and went back to their chant.

Prince Macta stood in a clearing where the fleet of Arvada had landed. The air above was churning with the bulk of the monstrous Sprites. "Let's get moving!" he shouted over the wind to Baltham. "The barbers spent hours getting my hair just right. I can't wait here any longer!"

In the hollow at the far end of the clearing, a rumbling sound rose from the earth. Two velvet-clad courtiers flanked the steps leading to the Cord. First a trembling bulge appeared in its surface, then the edge of a jeweled blade cut through the fibrous skin. In the opening a hand appeared. Other hands joined the first as attendants to the royal family stretched and pulled. A fleet of gondolas had arrived from Ljosalfar, each bearing a dozen or more Elves to the site of the royal wedding.

The Princess was the first to step across the breach, followed by her parents. Her wedding gown, woven from tree-spider silk, was a shimmering white. But the bodice was crisscrossed with strips of black moss. Asra had insisted on the detail, out of respect for her departed friend Skara. On her head, Asra wore her mandrake-leaf wig. Servants holding containers of wild oats, mulberries, and grapeseed oil waited behind the royal family. Before she ascended the tower, Asra's wig would be anointed with the oil and decorated with grain and berries, as a symbol of fertility. On her feet were the diamond wedding shoes. As the Princess stepped from the opening in the Cord, arriving at her ancestral home for the first time since her disastrous first wedding ceremony, she slipped on the stair. "Infernal shoes," she muttered, jamming her heel back into place.

'Tis a bad omen, thought the Queen, scowling. Soon the trees in the Grove would take on a golden glow as light from the east heralded the arrival of dawn. Asra looked around with a mixture of sorrow and gladness. Everything here was the same as she remembered; the monks and the Elves who formed the advance team had cleared Alfheim from the curse of Blood that lay on their land. They had scrubbed, trimmed, organized, and rebuilt the city in the trees so that it looked like it had never

been abandoned. This was the place Asra had grown up, and she was glad to be home. And yet, the horrible memories of that day came creeping into her heart, and she shivered.

The royal family began the slow march to their places in the wedding parade. Meanwhile the attendants and courtiers holding the edges of the rent in the Cord realized that the opening was making no attempt to heal itself. The emergency reinforcements in the Cord had held, yet the skin of the Cord itself was weaker and more vulnerable than ever. And so the servants merely stood back, and let the crowds pour through. Countless Elves and Faerie creatures climbed from the passageway and exited toward the torchlit Grove, as the pulsing wind of the Cord billowed out into the air.

Strolling Pixie musicians, clad in tunics decorated with feathers, beads, and bells, wandered through the Grove. Standard-bearers held flags in the Clan colors so that all would know their place, and Faeries everywhere hurried to join their fellows. There was hope in the air around Alfheim. Every participant had a role to fulfill, a part to play, and all of the trappings of ceremony and tradition made it easy to forget the troubles that had led to the wedding in the first place. There were going to be no mysteries, no surprises, no unpleasantness of any kind on this fine morning. The wedding would reaffirm the belief that the world was an orderly and predictable place, and everyone was anxious to believe.

Jardaine was anxious for another reason. She made her

way like a black cloud through the crowd. She was searching for Macta, who had agreed to meet her in the clearing where the fleet of Arvada was moored. But predictably, he was not there. The monk was livid with rage when she found the Prince crouching behind an immense tree trunk, rolling knucklebone with his brother-in-law. "I won't ask why you weren't at the place we were supposed to meet," Jardaine snapped. "I've got to be back at the top of the tower as soon as possible, and I spent far too long looking for you already. Just tell me how your father's plans are proceeding."

"I don't have a clue as to what my father's plans are," Macta snorted. "He doesn't seem to trust me with the details, though as his son, it should be me in whom he confides. Each of the Arvada is equipped to carry a hundred and fifty soldiers, and yet the only passengers on board when we left Helfratheim were the flight crew and the members of the wedding party. I'd wager that in all there weren't more than four score that made the journey. It hardly seems a proper plan to start a war with no soldiers, but what do I know? He said only yesterday that this would be a different kind of war."

"Well, what was his response when you asked him why he brought no soldiers?" asked Jardaine, her eyes narrowed.

Macta shrugged. "My father's Arvada was the first to land, and his advisors shuffled him off into the Grove before the rest of us touched ground. I was forced to travel with the water-logged Human, Liqua, who rode flat in one of the other cabs. When my father found out I had Liqua, he wanted me to turn her over to him immediately. I informed him that I had no intention of doing so, and of course, it made him mad. But then, *everything* makes him mad. Liqua's got that water-filled helmet fastened over her head, and all the sloshing around inside it seems to make her nervous. Herma and Holda have her hidden back behind the ridge now, waiting for your monks to come and lead her down to the Humans' house. They'll be ready to lure them out when the time's right. And I've been waiting here for you to arrive."

"So," Jardaine said, "that means you haven't spoken to the King at all."

"The King of Helfratheim is a busy man," Macta explained, "and he keeps his secrets close to his chest. You know I've never been able to penetrate his inner circle. I'm sure he has his strategy all worked out. But I don't suppose that's any consolation to you, Jardaine, for you and I shan't have the chance to talk again until all of this is done. You must think of my father as your ally, and trust him to do what he promised to do, which is to start the war between Humans and Elves, and to do it in the most dramatic way possible. You need to tend to your own part of the plan, and not worry about his. Now tell me what happened yesterday, with the Humans you were planning to—"

"'Twas more than just a plan, Macta," Jardaine interrupted. "Unlike some others I shan't mention, we in Alfheim aren't all talk, and no action. We killed five of them yesterday, and their awful machines won't be taking down any more of our trees;

you can be sure of that. The Troll Agar helped Nebiros and me poison them with a formula he invented. There's a place for him in our own inner circle once we're running the show around here! You should have seen the Humans chasing after us through the woods, hollering when they cut their ankles on the poisoned wire, and as they ran, their legs began to dissolve out from under them. 'Twas a sight to see. They got shorter and shorter, stumbling along on their stumps, screaming Bloody murder, 'til eventually all that was left were the heads, lying on the ground in puddles of ooze, their mouths flapping as their brains melted and ran out their ears and nostrils. When there was nothing left of them but their clothes, we dragged the stinking fabric back to the edge of the woods and hung it from the branches in the trees. When the others come across the borders today and see what we did to their friends, 'twill drive them mad with rage. What a time your father will have, killing them then!"

"Lovely," Macta sighed.

Baltham, meanwhile, clutched at his belly and made gasping sounds. This was all more than his delicate constitution could bear. "If a war's about to begin, Jardaine," Macta said, "I don't see why you had to go to the trouble of murdering the Humans. I'd wager your Bloodthirst has got the better of you. From now on you should let the experts handle the killing."

"Stay in my place, and mind my manners, eh?" Jardaine scoffed. "And let the Dockalfars take all the glory? I don't think so, Macta. I want all the world to know that Jardaine is a force to be reckoned with."

From somewhere down the path came the sound of laughter. Baltham recognized his own children's voices, and stiffened when his wife, Yenri, came into view. Jardaine bent to whisper in Macta's ear. "I don't like surprises," she hissed, "but I suppose we'll just have to trust that your father has a plan and that he knows what he's doing. Just so long as we've played our own parts. Now I've got to get back to the tower."

As Jardaine turned away, Sarette peered up from her Master's robe and flicked her tongue. "Trussst isss the lie that weaklingsss rely on when hiding from their fear."

"Here's a bit of prudence for you," Macta snapped. "'Tis wisdom to ignore the philosophy of snakes."

Fire Sprites danced on the tips of the wedding tower. Their light gleamed: twinkling, alive, illuminating the scene for all to see. From the viewing stands on the ground to the highest branches of every tree, all eyes watched, waiting for the procession to begin. Macta slipped into the seat next to King Valdis, in his viewing stand at the back of the Grove. "Father," he whispered, "thank the Gods I've found you. Why are you all the way back here? And where are the soldiers you promised to bring, to start the—"

"You're not wearing the black and yellow," his father hissed, his body stiff with anger. "I'll hazard a guess you haven't forgotten any other of today's details! Tell me when, exactly, will the Humans arrive—to get the show underway?"

Macta shook his head. "Once the vows are spoken, Father. I told you that before. But I was under the assumption that you would have troops assembled here to start the battle with the Humans as soon as they arrive!"

"Everything has to appear aboveboard, my son. We dare not risk that it looks like we orchestrated this event, not to the Humans, not to the Faerie Folk who will be watching. Aye, the Humans will die, but we must make sure that one is left alive at the end of the day to return and tell the others what transpired here. Some of the Faerie Folk must die, as well. There's a formula for success, and we need justifiable anger to stir the cauldron of rage and retaliation."

"But the *soldiers,* Father, where are the soldiers?" Macta begged. "Do you have them hidden away somewhere?"

"Keep your voice down," Valdis snapped. "There are no soldiers. We're entering a new age, son, an era of *techmagick.* Don't you remember what I told you? Soldiers? *Bah.* Who needs them anymore? The battle this morning will reveal the miracle of Experimentalism in action. We have our secret weapons in place, Macta. Just go about the business of getting married, see to your own plans, and don't worry about mine. I didn't get this far without knowing exactly what I'm doing. Are you sure you can trust your Elves to get the Humans here in time for the vows? And how many Humans can we expect? Twenty? A hundred?"

Macta blanched. "Don't worry, Father, the Mage of Alfheim's second-in-command, Nebiros, is overseeing the entire thing. We can count on them completely. Since they killed the Human workers yesterday, the Elves—"

"What?" the King huffed. "Did I say anything about killing Humans before today? That wasn't part of the plan. I don't like surprises, Macta!"

"'Twas Jardaine's notion, Father, to get the rest of the Humans angry, to make them careless with rage when they come after us, to make them so furious that—"

"None of you has any idea of what real fury is," Valdis hissed. "Today you'll see destruction up close and firsthand, and if you're truly my son, I wager you'll like what you see. Now I'll ask you once more, how many Humans will there be today?"

"Enough, Father," Macta answered, "enough."

From the orchestra the sound of the wedding march rose in majestic tones, flooding the hearts of all in the Grove with delight and expectation. "Then go and get married, my son," said Valdis, patting Macta on the shoulder.

"But aren't you going to join me in the procession, Father?"

Valdis sat back and crossed his arms. "Believe me, Macta, I've got the best seat in the house!"

46

TOMTAR SHUDDERED as he approached the McCormacks' house. It looked exposed and vulnerable at the end of the muddy field, its windows dark at this hour, its shingles streaked with dew. Fragile saplings in the yard were skeletal things, bare of leaves. Like the other houses lined up in a row, the McCormacks' house looked to Tomtar like a thing without a Soul. Only a smear of crimson on the horizon indicated that dawn was approaching. The whistle of the wind was sharp, and hurt Tomtar's ears. If he had had both hands free he would have pulled his cap down, but one hand was gripped firmly by the Human girl they called Liqua. Tomtar felt uneasy holding the Human's hand. He knew that the girl clung to a twisted fragment of life only because of the power of an Elfin curse. For thirty years he had been her sole companion; he had told her all of his secrets, shared all of his thoughts, but he never really thought that she might be listening. And he certainly never imagined that one day he would be walking through a field beside her, their fingers entwined. Since he discovered the Alfheim Clan Jewels hidden in a trunk in the McCormacks' basement, Tomtar's feelings about Humans had changed. He hated them. More than that, he hated himself for having believed that Matt and Becky McCormack were his friends.

The girl groaned and squeezed Tomtar's hand as she stumbled over the bulldozer tracks. In her other arm she clutched the tattered doll she had found during her previous trip to the McCormacks' house. The sound of liquid sloshing inside her crystal helmet muffled her cry, but it was not enough to squelch the note of distress. Her hand seemed to fade, then reappear, then fade away again in Tomtar's grasp. Tomtar felt ill. "Why couldn't we have stayed for the weddin', Nebiros? What's so important about gettin' Becky out of the house?"

"Keep your voice down," the Elf hissed. "'Twas Jardaine's orders. As soon as the wedding's over, she wants to talk to the girl about the Alfheim Jewels, and she thinks the little one might be more willing than the others to tell the story. The sooner we get her back to Alfheim, the better 'twill be for us all. But you can't let on that we know the truth about the Jewels. Tell the girl that she's comin' to see a real Elfin wedding!"

Nebiros, protected by the magick Jardaine had provided, took a knife from his pack and used it to sever the bundles of wires that entered the Humans' home. Then he went to the vehicles in the driveway, opened the hoods over the engines, and did the same. He had learned a valuable lesson in mechanics when he watched Tuava-Li pull wires from an engine with her bare hands. Now he disabled the vehicles safely and effortlessly. Slipping the blade into his pack, Nebiros grinned. He gestured for the others to follow him, and the trio climbed the porch steps. Tomtar remembered the day when Matt saved him from falling from the second-floor window. Then his mouth watered as he thought about the food Matt brought to feed him. Now those days seemed like a long time ago. He forced the memories away, hardening his heart against the sudden pang he felt there, and brought his focus to the task at hand. The porch creaked slightly as Liqua went to take the key from beneath the mat. "Now remember," whispered Nebiros, staring up into the girl's face and exaggerating the motions of his mouth, "you must open the door, invite us in, and then Tomtar will go up the stairs. We'll wait together down here, but you mustn't make a sound. We can't let the Humans know we're here."

"What about the rest of the Alfheim Jewels?" Tomtar whispered, as Liqua turned the key in the door. "Should we go into the basement and get 'em from that trunk?"

Nebiros shook his head. "The girl wouldn't come with us if she realized we knew her family had stolen the Jewels. 'Twill be our secret. Jardaine can come back for the treasure later, when this is all over. Now get up the stairs!"

The air in the house was still. The walls, the furniture, the pictures on the mantel, everything was hidden in shadows, everything felt heavy, and dark. Five Humans lay close by, sleeping in their beds, unaware that someone was creeping up the stairs. Tomtar walked past Matt's room. Then he paused in Becky's doorway and looked at the sleeping girl, with the blankets pulled up under her chin. He took a piece of bark from his pouch. It was stained red, inscribed with the emblem of the Mage. He placed it on the dresser just like Nebiros had told him to. Then he went to Becky's bed. He touched her shoulder and saw her stir. "Becky," he whispered, "wake up. There's somethin' in the woods I want you to see. The Princess is gettin' married, and she's wearin' the diamond shoe that Matt found. Do you want to go?"

Becky pushed up on one elbow and rubbed her eyes. "Tomtar? You're back!"

The girl threw her arms around the Troll and squeezed him so hard that he thought he would lose his balance. "The Elves called me to Alfheim," the Troll said quietly, "but I came back for you. If you want to see a real Elfin wedding, we've got to hurry!"

"But what about Matt?"

"Oh," Tomtar answered, "you know Matt. He wouldn't want to sit through a wedding. I'll come for him later, for the party!"

A minute later they slipped out the front door and headed out across the construction site. Nebiros and Liqua lingered behind the porch until the Troll and the girl had disappeared into the forest. Then they followed. Halfway to the line of trees, the Elf fumbled in his pack. He took out a small, tightly wrapped package and laid it on the ground. "Come with me, Liqua," he said. "Our job here is done."

When the package exploded in the field, sending a spray of soil and rocks fifty feet into the air, Tomtar and Becky were making their way along a trail in the dark forest, halfway to Alfheim. Nebiros and Liqua were not far behind. The explosion rattled the windows of the McCormack house. Matt sat bolt upright in his bed, his heart pounding, his eyes alert. He peered through his bedroom window and saw the black cloud of smoke already fading above the tree line. There was a pit in the ground at the center of the construction site. The portable toilet at the far end of the field lay on its side. Closer to the house the swing set lay toppled over in the grass. "Matt!" He heard his father at the foot of the stairs. "Becky! Did you hear that? It was some kind of explosion!"

Matt tossed his blankets aside and stumbled across the floor. He flicked on the light switch. Nothing. "The power must have gone out. Dad, I'm—"

From the doorway he saw his father standing in Becky's room, looking oddly tall, out of place amid the dollhouse and pink child-sized furniture. He was staring at the empty bed. "Becky?" he called. "Becky? Matt, where's your sister?"

"Dad, I don't know. I saw something out in the field; from

my window, it looked like smoke. And there's a crater, or something. You've got to come and see!" Matt backed out of the way as his father barged past him. "Charlie, is everything okay?" called Jill from the foot of the stairs.

"Becky?" Charlie yelled.

Emily, already in her mother's arms, began to wail. "Becky?" Charlie bellowed. "Jill, check the bathrooms. Check the basement. The power's out, so you'll need a flashlight. I think there's one in the drawer next to the stove. Matt, come on, show me where you saw the smoke."

Down the front steps and across the yard they went, moving like the world had switched over to slow motion. Matt was still in his pajamas. His father had pulled on some jeans and jammed his feet into a pair of boots. Matt saw the laces trailing in the dried mud. His own bare feet stung with every step. Matt followed his father across the field, and the cold air made their breath billow in puffs of white. "Wait up, Dad!"

"Is this some kind of prank?" Charlie grunted as he hurried across the field. "Was it the kids that've been screwing around with our construction equipment that did this?"

"Dad," said Matt, "I don't know any more than you do!"

They came to the edge of the smoldering pit in the ground. "Well, there's nothing here," Charlie said. "Nothing's damaged, nobody's hurt." He glanced up, scanning the horizon. "It was more than some Fourth of July fireworks that did this. It had to be dynamite. But why—"

"Charlie," Jill cried out from the front yard. "I can't find Becky!"

"Okay, that's it," Matt's father said, wheeling around. "It's time to call the police."

In the living room, Jill stood next to the couch, Emily in her arms, trying to get the toddler to drink from her bottle. The front door was ajar, and chilly air crept along the floor. Charlie pounded on the telephone and cursed. "It's not working. Jill, where's my cell?"

"I don't know," she answered, nearly hysterical. "Did you plug it into the charger? Did you leave it in the pants you wore yesterday?"

Charlie raced to the clothes hamper and found the cell phone in his pocket. He flipped open the lid; the screen was dark, the phone decharged. He hurried outdoors, the keys to his pickup truck clutched in his fist.

Matt got dressed and went back into Becky's bedroom. There was no sign of a struggle, or anything out of the ordinary. He was about to leave when he saw the piece of painted bark lying on the dresser. He held his breath and picked it up. In the dim light, Matt recognized the strange calligraphy on the surface. Becky was gone, and it had something to do with the Elves. The bark with the Mage's sign had obviously been left behind for Matt to find. This whole thing was his fault, and he had to tell his father now, before it was too late. If it wasn't already too late. Matt raced past his mother, who was pacing back and forth in the kitchen, punching numbers into the dead telephone, Emily stumbling behind her, begging to be picked up, sobbing pitifully. Matt ran down the front steps toward the driveway, where he found his father in the seat of the pickup truck. He was bent over the steering wheel, using both hands to force the key. "Dad!" Matt cried. "The hood's not shut."

Charlie cursed and leapt out of the cab. He flung open the hood and saw the cables and wires inside, neatly snipped. "It's a kidnapping, it's got to be! The whole time, it's been leading to this. Somebody's taken Becky. How are we going to get help? How are they going to call us, to ask for the ransom, if they cut the phone lines?"

"Dad," Matt interrupted, holding out the piece of red painted bark in the palm of his hand. "Dad, I found this in Becky's room. I know who did this. There are some . . . some people out in the woods; they live there, they're hiding out there, and . . . I know why they did this. They don't want you to cut down the trees and build houses, Dad. I think that's what this is all about."

Matt winced as his dad grabbed him by the shoulders. "Who?" Charlie demanded. "What people? I thought you met *Tom* in the woods. Is that who you mean?"

Matt squirmed out of his father's grasp. "I think maybe . . . Tom is involved, somehow."

"How!" Charlie's voice was a choked scream. "Who did

this? His parents? His family? Why would they set off an explosion, unless they wanted us to know they took Becky? Unless they wanted us to find them? Matt, you've got to tell me what's going on! You've got to show me where they live!"

"Okay," said Matt, peering into the darkness of the woods. He pointed a trembling finger. "I think it's that way."

Matt ran behind his father. He was breathless when they reached the row of pines that bordered the construction site, and Charlie saw what looked to him like people crouching in the darkness. "Hey!" he shouted. "Hey!"

But the figures in the darkness didn't move, and when Charlie reached them, he saw that there was nothing there but dirty, discarded clothing: plaid shirts, T-shirts and jeans, shoes and socks and boxer shorts, hanging from low branches where Jardaine and Nebiros had left them to be seen. A desperate cry rose up from inside him. "Whose clothes are these? What in God's name is happening?"

Matt lifted the hem of a dirty shirt, and a powerful chemical stench burned his nostrils. The shirt was damp, and sticky. Matt pulled his hand away, and there was red on his fingers.

Charlie sniffed the noxious odor, and grabbed his son by the arm. "Come on. We're going to have to take care of this, just you and me. We're on our own, here. No neighbors, no police, nothing. Let's go back to the house and get Grandpa's guns out of the case in the hall. I know you've never fired a gun before; you're about to get a crash course. Mom and Emily will go into the basement to hide, and we'll make sure all the doors are locked. Then we're heading into the woods, Matt, and we're going to get your sister back!"

47

THE DEER WERE ALWAYS present to witness a royal wedding. Of all nature's creatures, the deer were the only animals who had always been able to cross the borders of the Faerie and Human worlds at will. The mighty Deer King had gathered his herd and brought them to the Sacred Grove, and now they spread out along the periphery of the crowd, gazing over the assembled multitudes.

When the first shaft of daylight fell across the scene the viewing stands were packed with Faerie Folk. Beneath a purple canopy sat King Valdis, resting on a cushioned throne. He was as far away from the wedding tower as possible. Sitting in the row beneath him was his Secretary, Cytthandra. Next was the King's daughter, Yenri, and her gang of squirming children. Many Faeries of note, including the King and Queen of Ljosalfar;

Tacita, the Secretary of the Synod; Slajjar the Laureate; Hedwig, the Pixie Queen; and Narvad, the Unseelie Duke, were in attendance, filling the space between the King's entourage and the wedding tower. Macta's servants Holda and Herma sat side by side with balls of colored twine in their laps, their knitting needles clicking in unison. At the end of the row, Agar the Troll was hunched. His face was a mask of discontent; it was only because Jardaine demanded it that he had come at all. At the front of the crowd sat the kitchen staff of Alfheim. They looked expectant, proud, and happy. Byggvir, who had been the first to see the Human boy with Princess Asra's wedding shoe, had the seat of honor. None of this would have been possible without him.

At the top of the wedding tower, Princess Asra stood across from her betrothed, Macta Dockalfar. Between them was Jardaine, the silver-cloaked Mage of Alfheim. On her head she wore an antlered helmet. She smiled beatifically as Asra and Macta spoke the words that would complete the ceremony. On one side of the spiraling tower steps the bride's family was gathered, looking out over the crowd. Along with King Thorgier's royal entourage, they filled their side of the tower to capacity. On the other side stood Baltham. Tradition dictated that Valdis's contingent should have been stationed here, and yet the steps leading to the apex of the tower were conspicuously vacant. Baltham, feeling lonely and confused, shivered. He was following King Valdis's personal orders, not Macta's. He held onto a carved railing and peered across the crowd toward his family. There in the shadowed viewing stand was his own son, tugging on his sister's hair. Then he happened to notice something out of the corner of his eye. He glanced into the brightening sky and saw a hawk circling high above the tower, then, off to the side, a horned owl. He felt his stomach contract in a knot of fear. *Predators!* he thought. *What are they doing here?*

Jardaine had already spotted the birds, and the sight of them filled her with dread. She could feel her mind being probed, her secrets pried from their hiding place. She knew it was Tuava-Li and the Mage working together. Under normal circumstances a Mage would never violate another Elf's privacy like this. *How dare they,* she thought. Jardaine said nothing to the twelve monks who encircled her on the platform. She gave no indication to the miserable bride and her cheerful groom that she was just about to run away. ". . . And through sweet seasons spreads our joy, o'er meadow, copse, and hedge, for thee," Macta recited, "and—"

Jardaine heard the piercing cry of the hawk, and the entire crowd looked up. The birds were coming straight for her. She thrust out her arms, pushed her way past Princess Asra, and thundered down the steps of the wedding tower. "What's g-g-going on here?" cried King Thorgier, as the moonfaced monk ran headlong into his enormous bulk.

"Nooo!" Jardaine shrieked. She turned in time to see the kestrel making its descent to the railing, and the owl swooping close behind. Jardaine was trapped. When the owl landed it began an immediate transformation into the Elfin Mage of Alfheim.

"You have no right to interfere in my wedding!" screamed Macta. "You're not the Mage here anymore. You're a deserter, you abandoned your duties, abandoned your own home, and now you return to—"

The kestrel hopped down from the railing, struck the Prince with her beak, then pinned him to the platform. She stood astride his chest and glared at him with fierce eyes. Princess Asra, meanwhile, ran into the arms of her mother. "What are we supposed to do now?" whispered the monk Parslaine to her companion Ebba.

"I don't know," murmured Ebba, looking furtively around. "Jardaine is finished. If only Brahja-Chi were here to guide us!"

"Have faith," hissed Crotalus. "The Gods won't let us down today. We'll follow Brahja-Chi's orders. All will be revealed!"

The Mage stood at the top of the tower and spoke to the masses gathered in the Sacred Grove. "Children of Alfheim," she intoned, "dear friends from o'er the Faerie world, I stand before you to say that there will be no wedding today. This event was planned by the Dockalfars as part of a scheme to start a war with the Humans. Now that I have returned, order in Alfheim will be restored. But there will be no wedding."

"Don't listen to the old crone!" Macta screamed, struggling to free himself from Tuava-Li's kestrel claws. "She's insane!"

King Thorgier's face was red. "Macta Dockalfar has deceived

us!" he shouted. "I command him, his family, and guests to leave Alfheim immediately, and never r-r-return."

Jardaine gave Macta a kick. "'Tis finished," she said. "This is all your fault. If you had killed the Mage like you were supposed to do, this never would have happened. We've lost."

"Nooo," hissed Sarette, from inside the silver cowl. "'Tisss not done 'til you have given me the legssss you promisssed."

Jardaine grabbed the snake by its head and pulled it out of her robe. Then she tossed Sarette over the top of the tower. For a moment she contemplated flinging herself over the edge as well. But her courage left her, and she sunk to her knees in despair.

"Tuava-Li," the Mage commanded, "escort Macta Dockalfar and his family to the Cord. After they're gone, there must be an orderly departure for the other guests who've come to witness this sham wedding." She turned to face the traitor Jardaine. "I've read your thoughts," she said. "I know what you are planning."

"You violated my mind," the monk spat. "You had no right!"

"If Humans are on their way to the Sacred Grove, then we must all leave here as soon as possible," the Mage said to Tuava-Li. "We cannot fight them."

Tuava-Li released Macta from her claws. The Prince hurried down the steps, his tear-streaked face hidden in shadows. It was at that moment that the first shot rang out, a warning that echoed over the treetops. Humans were crashing through the undergrowth, very near the Sacred Grove. Pandemonium erupted as the Faerie Folk fled in terror. Down the steps of the

wedding tower the Elves careened, leaping, pushing, tumbling over one another to escape. Tuava-Li lifted the Mage in her talons and flapped away. She deposited her safely in the branches of a tree at the edge of the Grove, then soared back to the tower. She would rescue the monks who might be trapped on the platform.
"The Gods have spoken," said Crotalus, a smile spreading across her face. "'Tis our signal, sisters. In the name of the Canon, and the mistress who serves the word . . ."

Then the three monks reached into their robes and pulled the tasseled cords that hung there.

"Owww! Owww!" Nebiros hollered, pulling back his Bloodied finger. "Don't you dare bite me!" He kicked Becky in the side with the heel of his boot, and in that same instant an explosion rattled the forest. Leaves rained down from above. "What was that?" Becky cried. She lay on the dirt with a rope binding her ankles, and another wrapped loosely around her chest and arms.

The breeze carried the sounds of panic. The screams and terror-struck wails of desperate Faeries echoed through the woods. In her crystal helmet, Liqua felt the vibration of the blast and moaned.

"What's happenin' in the Grove?" asked Tomtar, looking startled.

"None of your business," Nebiros answered. "I'm not asking you anymore, I'm telling you. Help me tie up the Human."

Tomtar felt faint. A sense of betrayal swept over him. He had lied to Becky because he had been told that he must, that he must prove his loyalty. Now the Elf was demanding that he bind the girl so tightly that she couldn't even move. But why? How could he follow orders he didn't understand? Becky was just a child, there was no need to tie her up, unless . . . unless it was Nebiros who was deceiving him, not Matt and Becky. Who could he trust? "No, Nebiros, no, you never said anything about—"

The Elf pulled a damp rag from his pocket and pressed it over Becky's horrified face. Before she could protest, a pungent odor overcame her. Nebiros crouched on her chest, holding the filthy cloth over the girl's nose and mouth. "Poison," he said, "just enough to knock her out so that I can tie her up more readily. It wouldn't have been necessary if you had done as you were told."

Nebiros glared at Tomtar and the strange helmeted girl, who was swaying back and forth behind the Troll. "Don't you remember, Humans are the enemy?" Nebiros grunted. "Don't worry, Troll, I'm not going to kill her. We'll just hide her in the hollow of the tree 'til it's all over. Who knows, we may have further use for her, before we're done."

"Before we're done with what?"

Nebiros tied a knot, then tied another on top of the first. He gave the rope a yank, and watched the color fade from Becky's flesh where the rope bit into her. "I'll never get used to the color of their skin," the Elf mused. "If their Blood was the proper shade of green, instead of red, 'twould make their appearance less repulsive."

"Before we're done with what?" shouted Tomtar, grabbing Nebiros by the shoulders. "I thought Jardaine just wanted to talk to her. Is there somethin' else you're not tellin' me?"

Nebiros's eyes burned with contempt. "Get your paws off of me before I—"

Tomtar backed away, throwing up his hands. "We've got to set her free, we—"

Nebiros shook his head. "You stupid, sentimental Troll. None of us is free. You're a pawn in a game, that's all. Don't you have a clue as to what's going on? The sounds you hear? The banging, the screaming, the smell of battle? All right, gentle heart, if you won't help me with the Human, then why don't you just go, too? The Elves of Alfheim have no more need of your services."

"I'm not goin' anywhere," said Tomtar, looking down at Becky. "The *Tems* might be enemies to the Elves, but I'm not about to stand by and watch this one come to harm. She's just a child. I don't trust you any farther than I can throw you, Nebiros, though I'd love to see how far you can fly."

Another blast reverberated through the forest. Nebiros puffed himself up. "'Tis good to see where your loyalty lies, Tomtar. Perhaps we'd all best stay where we are, out of harm's way."

Charlie McCormack yanked away another piece of painted bark. Since he and Matt entered the woods, there had been markers attached to the trees at regular intervals. Charlie glanced at the writing on the bark, then tossed it to the ground in disgust. "They're trying to lure us out here," he said. "Why else would they mark the trail so clearly? And what's with this weird writing? What does it mean? Is it some kind of cult? Is this all just a plan to get us, to get *me* out in the woods, away from home? Because I'm cutting down the *trees*? Why would they need to take a little girl just to get to me?"

He pumped his shotgun and fired another blast into the branches. "Dad," Matt huffed, "it's not *just* about you. I don't think they like any of us."

"Well, if they want us so bad," Charlie grunted, "this'll let 'em know we're on our way. And that we mean business. We're probably being watched, already." He fired another shot, and the sound echoed through the woods.

"Listen up, Matt," Charlie said. "These are the things you've got to know to fire your gun, and I'm only going to tell you once." He quickly went through the steps.

"Okay," said Matt, hoping he would remember the sequence.

In the distance there were strange cries. "What do you know about all of this?" Charlie demanded. "I need you to tell me! This isn't play; this is a matter of life and death for your sister, maybe for all of us."

Charlie remembered his own father, who had disappeared in these woods and never came back. He thought of his sister, Anna, who never got the chance to grow up. Flooded with panic, he looked at his son and wondered if it had been the right decision to bring him here.

"Dad, they're . . . they're not like regular people," Matt hesitated. "They're not—they're not like we are. I didn't tell you, because you won't believe me. They're not from our world, Dad, they're not—*they're not human!*"

The deer began to gallop out of the forest. Like specters they appeared, like ghosts, weightless and pale. They fanned out and bolted past the man and the boy, and disappeared among the trees. The light in the forest seemed suddenly eerie and alien. The branches of the gray-green trees reached out like tentacles. The cries of the Faerie Folk, unearthly and horrible, grew louder, and louder still. "I think we're here, Dad," Matt breathed.

Suddenly there was a burst of heat. The air was full of smoke and crackling sounds. "It's fire!" Charlie yelled. "There's fire up ahead!"

And then there came the figures, little people, like people from another time, another country, another universe, running for their lives from the billowing smoke that poured from the forest ahead. Something moved into the patch of sky above them; something huge, and nearly formless, and tethered to the belly of the thing was a metal box, like the cab of an old-fashioned dirigible. An aperture yawned open at the front of the shape. A blast of fire shot out.

Macta made his was through the chaos. He arrived in tatters, Blood-smeared and muddy, beside his father in the field where the Arvada were moored. One by one the ropes and sandbags of the remaining Arvada were loosened by the flight crews, so that the enormous, translucent Sprites could lift into the air. "'Tis a glorious sight, is it not, my son?" hollered Valdis over the roaring of the huge, gaseous creatures.

"I wasn't certain, at first," Macta huffed, still out of breath from his race through the chaos of the Glen. "I wasn't sure what happened at the top of the tower. The sound of the gunfire from the Humans made me think of the wedding of Asra and Udos. Only this time the damage was greater, far greater than before. Then I realized that it wasn't the Human weapons that had torn apart the top of my wedding tower. I *know,* Father. The monks were hiding explosives in their robes, and they blew themselves to bits, didn't they?"

"Well, of course they did," Valdis exclaimed. "But no one else knows. All the Faeries think it was the Humans that did it. Everyone thinks it was the blast from those weapons they carry that caused the wedding tower to fall. In reality their little popguns could kill a few Elves, at best, but that's all. So we enhanced the panic, the fear, the fury, by making it seem that the Human weapons destroyed the tower, blasting the royal families to pieces. 'Tis all part of the *game,* son! I sold the explosives to Brahja-Chi, who passed them on to the monks so they might make the ultimate sacrifice for their beliefs. Politics makes strange bedfellows, Macta. Brahja-Chi wants war with the Humans as much as we do. She thinks that a holocaust will bring the Gods back to the Faerie realm, and that any sacrifice to the cause is warranted. Everything's going according to plan, my son. Maximum benefit to us, and all at a minimal cost! Now I must be off. Do you care to join me in the royal Arvada, or would you prefer to stay on the ground to see the battle unfold? Cytthandra and your sister, with all of her brats, are already inside. Baltham's busy doing a little favor for me, I hope you don't mind!"

"My *wedding,* Father," Macta growled. "The vows weren't spoken. I'm not married to Asra. It's all been ruined. She and her parents were more than halfway down the steps when the explosion blew the top of the tower to rubble, so I think they're all still alive, but in the confusion I haven't been able to find Asra. This is all your fault, Father, *all your fault!* You didn't stand on the tower where the Dockalfars were supposed to stand, because you knew about the explosion. But you didn't mind risking the life of your own son, and seeing me blown to kingdom come! What am I supposed to think about that?"

"Oh, look on the bright side, Macta," said Valdis, putting on his most sincere face. "You're a capable lad, and I always knew you could take care of yourself. You're here, aren't you? Besides, there was much speculation over the odds of your getting married today, and I dare say that I won quite a hefty sum as a result of what's happened here this morning! So cheer up! We'll all profit now that the war between the Humans and the Faeries is underway. You should be proud of the part you played! Now, is there any word about the fate of the Mage? What about your friend Jardaine? And when are the rest of the Humans going to arrive? So far we've seen only two. Are the others close behind?"

Macta brushed at his shoulder, where blackened, sticky clots hung to his collar. "Does it matter, Father? Are you not prepared for the worst?"

"You're right, my son, you're right! Hope for the best, and prepare for the worst, I always say. Then again, I always say, when lady luck is filling your sails, throw caution to the wind!"

Valdis tilted his chin toward the fleet of Arvada as he nudged Macta in the ribs. "*The wind,* you see? And one must approach the wind with a great deal of caution. *Ho ho!* A little levity in these situations always lightens my spirits. *Levity,* you understand? Levity? *Levitation*?"

Macta had a faraway look in his eyes, as singed tendrils of hair whipped across his face. "Well," the King continued matter-of-factly, "what the Sprites don't incinerate, the poison gases will destroy. You know, the base of the wedding tower is rigged with a tankard of gas that's set to explode when the Humans get close enough to take the full force of the blast. My Experimentalists assure me there's a spell involved, so it won't affect the Faerie Folk in the least. But wait until you see what it does to the enemy!

'Twill burn their lungs black. They'll suffocate in minutes. I have three words for you, Son, *techmagick, techmagick, techmagick!* You're witnessing the future!"

King Valdis noted the sorrowful expression on his son's face, and lay a hand on his shoulder. "I'm sorry about the wedding, you know. It couldn't be helped. But you're better off this way, believe me. Now join us in the Arvada, won't you? You're a Prince. You don't belong here."

Macta gazed across the field to the tumult and the chaos in the Grove. "No," he said. "Go without me. I'm going to find Asra."

"Then at least let me give you something for protection," Valdis sighed. "You know how to fire the Dragon Thunderbus, don't you?"

He snapped his fingers, and one of the Imperial Guard raced toward the nearest Arvada.

48

BY THE TIME CHARLIE and Matt reached the Sacred Grove, the wedding tower was in ruins. It was a violation of every natural Faerie law for Humans to be in this consecrated place; and yet there was no one left to object to their presence. The blackened foliage smoldered around their feet. Matt let out a cry as his shoe came down on something soft; it was the charred remains of an Elfin arm, oozing green, and attached to a piece of shoulder.

"Come out!" Charlie bellowed. "Show yourselves! Bring me my daughter, I promise we won't hurt you!"

"'Tis the Humans!" came a cry from a cluster of Pixies, dragging their injured to shelter. "They're going to kill us all!"

At the four corners of Alfheim the Faerie Folk jostled

for entrance to the frail Cords. This was their best hope of escape. The Cord leading to Ljosalfar was by far the most secure of the tunnels, having recently been reinforced, yet the crowds there were in chaos. Palace guards attempted to hold back the desperate crush of wedding guests so that the royal Faerie families might make their escape. Hot winds coursed along the length of milk-white Cord. Queen Shorya scurried down the path toward the threshold and her waiting gondola. Though the hem of her gown was ripped, and her forehead Bloodied by wreckage from the tower, she held onto her regal bearing as if it was the last certainty she had. Behind Queen Shorya stumbled her husband, Thorgier. His collar torn, his crown askew, he reached for the spider-silk sleeve of his daughter's gown. "'Twas the Humans that did this, just like b-b-before. *The Humans.* 'Tis a good thing we were close to the ground when their weapon d-d-destroyed the tower. We might have been killed!"

The Queen drew her daughter close as they hurried down the steps. "The Humans' weapons are more fearsome than before. There are so many dead, so many wounded. We're lucky to be alive."

"Three hundred and sixty moons ago, Udos was our only loss," Asra sniffled. "Who would have thought we'd look back and say that just one dead Elf was a stroke of good fortune?"

The royal family was stopped by the jostling crowd. All

around, held back by the guards, the multitudes were growing hostile. A clod of dirt whizzed through the air and struck Princess Asra's forehead. With a cry she touched the spot, then collapsed. "Rotters!" shouted a Gnome in a Bloodied waistcoat. "Cowards! Royalty—*bah!* What makes you think you're entitled to safety while we wait here to die!"

The Faerie Folk closed in on the guards; they were going to force their way past. The King and Queen hoisted their daughter to her feet and backed away from the crowd. "I'm all right," Asra murmured, rubbing her forehead.

A shot rang out like thunder. A stench of sulfur permeated the air, and the masses shrank back in terror. Through a cloud of soot stepped Macta Dockalfar. Brandishing the Dragon Thunderbus his father had given him, he shouted to the hordes of Faerie Folk. "Stay back, all of you, or face the wrath of my weapon! If you think you have reason to fear the Humans, know you have more reason to fear me. Now clear the way so that my beloved and her family can reach the Cord."

Macta paused to adjust the three false teeth that had once again been knocked loose by the recoil of the fearsome weapon. Then, as he struggled to pour more of the serpentine powder into the barrel of the gun, he inched toward the threshold. King Thorgier glanced nervously at his wife. The Queen looked to her daughter for a cue, but Asra was too stunned to speak. "Where do you think you're going, Macta Dockalfar?" she demanded.

"The wedding has been *delayed,* not canceled, Shorya," snorted the Prince. "My bride-to-be has need of my protection, as all can see."

"The royal family doesn't need your help," the Queen said. "Things haven't gone the way you planned, and now 'tis time you leave us be. Go back to your home. Alfheim is finished. There will be no wedding. The Princess does not require your company."

There was desperation in Macta's eyes. "Require, or desire? Let the Princess tell me with her own sweet lips!"

Asra stepped from behind her mother and lifted her hands in dismay. There was a smear of Blood on her brow, and her face was streaked with dirt and tears. "Perhaps everything that happens, happens for a reason," she cried. "'Tis for the best, Macta, that we part this way. Good-bye."

"Stop, Asra, please," Macta pleaded, lifting the lid of the box that contained a tiny Fire Sprite. With shaking hands he held it to the firing mechanism of the Dragon Thunderbus, ready to open the lid. "I will not lose this time."

"Love is not a game to win," said Princess Asra, turning away.

"That's where you're wrong," warned the Prince. "'Tis *all* a game, and there's much more to lose here than a bride. If you don't allow me to come to Ljosalfar, then you'll go with me to Helfratheim. Now, I'm not asking you, Asra, 'tis an order. So step aside from your family. Don't make this difficult, I've had a *very* trying day."

Asra shook her head. "You'll have your chance for happiness, Macta. Just let me have mine. Put your weapon down, and let us go."

"I go nowhere without you."

Behind the Princess, King Thorgier was shaking so hard that he could barely breathe. His frustration had reached its limit. All he wanted was to get into the Cord and get away from there. And Macta wouldn't let them go. With a roar Thorgier lifted his gold-tipped walking stick over his head, and lunged at Macta. It was was the last—and perhaps the first—courageous act in his life.

In surprise, the Prince took a step back. The lid of the tinderbox flipped open. The Fire Sprite leapt out of the box, as it had been trained, and touched a fiery finger to the fuse at the base of the weapon. The ball of fire that exploded from its barrel struck the King in a flash of light and color so intense that the crowd of Faerie Folk were stunned to silence. Then, as the smoke dissipated, and they saw what had become of the King, they tumbled over one another in a mad rush to the Cord. Macta dropped the red-hot rod. Stumbling, he turned and ran back toward the Grove.

"Dad, there's somebody else shooting," Matt whispered.

"I don't think they're shooting at us," Charlie said, peering around the side of a gnarled trunk. The heat from the fires in the Grove was stifling. "I was afraid we'd be walking into some kind of trap, but there's nothing here. The gunfire's coming from over that way, and you can tell by the screaming and hollering that there's something bad going on. It's like we walked into the middle of a battle."

Another blast of fire roared down from above, scorching branches and making glowing ash heaps from the detritus on the ground. Charlie glanced up and saw what looked like fast-moving clouds in the sky. He shook his head and blinked. The clouds were writhing, twitching like serpents. "The fire is coming from up there! But I don't see anything. There's nobody in the trees at all, no weapons, nothing!"

Charlie approached the blackened wedding tower. He shook his head, bewildered. "Look at this, Matt. What do you think it is?"

In the shadows of a ruined oak a figure was cowering, holding a bundle with a mechanical apparatus inside. After King Valdis's last conversation with his son, he had ordered Baltham to go to the grove and activate a hidden bomb. At the heart of the device was a battery made from a living slug, infused with magick to concentrate its dim life force. Wires from its body trailed through the leaves and down toward the ruined tower. Baltham felt queasy as he tripped a switch that connected the wires.

Charlie saw movement out of the corner of his eye. He threw an arm around Matt and pulled them both to the ground. It was a hawk sailing overhead, screeching and flapping its wings, hurtling toward Baltham. But it was too late. A flicker of electricity ran along the wire, and something beneath the fallen tower erupted with a metallic belch, spewing a noxious cloud into the air.

King Valdis's Arvada hovered over the charred ruins of the Sacred Grove. Billowing smoke obscured his view. "What *is* this?" Valdis screamed, banging his fists against the crystal window. "All this work, all this planning, for two miserable Humans? Is that all? Where are the rest that Macta promised? What did that meddlesome Mage do to Baltham? Did he manage to release the poison gas? I can't see, for all the infernal smoke."

The King pressed his nose against the glass. "Oh well, no matter. Waste no more time. *Burn it all to ashes!*"

A circle of black-robed Sorcerers sat on the floor of the cab. Their eyes were closed, their mouths moved in silent unison as they formed a mental union with the grotesque Sprite that held them aloft and waited to belch its flame on the scene below. "Ready . . . set . . . ," breathed Valdis.

"Wait!" interrupted one of the King's generals, who was seated behind the Sorcerers. "What about your plan to let one Human escape, to tell the other Humans about our war with them?"

"The Sprite can't incinerate just one of them," Valdis bellowed, "when there were only two Humans to begin with. Now! *Now!* Burn the Grove to the ground!"

The flame came like a molten river of red, spilling out of the cavern of the Sprite's mouth. Matt and Charlie leapt out of the way as the fire touched the cloud of gas that spewed from the wedding tower. With a deafening roar the Sacred Grove was enveloped in a white scorching blast.

When Matt regained consciousness the shotgun clutched in his arms was too hot to touch. He dropped it. His breath came raw and ragged, and the smell of burned skin and hair assaulted his nostrils. When he blinked, it felt like his eyes were coated with sand. Everything looked blue. He was inside some kind of rubbery, translucent bubble, and he could see that he was hovering above the ground. Only seconds had passed since the explosion had sent him toppling head over heels through the Grove. When he peered through the curved wall of the orb he could see that two other bubbles floated nearby. Inside one, he could see his father, pounding with his fists on the yielding blue surface, his lips silently mouthing Matt's name, and in the other, he thought he could make out . . . a bird? An Elf?

Hot winds whipped tendrils of moon-white hair against the face of a figure on a nearby branch. Her robe fluttered as she held her hands high. The Mage of Alfheim was using the power Tuava-Li had given her to protect them all from the force of the blast. She knew now that the Humans were not her primary enemy; it was an unthinkable, unspeakable evil that had driven the Dockalfars to burn the forest of Alfheim. It was Elves who were to blame for the destruction of their own kind. At the last possible second the Mage had conjured the shielding orbs and saved her Apprentice, and the man and his son, from certain death. The other Elf, Baltham, was not so lucky. His body lay between the charred trunks of two of the mighty oaks. The toxic effects of Valdis's poison gas had been dissipated in the explosion; but danger still remained. All five Arvada circled the Grove. Like hunters surrounding their prey, they closed in for the kill. Tuava-Li made mental contact with the Mage. *Let us go! The orbs won't be able to protect us from the rain of fire from above!*

"Then the humans will die," replied the Mage.

Tuava-Li's response was immediate. *"There is nothing else we can do!"*

The air around the blue globes shimmered. In a moment, Charlie, the heaviest of the three, slipped from the glistening orb and struck the ground. Matt was the next to follow. When Tuava-Li's blue orb shivered and popped like a soap bubble, she had already transformed into a kestrel. She soared over the Grove and snatched the Mage in her talons. Together they rocketed away from the site, over the ridge, and down into the trees that the fire had yet to reach. Above the heads of Matt and his father the sky was churning with the enormous bulk of the Arvada. Death stared down at them. Burning with anger, fear, and helpless rage, Matt rolled over and grabbed his shotgun. It was a futile gesture, he knew, but it was better than just lying down and waiting to die. Ignoring the pain from the burning metal Matt pointed the barrel of the gun upward, and fired. The effect was nearly instantaneous. High above the trees, King Valdis felt the weight of the cab shift. He looked to his Sorcerers, his daughter, and then his advisors, all of them horror-struck and breathless. Cytthandra clutched Valdis's arm. A high-pitched roar, a scream of air, shattered their eardrums as the Arvada began to fall. The shotgun blast had torn open the belly of the Sprite like a sack of rotten meat. Its transparent, nearly weightless innards sloughed from the wound and floated away, and the weight of the cab brought it, and its helpless passengers, crashing through the treetops. The other Arvada captains backed away from the hideous scene. They hovered over the smoking forest. Uncertain of what to do next, they watched warily as the two Humans with their terrible weapons fled to safety.

The fire had not yet spread to the part of the woods where Macta Dockalfar found his accomplice, Jardaine, along with five of the surviving monks. The monks had seen the confrontation between Jardaine, the Mage, and Tuava-Li; they knew that Jardaine's position of leadership was now dubious, at best. Yet their fear forced them to stay at Jardaine's side. They crouched in a trench behind a fallen log, chanting together. "I thought you were dead," Macta sputtered, as he came in sight of the moonfaced monk.

"And I thought you were riding in the Arvada that just crashed near the Grove," Jardaine said with a rueful grin. "The Gods must have spared us for some greater purpose."

"I saw it go down," Macta said. "My father was in it, not to mention his most important advisors and generals. His Sorcerers . . . My sister, too, and her children, and . . . and . . ."

Macta was overcome with emotion. "The game is over. We're ruined. Everything went wrong. We thought we were smart enough, prepared enough to fight the Humans and win. Faerie Folk aren't meant to live, if this is all it takes to defeat us."

"Your father knew how to make weapons and sell them," Jardaine replied, "but did he think those flying slugs were invincible? He gambled, and he lost. Now will you let me advise you, Macta?"

"'Tis too late!" cried the Prince, looking at his soiled hands.

"Bah," spat Jardaine. "I've been learning for decades, charting the course of my own education, behind the Mage's back. Tuava-Li only ever did what she was told. She may have the raw power the Mage seemed to value so highly, but power is worthless if you don't know how to use it to get what you want. I have resources you can't even dream of, Macta. What would you say if I told you that we've made contact with the captains of the other Arvada, and they're all waiting to take my orders? They'll hear my commands in their brains just as if I'm talking to them."

"Then . . . then, if that's so, they could descend to a safe place, pick us up, fly us to Helfratheim, and I would be . . ."

"Aye, you'd be the new King! We'll be even better off than just ruling over this little dirt pile, Alfheim. *We'll have control over your father's entire empire!* Things couldn't have gone better if we'd planned them this way!"

Macta stared at Jardaine. "Did you *plan* this to go the way it did, Jardaine? You and your little snake, Sarette?"

The monk grinned. She pulled back her cowl, exposing her bare neck. "Sarette met with an unfortunate accident. Now there's just one more thing before we leave. We must retrieve the remainder of the Alfheim Jewels. They're still hidden in the cellar of the Humans' home, right where we left them. And since Alfheim is gone for good, the Jewels might as well be mine! Don't give me that look, Macta. I won't let you squander any more of my fortune than you already have. I have a sentimental attachment to those gems; I've been coveting them for a long, long time. Come on, the Arvada will follow us to the field by the house. We just have to stay out of the way of any Humans with weapons."

"But how will we get *into* the house?" asked the Prince. "I haven't seen Liqua since this all began. We need her to let us in. She's probably dead; she was nearly dead to begin with."

"I may know where Liqua is. Nebiros used her this morning to get into the Human house, where he kidnapped the little girl. That's what drew the other Humans to Alfheim with their weapons. If Nebiros is by the trees where I told him to wait, we'll all go to the house together."

"What if there are more Humans still inside?"

"Then I've got these," Jardaine answered, taking a fistful of poison-tipped darts from a pocket in her robe. "I took them from that Troll, Agar, before he scampered away. 'Tis not enough poison to kill a Human, but it will certainly stop them in their tracks. And Liqua will have the weapon she lost in the forest three hundred and sixty moons ago. I've stashed it nearby!"

"Ah," said Macta. "So this is why you asked me to steal the weapon from the Experimentalists' Chamber. But what makes you think that Liqua can still fire a thing like that? She barely has the strength to stand!"

The monk gave the Prince a smile that barely disguised a dare. "If she can't manage to shoot the weapon, I know you have some experience with the Dragon Thunderbus, eh? Now, a Prince ought to be Elf enough to handle a weapon like Liqua's, don't you think?"

Becky woke up with a scream. Bound and shoved into the hollow of a tree, she felt the heat from the fire that was ravaging the woods. Over the crackling roar of the blaze,

Charlie and Matt heard the familiar cry, and changed the direction of their flight from the inferno.

"I'm not goin' with you," insisted Tomtar, shaking his head at Nebiros.

In her crystal helmet, Anna knelt on the ground and cowered from the blast-furnace heat. With a loud popping sound, a crack opened up in the helmet. A trickle of water ran out and evaporated instantly. She hugged her doll tight to her chest. "I won't leave!" Tomtar cried. "We've got to let Becky go. 'Tis too late to worry about followin' orders. She'll die if we leave her here."

"What's one more Human?" snapped Nebiros.

"What indeed?" came the voice from behind. It was Jardaine, followed by Macta and the monks who had survived the explosion at the top of the wedding tower. Many were injured, all were frightened. "Come on," barked Jardaine. "There's a weapon in the tree trunk behind the girl. Get it. Then get Liqua up off the ground, and let's get out of here. We're going to the Human dwelling beyond the field."

"I'm staying," said Tomtar. "You can't make me go."

A tongue of flame spread across a branch overhead. "Suit yourself," Jardaine snapped.

The Elves pulled Becky from the tree and let her fall to the ground. They retrieved the old gun, then led Liqua, who staggered and faded in and out of sight, through the woods toward Matt's home. Tomtar struggled to untie Becky's ropes.

"Tomtar, what's going on?" the girl cried. "Why is it so hot? What are you doing?"

Over the roar of the fire the forest rang with another gunshot. "Matt!" Becky cried, looking up. "Dad!"

Charlie and Matt came crashing through the undergrowth. "Get away from her!" Charlie shouted at Tomtar. "Get away from her now, or I'll shoot you dead!"

49

TUAVA-LI AND THE MAGE soared over the burning forest. Tuava-Li heard her Master's voice in her brain, and she did not like what she heard. Tuava-Li's thoughts rang out as clearly to the Mage as if she had spoken them. *NOOO! 'Tis too dangerous!*

But the Mage remained calm. *'Tis all right. You'll see. Bethok will not allow us to be harmed, even now. There's something we must do for her.*

The limb was black and charred where the kestrel and the owl came to rest outside the Mage's quarters. Nothing remained but a burnt hole where the doorway had been. The smaller branches of the trees of the Grove had been consumed by fire, though the massive trunks had resisted the engulfing flames. Fifty feet below, the ground cover still burned. Fire Sprites danced in the smoldering wreckage of the forest, delighted by the sheer joy of so much heat, the magnitude of the fiery destruction. At the mouth of the black hole, the Mage and her Apprentice returned to their Elfin forms. The Mage whispered in an ancient tongue, and let her hands skim the surface of the charred wood. She was talking to the tree. Her voice carried a tone of strength and reassurance, like the voice one uses to calm a frightened animal. She stepped into her quarters within the smoldering trunk and could not prevent a small gasp from escaping her lips. Tuava-Li followed behind, her face a mask of sorrow. The floor of the Mage's quarters was a pool of melted candle wax. The walls seemed to breathe in and out, as bright flecks of fire were born, sparked and crackled, and then died in the fiber of the wood. The tree was attempting to shield the Mage's treasures, trying to keep the heat away, preventing the fire from invading a space it had been charged to protect. *"Vingata del t'mori, vijn hajjin sol t'mort,"* whispered the Mage.

She held her hand above the cover of a book which lay amid the ashes on her desk, feeling for the heat. Then she gingerly lifted the cover and watched it crumble. "'Tis all gone," Tuava-Li sobbed, "all of the wisdom, the knowledge, all we worked for, all gone."

"Ah," said the Mage, smiling wistfully, "but wisdom never lived here alone. Wisdom didn't die in the ashes of my library. You speak words, Tuava-Li, and your words are magick. They move, like spirit, to any who are listening, and that's how they live. Words are the way spirit moves. We've lost some of the words to the fire, but the spirit still lives. So do not grieve too much. Now place your hands on the walls of the trunk, and repeat the words I say. They carry magick in them. 'Tis time for the spirit of our beloved Bethok to leave her burned body."

The Mage and her Apprentice knelt before the ruins of the old shrine. They whispered to the tree to let her know that she was finished with her obligations to the Elves, and that the time had come for her spirit to return to the Earth, to the Cord. Soon there came a rumble from the base of the once-mighty oak. It was followed by a series of sharp, earsplitting creaks, like a claw hammer yanking nails from a plank. Bethok was pulling up her roots. She was loosening her ties to the earth. When she fell, her body would make a firewall to stop the spread of the inferno, should the wind send it back this way through the woods. "We must go," said the Mage, "quickly."

The murky light could not hide the fact that the forest was smothered in a blanket of ruin and despair. The two Elves hurried onto the tree limb, and began the transformation to their bird forms. They flapped away from the branch just as the tree swayed, leaned into the grove, and fell. Then the other four trees pulled up their own roots. With a thundering crash, the Sacred Oaks collapsed to the ground. There was no way for Tuava-Li to express her misery, save to flap her wings and fly away. *If only a bird could weep,* she thought.

The immediate reply of her Mage echoed in Tuava-Li's mind,

as the owl and the kestrel sailed up through the smoke and flame. *Let us take the power of our sadness and use it to search for survivors. A predator's eyes are well suited to the task. There may still be some trying to flee from the fire.*

Anna, barefoot, traipsed through the smoldering debris, trails of vapor sizzling in the hot, smoky air and disappearing up the length of her translucent legs. She followed Macta, Jardaine, and the monks to the edge of what remained of the woods. *I've been here before. I've done this before. It's nothing but a memory, there's nothing I have to be afraid of, it's nothing but a moment, unreal as all the others, just thoughts floating downstream, I'm at the bottom of the stream, safe and sound, this is just a dream merrily, merrily, merrily, merrily, life is but life is but*

life is but a dream

Stumbling, the cracked helmet leaking fluid, she followed the Elves. She was oblivious to the fire. The shotgun she had dropped on the forest floor thirty years before was once again planted firmly in her grip. *This time I won't drop the gun, when I find Daddy, I'll*

protect him, I'll shout to the deer, and the little people, and they'll all turn their heads and look at me, and I won't let it happen again, not like before.

Macta is my friend, Macta saved me.

Now he's going to help me save my

Daddy.

Macta turned to look at the girl. His eyes stung horribly, tears ran down his cheeks, leaving dark trails. He could barely see through the smoke and the blur of his tears. But it was plain that Liqua was falling behind. He needed her. He needed her to open the door and invite the Elves into the Humans' home. He needed her for that one last task. And he needed to know that if there were other Humans in the house, the gun he had given the girl would be put to use against them. It was a calculated risk; he had done all he could to assure the girl that he was her friend, that he would take her to her daddy, and that there were people, bad people, who wanted to stop her from seeing her father again. If Macta's lies achieved the desired ends, it would all be worth it. Liqua was a wretched thing to behold. Just one look at her in this condition would frighten any Human who might see her. Even if she never pulled the trigger of the weapon she carried, just the sight of her would give Macta and the monks time to get the remaining Alfheim Jewels out of the house and loaded into the waiting Arvada. And then he would be done with her. It wouldn't matter any more what became of the girl, she could dissolve, she could fade away, she could just disappear, and that would be as it should. It was a miracle she had survived this long. She should have died three hundred and sixty moons ago. "Come on, dear one," Macta soothed, suppressing his own anxiety. "We must keep up!"

The temperature along the forest floor was unbearable.

Though winds were moving the course of the fire slowly eastward, away from Alfheim and the houses at Sylvan Estates, there was still no escape from the suffocating, scorching heat. Macta had discarded his tunic, and his shirt and breeches were soaked with sweat. The monks, reluctant to give up their hooded robes, plodded onward, drenched to the skin. At the front of the group stalked Jardaine, shielding her eyes from the smoke and cinders. She led the way through a charred maze of fallen trees and smoldering rubble. The pale, greenish faces of the monks, normally as clear and smooth as spring buds, were stretched and dry, beginning to crack as the heat drew the moisture from the air. If they could get out of the forest, they would survive. It wouldn't be long before Liqua vanished completely. "Come on, your father needs you!" Macta pleaded. "We must hurry, or 'twill be too late! Come on, you can do it, this time you must save him!"

50

HUMPTY DUMPTY SAT ON A WALL, Humpty Dumpty had a great fall. All the—"

The back cover of the old book came loose from the pages and dropped to the basement floor. The brittle Scotch tape that had held the book together had finally given way. Jill McCormack sighed, as she sat with Emily on her lap. Emily was pointing at the picture and cooing softly. It was just an old Golden Book from when Charlie was little. She'd found a pile of them in a box on a shelf. Dirty. Musty. Coming apart. Why Charlie bothered to move them from his mom's house, she couldn't guess. But what else was there to do down here? Everything was coming apart. And there was nothing to do. Nothing to relieve her tension, not until Charlie came back. Not until she knew Becky was safe. Jill noticed that her hand was trembling. Emily squirmed on her lap and made an effort to slide away. "No, honey, no, look, I'll read to you some more! Here, look at the pretty pictures!"

Jill wrapped her arms around her toddler; it felt like the only thing that was keeping her sane. Becky was gone. Charlie and Matt were gone, too, gone to find Becky and bring her home. And here sat Jill, like Charlie had asked her to, next to the window in the basement, waiting. Waiting until . . . what? When? Jill realized she should have run for help. The nearest farm was only a mile or so down the road. Why did Charlie feel so sure she'd be safer locked up in the house? She should have said no, she should have insisted that she try to find somebody who could help them. She could have flagged down a passing car, a truck going by, anything. It wasn't a busy road, but vehicles went past every once in a while. Anything would have been better than to be stuck in the basement, helpless, waiting.

"Humpty Dumpty sat on a wall . . . ," Jill began again, in a singsong voice. But Emily slipped out of her mother's lap and toddled away. "Up, up!" the baby gurgled, pointing toward the stairs. Jill got up and took Emily's hand, all the while scanning the dark basement for some distraction. "No, honey," she said. "Daddy wants us to stay down here."

Then Jill spotted the old, black trunk in the shadows near the wall. "Emily, look over here . . . Let's see what's in here!" Jill crossed the basement, undid the rusty latch, lifted the lid, and peered inside. "Aha!"

The dolls were old, and dirty, and somebody had been in the trunk and had made quite a mess of things. Loose cloth caps, capes, shoes, and pieces of broken toy furniture were strewn among the dolls. Normally, Jill wouldn't have given these things to the baby; not without a lot of cleaning up, first. Her hands were shaking as she picked up a doll. "C-come over here, honey," Jill said. The toddler was headed for the basement steps. "I want to show you some dolls! Look!"

The pink-skinned baby doll was dressed in a faded velvet dress, with a string of plastic pearls around her neck. One blue eye was stuck open, staring ahead, while the other eye flapped open and shut. Emily toddled toward the trunk with both hands outstretched. She squealed in delight as Jill handed her the doll. Then something buried in the trunk caught Jill's attention. An enormous shining ruby. A little pile of emeralds, next to it. *Costume jewelry,* thought Jill, *I don't remember this in here.*

Jill reached deeper into the trunk, and her fingers found a fist-sized burlap sack. It was heavy, and it rattled when she picked it up. Emily was at the side of the trunk now, hands grasping the edge, wondering what other treasures waited inside. She had dropped the doll on the floor. It lay awkwardly, arms twisted, already forgotten. *"Eeeah,"* Emily cried, reaching for the gleaming ruby.

"Nooo," Jill said, shaking her head. "That's a choker. Let's find you another doll."

There was a naked baby, smaller than the other dolls, with

arms and legs that could be posed. Jill picked it up to hand to Emily. "Look, it's a little baby! It's *your* baby!"

Then she saw the other burlap bags tucked beneath the doll. She plucked one from its hiding place and pulled the drawstring. It was impossible, they looked so realistic. She shook the diamonds out onto her palm. She grabbed the sacks of jewels as she stood up. She could look at them upstairs in the better light. Jill scooped up Emily. "Maybe you need a snack. I guess it would be okay to go upstairs, just for a minute or two."

The clock on the wall was stopped: 5:04. Jill felt as if she were moving in slow motion as she dropped the little sacks on the kitchen table. She'd open them soon. There was something about those jewels; they looked almost real. But first things first. She took a pitcher from the cabinet and went to fill it with ice from the refrigerator. She pressed the lever. Nothing. *Now what?* she thought, forgetting again that the power was off. Then she took the pitcher to the sink to fill it up. Cool water would be good to have in the basement, something to drink in case they got thirsty. Emily was already in the pantry. She was searching a bin on the floor for the little packages of pretzels and chips she loved so much. "Here, honey, I'll get them," said Jill. She put the pitcher on the table and stepped into the pantry to join her daughter. Neither of them heard the front door latch pop open. But a second later Jill realized voices were coming from the living room: odd, high-pitched voices. "*Sssshhh,* quiet, you idiot! If there's anyone home, we don't want them to know we're here."

"I don't feel well."

"Have you any of that bark, with the spell for metal, Jardaine? I can't stand it in here. I'm going to be sick!"

"Then wait outside, and keep watch. We'll go in and get the Jewels."

There was a loud bump from the living room. It was immediately followed by a strange, choked sound, a gurgling, a groan. Jill hoisted Emily into her arms and stood there in the closet with a hand gently covering the baby's mouth. With her other hand she reached for the knob of the pantry door. She pulled gently, until the latch shut. *Thank God,* she thought. It closed without a squeak. But then there was another bump, this time in the kitchen, just a few feet away. "Keep the weapon steady!" a voice hissed.

Jill held her breath. It was a strange voice, coming through the pantry door, a voice as high as that of a child, but with some indistinct quality that was more like that of an adult. Perhaps it was the authority of the voice, the implicit danger in the commands. Then there was another voice—deeper, but equally strange. "Down the steps, and be careful," said Nebiros. "We'll be out of here in the twinkling of an eye."

"Aye," Jardaine agreed. "My Arvada are waiting for my command."

"They're my *father's* Arvada, Jardaine," hissed Macta. "Simply because you can call them down with your magick doesn't mean they belong to you."

The Prince turned toward the broken, tattered girl in the crystal helmet, and stamped his foot. "Wait here, Liqua," he ordered. "Keep your weapon at the ready. This is where the enemies of your father live, the Humans who want to stop you from seeing him again. Don't let any Human get past you."

Jardaine and Nebiros led the monks to the basement steps. They climbed down backward, one step at a time, and Macta, holding a finger to his lips, turned away from Anna. The girl stood leaning against the counter as he, too, descended the stairs. Anna let the shotgun drop to her side; the weight of it was sapping what little strength remained in her. The doll she had taken from the house before was draped over her other arm; she gave it a squeeze. Through the liquid remaining inside her helmet Anna gazed blankly at the chairs. Her eyes scanned the fruit bowl on the counter, the little magnetized photographs on the shiny steel refrigerator. Her head felt very heavy. A rivulet of fluid made its way through the crack in the helmet, running down her neck, soaking into her tattered shirt. Anna was overcome with fatigue, and pictures, memories, half-formed dreams began to flood her mind. She remembered another kitchen, long ago. Then her wandering eyes fell upon the pitcher of water on the table. *Water!* She dropped the shotgun, stumbled across the room and plunged her trembling hands into the pitcher. *Aaaaaaaaah!* she moaned. *Water. Home.* But she lost her balance and fell against the table, and the pitcher crashed to the floor.

In the basement the Elves froze. "What has she done now?" Macta snapped. Nebiros and Jardaine stood inside the doll trunk. They had heaved its contents onto the cement, and there was nothing left to find. "They've taken the Jewels," Jardaine gasped, staring at the bottom of the trunk. "There's nothing here but a few scattered stones. We've got to go."

Upstairs Anna squatted on the tiled floor. Her fall had broken her crystal helmet, which now lay in pieces amid the shards of the shattered pitcher. Only the metal rim remained, a collar that hung loosely around her neck. Tendrils of hair hung over Anna's face. Water dripped down her cheeks. The veins and muscles beneath her skin faded from view where the trails of water ran. She bent low, moaning, and rubbed her face into the liquid that puddled around the broken glass.

The sounds coming from the kitchen were more than Jill could stand. She eased open the pantry door, and as daylight flooded her eyes, she gazed upon the wretched, damaged girl. The stench made Jill feel faint. This girl was older than Becky, and she looked like she'd been living in the woods her whole life. "My God, w-w-what happened to you?" Jill stammered, stepping out of the pantry. "Who are you? What are you doing here?"

Emily toddled into the light and clung to her mother's ankles. "Shoot her!" came a voice from beyond the basement door. Macta was hoisting himself up the stairs. "*She's* your enemy, *she* doesn't want you to see your father again, pick up the weapon, Liqua, and *shoot her*!"

Jill heard the awful, tinny voice, but she did not at first see the Elves climb up out of the basement and gather around the soaked, disheveled girl. Jill's eyes did not register the reality. The figures began to materialize only slowly, as Jill realized with mounting terror what she was witnessing. The strange, filthy girl scrabbled across the floor like a spider, grabbed the shotgun, and struggled to her feet. Jill stepped back. The girl aimed the shotgun squarely at Jill's chest, and then she reared back and let out a scream. It was a hideous, unearthly sound, full of anger, and fear, and loneliness. As she did so, her body seemed to fade away, and then return with a pale, sickly glow around it. But the barrel of the shotgun was still pointed straight at Jill.

"Stay back!" shouted Jardaine, holding her hand over her mouth. The other monks pressed the edge of their robes over their faces, fearing contamination. "Where are the Jewels?"

"W-what are you?" Jill whimpered. "Why are you here? Do you—do you have my daughter? Did you take Becky?"

"Give us the Jewels, or we'll kill you," said Macta, "and your little girl, too."

"Give us the Jewels," Jardaine said, casting an angry glance at Macta. "And we'll tell you where you can find your girl. And your son and your mate as well."

"You—you know where they are?" Jill said, taking a step forward.

"Stop right there!" Jardaine shrieked. "Don't come any closer!"

Jill looked down at the Elves. There were only seven of them, all together, and they were too small, too short, to see the burlap sacks on the tabletop. Jill took a deep breath. She wondered if she was hallucinating, if she was having a nervous breakdown. Maybe she should just ignore the strange beings in her kitchen and take Emily back to the basement. She started to turn away.

"Stop!"

The voice was wet, and muffled, and raw, yet the girl with the shotgun had spoken her first word in thirty years. "Stop!"

The sound that erupted from her mouth took Anna by complete surprise. It was like an alarm going off in her own mind, waking her up after a long, troubled sleep. Anna felt the shotgun in her hands, and looked into the face of the woman who loomed before her. And she spoke. Her voice was strangled, her tongue felt as awkward as a block of wood in her mouth. But she spoke. *"Where . . . where is my daddy?"*

Jill stared back. The girl's face looked suddenly familiar. So did the shotgun in her arms; it matched the one in the hall gun closet, the one that had belonged to Charlie's dad. *Charlie's sister. It can't be. It looks just like the pictures of Charlie's dead sister.* "I don't know where your father is," she answered, swallowing hard. "But . . . if you put that gun down, I'll help you find him. I promise . . . *Anna.*"

The girl faltered. For a moment she began to fade away, her hands, her feet disappearing. *Anna. Who is Anna?* She hadn't heard the name spoken aloud in so long, so very long.

"Liqua," Macta snapped, watching the girl fade away, "*Come back!* You can do it. You mustn't trust the woman. *We're* your friends. Do as you're told and keep the weapon pointed at her. She wants to hurt us, Liqua. She wants to steal our precious things. You have to protect your friends."

"I'll give you the jewels," Jill said calmly, turning to Macta, "if you tell me where my family is. No, that's not all. Take me to my family, and I'll give you the jewels. That's my offer."

"'Tis not a bargain," Macta sneered. "You have something that belongs to us. We want it back. Now! I'll wager you value your own life. The Human girl is mad. She'll kill you without blinking. You have ten seconds to decide. The Jewels, or your life. Ten. Nine. Get ready to shoot, Liqua!"

Emily crawled away from her mother's ankles. She had seen the shotguns in the hall gun case, but she had no idea what they were for, or of the danger present in the room. She got up on her feet, toddling along the wall. She was curious about these funny little people, no bigger than some of her sister's dolls, standing there in the kitchen. Why were they shouting? "Eight. Seven. Six."

Emily reached out a pudgy finger to touch Macta. She giggled as the Prince leapt back in alarm, as the monks reached into the sleeves of their robes and pulled out slender reeds. They were the blowguns taken from Agar the Troll. "Liqua, I want you to keep the weapon aimed at the Human," Macta ordered.

Jill took a step toward Emily. The monks placed the ends of the reeds into their mouths and took aim, ready to shoot the poison darts into the baby's flesh. "My daughter," pleaded Jill, "just let me get my daughter!"

"Don't move," Macta replied. "Give us the Jewels or we'll shoot your child with poison darts, right here, right now."

Macta knew that the effect of the darts would not be fatal to a grown Human, though it might well make them very ill. Who knew how the poison might affect a Human baby? It was a game, everything that was happening, a game of life and death, and it made him giddy with excitement.

Emily stood up, with one hand tracing a line on the wall, and toddled away toward the open front door. There was a new distraction, something else to capture her interest. A monk in her hooded cowl stood in the doorway, twenty feet away, looking horrified at the Human child coming straight for her. The monk turned and ran. Emily giggled again, and toddled after her. "Shoot her with the darts," Nebiros snapped, "don't let her get away!"

"No!" cried Jill. With one quick move she reached out

and swept the burlap sacks from the tabletop. In a shower of color the Alfheim Jewels hit the floor, skittering across the kitchen. One of the sacks struck the side of Macta's head and knocked him flat on the tiles. Then Jill leapt over the Elves, kicking Jardaine, and stumbled for the front door. "Emily!" she screamed. "Emily, go outside! Now! Mommy's coming!"

51

CHARLIE WAS BREATHING HARD as he bounded across the construction site. The sky above was darkened not only by the smoke from the forest fire but by the massive Arvada that hovered over the McCormacks' home. The air was full of flickering shadows and the sharp whipping sounds of the Sprites as they twitched their tails and waited for Jardaine's commands. "Dad," puffed Matt. "We can shoot those things, like the one I nailed back in the woods!"

"What if they come down on our house?" his father grunted. "Mom and Emily are still inside. We can't take that chance."

Back in the woods Tomtar had done his best to explain to Charlie and Matt what was going on. The Elves were headed for the McCormacks' house to look for the Alfheim Jewels, and they wouldn't hesitate to harm anyone who stood in their way. Now the inferno was behind them, but other dangers waited ahead. Shotgun shells rattled in Charlie's pocket. He pumped the gun and called to Becky, who was struggling to keep up with her father. "Just stay behind me, honey. I won't let anything happen to you."

"I was wrong to doubt you, Matt," Tomtar panted, as he hurried behind Matt. "I let the Elves make a fool of me. I never had a Human for a friend before. But we're goin' to defend each other, from now on, aren't we?"

Matt didn't know what to say. Still, he glanced over his shoulder and nodded, as he hoisted his shotgun and stumbled over the scarred earth.

Charlie was a hundred feet from the house when he saw movement on the front porch. It was one of Jardaine's monks. The little cowled figure swept across the deck and down the steps, like a leaf blown across the road. Then Emily toddled out the open door and swayed uncertainly at the top of the stairs.

"Emily!" Charlie yelled. "Emily!"

The baby turned around and carefully lowered herself down the steps, one at a time. "Da Da!" she gurgled.

Charlie let out a sob as he ran. Just then he heard a shotgun blast from inside the house. Charlie watched helplessly as he saw his wife run from the front door and suddenly topple facedown onto the porch. "Cover me, Matt!" he shouted.

In a matter of seconds Charlie was there beside Jill, whispering her name, checking for a pulse. Matt crouched next to the stairs, his shotgun at the ready. Becky gathered up Emily in her arms and hurried to hide behind the truck in the driveway. "Jill!" Charlie whispered harshly, dragging his wife's body away from the open door. There was no blood; it was clear she hadn't been shot. A little, feather-tipped dart protruded from her throat. Another was stuck in her arm. "Jill!"

"Charlie . . . ," she moaned, her head rocking back and forth.

"Jill, are you all right?" Charlie breathed. Gently he took one of the darts by the shaft and pulled it out.

Tomtar stood next to the open front door. *"Pssst!"* he called.

Charlie glanced up. "What?"

"I'll go inside to see if there's any danger, sir, but you've got to give me your permission."

"What?" Charlie repeated.

"Mister McCormack, just tell me it's all right to go in your house! I can't go in without your invitation!"

"All right, go, *go!*" Charlie whispered. He turned to his son, who stood, eyes wide with terror, looking down at his mother. "Matt, I want you to stay out here. We don't know how many of them there are, or what kinds of weapons they might have. I heard a shot from inside. I think Mom's okay. You've got to keep an eye on her and guard the girls, too. I'm counting on you."

"Okay, Dad!" Matt nodded weakly.

On the kitchen floor, Macta and five of the remaining monks were busy gathering up the diamonds, emeralds, rubies, sapphires, and other precious Jewels, and cramming them back into the burlap sacks. Nebiros helped Jardaine to her feet, and she stood in the flickering light that came from the window. With her eyes closed she focused her energy to contact the pilots of the Arvada and bring them earthward. Sweat rolled down Jardaine's brow as she grit her teeth, her body shaking with the exertion. Then she opened her eyes and peered out the window. The Arvada began their slow descent. "I can do it," she said, breaking into hysterical laughter. *"I can do it!"*

Anna lay on the floor next to her smoking shotgun. The stench of sulfur filled the air. None could have known why she pulled the trigger and fired a shot into the ceiling. Maybe she meant to hit the woman, as Macta had commanded. Maybe she meant the shot as a warning. Maybe it was an accident. But the monks felled Jill with their darts, anyway, and the recoil of the gun brought Anna down. Without the helmet, without the flowing water to keep the memory of her body together, there was little left of Anna McCormack. She was a fragment, a shard, a reflection of a human being. Just as the broken glass around her was just a memory of the pitcher it had once been, Anna was little more than a memory, an echo of a human. Yet amid the jumble of thoughts that careened through her broken mind, a thread of sanity began to reveal itself, even as the molecules that formed her cursed body began to drift apart, vaporizing, coming undone. *Mother mother, where is no she's not my mother why not my friend not my friends not little people not helping help me water I need water my family my house my help me!*

Anna rolled over, hoisted herself up against the counter, and found herself staring into the kitchen sink. *Of course,* there was water here. It had been so long since she had been inside a house. She reached out a shimmering, nearly transparent hand and found the cold-water tap. *Water,* her lips formed the word, and the sound of her own voice brought the girl back from the brink of extinction, if only for the moment. She held her hands in the cold, flowing stream, tossed the water up onto her face, her hair, the rags she wore for clothes. She saw the veins, the nerves, the muscles, a blur of red appear in her hands, the beautiful, pink opacity of human skin forming before her eyes, and she luxuriated in the sensation of being solid, real, of being *alive.*

"Stop right there!" a man's voice boomed from behind her.

Anna swung around, her vision blurred from the water in her eyes. The monks stood up and stared at Charlie, who had slipped silently into the room. Overcome with terror the Elves dropped the Jewels clutched in their hands. They pulled up the edges of their robes to cover their faces once more, deathly afraid of Human contamination. "The blowguns!" screamed Macta, from beneath the kitchen table. "Shoot him, you fools! Liqua, get your weapon! Quickly, the Human's going to kill you!"

Charlie's eyes darted around the room. There was a powerful stench in the air, wet, moldering, foul. He saw a figure under the table, he saw a blur of movement as another one raced to hide behind the trash can. A much larger figure, dark and hulking, seemed to be materializing by the sink. The tap was running; the sink was overflowing, and a pool of water was growing larger on the floor, at the feet of the . . . *the girl? A human girl?* She was splashing water onto herself, and with each passing second Charlie could see her coming into focus.

The monks raised the blowguns between their trembling lips as Charlie swung the barrel and fired his shotgun at the Elf who dashed past him. It was Nebiros. There was an explosion of green on the tiles; a volley of darts whizzed by Charlie's head and stuck in the cork bulletin board behind him. Anna startled and let out a cry. She bent convulsively and picked up her shotgun from the floor. The others scattered, screaming, running for cover. Charlie pumped the shotgun and turned to stare into the eyes of the girl who aimed her own gun straight at his chest. In a moment frozen in time the girl opened her mouth and cried out, *"Daddy?"*

Charlie blinked. The girl was filthy, disheveled, and the look on her face was completely mad, insane, demented. She was just a child, not much older than Becky. Yet why did he think he could see through her limbs? As the girl lowered the shotgun and stumbled across the kitchen toward him, Charlie stared in awe. It was impossible, he knew, but there she stood. It was his little sister, Anna, not a day older than the last time he had seen her, thirty years before. "No!" Macta screamed again, from beneath the table. "You belong to *me*! You're on *my* side, not his!"

There was a blowgun with a poison dart lying on the Blood-spattered tile near Nebiros's body. Macta grabbed it, raised it to his lips, and spun around to face Charlie. "You're not going to shoot my daddy!" Anna sputtered. She squeezed the trigger of her shotgun.

At that same moment Tomtar leapt out from behind a cabinet to grab Macta's arm, and stop him from firing the dart. The rain of shotgun pellets sped over their heads and crashed into the freshly painted wall behind them. "Aaaaargh!" screamed Tomtar, clutching at his shoulder. A trail of emerald-colored Blood ran down his arm. The Prince gathered up two bags of Jewels and lumbered through the front door. Jardaine and her monks were cowering behind the garbage can, hidden from view. Jardaine stared out through the glass of the French doors into the turbulent sky. The Arvada were landing. Jardaine peered around the edge of the garbage can, past the splattered remains of Nebiros. She cast a glance toward the front door of the house, and smiled ruefully. Jill's body, limp and motionless, was still stretched out on the porch.

Charlie stood in the middle of the kitchen. He was too stunned at the sight of his sister to move. Anna dropped her shotgun and fell into Charlie's embrace. But it only took an instant for the realization to hit him; the girl was fading away. The moldy odor was disappearing, too, just like the pale arms that held him so tightly. *She thinks I'm her dad,* Charlie said to himself. *Our dad.* Tears ran down his face. The girl was real, flesh and blood, and yet she had no weight; there was nothing substantial about her. She was fading away, like a ghost. She didn't exist. She couldn't exist. She'd been gone so long. And yet here she was, crying out in a tremulous voice, "Daddy, Daddy, Daddy, I never thought I'd see you again, Daddy, I missed you so much."

Charlie knew that he was just about the same age his father had been all those years ago, the day he disappeared in the forest. He knew how much he resembled his dad; every time he looked in a mirror he would see it in the way he was getting older, the gray stubble on his chin, the creases of worry across his forehead, just like his dad. "I missed you, too, Anna," Charlie answered, his voice choked with emotion.

It didn't matter that Anna was mistaken. It was too late for explanations, too late for everything. All of the rules, all the foundation for his reality was shattered, anyway, like the heart and the mind of the disappearing girl. "You'll never know how much I missed you," Charlie murmured.

He sank to his knees. The girl was letting go now of the frail cord that bound her to life. Safe in Charlie's arms she was free to let go. Charlie held her close, and felt her fading away. He closed his eyes and found himself singing softly, like a lullaby, the song his father had sung when Charlie and Anna were little. *"You take the high road, and I'll take the low road, and I'll get to Scotland before you, for me and my true love will never meet again . . ."*

Matt leaned up over the bumper of the pickup truck in the driveway. He had dragged his mother to the edge of the steps, and soon she was conscious enough to stumble down the stairs and across the lawn to where her girls were waiting. Hot winds whipped against their faces as the Arvada flicked their tails and churned up dust from the construction site. *"Stop, Macta!"* Tomtar cried as he hurried down the porch steps, gripping his injured shoulder. "You won't get away with this! Stop!"

"Tomtar, *no*!" Matt hollered. "Forget about him; he can't hurt us!"

Charlie stepped through the door of the house. His face looked dazed, stricken, but he hurried down the stairs and went to join his wife and daughters behind the truck. Churning winds filled the air with dirt and cinders.

Tomtar ran as if his life depended on it to get between Macta and the fleet of Elfin war craft. Matt raced toward them as he saw the Prince drop one of the sacks of Alfheim Jewels, and draw the blowgun from his trouser pocket. "Get out of the way, Tomtar!" the boy shouted. Macta glanced up, just in time to see Matt racing toward him with the shotgun in his hands. The Prince dropped the blowgun, snatched up his bag of gemstones, turned in the other direction, and ran. Past the low stone wall he sped, past the shrubs and the signs and onto the highway. Macta hesitated for a moment at the edge of the road, and then dashed across the blacktop. If he couldn't reach the Arvada now, at least he could disappear in the woods on the other side of the road, where the fire had not burned the trees to the ground.

Screeeeeeeeeee! It was a white panel van that hurtled down Highway 256. When it ground to a halt, Macta Dockalfar's body lay on the roadway. "What the hell are you doing on the road, kid?" The driver of the van leapt out of the vehicle, stepped obliviously over Macta's still form, and shouted at Matt. "You could have got yourself killed! And what are you doing with that shotgun?"

Matt was startled. He pointed at the ground. "Don't you see—"

"See what?" the truck driver answered, looking at the roadway as if nothing were there.

Suddenly Matt felt dizzy and ill; he thought he might throw up. All it took was one uncomprehending human to make him doubt his own senses. "Tomtar!" he cried, but the Troll was nowhere in sight. *What you don't understand, you don't see. That's why*

Macta got hit by the truck, that's why I . . . Matt glanced at the road again, and this time didn't see the battered remains of the Prince. He looked at the gun in his hands, then threw it onto the gravel shoulder of the highway. Macta had to be dead, Matt had seen the truck hit him, even if he couldn't see the corpse anymore. "Mister!" he cried out. "Don't you see the smoke? There—there's a forest fire back here. And look, look in the field! You've got to help us!"

"Us?"

"Mister, please, have you got a cell phone, or something? You've got to call the police! You've got to get help!"

The truck driver looked confused.

"Look!" Matt screamed, pointing toward the construction site. He blinked, and blinked again, and the Arvada were there, twitching their tails. "Don't you see them? They tried to kill us! Look at the sky! Don't you see the smoke? Don't you see the fire in the woods?"

"Calm down," the man said, as suspicion crept across his face. He waved his hands in front of him and backed away, and Matt could see that he was scared. "I don't see anything," he said. "I don't know what you're talkin' about, kid. Look, if you want, I'll call the police for you when I get where I'm goin'. Maybe you should just go back in your house and wait for help."

The man climbed into the van and shut the door, locking it behind him. "You're not going to help us?" Matt screamed, pounding on the side of the van. "You're not going to do anything?"

The driver in the panel truck floored the gas pedal and hurtled down the road. Matt cursed and went back to the gravel shoulder. He picked up his shotgun and called out. "Tomtar! Tomtar! Where did you go?" Matt looked down, shook his head, and blinked. "I think I can see you . . . wait, here, take my hand!"

The Troll reached up and grabbed Matt by the thumb. "Come on," he pleaded. "Somethin's happenin' at your house. We've got to get back, Matt."

As he faced the house and the forest behind it, Matt saw the vast column of smoke rising from the woods, and he saw the massive, gaseous monsters, like living hot-air balloons, there on the field. The beasts roared, a terrible, high-pitched sound that made Matt cover his ears. "Why couldn't the man in the truck see this?" he yelled. "Why couldn't he feel the heat, or see the fire?"

Tomtar had to hold onto his cap to keep it from flying off in the wind. "He didn't *see*!" the Troll shouted. "You see what you believe in, and that's all."

"But the fire's real, the forest fire, it's burning down the trees. Anybody could see that!"

"Not if it's happenin' in *our* world!" Tomtar cried. "The Faerie world."

"But where's the border? Where's the border of your world and ours?"

Tomtar stared out into the field, shielding his eyes from the dust and debris. "I don't know!"

The pair hurried back down the long driveway toward the house. When they reached the family pickup truck, Matt cried out. "Dad? Mom? Becky? Where are you?"

There was no reply. Matt squinted through the turbulent air, and saw a group of dark figures marching toward the monstrous craft. "Wait!" he screamed. "What are you doing?"

Matt checked his shotgun for shells: all gone. There was nothing he could do to stop the Elves now. As he raced for the field he saw his mother, with Emily in her arms, get down on the ground and crawl through a large open panel on the side of a brass cab. One of the black-clad monks was clinging to his mother's back, guiding her movements. A monk led Matt's father into another cab, and Becky climbed into a third. Light flashed from the gleaming metal shafts of the blades that the monks held against his family members' throats. Suddenly a ghostly figure stood in front of Matt, brandishing a dagger of her own. It was Jardaine, but she was as big as Matt now, five feet tall or more. It was an illusion; it had to be. Matt swung the barrel of his gun at the monk, and it passed right through her as if she wasn't real. Matt heard laughter and looked down. Jardaine was there, no bigger than a doll, and she had the knife-edge pressed at his ankle.

"You can't change what I see," said Matt. "You can't change what's real!"

But Jardaine leapt, grabbed Matt by the hair, and swung herself up so that her legs clamped around his shoulders. In a second she had her blade at his throat, and whispered in his ear, "Aye, I can. The magick isn't make-believe. These blades are tipped in poison, enough poison to kill even a Human. We've been waiting for you, boy. You're coming with us, all of you! Your world's not ready yet to know about Faerie Folk, and it appears we're not ready yet to settle the score with your kind."

"But what are you going to do to with us?" Matt cried.

"What are we going to do?" Jardaine mused. "All I know for sure is that we have no intention of leaving you here to tell the world what happened."

A shadow rushed past. Matt saw one of the monks, carrying the two bags of Jewels that Macta had left on the highway. "You don't have any weapons," Matt insisted. "Those knives aren't real. Elves can't touch steel! The blow darts, I saw them, I saw what you did to my mom, but you're trying to get into my head, make me think the knives are real, when they're not!"

The Elf chuckled. "Can you be sure of that, young hero? You forget that Tomtar had his spells to protect him from being seen, to protect him from metal. Do you want to take the chance that this is all pretend? Now come along, and climb into the Arvada. They're made of metal, too, you know. We've got a long journey ahead of us. Your mother's Blood has been contaminated by the darts, like yours was when you stepped on Princess Asra's shoe. If you want us to help her, you'll do as I say."

Matt stumbled toward the fourth Arvada. He shielded his face from the winds. Jardaine still clung to his shoulder, with her blade against his throat. When he reached the cab, Matt tossed his shotgun aside and got down on his hands and knees. He peered into the cab. It was obvious that the interior of the cab was damaged, the flat bottom blackened and twisted. "It isn't safe," Matt said. "This won't support my weight. Are all of these things damaged? You won't be able to get us off the ground!"

"All of the cabs were compromised by the fire from below," Jardaine said, hopping to the ground. "This one's the worst, and we saved it for last. If you hadn't shot down the fifth Arvada, there wouldn't be a problem. Now get in."

Matt squeezed into the cramped space, flat on his back, feeling the distressed metal catch at his shirt. The top of the cab was just inches from his face. Out of the corner of his eye he saw a group of Elves hurry around the side of the vehicle to swing the brass doors shut, and seal him into the craft. "Where do you want to take them?" a gruff voice came from outside.

"A family of live Humans might prove useful to the Elves of Helfratheim," Jardaine replied. "Though now that the King and his son are dead, things may be a bit . . . *chaotic* there. Perhaps we'll just jettison the cabs over the nearest body of water! They'd sink like stones, and no one would ever be the wiser!" Jardaine laughed, and Matt could hear her voice growing faint as she went to enter another of the Arvada.

Matt pounded on the sides of the cab, trying to force open the door. If Jardaine was contemplating killing them all, there wasn't a moment to spare; he had to stop the Arvada from taking off. But the doors were unyielding, no matter how hard he tried. Matt let out a cry of despair. A moment later the Arvada rumbled, then began to lift slowly off the ground. *Broaaaaaagh!* the great Sprites roared. *Broaaaaaagh!* Matt wanted to press his hands over his ears; the sound was deafening, but there wasn't enough room in the cab to move his arms. He realized it must have been excruciating for his parents to squeeze into these vehicles; they were as confining as coffins, and perhaps soon, that was what they would become. Matt pushed his knees against the top of the cab and found that the sheet of metal beneath his back, damaged by the forest fire, was giving way. He gave a mighty push and heard the groan of the metal, felt it ripping his shirt, and suddenly he was lying on the ground, in the shadow of the cab. Sucking in breath Matt jumped up, made a mad dash, then leapt for the Arvada nearest to his own. His fingers took hold of a brass railing along the top of the cab, and with a lurch the Arvada lifted Matt off his feet. The gigantic Sprite thrashed and roared, but Matt held on tight, his weight slowing the vehicle's ascent. Through the little windows on the side of the vehicle Matt could see his sister Becky's terrified face looking out at him. "Becky, you've got to push, push on the doors!" Matt screamed. "I think there's a latch here, but you've got to push! Now!"

Matt loosened his grip with one hand, then grabbed at the

latch that held the doors shut. At that same moment, Becky shoved with all her might, knocking the doors open, and the two of them tumbled, screaming, to the ground.

Jardaine shook her head as she peered at the children from an Arvada window. "If only they'd fallen from a greater height, we wouldn't have to be bothered with these Humans."

"What would you like to do?" asked the driver of the craft. "Should we circle around and pick them up again?"

"Nooo," Jardaine answered. "We have run out of time, but we mustn't let them live. How do we command these Sprites to attack?"

Matt lay on the dirt, coughing. Becky let out a cry, a long, wailing cry of sorrow, and anger, and pain. Matt got up on his knees, testing his weight to make sure that nothing was broken. "Becky, are you okay?" he hollered, spitting dust from his mouth.

"I don't know!" she cried. "Mom! Dad!" Becky got up and raced across the rough ground, grasping for the vehicles that now were out of reach. Pelted with dust and gravel and ash from the winds, Matt saw the wrinkled creases at the front end of the creatures open up, revealing yawning, red-rimmed holes. Then he had to shield his eyes again as white-hot bursts of flame shot from the mouths of the beasts. "Run!" Matt screamed. "Run for cover!"

The pillars of fire were blinding. They scoured the ground, then enveloped each of the houses in the development, each of the houses his father and his crew had built, investing all of the money, all of their hopes, all of their dreams. Matt grabbed his sister and they huddled behind a boulder until, with a roar, the Arvada switched their tails and drifted off into the distance. "Over here!" someone shouted. Matt glanced up and saw Tomtar peering from behind a tree at the edge of the woods. "Over here, the heat, 'tis not so bad. Come on!"

As the children stumbled across the scorched earth a shadow flashed overhead, then two. Matt ducked as his heart leapt into his throat. What now? "Get down, Becky!"

A horned owl and a kestrel sailed over the children's heads and landed on the branch of an elm. Matt looked up to see both of the birds begin their transformation. He rubbed his eyes, and in a moment the Mage of Alfheim and Tuava-Li crouched on the branch, staring down at them. Matt bent to pick up two rocks from the ground. They were sharp-edged and heavy, ready to throw, just in case. "What do you want?" he demanded.

Becky began to sob, deep, wrenching, uncontrollable sobs. Matt put his arm around his sister. "Why are you looking at us?" he cried. "Why are you here? You've ruined our lives. We've got nothing, nowhere to go. The others are going to kill our parents and our sister. They—"

"We saw it all," the Mage interrupted.

"'Tis no responsibility of ours to help you," said Tuava-Li, "but . . ."

"I can help, Matt," volunteered Tomtar. "I think I can. There used to be maps, charts of all the Faerie lands, back in Argant where I grew up. There's someone there who could show us. If Jardaine's taken your parents to Helfratheim, we could find out how to get there, and follow the path overground. Maybe we could still save 'em!"

"Helfratheim would probably be their first destination," offered the Mage, "just to return the Arvada to their home port. And Jardaine wouldn't harm your family if she thought there was some advantage in keeping them alive. There are maps of the Faerie world at the Council headquarters in Ljosalfar, as well. No Human has ever stepped foot there before, but under the circumstances . . ."

"What circumstances?" asked Matt.

"We need to talk," said the Mage. "We may be able to make an agreement that is mutually satisfying."

"Ma'am," Tomtar said, looking up, "do you know how to get to Ljosalfar, overground? 'Twould take many days."

"The Cord to Ljosalfar is still intact," said Tuava-Li.

"But—the fire, didn't the fire—"

"Noooo," said the Mage. "The trees of the forest gave up the sap in their veins to keep the Cord moist, to keep it from being destroyed. The Cord is weak, 'tis not well, but the way to Ljosalfar is clear." The Mage nodded at Matt and Tomtar. "The future of the Faerie world requires three souls to make a perilous journey: an Elf, a Troll, and a Human. As it was in ancient times, 'tis the only way to save us now. 'Twill be a journey to save the

Cord by planting the Seed of the Holy Adri at the center of the earth, beneath the pole. Tuava-Li will lead the quest, but two others are needed to join her. I ask you, Tomtar and Matt, to be Tuava-Li's companions."

Matt glared at the Elves. "What seed? What pole? You're talking nonsense. You got me into this; you've got to help me find my parents. We don't have anywhere to live. We haven't got any relatives around here, friends, no one. You can't ask anything of me. I've got to take care of my sister."

The Mage smiled sadly, shaking her head. "I know, it makes no sense to you. But it will. Tuava-Li, and Tomtar, and Matt, if the three of you undertake this task, you will have the chance to save the Faerie world from disaster. Perhaps the Human world as well. 'Tis bigger than your own family, Matt. As long as the Cord slips toward death, and the Human and Faerie worlds flow together, our enemies will stop at nothing to provoke a war. Jardaine, Brahja-Chi and her followers, and whatever remains of the Dockalfars will be intent on the path of destruction."

Tuava-Li and the Mage looked at one another. "This is the offer we make," said Tuava-Li, turning toward Matt. "We'll help you find your parents if you agree to go on this journey with me. And the Mage will care for your sister until your return. There'll be many times I'll need to travel overground, and 'twill be far, far easier to accomplish our goal with a Human accompanying me."

"You were supposed to grant Matt a wish," murmured Becky.

"From the faeries, because Matt found your diamond shoe. That's what he told me! You've got to grant us a wish! You've got to bring our parents back!"

"Wishes don't come true," said Tuava-Li, "unless you make them come true."

"That's the domain of *magick,*" said the Mage. "That's the nature of magick itself, to make a wish come true. But we're complex creatures, Elves and Humans. The wish you receive is not always the wish you *thought you made.* If I'm not mistaken, you've already got what you wished for."

"You mean the medicine you gave me for my foot?" argued Matt. "That was a bargain you offered, it wasn't what I *wished* for. If I'd gotten what I wished, we'd have our parents here with us, and you'd be so far away we'd never even think about you again. I never wished for this. It's all been just a . . . a horrible accident."

"There are no accidents," said the Mage. "Do you think you stepped on that diamond shoe by accident? You did not. Your ancestors claimed this land for a reason. Your father built your house for a reason. You found Asra's shoe for a reason. Your parents and sister were taken for a reason. We're here talking to you for a reason. All of this is what you wished for. It's all unfolding the way it was meant to be."

"No," said Matt. "I never wanted any of this. You're lying, just to get me to do what you want."

"Is that what you think?" said the Mage, her eyes large and round, like an owl's.

From far away the wail of an ambulance siren, and then the urgent honk of a fire truck, drifted on the air. "You see," the Mage said, "the borders of our worlds are in flux. Now the Humans see the fire, and they'll attempt to contain it. Perhaps 'twas the burning houses that got their attention. Everything that happens is a gift, if you see it the right way. Now we must go. Will you come with us, and we'll discuss our bargain at greater length, or will you stay here and wait for the Humans to arrive?"

"What about the fire?"

The Mage was getting tired, and it took Tuava-Li's intense concentration to help her Master become an owl again. "What about the fire?" Matt repeated.

"We'll fly overhead," Tuava-Li said, "and guide you safely. The winds are blowing in the other direction now, and the trees all the way to the Sacred Grove have fallen to help break the fire. Alfheim is no more. But there is still the Cord. May it always be so!"

And so it was that a Troll, and a Human boy, and his sister hurried into the forest, moving in the shadow of a pair of predatory birds. Through smoldering heaps of blackened foliage they made their way, over burned trunks that blocked the path to a scooped-out gully at the edge of a ruined kingdom that had not survived the attempt of the Mage and her Elves to save it. The entrance to the Cord flapped in the wind that still howled through the ravaged forest.

The children stood awestruck at the brink, holding hands. The Troll climbed through a ragged tear, beckoning to his friends to follow. "Don't be afraid," he said, "try to keep me in sight!"

In a moment, with a deep sucking sound, he was whipped away. *What is the Cord?* Matt wondered, even as the birds turned back into Elves, opened the flap, and took the hands of the children, even as they assured them they would be safe. Matt gave Becky a kiss on the forehead. "It's okay," he said, nodding for her to go. "I think we can trust them."

Becky looked doubtful, as tears welled up in her eyes.

"Go on." said Matt. "We've *got* to trust them. I'll be right with you, the whole time."

And with that, the children knelt, leaning into the harsh, rushing wind of the Cord, and slipped away. The Mage and her Apprentice followed, staying close behind.

End of Book One

ACKNOWLEDGMENTS

A FEW YEARS AGO, on an autumn road trip across Pennsylvania, I was struck by the number of deer that I saw along the highway. Some were alive, but many were dead, struck by cars or trucks. It seemed so sad that these graceful, gentle creatures couldn't learn to be more careful! As the road snaked through the trees, I saw a herd of deer disappear in the early-morning mist. *Where are they going?* I asked my kids, and we took turns making up answers. We all thought it would be nice if they were going somewhere safer than the edge of the highway. I suggested that maybe the deer were headed for a wedding deep in the forest. At that moment it seemed plausible that there might be faeries living in those dark and mysterious woods, and a faerie wedding would be the perfect place for deer to go. With that thought, the book you are holding in your hands was born.

I would like to take this opportunity to thank all of the people at Abrams who encouraged and helped me bring *The Low Road* to completion. Howard Reeves, my brilliant, perfectionist editor, shares my passion for the fantasy genre. Chad W. Beckerman, art director, has a quirky, outside-the-box touch that is always welcome. Readers Suzanne Harper, Susan Van Metre, and Scott Auerbach helped me tidy up the text and make my imaginary world consistent, and Jason Wells, marketing director, has been there to spread the news about this book, with enthusiasm that is always contagious. I also wish to thank the students at Glen Ridge Upper Elementary School, Nitrauer Elementary School, and Brandon Academy, to whom I read chapters of this book while I was still working on the manuscript. And thanks to my friends at the Glen Ridge Public Library and the expressive models who inspired the artwork, including Ivy, Raleigh, Russell, Greg, and Miranda.

About the Author

Daniel Kirk has written and illustrated a number of bestselling picture books for children. This is his first novel. He lives in Glen Ridge, New Jersey, with his wife, three children, and two rabbits. For more information about him, visit his Web site: www.danielkirk.com.

THIS BOOK WAS ART DIRECTED and designed by Chad W. Beckerman. The text is set in Cochin, a typeface designed by Georges Peignot and named for the eighteenth-century French engraver Nicolas Cochin. The font incorporates a mix of style elements and could be considered part of the Neorenaissance movement in typography. It was popular at the beginning of the twentieth century.

The illustrations in this book were made with charcoal pencil on Arches watercolor paper.

THIS BOOK WAS ART DIRECTED

Enjoy this sneak peek at

The High Road

the second book in the *Elf Realm* trilogy

MATT WAS FALLING. The ground had opened up beneath him, and as he plummeted headlong through a narrow tunnel, arms and legs flailing, there was no ending, just falling, falling, falling. When he tried to scream, the roaring wind filled his throat, and only a sob escaped his lips. His mind was a blur. His panic was so intense that he couldn't concentrate on anything but the certainty that he was going to die. A heartbeat later he heard someone screaming. She plunged past him, bouncing off the milk-white walls of the tunnel. "Becky!" Matt cried.

"Matt," she shrieked, tumbling head over heels, her voice raw with fear. "Matt, Matt!"

Suddenly the boy and his sister hurtled around a curve, and a ragged figure brushed past them, followed by another, and another, and another. Pale faces with huge gleaming eyes and pointed ears stared, then shot out of sight. With a sudden burst of shock and relief, Matt realized that he wasn't falling after all. It wasn't gravity pulling him down; it was something else, some unknown force, pulling him and his sister forward in a vast tunnel, parallel to the ground but beneath it. They were in the Cord. They were traveling the Low Road, the Faerie passage hidden in the earth, and Matt and his sister weren't falling; they were *flying*. "Becky," Matt cried, "hold your hands out in front of you, keep your body straight, and your eyes ahead. Look where you're going!"

"I can't," Becky sobbed, and bounced off another wall.

"Yes, you can! If I can do it, so can you!"

"I can't," Becky insisted, as Matt drew alongside her and took her hand in his.

"Then stay with me," he said, trying to keep his sister steady as they hurtled together through the tunnel. Even though Matt's heart was pounding, confidence welled up inside him; he felt a crazy certainty that he could do this, that he could navigate the Faerie passage, that he could lead himself and his sister to safety somewhere up ahead. "We're flying!" The words burst from him, fragile and explosive. "Becky, we're flying!"

Then in the distance he saw a dark line spread along the wall of the Cord, like an ink mark drawn by an invisible hand. There was a ripping sound. Dozens of tiny, filthy fingers reached into the tunnel and grabbed Becky by her hair. They yanked her from the Cord as Matt hurtled forward, unable to turn back. In despair he clutched at the walls with his fingernails, trying to slow the insane velocity. His grip gave way. Then his perspective shifted again, and in horror he saw that he wasn't flying after all. He was falling, down, down, down.

Silence. Matt opened his eyes and sat up in the darkness. He was breathing so hard that he felt dizzy. In the seconds it took to orient himself, a glimmer of hope welled up inside, then vanished, leaving him in a place blacker than he could ever have imagined in his brief fourteen years of life. As he left the realm of dreams behind and entered the waking world, Matt had no doubt that this was the real nightmare. He wasn't at home in bed. He was in a cramped, moldy space beneath the roots of some enormous tree in the woods, where he had spent the night sleeping fitfully next to his sister on a pile of damp leaves. He brushed a leaf from his face, and peered into the darkness to see if Becky was still lying asleep beside him. He heard her quiet breath, regular and calm, and he decided to leave her alone. She was only nine. It wasn't fair to subject her to this insanity. Daytime would come too soon.

Matt crawled out from under the tree roots into the dark forest. His jeans and T-shirt were filthy, caked with dirt, even though he had turned his clothes inside out, like the Elves had asked him to. Evil spirits, they said, would be less able to recognize someone with their clothes turned inside out. Around his neck hung a tangle of beads, amulets, and charms designed to protect him from spells. Or at least that's what the Elves had told him. *All superstitious garbage, all of it,* Matt thought. There was a soggy lump of herbs tucked between his teeth and gums. He spit it out into the foliage. All night long he had kept the bitter herbs in his mouth, just like they had instructed. This was supposed to dull the pain from the markings they had tattooed on his chest, which they'd guaranteed would hurt. *They were right,* he thought. This was madness, all madness. And it was all his fault. Matt slipped his fingers beneath his T-shirt and felt the place where his skin had been marked. *To protect and help you,* the Elves had said. The tattoos were necessary to protect him from the dangers that lay ahead. *What dangers?* Matt thought. And how would they help? Was he crazy to agree to this? What was he thinking?

Matt peered into the darkness. Over the tops of the trees, a streak of purple appeared; dawn was near. He heard what sounded like footsteps in the distance, clomping over the leaves on the forest floor. Elves—no doubt soldiers on guard—were patrolling the outskirts of the Elfin city of Ljosalfar. Matt moved carefully among the trees. His fingers touched carved wood; it was one of the totem poles sculpted by Neaca. She was an old friend of the Mage. The Mage had ruled Alfheim, the community of Elves that was destroyed in the firestorm that took Matt's own home. Now the Mage and her apprentice, Tuava-Li, were homeless, too, and they, along with Matt, Becky, and Tomtar, were all Neaca's guests. Neaca's forest home was surrounded by totem poles like the one Matt stood behind. She called them her *Klumma.*

"Matt, is that you?" a voice whispered from the gloom.

"Tomtar?" Matt replied.

Matt and Becky had gotten to know the Troll in the weeks after Matt had stepped on the jeweled shoe. Before the failed Elfin wedding and the battle that followed. Before the fire. Before the black-robed Elfin monks took his parents and his baby sister in the flying machines. Before Prince Macta and the monk Jardaine entered his house with the ghost-girl, Anna. Before the guns, and the fear, the running and the screaming, back when the world Matt knew was simple, and peaceful, and good. If Matt had a friend in this bleak place, it was Tomtar.

"What are you doing up so early?" Tomtar asked.

"I had a bad dream. I couldn't sleep. And these . . . these tattoos hurt. I think the Elves are trying to kill me!"

Tomtar squatted in the brush between two *Klumma.* He glanced up at the boy through a mop of curls, wondering if he was making some kind of joke. "'Tisn't funny, Matt. I know you don't trust 'em, but you've got to try. The Mage knows better than us what's at stake."

Matt saw movement in the shadows ahead and ducked down. Lights, like torches, appeared. *Fire sprites.* Matt mouthed the words. He'd seen them before, in the battle in the woods. A moment later a squadron of perhaps a hundred Elfin soldiers marched past. Matt was sure they would hear his beating heart, and the throb of blood pulsing in his veins. He squeezed his eyes shut. Soon the soldiers passed by, oblivious to the boy and the Troll. When their footsteps faded in the distance, Tomtar grinned up at Matt. He rapped his knuckles on the *Klumma* and stood up to his full height of twenty-seven inches. "We've got to trust 'em, see? Old Neaca's lived here for ten thousand moons without bein' noticed, right here on the edge of Ljosalfar. These things she's carved, they keep the world away. We're as good as invisible as long as we stay inside their perimeter."

Matt stood back and gazed at the *Klumma.* It looked like a stack of grotesque heads piled one on top of the other, each face more ugly and threatening than the one below it. How could he and the Troll be invisible to other Elves, just because they were standing behind these terrifying wood carvings? "Where are the Elves?" he asked.

Tomtar lifted his chin, pointing to the treetops. "Tuava-Li and the Mage are up there with Neaca in the high branches. They're getting ready for the sun to rise."

Just then Matt heard a faint sound. "It's Becky," he said, and he hurried through the undergrowth toward the gnarled old tree. Scraping his forehead on the tangle of branches, he tumbled into the leaf-dense pit and found his sister sitting up in the darkness, rubbing her eyes. "I'm here," Matt said, kneeling. "Don't worry."

"I felt a bug on my face," Becky whimpered. "Where did you go, Matt? I called for you!"

Matt could just see her thin lips quivering, a streak of dirt on her high cheekbones. "I was outside," he said, "talking to Tomtar."

"I'm starved," Becky whimpered. "I want to go home!"

Matt didn't know what to say. There was nothing he could do about a bug; surely there must be thousands of them in this hole in the ground surrounded by tree roots, rotting twigs, leaves, and dirt. There was nothing he could do about his sister's hunger, either. Matt felt his own stomach rumbling. If they were lucky, they'd breakfast on some berries and dried twigs, or a few nuts. And home? Home was gone forever. "Come on out, Becky," he said, hoping to distract her. "The sun's coming up, and the sky looks pretty over the hill!"

Tomtar was waiting outside the tree trunk, and when he saw Becky he squeezed her around the waist. It was a heartfelt hug, and Becky squeezed him back. She stroked the Troll's hair and blinked as she watched a splinter of sunlight filter through the trees. "Is that the way home?" she asked.

"Yeah," Matt replied. "That's east. I think that's where the houses are—I mean, were. But . . . I'm not sure."

"I guess it doesn't really matter which direction it is,"

she murmured. "We don't have anywhere to live anymore. Everything's burned up and ruined, and Mom and Dad and Emily are gone."

Matt stared at the ground. A breeze drifted through the trees, and the forest was filled with the whispering of leaves. "Don't worry," Tomtar said, "everything will be all right. The Mage says there are maps in Ljosalfar, and I know there are maps back in Argant, where I come from, too. One way or another, you'll find your family and get them back."

"I know," Becky said, her face brightening. "Do you think the Mage and Tuava-Li will let us leave today, Matt?"

"I'm not sure," Matt said, fighting the despair that clawed at his heart. "Probably soon."

The sound of singing came from overhead, and the brother and sister glanced up to see the source of the eerie, warbling voices. Three Elves sat along a wide branch, bowing to the rising sun. "What are they doing?" Becky asked. She was unaccustomed to waking so early.

"Welcomin' the day," Tomtar whispered. "'Tis one of their rituals. You know Neaca was a Mage, too, a long time ago. She was the leader of a place like Alfheim."

"What happened?"

Tomtar shrugged. "I don't know. Anyway, she was left alone, with no reason for livin' and nothin' to do, so she came to these woods and began carvin' her *Klumma*."

"They're ugly," Becky said, and Matt couldn't help but agree. In fact, the Faerie Folk themselves seemed uglier to him every day—their tiny fingers, their pointy little teeth, pale skin, and dark, wet eyes—it was all weird and strange and ugly to Matt. It was hard not to judge them by their appearance, and the feeling of revulsion welled up in him again as he watched the Elves going through their ritual on the tree branch. If he didn't need their help to find and rescue his parents, Matt would never be able to stand them for long. *It's probably the same for them as it is for me,* he thought, remembering how the Elves had covered their mouths when they first saw him, afraid that he'd contaminate them with germs. *It's only natural. We're not meant to live together.*

"Did you wash your hands yet?" Tomtar asked, his bright eyes darting from Matt to Becky. "The Mage says 'tis important."

"Oh, yeah," Matt snorted. The Elfin rituals were quickly getting under his skin, and he threw up his hands in mock alarm. "Because the dead touch us in our sleep, and we have to clean it off or they'll give us some kind of cooties, right?"

Becky's eyes widened. "What?"

"You shouldn't mock our beliefs," Tomtar said, frowning. "You said you had a bad dream, Matt."

"But a bad dream isn't the same as being touched by somebody or something dead. If I have to follow all the little rules and restrictions that the Elves want me to follow, I'll go crazy. Half the things they say sound crazy to begin with."

"I'll wash mine," Becky said, holding her hands away from her body.

Matt sighed. He knew it wasn't worth making an issue of everything. Going along with the Elves' superstitions wasn't going to hurt them, even if he found it annoying. He sighed and got up. "Then let's all do it together."

"I'll lead you to the stream," Tomtar chirped. "After that we'll find somethin' to eat. You know what they say: You can't argue when your belly's full!"

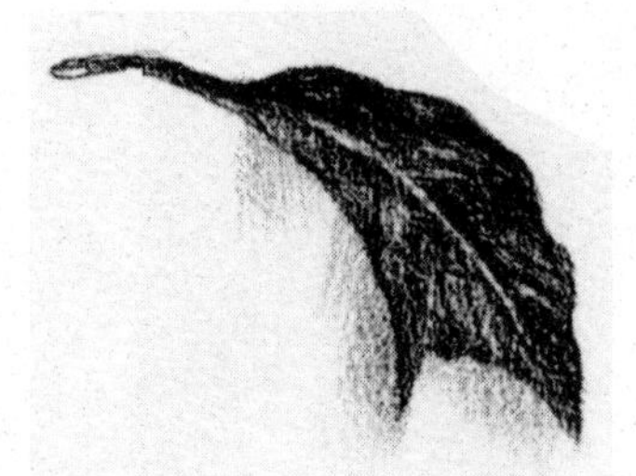

check out these other titles.

The Unknowns
by Benedict Carey
978-0-8109-7991-8
$16.95 hardcover

The Lighthouse Trilogy:
The Lighthouse Land
by Adrian McKinty
978-0-8109-9361-7
$7.95 paperback

The Chronicles of Faerie:
The Hunter's Moon
by O.R. Melling
978-0-8109-9214-6
$8.95 paperback

AMULET BOOKS. AVAILABLE WHEREVER BOOKS ARE SOLD | WWW.AMULETBOOKS.COM

Send author fan mail to Amulet Books, Attn: Marketing, 115 West 18th Street, New York, NY 10011, or in an e-mail to marketing@abramsbooks.com. All mail will be forwarded. Amulet Books is an imprint of ABRAMS.

DANIEL KIRK
ELF REALM
THE HIGH ROAD

ESCAPE THE MASK
DAVID WARD

DAVID CLEMENT-DAVIES
Fell

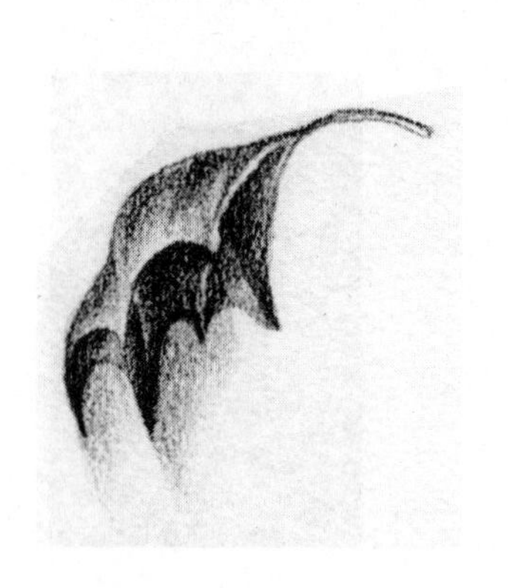